ONE NIGHT ONLY

G.P. RITCHIE

NIGHT'S
BORDER
press

This edition first published in 2018 by Night's Border Press 24a Ainslie Place, Edinburgh, EH3 6AJ

Rev: 1.08
ISBN: (e-book) 978-1-9164246-0-9
ISBN: (paperback) 978-1-9164246-1-6
Cover Design by James, GoOnWrite.com

This one's for Big Bad John.
Even if it is a Mammy-Daddy.

PROLOGUE
1977

The sea routes from Danang to China were marked by corpses. The captain shoved the chart into his pocket, gazed over the bow rail and sighed.

So many died in these waters. He saw it night after night; such a waste of life. Both here and round the headland into the Gulf of Thailand, primitive fishing vessels fit only for coastline shallows would take desperate routes across open water.

And tonight would be no different.

Even though the sea was troubled and mist thickened on the water, even though the night was deeper than ink, still, they would come. So he dropped anchor here, where currents trapped the smaller boats. Those drawn past this point would be lost. He would be their last hope.

Soon.

His crew knew the time approached. Below decks some chatted and played cards, while others prepared the food.

He raised his binoculars, squinting into the mist.

There.

A firefly lamp topped a short mast. Off-course and drifting.

Roll the focus ring: a formless blur sharpened. A worried huddle under tarpaulin; the faces of generations travelling together. One man passed his top-coat to an elder, then rubbed his own bare arms against the chilling mist. As the fit protected the frail, so the frail endangered the fit. The captain saw no logic in such a trade.

He powered the spotlight to illuminate twin flags, red cross and red crescent, then signalled for lights in the main cabin. A banner spread the length of that window would now burst into view. Written in Vietnamese, the refugees' likely first language, it read: *Safe passage to Hong-Kong.*

The whispers of the night sea receded, overcome by the creak of old wood and a rising clamour of voices. The struggling craft listed badly to starboard. He sounded the horn, ushering the nearest lifeboat into the water.

Once all refugees were aboard, the bare-armed man bowed, offering his single pressed leaf of gold in repayment, but the captain waved it away.

"Our deepest thanks, Captain. My name is Chien. This is my wife, Mai." His English was accented but excellent. The younger woman nodded, her eyes averted. Pretty.

The captain beckoned them inside. "I am Captain Vorsky, and you are my guests." The boat people, with drawn faces and darting eyes, clustered around the provisions laid out in the main cabin. "Friends, our crew have eaten. Everything here is for you." They nervously sampled the cheese and bread, the artichoke tea and rice wine, but avoided the fish stew. The behaviour was familiar. It had become taboo to eat sea fish that might have grown fat upon friends or relatives. "Chien, please, reassure them. The fish is Basa, fresh-water catfish."

With Chien's encouragement, the group filled their bowls and ate all they desired.

Eventually the youngest crawled under the table to sleep while the adults talked. Soon the adults also quietened, some sitting on the carpet, others stretching out beside their children. Chien asked, "Captain, can we sleep here? We are unusually tired."

The captain nodded. "Your journey has nearly begun."

The man yawned his thanks. But as he crouched to settle alongside his sleeping wife the captain touched his shoulder. "Might I perhaps ask your age?"

Chien's eyes drifted open before briefly narrowing in confusion. "I am thirty-eight."

"A pity. No matter. My friend, sleep well."

All around, unconsciousness took hold.

The captain signalled his waiting crew. "Her. Him. The children. Both of these men. And this couple at my feet. Take them to the hold." He pointed towards Mai. "But have her taken to my cabin." The bodies were lifted with no struggle.

He watched silently while the others were dragged outside. All slept deeply now. The sedatives were strong, and this end was merciful. Better by far than the fearful drowning offered by their own vessel. Here, there would be no screams of pain or panic. No desperate sculling until muscles failed and lungs flooded with brine.

When Chien dropped overboard, the captain unlit the flags and returned inside. He paid no heed to the splashes that followed. No one would miss them. After all, many died in these waters. He saw it night after night.

PART I

THE RED SMEAR

30TH AUGUST - 2ND SEPTEMBER

1

CHARLOTTE SQUARE

TUESDAY 30TH AUGUST, 02:50

The dark-red smear defiled the broad Charlotte Square paving, a sickly glistening under the wrought-iron railing lights. Edinburgh Councillor Joan Wood was dead. This ragged line of blood, skin and black rubber was the final mark she'd leave on her city.

Detective Inspector Andy Lorimar crouched with his torch. He saw tyre prints from all four wheels, marking the trail of a body dragged over thirty feet. It arced first towards and then away from the kerb.

He hoped she'd lost consciousness quickly.

Nearby, a solitary scene-of-crime officer wrestled his camera. He spoke flatly, without looking up. "You missed the body."

"So I see."

"Five minutes ago. Gone where the goblins go. Cowgate. You also missed the paramedics. And you missed all the other SOCOs too. You're late. Just me and the skin slick left now." He framed the remains carefully in the rear viewer of his camera. "So you're the CID assigned?"

"I volunteered. I heard it over my radio." After a pause, Andy added, "I couldn't sleep."

"Taking an Airwave to bed? Your life must be a barrel of laughs."

The strobing camera flash burned the ugly streak onto his retina. He didn't envy the pathologist dealing with the leftovers from this mess. "Was anyone close enough to recognise the victim? Apart from us?"

"Not that I know."

"The paramedics?"

"They didn't hang around. There was nobody to save, just evidence to keep the hell away from." The man scowled. "No offence mate, maybe you pull all-nighters for kicks, but I'm just finishing up here. It's three in the morning. Once I've got these last—" The officer froze. "Shit! Is that a finger?" He crawled to the kerb, ferreted in the gutter and retrieved the bad news. "Bugger. That's me going to Cowgate as well, now."

Andy left him bagging his evidence. When he reached the uniformed officers on the perimeter, the woman spoke first. "Our crime-scene colleague's having a bad morning."

Andy nodded, but glanced back towards the bloody skid mark. "Not as bad as some. Were you the first on scene?"

She nodded. "A couple called it in after a night out. They'd been walking down George Street, but when they passed the Roxburghe Hotel on South Charlotte, they heard the van mount the pavement. It reversed then drove forward again. They didn't know what they were looking at until it cleared the scene and they saw the body, but they were too scared to approach it."

"Any shouting? Religious or nationalist slogans?"

"Nothing like that."

Terrorism was a mandatory consideration with vehicle hits nowadays, and especially here, so close to the First Minister's residence. But this van had left the scene without further incident, it hadn't been on a killing spree. "Did the couple know the identity of the victim?"

"Didn't seem to. Neither did we at that point. Why d'you ask?"

"Someone leaked her details on the internet, within minutes of the event."

"The killer?"

Andy shrugged. Everybody chased 'likes' these days, why not killers?

All three turned as an approaching car engine puttered into silence. Chief Inspector Brian Nesbitt slammed the door behind him, his frown deepening as he ducked under the tape. "You didn't save me a journey after all."

"How come?"

"A tweet says she'd concealed corruption on the trams project."

"A *tweet*?" The Edinburgh Trams controversy had rumbled on for years. The multi-million budget overrun created an enduring political grievance that didn't need a Molotov like this chucked at it. "So who sent it? Were they claiming responsibility? Or suggesting a motive? And how the hell do they know so much?"

Nesbitt shrugged. "All questions for the just convened major investigation into the death of Joan Wood. The team will work out of Fettes Avenue, with me as SIO."

"Do I need to audition?"

"On balance, a nosey insomniac could be useful. So congratulations. You're in."

THE MORNING BRIEFING featured a trio of higher-ups labouring the need for rapid progress, thus preventing the job from actually starting. Upon escape, Nesbitt's first task was scarcely more joyous: human resource. With multiple major investigations already underway, he disappeared to identify some living bodies for a change.

Andy contacted Edinburgh's central monitoring facility to track the van and establish Wood's final movements. The available CCTV record showed the victim had walked past a camera proceeding east to west down George Street in the minutes before the incident. But over the course of a long call, the operator's scans of additional footage revealed nothing further. Her clothing suggested she may have recently come from a social engagement. Pursuing that thought, he booked afternoon appointments with candidates suggested by Wood's recent council diary. He was preparing for the trip when Nesbitt resurfaced and stole it, playing the twin cards of sympathy and seniority.

Instead, Andy took the opportunity to check the statements gathered at the scene against primary sources. After only a few calls, confirmation was forthcoming. The husband from the couple who reported the attack repeated what he'd heard from uniformed officers at the scene. They'd left Fingers Piano Bar and had planned on walking home, but as they neared Charlotte Square they heard screeching tyres. The idea of approaching an obviously mangled body horrified them, so they kept their distance while the husband called from his mobile. They didn't see anyone enter the square until the police arrived, and only discovered the victim's identity themselves from breakfast news reports. Similarly, paramedic dispatch corroborated what he'd heard from the SOCO: their guys were not present long enough to recognise anyone. Now, nearly fifteen hours later, it seemed nobody could explain how Wood's name leaked onto the web.

With other avenues in hand, it was time to interrogate the victim. But that attempt collided with an apparent pathology staffing crisis. Nobody could answer questions about the councillor's postmortem, nor could he get a release time for her personal effects.

Discovering the factor of her apartment building operated as a master key holder was at least a minor victory. He radioed the information to Nesbitt, who agreed to check her home on his way back from council offices.

A morbid thought intruded. He imagined his flat becoming the subject of such a visit. What might an investigator conclude about the solitary inhabitant? If his neighbours were interviewed, would they even know him at all?

His self-indulgence was dispelled by the callback from central monitoring. They had captured the van travelling into town on North Bridge, then Queen Street and George Street. It parked on Glenfinlas Street just before midnight. The driving appeared slow and careful. Somebody with time on their side, perhaps early for an appointment. Since Wood had been walking away from her route home, might she have deliberately approached her murderer?

Following the attack, the vehicle took a far less sedate pace along Queensferry Road, and they lost track shortly after. The number plates on the vehicle were either illegibly dirty or deliberately obscured, with no scope to extract even a partial. The fact a white van was the John Smith of motor vehicles left precious little to go on.

BY THE TIME Andy finished updating the incident system, dark rain pattered against the window. He attempted to stifle a yawn, but was forced to admit defeat. That early-morning crime scene had just drawn a line through the to-do list.

Upon reaching the car park he spotted spiky blond hair cutting through the drizzle like a shark-fin. His mental jukebox played the theme from *Jaws*: Jamie bloody Devlin. He did the sensible thing, and attempted to sneak to his car unnoticed.

"Ho! Link-man!"

He didn't appreciate that nickname, but protest had fixed it like glue. "Sergeant Devlin? Drylaw business brought you over to Fettes?"

"I'm working here from tomorrow. You guys need the boost."

Disaster. They had worked together before. Or, more correctly, one of them had worked. God knows what Devlin had been up to. "Family let you out late then?"

"No biggie. Five minutes, drop in, press the flesh. We're in Comely Bank now. You still got your hermit hole in Ferry Road?"

"I've not moved." The cheeky bugger had spent two years in uniform, then straight into CID. He'd heard rumours about well-placed connections, but more likely recruitment had simply misread the word defective. "So Brian Nesbitt requested you?"

"My gaffer donated me. Greater good and all that."

Donating Devlin made sense. But accepting him? Brian must be desperate. As their conversation faltered, Andy cast around for inspiration, only to have some land in his eyeball. "Best get out of the wet, I suppose. We'll try to make sense of this tomorrow."

Devlin scoffed. "We're looking for white-van man. How complicated can it be?"

2

A FREE TICKET

WEDNESDAY 31ST AUGUST, 00:03

D espite the gruesome hit and run dominating the city news, for one final night, the festival good times were determined to roll.

But, John Reynolds, lacking his own festive spirit, seemed destined for a supporting role in the alcohol misadventures of others. An evening begun staggering beneath the weight of a catatonic drunk at his hotel had now ground to a halt behind a street clown whose entire performance consisted of downing pints. John could tell this was the man's eighth, not through deductive reasoning, but because of the people chanting and holding up fingers.

Even for Edinburgh's crazy season this was an unusual sight, so John grudgingly accepted the distraction of the desiccated harlequin holding court in the middle of the Pleasance. Sweating through greasepaint, steely eyes above Pierrot tears, the clown guzzled and gulped, determined to see the bottom of the next glass or keel over in the attempt. Despite holding them at bay by the girth of his hooped trousers, he had no shortage of admirers willing to get the next round in.

On a conventionally bad day, this unlikely vision might have been a relief. But after this day, as part of this week, John saw only proof of a harsh fact: life won't only kick a man while he's down, but sometimes, will strap on comically large shoes to do it. When even a tight-lipped, sad-eyed, alcoholic clown was awash with friends, he knew the universe had a message for a solitary sad-case like himself. And after three miserable days, he was ready to take the hint.

As Tricia might have said, he only had himself to blame. She'd have gone on to explain that a moderately perceptive man would have found the name of the last show to be warning enough. *Slippery Giblets* (jauntily straplined 'Abattoir The Musical!') had a small audience, and by the end John found himself, like the unfortunate papier mâché animals on stage, stunned into silence.

When he'd last lived in Edinburgh, fifteen pounds guaranteed a decent night at the festival. But you couldn't depend on things to stay the same, not just because you wanted them to. Tricia would have said that too. If she'd been here.

At least their break-up meant an end to the endless dissection of his mistakes. And he made a lot of mistakes. Like yesterday's two-hour mime about venereal disease. Like *Slippery Giblets*. Like thinking a holiday they'd planned together would be bearable alone.

Perhaps Tricia was right about him, about his inability to share himself emotionally. Maybe there was something missing, something he couldn't acknowledge. Or perhaps things had just run their course.

The last seventy-two hours battling crowds in Edinburgh hadn't improved matters. So he'd catch the train home tomorrow and they could sit down, talk, and perhaps salvage something. Friendship, at least. Just turning his back on the last five years wasn't an option.

For now, though, it was dark. He was tired. And it was probably time to head back to the hotel and crash.

"Hi there! I'm Nick. How about a final show this evening?"

The speaker had a mature student look: floppy hair, inappropriate duffel coat, weather-beaten satchel. A typical Fringe marketing rep trying to move cheap tickets. On a slow day they'd settle for boosting atmosphere and generating word of mouth.

John wondered if Nick's show could be worse than *Slippery Giblets*. He wondered if anything, ever, could be worse than *Slippery Giblets*. "Maybe. What have you got?"

Nick fumbled inside the satchel. "Depends. How many of you are there?"

"Just me. I head back to London tomorrow, so make it something good or I'm calling it a night!"

Nick handed him a flyer. "That one's special: Max the Magnificent, Illusionist Underground. Two seats to fill for a one night only magic show—"

"Sorry, I stopped watching magic as a kid. Izzy-wizzy, let's get busy with some no-name guy after midnight won't—"

"Go on! Please!" She appeared from behind the mature student and stood at John's side. Her formal long coat might have seemed severe except for the outrageous number of bobbles dangling from the woollen hat above it. Little tufts of auburn hair poked out beneath the hat's purple perimeter, taking front row seats for what, John supposed, was the world's most beguiling Newton's cradle. As she tugged at his sleeve, he struggled to make sense of her intervention, a task that so engrossed him, he completely forgot not to stare.

Nick coughed. "Two seats are available free of charge, but this lady is alone, so if you join her I can release the tickets. Failing that, I've got more chance of getting both seats filled by a couple."

The woman took his hand. "Hi, I'm Sara! I love magic!"

Warmth mushroomed in John's cheeks. This was confusing. Tomorrow he would go home and put his life back in order, but tonight he needed some company and Sara seemed like fun. The problem was acknowledging his sudden compulsion to go to the show. Hadn't she just heard him announce how much he hated magic?

His mouth made a reckless leap into the breach. "I'm John. I suppose I always liked that thing with the egg cups."

15

Nick's eyes rolled skyward but Sara was gentle. She laughed a little. "Me too. I love the thing with the egg cups!" And just like that they were going to a show.

They pushed past the clown rattling his case for payment, and headed out of the courtyard. John fretted about protocol. Should they walk together? If so, how closely? Perhaps she'd prefer to keep her distance now the tickets were secured?

But Sara resolved those concerns by taking his arm and pulling him down the hill. "I know the way. Come on, we've got a walk ahead of us!"

He wondered about people with this easy, friendly manner. How did they come by it? Why didn't he have it? Had Sara noticed?

"We turn left at this junction and walk along the Cowgate. Did you know this was the main road for cattle in the olden days? The sheep were promised equal access, but that was just the wool being pulled over their eyes." Then she nudged him softly, frowning. "Sorry, my jokes are terrible aren't they?"

Was she nervous? Could she be interested in him? That would be a whole new variable to contend with. "You're funnier than anything else I've seen this trip, believe me. Can I ask where you're from?" He hoped the question sounded relaxed.

"We moved around Europe as a child, but settled in Switzerland for a bit. I call Richmond home nowadays. You?"

"I grew up in Inverness before studying here. Now I'm in Greenwich." He grinned. "We're practically neighbours!" Over-enthusiastic. Damn. He closed his eyes at the masterful piece of blurting. She'll think I'm a creep and clam up.

But she didn't. "I know, isn't it great? Look! Niddry Street!"

John followed her past a parked van and around the corner.

The narrow cobbled lane travelled uphill and away from the shadowed arch of the South Bridge. But in truth the lane remained part of the bridge structure. Trickery like this must be why the underground vaults remained anonymous. People might roam the Edinburgh streets for years and never know they even existed.

At this time of night the area was beginning to quieten. A single burst of distant revelry soared and faded as they walked towards the unremarkable door. A rough placard leaned beside it.

VENUE 1331: WONDERGROUND
MAX THE MAGNIFICENT
ONE NIGHT ONLY – BEGINS 12:45am

Plastered across the sign, a sticker read 'Sold Out'. Nick must have phoned ahead.

As the door swung shut behind them, Sara checked her watch. "Two minutes to go. Come on!"

They picked their way down the damp steps towards a network of abandoned chambers. Ramshackle electric lights flickered and buzzed as they passed, tiring in their battle against the implacable darkness. The sound of their footsteps echoed against old stone. It was hard to imagine a more atmospheric beginning for a midnight magic show.

The first chamber they reached was small and bare, and the scuffed dirt floor was marked by heavy bootprints. The venue preparation was perhaps only recently completed.

Sara hurried ahead.

The echoing welcome of orchestral music grew louder, and the outsize shadow of a gramophone horn loomed on an approaching chamber wall. Whether this was the source of the music or just stage dressing he couldn't be sure, but he appreciated the theatre. A plaintive clarinet rose and fell above an ominous string section. "Should we recognise that?"

Sara grinned. "Shostakovich! Seventh, I'd guess but don't ask me the movement. My father would know!"

The music now contended with a growing hum of audience chatter. Realising they held the last two tickets tempered John's excitement. It was surely unlikely they'd find seats together.

This largest room so far was still small compared to most standard festival venues, and they found a mixed audience crammed onto four plastic benches and two wooden pews. The stage was a small raised platform about one metre deep. Most seats were taken, but happily, he and Sara squeezed onto the outside of the back row.

The chamber itself was unusually dressed. The wall behind the stage was draped in obligatory black velvet, but all the flooring and the stage itself were covered in white vinyl sheeting. It was so spotless that John regretted stepping onto it. Their new neighbour in the back row pointed his gold-topped cane towards a pile of shoes by the entrance. Just then, a grand voice interrupted the music.

"PATRONS ARE REMINDED MAX THE MAGNIFICENT DEMANDS THE REMOVAL OF ALL FOOTWEAR BEFORE THE TAKING OF SEATS! HE STRESSES HOWEVER THAT ALL OTHER CLOTHING SHOULD REMAIN ON AT THIS TIME."

Peals of laughter added to an already buoyant atmosphere.

The strongly accented voice was difficult to place; it was definitely European, possibly Slavic or German. John glanced towards Sara, who was already rising to remove her shoes. He followed suit, grateful to find his socks were free of both odour and holes.

He thanked his neighbour as he settled himself once more. "A bit weird about the shoes though, isn't it?"

The man smiled broadly. "I hear it gets even weirder."

Then the solitary bulb above the stage blinked into absolute darkness.

"LADIES AND GENTLEMEN, KINDLY WELCOME ON STAGE, THE ONE, THE ONLY, THE INCOMPARABLE, MAX THE MAGNIFICENT!"

Applause built towards a crescendo before light returned, revealing a stately but somewhat elderly man standing beside a small cabinet. He was dressed in a white evening suit, with a folded black handkerchief jutting dramatically from his breast pocket. His posture, while not stiff, was strikingly upright, suggesting stagecraft acquired when deportment was still a foundation of the performing arts.

He accepted the applause in silence, stroking his finely groomed moustache. Finally, he dipped into a shallow bow. "Thank you all! You are too generous. I am delighted to share my magic tonight. While many of you know of me, for some this will be your first experience. I shall endeavour not to disappoint!" He leaned conspiratorially towards the audience. "But magic is a communal art. Tonight we work together to transform a spartan chamber into a palace of wonders!"

At the corner of the stage Max stamped hard, three times. "A magician must always have the best shoes in the house. I ensure this by having the only shoes in the house! I thank you for your cooperation! More than this, a magician must always have the best sleeves in the house. Please, would someone care to check my sleeves?"

He beckoned a blushing young woman from the front pew onto the stage. Then he flung open his arms. "Young lady, please check my sleeves and report what you see. Carefully now, leave nothing to chance!"

She felt her way closely along each arm, patting the creases and folds up to his shoulders, and then continuing onto the body of the jacket itself. "Nothing," she said. "There's nothing there."

"Thank you, my dear." Max lowered his arms. "That was very thorough, and justly so, for I am an old fox."

Lock picks tinkled to the stage from his right cuff.

"Who has excellent sleeves."

Four decorated throwing knives clattered from his left cuff.

"And who is not afraid to use them."

A spray of playing cards riffled to the ground from each arm, many hundreds of cards in all. The audience gasped. Max affected bewilderment and knelt to gather the objects together. "Oh dear, oh dear, now how did this happen? Ah well. I was to request some applause for you young lady, but now I must ask: is there an optician in the house?"

A wave of laughter washed the embarrassed volunteer back to her seat.

John relaxed, secure in the hands of a professional. He glanced towards Sara, and she returned his gaze. "He's wonderful John, isn't he?"

The next sequence involved cards and cups. There was something in the way Max carried himself that captured the eye. The stage was tiny, but he moved with fluidity and grace, with no sign of being constrained. Even storing and retrieving paraphernalia from his cabinet had a performer's precision, conveying the constant sense that the heart of the unfolding illusion would be found in this motion, or the next, or the one after.

"Young sir," announced the magician, "is this," he brandished the ace of clubs, "your card?"

A teenager, all ripped jeans and swagger, shook his head, struggling to suppress delight at making the performance falter.

Max asked, "In that case, might I keep it?" The youth hesitated before nodding. "Excellent. You have agreed I keep the card. To make it most useful will you also please share with me your PIN number?" This time the youth refused, but confusion had destroyed his smirk entirely. Max flipped the ace around to reveal, taped behind it, a bank ATM card. In a stunned double take, the youth glared back towards the bench where his jacket lay. "By all means, return and check your wallet. And tell us what you find."

After a moment's rifling the youth produced the Jack of Diamonds which had somehow found its way into his wallet.

"Finally, might I invite you to read out what is written on the back?"

The youth began, "Seven—", before halting abruptly. Flushing, he crumpled the playing card, and shoved it into his pocket.

Max smiled. "You do not wish to. I see. In any event, lacking your security number I shall return this bank card with thanks. For my next show might I suggest you bring contactless?"

Laughter grew while the youth urgently questioned his neighbours, his journey from swagger to cluelessness complete. The room filled with warm applause. But the magician allowed only moments before raising his hand. "I thank you for your appreciation. But my presentation so far is common parlour magic, imitated many times. What follows however, is something quite unique to my own performances, and for that, I need another volunteer. So please, a healthy gentleman to join me on stage?"

Max scanned around the room, before, in a welcome near miss, settling on John's neighbour. "You sir! In your fine striped shirt! You sit at the back to avoid attention. But your ruse has failed. Do you care to join me?" The man protested, holding up his walking stick. "A poor excuse, but it will serve, I suppose. Surely another shirker from the back two rows will come to my aid?"

Sara whispered, "Why don't you do it?"

John wrinkled his nose, hoping someone else would take the challenge. He came here for entertainment rather than humiliation.

But Sara leaned in closer. She squeezed his hand. "Please John, for me?"

And he rose automatically, fingers still tingling from her touch. How could he refuse? The applause from the crowd became a physical force, sweeping him onto the stage.

The magician extended a hand to greet him. "A brave young man assists this old one! What is your name, good sir?" John introduced himself sheepishly. From the back row Sara waved and laughed.

The magician's spiel continued. "Now, one of the highest and most dramatic forms of magic is escapology. Even today we still marvel at the feats of Houdini, ninety years after his passing. Houdini was a great escape artiste, but a traditional one, for where Houdini worked his escapes with the abilities of his own body, I work mine through the untrained and unskilled bodies of volunteers. Ladies and gentlemen! You are about to witness a remarkable exhibition of 'Remote Escapology' and it is a feat you will never forget!"

Max tugged at the black velvet drape to the rear of the stage. Its removal revealed not a wall, but a simple frame. The stage itself stretched back a further two metres, and in the centre of that space stood a chair of elaborate design.

Finely carved pale wood did not mask the peculiar construction. Oddly, the armrests formed curved channels. Inside those channels, buckled straps rested on rectangular blocks ready to secure him in place. As he sat, even through his clothing the polished wood felt cold and unyielding. The back legs of the chair were longer than those at the front, pitching him slightly forward.

His feet rested inside a base, which was a wooden box with shallow curving sides. John pressed downwards finding it solidly connected. The structure presumably prevented lifting or unbalancing once secured. Max led the audience through the confinement, some craning forwards to watch the ankle straps buckled and drawn tight. "And now the arms! John, please, roll up your sleeves. Yes. Position your hands palm upwards please, everything must be visible. Just so. Now my friend, can you move?"

He tested the restraints. His legs were held fast, and while he detected a little give in the arm straps, his elbows were too close to the broad chair back to use it. He shook his head.

But Max frowned. "I remain unconvinced!"

Reaching behind his cabinet the magician returned with a panel. It clicked into a snug fit against the base of John's throat, covering his chest. Looking down, the panel shared the same wood and curving design as the rest of the chair. A deep breath forced his belly against the bottom of the panel, but despite that pressure it retained a perfect interlock with the arms, maintaining a seamless U-shaped channel. It curtailed his upper body movement almost completely; despite pushing hard the panel barely budged.

But once more, Max retreated, frowning. "No! It is still too easy! An escapologist's eyes are the keys to any lock!" He drew a blindfold from his pocket and fitted it snugly around John's head.

Darkness.

Pacing.

Audience murmur.

More pacing.

And then, abruptly, silence.

"Finally, Max the Magnificent is satisfied – so two more volunteers? Yes, you sir. And thank you, madam."

Soft footfalls approached and mounted the stage. Cabinet drawers slid open and slammed closed.

"Now my friend John, your first step on the road to escape is identification. In a moment our volunteers will put something into your hands. You must identify these items and then turn that knowledge towards a solution. Can you do that?"

John nodded. Curiouser and curiouser.

"So, dear helpers, take one of these and put them into our volunteer's hands."

Something brushed John's left palm only to be quickly removed at the magician's protest. Could it have been a key? A lock pick? The touch had been too fleeting to draw any conclusion.

"No, no, no! Not like that! You make it too easy. Like this. You see? Like this, like this!"

Laughter rippled though the audience in response to the magician's strident demonstration.

"So you both understand, yes? Then together now. On the count of three. One. Two. Three!"

John felt blades pierce both hands simultaneously. They bit deep into his palm, punching through muscle and bone and sinking into the blocks beneath. There followed two sharp cracks, metal against metal, driving them deeper. He jerked violently in reaction, a movement aborted by the tearing pain of the stationary blades.

This agony was like nothing he had ever experienced, like nothing he could ever have imagined. What was happening here? What had gone wrong?

But the crowd applauded, cheering more fervently than at any previous point in the evening. Some stamped their approval; seats rasped as people rose to their feet.

John screamed and screamed and screamed.

He wanted to tell Sara to get out, get away, get help. But he couldn't form words. His mind was trapped in a chaos of pain and fear.

Somehow through that maelstrom he heard the conjuror's words. "And so it begins, ladies and gentlemen, our lesson in escape. Brave volunteer, can you identify what has happened?"

But the words foundered against a wall of agony; senseless noise colliding with the pain before falling away.

"I beg your pardon? It is difficult to understand when you shriek and grunt this way. If you don't know the answer just say so! You are, after all, a beginner, and you will be forgiven."

Again the crowd laughed. This was what they wanted to see.

The damp cold of the vaults was inside John now, soaking through his shirt and trouser legs, rising, a clammy tingling in his brow and neck. His heart pounded out each gulp of air, and he gagged, swallowing desperately, drowning in his own breath.

The chair began to turn and spin and twist, like the bed of a little boy in the grip of fever.

JUST IN BED.

"Lots of rest and liquids," the doctor said, "and he'll be right as rain in the morning."

And here comes mum, brisk and caring, moving the sweat-plastered hair from his eyes, mopping his brow, touching his cheek, making him safe.

"Sleep, Johnny", she said, "just sleep, son"

And as the doctor left the house a door slammed in the distance.

BUT IT WAS in the distance above.

And it was the door to the vaults.

Someone (Sara, please God, Sara) had got out. John needed to stay alive until help arrived, which meant remaining conscious. Struggling against the pain, he pushed it down, just a little, just far enough so he could think.

First control the breathing.

Breathe.

Breathe slowly.

"Ladies and gentlemen, marvel at this first stage! Our budding escapologist struggles to absorb all we have taught him. But, alas, his own body rejects the lessons! A wounded animal, it craves only oblivion. The oblivion we grant to all who threaten our work."

Wounded animal, yes. But threat?

THEY'D DRAGGED *the drunken giant to all the way to suite 552 before he'd tried to speak. The words sounded like: "S'not my room."*

"Is this right?" John asked the man with the glasses.

"Oh yes. He's ours. We'll look after him."

THE ORATORY CONTINUED, a vague rise and fall in the background of his breathing and his pain. If he wanted to live, part of him must be aware, must assess the damage to his body, and must seize any opportunities for delay or escape. That part of him became a pinpoint focus, a focus inside his body but insulated from it. A focus that could explore.

Left hand? Fuck no! Too much, far, far too much. He howls and grunts and they laugh. But ignore him and them. They don't matter.

Right hand? Oh-sweet-jesus! Away, away!

But stop.

Go back.

There was something, something important.

Was the blade at an angle? When he'd jerked before, could he have wrenched it out, even slightly?

So try to move; just a tiny, tiny movement. He screams again, but ignore him. Just focus, stay here, at the hand. The hand with the moving blade. The hand with the loose moving blade. And think.

Max called for volunteers. What now, you old bastard? What are you going to do now?

Focus.

Arm straps slightly loose, but no room to pull straight back, even forgetting the blade. So what else?

Footsteps arrive on the stage. Max spoke again. Something about scalpels.

Do it now. No time for anything else. Quickly, so it happens before you can feel it.

John forced his elbow off of the right-hand armrest. He pulled fast and hard, down and to the side, elbow hitting but just clearing the extended back of the chair and wrenching the blade out of the wood. The blade through his palm hit the restraining strap as he pulled further, twisting round and slicing inside his hand. The sound was sickening; ripped cartilage, scraped bone. It was unbearable. His arm recoiled forward again, away from the strap. Warm liquid sprayed into his open screaming mouth.

But he had to carry on. He had to try again. Pull harder.

He noticed a change in the room. Max's spiel faltered as the blade caught in the restraint for a second time. The audience gasped as the blade wrenched loose and his arm came free.

The push to lift the blindfold from his eyes left a bloody streak in the middle of John's face, but he could see them now, and they all stared back: the audience, the magician, and the two volunteers with their little knives.

Despite the agony, he drew something from their frozen moment of panic; galvanised, he grasped and wrenched out the knife pinning his other arm. The pain was excruciating, but whether he'd be able to use the weapon in any meaningful way or not, he brandished it as best he could while freeing himself from the left arm restraint.

"Now, now. Put that down," soothed Max, recovering his composure "We don't want anyone getting hurt."

If he could just hold them off, keep them back then help would arrive; he'd heard her leave. He looked over to Sara's seat that should be, would be, *must be* empty.

It was. Thank God.

John lashed out again and the volunteers jumped back, one of them stumbling off the stage and onto the front pew of spectators.

He heard the voice in his ear. "John, stop this. It's all pointless."

Twisting around as much as the chair would allow, he saw Sara. She hadn't escaped, hadn't gone for help. But it was hard to understand: she wore the glittering eye mask and sequined silver dress of the magician's assistant. He saw the assistant catch an object thrown by the conjuror. He saw the assistant swing.

And a hammer crunched into his right shoulder.

Perhaps the shoulder dislocated or perhaps the collarbone fractured. Whichever. He dropped the knife. And screamed.

Max, grinning now, carefully unfolded his black handkerchief to reveal a tiny bottle. He removed a stopper and poured the contents onto the black cloth. "We must make our guest more comfortable!" A single stride pressed the handkerchief against John's face. He recoiled from the acrid pungency, but the magician's hand at the back of his head forced the matter.

And now, everything began happening in a haze, almost as though he were separating from his captive body, separating from the pain, watching it all from a distance.

THE MAN in the chair screams as they refasten the straps and fix the knives once more through his hands.

Whoops from the audience when Max produces a string of handkerchiefs from the captive's trouser pocket, and uses them to stuff his mouth silent. A protruding rainbow of stubs darken in the damp of each grunting breath.

Volunteers slice the length of the man's forearms, letting the blood cascade into the semicircular channel formed by the chair. Max indicates just where to cut on the captive's throat, and they watch as blood trickles downwards, down the restraining front panel and into the curved channel of the interconnecting chair arms. The pitch of the chair causes the blood to run and gather at the front.

Holding a pair of spigots the magician turns to the audience with a grand bow. "Ladies and gentlemen, the interactive part of our evening begins. Please form an orderly queue by the side of the stage."

Applause.

A small crowd gathers. They point admiringly at their captive, the bravest leaning across to test the knives in his hands. The procession contains a familiar figure in a duffel coat, carrying a satchel. Who? Perhaps a late arrival when the door slammed earlier?

It doesn't matter.

It's cold.

So cold.

ON THE NIGHT *Tricia's dog died, snow had lain thick on the ground.*

They'd walked for hours in the playing fields, throwing snowballs, watching each missile implode against his muzzle, laughing at his confused barks of encore. As they set off for home, high spirits sent the dog running ahead, up the steps and out of the gate.

Life changed in a short series of sounds. Each one was a domino falling: a car slides on ice, the dull thump of collision, agonised whining, engine roar as the vehicle speeds away.

They ran to find him.

The poor beast was on his side, breathing froth. His blood polluted the white snow in a widening circle. He was beyond saving.

But when they discussed what needed to be done, Tricia became upset. Why did John want to kill Teddy? How could he even think it? As she stared at him, something entered her eyes, something that never left again.

She'd never understood.

He didn't want to kill Teddy.

He loved Teddy: he'd just wanted to take away the pain.

He just wanted to take away the pain.

SARA DISPENSES CUPS and brushes as Max explains where to make the incision.

Carefully, they remove the front panel and open the captive's shirt. Dry blood cakes his chest from seeping throat wounds.

A volunteer asks a question and everybody laughs as Max corrects his grammar.

THE OTHER SHOW made nobody laugh. It was too awful. By halfway through he'd been daydreaming, waiting for it to end. But even when you don't listen things linger somehow, like that awful song.

Slice with the knife and open 'em up. Slippery giblets, schlup, schlup, schlup!

So tired.

So cold.

Tired and cold but they won't let him sleep.

There's a pattern on the floor now, they're painting something, red on white.

Just like Teddy in the snow.

Some of them are fighting over his wrists.

Why won't they let him sleep?

———————

MAX LEANS OVER HIM, shakes him, slaps his face, whispers in his ear. "John! Have you learned how to escape? Do you know the secret? There is only one way, so take it. Take it now."

And then the magician turns to his audience. "My friends, our show draws to a close. All that remains is gratitude for our brave volunteer, who even now sets out to follow Harry Houdini, Useslau, Emil Kio and all other departed greats of the art."

It was easier than John had ever imagined. One moment he was there, and the next—

———————

WHEN THE SMALL crowd from the vaults dissipated, an older man and his son paused for a few moments at the doorway. The father briefly steadied himself on his cane, recovering his breath from the staircase.

"We thought he'd ruined the show, instead he was the star," his son said.

The man nodded. "That was even better than in Prague. Best thing I've seen at the Festival by a mile."

They both laughed and embraced warmly before turning towards the Royal Mile and the safety of home.

3

THE MISSING HUSBAND
THURSDAY 1ST SEPTEMBER, 11:45

George Street busied as lunchtime approached, and Andy wondered if they were wasting their time. Perhaps his uniformed colleagues on Rose Street and St Andrew's Square were faring better, but nobody in the bars, restaurants or shops he'd visited recognised Wood's photograph. Most staff hadn't worked late enough to have seen her, but all took the details to circulate around their colleagues.

It would be significant progress to establish where she'd been on the evening of her murder. Since Nesbitt was interviewing at the council, and Devlin was doing whatever Devlins do on their first day, he'd taken a shoe-leather dice roll. Sometimes that even worked. But not today. Not so far at least.

The throngs of festival tourists hauling luggage were another cause for depression. The population ballooned during August, but September stuck a pin in it. So many potential witnesses, all fleeing the city? Not a good omen.

His radio crackled. "Link-man? Are you easily scared? Over."

Now he remembered what Devlin did. Wasted everyone's bloody time. "No, DS Devlin. Not usually."

"I logged a spooky call from an Angela McKay. Her husband didn't come home last night, and a psychic lady, a certain Mrs Chambers from the Palmerston Centre, has implied he's dead."

This was weird, even for Devlin. "Are you serious?"

"Totally. But then again, her husband might be out on the piss. Apparently he has a history of falling off wagons."

"But it's not even twenty-four hours yet. What's the relevance to us?"

"He worked for the council. Robin McKay."

That changed things. "Where was he on the night Wood died?"

"Home in bed. But maybe he knew something and got cold feet the next day?"

Devlin left the details and signed off. It was probably nothing, but the Edinburgh Council connection placed it somewhere on the to-do list.

When a further two frustrating hours passed with no recognition of Wood's photograph, he thought back over Devlin's call. They had a statement from McKay's wife, but here was another witness, albeit unusual, who claimed knowledge of their missing person. He might as well eliminate her early. They weren't too far away from here, so he took the chance and called the spiritualist centre on Palmerston Place. If their Mrs Chambers truly had information, he'd hear her out.

But the friendly receptionist didn't know where to find his witness right now, only that she would be in again tomorrow morning for a 'demonstration of mediumship'. Whatever that was, he decided to be there to greet her.

Until then, back to the shoe leather.

4

DOIRIN CHAMBERS

FRIDAY 2ND SEPTEMBER, 09:15

Doirin Chambers was in the zone. Silk lilies? All present and correct, no thieving like last week. Clock? Ticking. Loud bugger actually. One minute to go. Dutch courage? Holding. Audience? Respectable mostly, which is something for this time of year. Settling down now. OK. Breathe. Smile.

"Welcome friends, to the Palmerston Centre and our Conan Doyle suite for today's demonstration of mediumship. My name is Doirin Chambers. As a wee lassie in Glasgow I took Sir Arthur's advice and eliminated the impossibility that my daddy's love was gone forever. What remained brought us all here today: the world of spirit."

The room was packed. So many faces, such a mixture of emotions. "Before we start, I know everyone is hoping for a message, and I'll be as busy as I can in the next sixty minutes trying to make it happen. The hard truth is that only some of us will get a contact today, so please understand spirit doesn't line up for us in order of greatest need. It isn't to do with how much they love you or how strong an emotional bond you had. Sometimes it's more like the

January sales. We open our hearts and hear from whoever has today's pointiest elbows."

Her gaze flowed over the attendees while she waited for guidance. This was always the hard part. Making sure nothing masked the vibration. Even the tiniest distraction could put the mockers on it. Like the egg on that jumper. Not spilled, no, a big, smiley Humpty Dumpty thing. On a grown woman, too. You see some characters around festival time. Being heckled by last week's bereaved comedian was not an experience she'd care to repeat. Thankfully the madness was all winding up now and it was getting back to business as usual.

"It can take a few moments to make a connection. The spirits are awful shy tonight, so fill your hearts with trust and love."

Check him. Shuffling in at the back. Big hands. Granite face. Solemn. Like a caveman who's just lost his mammoth. Aw pish! Focus-pocus! Here and now! Catch the vibration.

It's the shuffling though. Why do that? It doesn't help. The opposite. The quiet bit in the symphony isn't the time to start scraping the floorboards. C'mon. Conductor in the house.

A sudden flurry in her mind. Woah. Someone's in a hurry. More than someone. A lot of someones. But they don't want to connect for themselves, just to push another—Oh. OK. Her with the hat.

Doirin clasped her own arms and squeezed. It made spirit more talkative for some reason. We're never beyond a hug, and that's the truth. "I've got someone for you dear. A chap. This is recent. There's a lot of emotion." She flashed to her Davie, taken young at forty-five, seven years back. Then it burst out of her violently, like a sob. "Aw missus! You lost your husband! I'm so sorry!"

But hat-lady was puzzled. She was open to something, but that wasn't it. Mobile phone vibrating like crazy. She'll likely try to nudge me along.

"Not my husband, no. He's fine. But could it be a husband figure? Like a close uncle?"

You need to be gentle on these occasions. "An uncle close enough to be mistaken for a husband? That's one for the social work. I'm awful sorry. This message is insistent. He's saying it's your man. Did you have a previous marriage?"

Still nothing. A true professional might have gone with the uncle thing. Ah well. Hat-lady's phone goes ballistic again, so off she trots. Charming. Spirit doesn't like that. Doirin neither. Need a new vibration. Ah. The pull. Captain Caveman. "You sir, with the dark coat?"

He starts looking left and right, miming the big *who me?* They always do that when they're just in for a wee nosey. But there are no spectators in spirit, we're all in the game. "I'm hearing you're a services man. Not army. Police?" Actually, he looks like a prehistoric undertaker. "They're giving me a name. Lynne? No. forgive me, sir, sounds like Lunk? Does that mean anything to you?" That's terrible. He'll think I'm having a go.

Silence. Not used to answering questions, this one. More of an asker. Just chill, Doirin. The expectation in the room will have him singing like a budgie in no time. One-elephant. Two-elephant. Three - ah - there he goes.

"Could it be Link?" He muttered without enthusiasm, but the words still carried. He had one of those voices. "Link's me. At least, it's a nickname some people use."

His eyes glowered from under the brim of his brow. Link. Good name. And good on him for admitting it, knowing everyone in the room would visualise *The Evolution of Man*, with him one step up from Billy Knuckles.

"It's because I'm good at connections. Y'know, links between things."

Doirin nodded. Aye son. You keep telling yourself that.

Commotion at the back again. Keep it together Doirin. Just another day at your friendly neighbourhood spiritualist centre. Restful contemplation, sought but not guaranteed. Oh. Hat-lady's back. And she's crying.

The woman held her phone at arm's length, face twisted in shock.

She stumbled forwards, staring at the medium. "How did you know?"

Doirin hated this. Normally a person will cross and take time to get comfy, but break the protocol and you've got a scene to deal with. "Are you with friends? Bless, darling, we're here for you. This is very unusual. It takes a special love to call out so quickly. What I'm feeling is that he doesn't want to go. He wants to be with you."

Plenty of drama for the bystanders this. Lots of shocked admiration. The old-timers would say nothing pulls the crowds like the old instant widow. Painful though. The old-timers would also say the show must go on. And they were right on that one too.

Doirin continued the demonstration, her attention pulled here and there, trying to interpret and pass information as best she could. On two occasions she got the nagging suspicion Constable Caveman was talking to Hat-Lady. And by the end, as she worked down the post-demonstration line of grateful attendees, she saw him waiting by the door. Notebook out, polis face on.

Doirin sighed. If she didn't know better, she'd almost have said someone was about to get lifted.

To suggest that Andy Lorimar didn't welcome the placement of the interview rooms in Fettes Avenue would be an understatement. At the far end of an open-plan office packed with the professionally curious, it was a gauntlet run of smirks, sneers, raised eyebrows, and now, worst of all, Jamie bloody Devlin's piss-poor attempts at physical comedy. Today found him inexplicably simulating masturbation while pointing at a sprinkler on the ceiling.

With such high jinks an ever-present danger, Andy ensured anyone he brought in walked ahead of him. As a result, they were mostly spared the unedifying sight of grown police officers acting like chimps. Unfortunately, today's guest had insisted on carrying armfuls of fake lilies, hanging left and right in a messy sprawl, bobbing over desks and brushing the faces of his colleagues. This took their hilarity to another level, and that grated.

When one lily dropped to the floor, by instinct Andy stooped to retrieve it which somehow managed to worsen matters. The thin stem appeared so incongruous in his shovel-like hands, he found himself striding through a chorus of mimed pleas that he begin carrying it in his teeth.

After reaching the relative sanctuary of the interview room he took a moment to consider the woman across the desk. She was imposing in several ways. Her eyes were bright, but held a fierce cynicism. He guessed she was around five foot ten in those purple boots of hers. But the flamboyance of her bohemian dress was smothered by the thick sheepskin coat she wore above it like armour. He wondered if the scorn in those eyes ever softened into mischief. Then he wondered why the hell he was wondering that and got back to the job in hand.

Under the circumstances she appeared unusually confident. He could have covered most of his questions outside, but the oddness of the situation had earned her an invitation into the station. Such an invitation could sometimes shake a windfall out of the information tree. But not with this one.

She sat placidly arranging her lilies on the desk. "Tenner per stem these, can you believe it? Just about rooked me. But they're my signature now. They're beautiful. No pollen stains, and the beauty lasts. Nothing worse than a dead flower."

Andy couldn't help himself. "Ironic for a spiritualist, don't you think?"

She fixed him with a withering hybrid expression, half sympathy, half contempt. "Son. We're talking about plants."

Unusually chastened, he knuckled down to business. "OK, Ms Chambers, thanks for your voluntary attendance here today. 10:49 a.m. Interview begins. Ms Doreen Chambers and Detective Inspector Andy Lorimar."

"Forget this Mizz Chambers. You can use my first name. But

that's not how it's spelt." Her finger stabbed the notebook in front of him. "It's D-o-i-r-i-n. Mammy was from South Uist so we got Hebridean names. I'm not normally fussy, but you seem," her mouth puckered, "a very particular man."

He corrected his note before continuing. "OK Doirin. What's your knowledge of Edinburgh Councillor Joan Wood?"

Her eyes widened. Surprised. So she should be. A plausible start.

"Nothing. Except from the news. Was she knocked down on Charlotte Square the other night?"

"Yes, that was her. What information do you have on her colleague, council employee Robin McKay?"

"I've never heard of him. Son, I thought this was about me upsetting the hat lady?"

"We'll come to that. But Doirin? I'm a Detective Inspector. I've not answered to 'son' since I was twelve."

"Good for you, son. I'm not asking you to answer to anything. I think you're the one doing that." Doirin rearranged her lilies, one eyebrow showing he could take it or leave it.

Despite everything he found himself warming to her.

"You claim not to know council employee Robin McKay. And yet on August 31st his wife Angela McKay claims you told her," he checked his notebook. "Mickey is sorry he missed the prawn cocktail."

Doirin considered this for a moment. "Oh. Her? Charming! She blanked me. Said she was only there with a friend and didn't understand me at all."

"How did you know she'd been waiting for her husband at a restaurant?"

"I didn't."

"How did you know what she had ordered?"

"I didn't."

"If you didn't know these things why did you say them?"

Doirin sighed. It was an exaggerated sigh of the kind normally reserved for toddlers. He tried to glower back. He had the right face for glowering, everyone told him. But today his glower felt warm in both cheeks.

"Now, Detective Inspector, I may be a large in the world of fashion, but in the world of spirit I'm a medium. I say things I don't know on a daily basis. Sometimes the message gets through. Am I honestly in here for doing my job?"

He changed tack. "When you said," again, he consulted his notebook, "that 'he had looked down on her with love', did you mean from heaven? Were you suggesting Robin McKay is dead?"

"I'm not a phone service son. If I'm giving a message from someone, that usually means they are in spirit."

"Usually?"

"Nobody's perfect. It's not an exact science." It was Andy's turn to raise an eyebrow, at the idea that what Doirin did was a science of any kind. "See, it's like voices whispering on a radio. Some days the radio is beside me. Sometimes it's next door under a blanket. I try to catch snippets and pass them on. I try to be accurate, but I'm never sure. All mediums are different in how they translate things, but I will say for me, down just means down. Spirit isn't above us or below us. But, always, spirit is with us. D'you understand?"

It sounded like a line she'd used before. Andy thought he might as well tug the thread a little, see if she unravels. "You said Angela McKay blanked you. Was there more to say if she'd played along?"

"Here! Hold on a minute. Play along? It's not a game, son. But what she did was rude."

"But would you have told her more if she hadn't been rude?"

"Maybe something about their first date. But I didn't memorise it. I mean, she waved me away! Like I was a midgie!"

The display of outrage seemed broadly genuine. Andy took a few notes and then sat back to think. Time to cover the most obvious possibility. "Doirin, today you told Isabel Harper that she had lost her husband. She then discovered he had fallen or, perhaps, and you might confirm this, *been pushed* from a ladder and had been rushed to hospital. Is someone giving you information about crimes that have been, or will be committed?"

"When you say someone do you mean—"

"Yes, Doirin, yes. I mean someone alive." That such a point required confirmation became suddenly annoying. "Corporeal. On this side of life. Clogs unpopped. Bucket unkicked. Less of a spirit guide, more of what might technically be called an accomplice. Clear enough?"

"Yes, Detective Inspector. Perfectly clear."

He waited. So did she. Her judgemental eyebrow was back. And she was considering the lilies again.

Sighing, he said, "I don't intend to disrespect your beliefs. Please understand, when I ask these questions I'm trying to make sense of a unusual set of circumstances. I hope you can help me. Nobody should be"—he searched for the phrase—"in spirit, before their time."

She made a little sound at the back of her throat, as though judging an apology. "Nobody alive gives me information. I don't wear an earpiece, or have an accomplice. I'm passing on what I can barely hear to people who are often in no fit state to listen." She paused for a moment, and then continued, more quietly. "Rushed to the hospital, you said. So they tried at least. To save him, I mean. He really didn't want to go." Her fingernails gripped the desk.

"They did save him. He's in intensive care."

Doirin's hands relaxed, and her smile was like switching on a floodlight. "See, son, I'm wrong! I was wrong! That's great. He didn't die!"

Her happiness was believable, and he'd seen plenty of fake smiles to benchmark it against. But given she was daft as a brush already, the fact Jonathan Harper had been clinically dead for seventy seconds in the ambulance was best left unsaid.

Her expression shifted. "But if he's alive, why am I here?"

"What happened today was just an aside. You're here because you claimed to have information relating to an ongoing investigation."

Her sigh warmed his cheeks again. What was so special about her disdain that he actually felt it?

"Son, I don't mean to talk down to you, but it isn't my fault if you never learned to listen. I don't have information any more than a letter box does. Stuff passes through. And I can't just switch it on and get you more either. For me, it needs the loved ones. They're the magnet that draws spirit close."

"I understand your belief, Doirin. But we *will* need to speak to you again if we find Robin McKay is dead. Your claim of prior knowledge could make you a suspect in our investigation."

He examined her face carefully. Stress sometimes led to revelation. But in her case it led to outrage. "Aw for Christ's sake! This hardly ever happens and you're painting me as Doctor bloody Crippen." But her anger faded into a concerned silence.

He pressed the advantage. "It may be advisable for you to consult a lawyer. Will I get you some contact information?"

"You will not! Lawyer? They're worse than you lot. I don't need a lawyer."

"I'm not saying you do for sure. But you might."

"I don't son. Jimmy says I don't. Jimmy says you never take the easy answer."

"Jimmy?"

"Aye Jimmy. McErthy? McArthy? He—no! Not him." She hesitated, "That's strange. It's the others. They want him to talk about your mother?"

Andy rubbed his eyes. "Interview concluded, 11:09 a.m.."

He pointed Doirin Chambers towards the reception before walking to the gent's toilet and locking himself into a cubicle.

Inside, he raised the toilet lid and crouched, facing away from the cubicle door, away from his colleagues, away from his work, away from what had just been said. He queasily examined the stained porcelain, feeling the sweat breaking on his forehead, trickling down his back. He wondered if he would heave. This wasn't good. It hadn't happened in years.

But it was happening now, and he couldn't stop it. The sucking vortex of his past was drawing him in. And the more desperately he tried to block the memories, the more urgently they pressed in. A boy's memories, escaped from the locked box in a man's mind.

———

HE REMEMBERED BEING HUDDLED under a blanket in the corner of the room. It had been bright outside, but he hadn't known the time. The other beds had been empty.

Ilsa was away, but someone had brought up a tray of food. He hadn't touched it.

Outside, children were playing. Fourteen was too old for here, Ilsa had said, which meant he'd be moved on soon. But he couldn't understand why he'd been accepted in the beginning. He didn't feel like he'd changed at all since then. How could he? Everything inside was frozen.

He thought about Mum a lot.

It was like she'd walked into a tunnel, only to reappear a few days later, with a lifeless face of grey newsprint, staring at him from the front page. Now everyone thought they knew her, but they didn't. You can't read a headline as a life story. Everything that matters is missing.

Before, when he'd been able to cry, he'd thought it didn't help. But now he knew better. The tears were a pressure valve, letting the grief escape. His face might be dry, but the poison was trapped inside.

Grief hardens.

At first, it felt like grit in his joints and muscles, aching with every movement. But when the tears dried, the grit coarsened, sharpening into shards. Wherever it touched, it cut and infected and spread.

Before, Andy had enjoyed words.

Ossify.

A good word for a horrible thing. His insides were hardening and breaking. Everything he used to be was splintering inside him. It was too painful to move, so he stayed in bed.

Sometimes he thought he could hear her, but faintly because she was so far and so deep. That's why he tried to find the tunnel too. He would walk in, and disappear, and they'd both be reunited in the headlines. But it wouldn't matter. He wouldn't have to see the front pages this time, and it wouldn't bother anybody else. After Granda had died, no one was left who cared. They'd only had each other.

Later a doctor visited to explain that Andy was harming himself. He realised if he ate the doctor would leave. So he did. And the doctor went. And then Andy returned to the tunnel.

It was dark in there, but he felt like he was getting closer. Some visitors thought him rude. But they didn't understand. They were too far away to speak to, and he didn't want to come out.

The other children were disturbed by him. He could sometimes see worried little faces staring down from that circle of light in the distance. But this shouldn't affect them. They went outside to play and came inside to sleep. But he knew where his time, all his time, was best spent. In the gloom. Feeling his way. Following the line of damp brickwork beneath his fingers. That line took him deeper and further than ever. Although not far enough. Not yet.

But the day Ilsa placed an object on his bed, it somehow caught his attention.

He felt her do it, even down here in the dark. Just a slight tremor in the floor of the tunnel. "Andrew!" she shouted. It was loud, and it echoed, the walls reverberating with her strong accent. Ilsa had always understood he was moving farther away. That she needed to shout. That she needed to force him to come back.

Sometimes Ilsa stared so fiercely at him, he wondered if she knew about the tunnel. He thought perhaps she could see, somehow, the true surface of his world reflected in his eyes. Her face had such intensity. He noticed that again now, as she spoke and cajoled and shouted and tried to make him reply. But he didn't know what to say.

She was speaking again. Something about a friend giving a talk to the children. But it was hard to hear her over the sound of the dripping water, over the sound of his own footsteps. The echoes grew loud this far down. He knew if he went much further, soon this would be all he could hear. Just the sounds of the tunnel washing over him forever. He wasn't scared of that. Why should he be? Those might be the same noises his mother heard. Perhaps, she was listening to them even now. He should go deeper.

But Ilsa had placed an object on his bed.

It was a small blue box, with an unusual geometric design. He couldn't read the foreign writing, but he understood two words in English: Magic Cube. Perhaps Ilsa had brought it back from her trip to Hungary.

He picked up the box and removed the tape sealing the lid. Inside he found a cube with six coloured faces. Each face was built from nine segments, and each row or column formed part of a horizontal or vertical slice that rotated independently.

It looked like some kind of puzzle.

One twist. Two twist. No. Go back. Andy restored the faces to the starting position. He found he could retrace his steps for up to six moves, but once he pushed past seven, he made a wrong choice and the uniform faces became hopelessly lost.

This was a proper puzzle. And he had always enjoyed puzzles, especially difficult ones. They were challenges you could measure yourself against. Mental hurdles to jump for the fun of it, and the higher the hurdle the better. This one was a high hurdle.

But more than that. Each clicking rotation acted as a kind of ratchet, slowly pushing the darkness and the echo and the dripping water further from his awareness. He knew it wasn't gone. It waited for him. He was just allowing himself a little distraction.

For the first time in months he thought about a friend from before. About Mr Gallagher. He wondered briefly if the old man still visited the library with his newspaper and his little chess set. It was part of his life he hadn't considered for a long time. He'd avoided thinking much about the past at all. Why remember things spoiled beyond recovery and gone for good? So he returned his focus to the cube.

A few moves more and he had the white side restored, but it left the other faces in disarray. He needed the side blocks adjacent to the white face to match the coloured centre of their respective side surfaces before he could even think about a second full side. This would take some thinking about.

And it did. He thought about it until he was tired, then he thought about it while he lay awake in the dark, and even while he was sleeping. The following morning he was still working on it when he saw the girl staring. Face covered in freckles, arms covered in ink marks. Shona. She pointed to the completed top surface. "Well done! You've made it all white!"

"That's just one side. One side isn't enough. You need to complete the whole thing. So I'm working on the top edges now. They'll help me get the rest." He twisted again.

"Can you show me?"

"No." Her face fell, so he relented. "Maybe when I finish it." Shona smiled and ran from the room.

Ilsa came later and sat on the edge of his bed. "I find Buvos Kocka —the cube—back home and think of you. You like it?"

Andy continued working on the edges. The hard part was building on previous progress without losing what was already achieved. But he nodded to Ilsa. It was a good gift.

"I glad. Now, I wondering. Maybe ... you join for lunch today?"

He wasn't sure if he wanted to do that. When he didn't turn up for meals at first, they ignored it, but eventually they'd begun bringing him a tray. "Do I have to?"

Ilsa shrugged. "You should. After lunch my friend come. He talk all about his job. He police."

Andy shook his head fiercely. He hated the police. They hadn't helped and they never helped and he didn't want to see them and he didn't want to hear them and he would stay here. He dropped the cube and pushed himself back into the corner.

"No. Andrew. No! You don't need to! We bring you some food. It OK." She pushed the puzzle back into his hands. "Keep working. It hard. But you only one here who could do it. You get it soon, I know."

After she left he worked on the cube again. He tried not to think about anything else. But it was impossible, and his attention wandered to the hubbub of lunch, then the clattering of the dishes, and eventually the sound of a man's voice in the front room. He was talking about families, then about his uniform. Andy was on edge for over an hour until finally the front door closed and he heard an engine start. From his window he saw the rear of the police car retreating down the road.

A few hours later, the top face and all its edges were the way he wanted them. His instincts told him to work on the middle layer, but the more progress he made, the more he had to protect.

The man was in the room before Andy even heard him. He wore faded jeans and a T-shirt with a picture of a car on it. His face seemed nervous, but friendly. "Go on," he said, "Guess the show."

Andy didn't need to guess. "It's a Ford Gran Torino. That's the car Starsky and Hutch drive. Who are you?"

"I'm Jimmy. Put it there big guy." His voice sounded familiar. The man extended his hand.

Andy took it. "Are you new? Are you working here now?" But when he saw the man shake his head, he realised at once why he'd recognised the voice. He pulled away then, back towards the corner.

Jimmy frowned, raising his arms. "Hey! Relax pal. Just a social call."

"You're the police aren't you?"

"I'm not involved with your mum's case. And I think scaling back the investigation is a shitty decision too."

Andy looked at him. It was true. A shitty decision. "So why are they doing it?"

Jimmy shook his head. "The usual bollocks, Andy. Money, resources ... a case only stays at the top of the pile for so long. It depends on manpower and how many other crimes need looked at."

Andy glared at him. "And it depends on the victim too."

Jimmy held his gaze. "Aye. Sometimes. It shouldn't though."

"So why are you in the police if you think like that?"

The man sighed. "It's not perfect, but every day new bad things happen. If we can help stop some of them, and catch some of yesterday's bastards before they get to tomorrow, then that's a job worth doing."

Andy suddenly wanted to explain something. "It's not true, you know, everything they said. In the papers." His chin locked. Then his face flushed in a sudden battle with tears.

Jimmy grasped Andy's hands and looked hard into his eyes. "Nobody knew her, Andy. Not the newspapers, not the police, not the social workers. Your memories of your Mum, the ones you choose to keep close. They're all that matters. Ignore the rest, son. Nobody knew her but you."

And Andy cried.

So Jimmy waited.

Eventually the boy wiped his face on his bedsheets and said, "You grew up somewhere like this, didn't you?"

Jimmy frowned. "Why do you think that?"

"You're quite loud."

"Cheers for that."

"I mean. I could hear stuff you said to the other kids, downstairs. How they'd become experts at families and friendships because they'd need to have so many of them. It felt like ... I don't know. It felt like you were trying to pass on your experience or something."

"I didn't realise I had a psychologist in the building."

"But are you? Like us, I mean."

Jimmy sighed, gazing around the plain walls of the dormitory room. "I didn't have the best start I suppose. In care and fostered and all the rest. I was lost for a while back then. But I was young. All water under the bridge."

Andy felt the warmth of a smile at that idea. It was an unfamiliar feeling. "I might look forward to that then," he said, resuming his twisting at the cube.

"What?"

Andy glanced up at the police officer, feeling something inside softening. And with it, the reopening, perhaps, of other paths and other possibilities.

Jimmy wasn't letting it go. "Help me out then. What are you looking forward to, Andy?"

"You showing me the other side of that bridge."

———

ANDY PRESSED the cistern button and flushed. *But you did, didn't you? You showed me the other side.* He dried his eyes on a sheet of toilet paper as the crashing water faded to a gurgle. The impact of interviewing Doirin Chambers was unnerving. But it was over now, and there was work to do. He'd start with a cuppa.

5

PATHOLOGY
FRIDAY 2ND SEPTEMBER, 12:27

He spotted Brian Nesbitt as they approached the same coffee machine from opposite directions. Nesbitt was experiencing turbulence in his personal life, and looked in need of caffeine. Unfortunately Jamie Devlin and one of his cronies from Drylaw, Lenny Burns, were at the machine already.

Devlin pounced first. "Link-man! Talk of the devil, eh Lenny?"

Burns drew himself up to his full height, such as it was. Neither of these lads would have made it past the minimum five foot ten in Andy's day, but times change and opportunities were now equal. Sadly, in this case. "Aye Jamie. The big rain came and washed the scum off the streets. Oh! Sorry! Did I say scum? I meant old florists!"

Andy grimaced. "Have some respect Lenny. She was basically ages with me."

"Aye that's what we mean Link, fuckin' ancient!"

Devlin pushed between them. "Cool your jets Lenny! With a face like Link's you don't pass up the chance of female company. Even with a flower-power refugee from Godspell, am I right?"

Nesbitt continued walking, mumbling about upstairs having better cappuccino. Andy followed, doubting the DCI had ever graded the different machines but confident everything tasted better upwind of the chuckle brothers. "Chief, any chance I could visit Angela McKay?"

Nesbitt considered it, but only briefly. "Sure. Jamie took her statement before. A fresh eye wouldn't hurt. I'd be glad if we could rule her missing man in or out. Head over after the case meeting." Then he hesitated. "Are you puzzled by something?" Andy and Nesbitt shared a long history. Unlike most of Andy's colleagues he'd learned to distinguish the angry scowl from the pensive scowl from the satisfied scowl.

"It's about ... well. You remember Jimmy?"

"Which Jimmy? It's Scotland. We're drowning in them."

"McArthur. Jimmy McArthur."

"The old gaffer? God bless his soul. Sure, I remember him. I was only three years with Lothian and Borders when he retired, mind. That was some do. My head still nips thinking about it. Unusually, you were in quite a state yourself."

The upstairs drinks dispenser was identical to all the others, right down to the tide marks on the carpet. Andy opted for his usual hot water which he'd combine with a previously vetted brand of teabags back at his desk. When the stream ended he picked up the cup, feeling the sharp heat through the plastic.

Nesbitt's mockery was gentle. "Still on the chamomile tea? That stuff'll kill you." Then he punched his own complicated series of numbers, holding certain buttons for longer than others. Andy suspected the voodoo that sprang up around coffee machines would disappear overnight if suppliers made the slop drinkable by default. The DCI ended his incantation by repeatedly hitting the 'whitener' button. Labelling it 'milk' would probably have violated Trade Descriptions.

As the machine thought about it, Andy pressed on. "So... Jimmy. He used to say something about me. Can you remember?"

"Blow your own trumpet man!"

"It's important. Please."

Nesbitt answered over the hiss of the dispenser. "Well. I remember the whole team got a mention in his leaving speech. But you were something like 'Allergic to quick fixes and easy answers but by Christ Link'll get you the truth,' then the long pause, mind, 'eventually.' He was a good guy."

Andy swallowed. "Aye. The best" He considered the residue at the bottom of the drip-tray before continuing. "Retirement didn't suit him."

"It happens. Good police are like sticks of rock. But what brings Jimmy up, anyway? Is it his anniversary?"

Andy paused before answering. "I think he maybe knew the woman I just brought in. Doirin Chambers."

"From the little I heard her say she's not been in Edinburgh long."

Andy shrugged. "Four years."

Nesbitt nodded. "She's here four, but he's dead six and before that he'd been retired in Spain. Seems unlikely, no?"

Andy knew he was scowling again, another pensive one. There had to be a connection, and he'd find it.

Nesbitt nodded towards the staircase. "Maybe something will jog your memory in a minute… We're in that same room for the case meeting."

THE NATIONAL FORCE'S ruthless drive to increase efficiencies had created a fad for stand-up meetings. The idea was doing more with smaller rooms. As a bonus, it almost entirely prevented people falling asleep before the end.

When the team entered, Andy immediately caught the scent of Doirin's lilies. Then, recalling the flowers had been fake, realised it must be the aroma of her perfume. In any case, it wouldn't hang around for long now; the wet-dog funk of gathered detectives usually established itself quickly.

Nesbitt brought the room to order. "Resourcing. We've two new faces in the room. Welcome Detective Constable Lenny Burns."

Burns stepped forward, both winking *and* saluting towards Devlin before moving in for a fist bump. Nobody in the room had any doubt whose name he wanted inked inside his BFF tattoo. Andy rolled his eyes. Two clowns working the same case was far from ideal but at least keeping them occupied and out of his way was a problem for the DCI.

The chief continued. "We've also got an expert from the National Cyber Crime Unit. DS Elisia Petrakis will be around for a few days before heading back to the NCCU mothership."

A sombre young woman with short dark hair raised her head, nodded curtly to the room, and then returned attention to her smartphone. If you worked cyber crime you didn't have to feel guilty about that kind of thing. Preferring technology to people was what got you promoted.

Nesbitt's case summary brought everyone up to date with the circumstances around Councillor Wood's death, the white van and the social media postings. Then he glanced towards Petrakis, presumably seeking a technical analysis. "And I'd like to invite..."

Devlin coughed and stepped forward, always happy to hijack someone else's spotlight. He opened his notebook and turned the pages with an odd, slow reverence. Then having found what he was looking for he paused, letting the expectation build. Nesbitt frowned but reluctantly waved him on.

He began. "Yesterday, September first, a call to the investigation team reported the disappearance of another council employee. I immediately recognised this should become part of our inquiry." Andy sighed loudly. Devlin's mind was a steel trap, but only when viewed through the prism of his own notebook. "The caller was Angela McKay, wife of council IT employee Robin McKay. Her husband failed to return home the previous evening. Robin McKay has a history with alcohol, which in the view of Mrs McKay made him somewhat unreliable. She thought nothing of his absence initially. However, after a run in with a psychic at a spiritualist service she'd attended with a bereaved friend, she called on my assistance and I assigned Detective Inspector Lorimar to investigate and report back to me. This is—"

"Not entirely accurate, Detective Sergeant." Nesbitt shook his head. "For the avoidance of doubt, I assign resources on this investigation. DI Lorimar? Could you make our colleague's point for him?"

Andy nodded. "Doirin Chambers operates as a medium at a spiritualist centre on Palmerston Place. Her intuition told her Robin McKay was dead, but she admits she may be wrong, and she seems ignorant of any link to Councillor Wood. At this time the McKay and Wood situations seem unrelated, but I recommend a follow-up with Angela McKay to reach a conclusion on that."

Nesbitt nodded. "I agree. Take DS Devlin with you since he had initial telephone contact."

Andy's heart sank. Devlin would be a liability. Still, this was not the place. He'd make his representations in private.

"Excuse me, Chief Inspector?" Devlin apparently had no qualms about publicly questioning his superior. "I believe I should lead the follow-up with Mrs McKay. It might need a delicate touch. And it would be best if I show Constable Burns the ropes on this."

Nesbitt's response was, predictably, ice cold. "It would be best, would it?"

"Yes sir."

"Let's talk about synergy, Detective Sergeant. Synergy is when we put two things together and get a result greater than the combined parts. Synergy is what we hope for when allocating partnerships. Makes sense, don't you think?" Devlin frowned, ignoring the question. "However. When unwarranted ego meets doe-eyed adulation you end up with negative synergy. In your and DC Burns's case, it's not just worse than the sum of the parts, but actually worse than bloody useless. I'll work with Constable Burns and you'll work with Inspector Lorimar. This is your chance," he glared at each man in turn, "both of you, to watch and learn. Am I clear?"

Devlin's nostrils flared, but he said nothing. The room was glacial.

Andy winced. He had little sympathy for idiots, but plenty for himself and that ham-fisted intervention meant everyone's fate was sealed. There would be no wriggling out of the decision now, not for a while at least. Which made it an appropriate time to change the subject. "As requested, Chief Inspector, I eventually reached Doctor Nassar, our assigned pathologist. Due to departmental backlogs she hasn't completed her work on the body, but under pressure gave me a preliminary verbal report. Death was by," Andy checked his notebook, since he wanted clarity on the ownership of the words he was about to use, "being hit by a sodding great van and repeatedly driven over."

Nesbitt smirked. "Twelve years of the best medical training our country can provide, ladies and gentlemen. So far, it doesn't look like an accident, but we need a clear steer from the pathology. Keep on her. The delay is unacceptable. Finally, Sergeant Petrakis, where are the NCCU on the social media posts?"

Petrakis peeled herself from the wall, returning her phone to her pocket. She spoke the way Andy imagined a nursery teacher might if they secretly belonged to an underground hacking collective. "OK everyone. Please raise a hand any time you don't understand any of my infosec terminology."

Lenny Burns' hand rose at 'infosec' but when Devlin mouthed 'information security' he hesitantly lowered it.

Petrakis continued. "Every access to social media is logged by the provider. That logging includes a variety of technical details, network addresses and other attributes that together form a kind of digital fingerprint. NCCU maintain relationships with all primary platforms, so we achieved a rapid response on this. These posts came from a source we've seen before, which is a PC belonging to Maria Constanza de Santos Rosario."

Nesbitt rubbed his hands. "Let's bring her in."

Petrakis patted the air, as though calming an invisible pony. "Ms de Santos Rosario is a non-English speaking eighty-six-year-old who lives alone in Lisbon, Portugal. The outer limits of her computer experience will be ordering the weekly groceries. She'll know nothing about this matter."

Andy shifted uncomfortably. Something about the scenario was wrong. He could feel it. It prickled under his skin like an allergen.

Lenny Burns had no such uncertainties. "Grandkids! They're a nightmare now. Teach them iPads as toddlers and see what you get."

Petrakis frowned. "Grandchildren aren't relevant. We've encountered this person before because her computer became compromised. She was, and apparently remains, part of a botnet. Her machine is taking commands from a remote command-and-control server without her knowledge. Those commands were behind the social media postings in this case."

Nesbitt asked, "Do we know who's behind those commands originally?"

Petrakis shrugged. "Probably someone who spent some bitcoin on the dark web using the Tor browser. Even if we had full packet logging, which we don't, with a new layer of encryption at every relay in the circuit, the onion routing makes origin tracing virtually impossible."

Every hand in the room was now raised.

Sighing, she tried again. "No. We don't know who specified the social media messages. And realistically, we won't find out." Her message sank in, collective disappointment palpable in the growing silence. She reached into her pocket for her phone. "Right. I'm consulting with Edinburgh University on other matters until Friday. DCI Nesbitt has my details should anyone have further questions." She paused and turned towards Andy. "Talking of the University, DI Lorimar, they have a well-respected parapsychology department if you want me to find a contact for that spiritualist malarkey."

A seat of higher learning, studying the paranormal? Andy's mind boggled, but he nodded acceptance.

Nesbitt brought the meeting to a close. "We're continuing the interviews with Edinburgh council staff. I'll pull people in as need-ed... Let's keep moving. If you know what you're doing, get on with it. If you don't know what you are doing, stay behind, and tell me very, very slowly why not."

Everyone filed out, except for Lenny Burns, who hovered just inside the door, stepping anxiously from one foot to the other like a schoolboy in need of the toilet.

ON THE WAY to Angela McKay's flat in Leith, Devlin alternated between tense silence and noisy ranting. Andy had initially taken a certain amount of pleasure from his unhappiness, but now his colleague had reverted to being merely a pain in the backside.

"How can Nesbitt treat me like that? I *own* this lead. I brought it to him to begin with."

"For Christ's sake Devlin, you don't own any lead. You only answered a phone."

"Maybe, but I got her to talk."

Andy sighed. The idea that Angela McKay hadn't called to be silent was nowhere in Devlin's reasoning. "Look Jamie. For future reference, Brian Nesbitt is a reasonable guy, but you don't argue with the lead investigator's decisions in a public forum. If you had a problem partnering me you should have taken it offline."

"Oh yeah, Link-man? Is that what you planned to do?"

Andy said nothing. They would have to work together. It was pointless to plumb the depths of their mutual contempt. He turned into the car park at Maritime Square.

As they approached the door of the block, Devlin bustled past to press the buzzer for the ground floor flat. A tinny greeting sounded in response. "Mrs McKay? Detective Sergeant Jamie Devlin here. We spoke to each other by phone. My colleague DI Lorimar will assist me today. Could we come in?"

A buzz preceded the sharp click of a latch. Inside, the door to the corner flat stood open.

While Devlin handled introductions, Andy took stock. The place was compact, but well decorated and clean. Doors led into two bedrooms. No sign of kids. Angela McKay was average height, short brown hair, nose stud, early thirties. Her eyes were weary, but not through tears, more a kind of resignation.

Devlin reached the end of his spiel. "And please, don't be intimidated by Detective Lorimar. He looks worse than he is in practice."

Angela McKay was unimpressed. "I don't understand what you mean. He looks a bit like my husband in fact." She turned to Andy. "Are you a rugby man?"

"Not since school. Just big-boned, I guess."

She smiled, but without warmth. "Robin played at Uni and a bit after. He was good. I wish he'd kept playing, to be honest."

She sat on the armchair while they took the sofa opposite. "I don't suppose you've found anything?"

Andy shook his head. "Not as yet. I know you discussed various details with Sergeant Devlin by phone, so forgive us if our questions touch on some of that again."

She shrugged, eyes drifting towards the window as though she might see her husband walking past. "He hasn't contacted me, if that's one of your questions. No phone, no text. Nothing. That's not unusual though."

"In what way, not unusual?"

Devlin flicked through the pages of his notebook, preparing to speak, but Andy shot him a glare. This was for Angela McKay to say.

"Robin has a drink problem. It started a while back, but it's been getting worse. Weekend boozing at the rugby club somehow leaked into the rest of the week. This isn't the first time." She held their gaze as though she wanted them to understand. "It's not that he doesn't care. He cares. And he tries too. Really hard sometimes. But he can't control it. You can't count on him ... he can't count on himself."

In any other scenario, Andy knew this wouldn't be getting police attention. But they needed to rule it in or out. "In your call, you mentioned dinner plans for 8pm on Tuesday August 30th. When was that arranged?"

"Out of the blue, on Monday morning before he left for work. He seemed happy. Said we might have something to celebrate. He even brought a bottle home on Monday night to take with us." She pointed at the sideboard in the corner. An alcohol-free sparkling wine stood untouched awaiting his return.

"And where were you eating?"

"Martone's, on the corner of Leith Street and Waterloo place. It's an Italian we go to sometimes. We'd booked our favourite table upstairs."

"Was he meeting you at home before the meal?"

"I wasn't sure. I thought he might, but he sometimes worked late. He's in the E-government division, which means computers, and the impression I get is that stuff goes wrong all the time. He didn't answer his phone, so I presumed I'd just meet him at the restaurant."

"How long did you wait for him?"

"I gave up around half past nine. After I'd eaten, basically. I've been down this road before. I was buggered if I was going to be stood up *and* starve." She paused. "That's what freaked me, really, with that weirdo psychic woman."

"Doirin Chambers, at the Palmerston centre?"

"Yeah. Her. See, I had prawn cocktail to start. Just like she said."

Andy suspected this was how it worked, people remembering the hits and discarding the misses. "But she didn't get your husband's name right did she?"

Angela flushed. Her lip trembled. "No. But that was strange too. When I met him, ages ago, before we were going out or anything, I sometimes called him Mickey. McKay, so Mickey, right? Just a daft thing people do. Anyway one time I got him a scarf. An American football thing, bright colours. I even sang to him. That song. You know the one? Oh Mickey, you're so fine? We always counted that as our first date. I don't think about it much nowadays."

Andy bit his lip. Doirin said she'd planned to pass on something about their first date... Unlikely, but they'd come all the way here. No harm in tugging the thread. "Could you show us the scarf?"

Now it was Devlin's turn to glare. When Angela left the room he asked "D'you want to sniff his socks too?"

It was easiest to lie. "Just buying us time to confer. What do you reckon?"

Devlin shrugged. "Same as I've always thought. That he's probably sleeping it off somewhere."

Angela returned perplexed, carrying a plush-covered book but no scarf. "It's gone. It hasn't moved in ages, but ... I don't know. Here's a photo." She flipped the album open and handed it over.

He used his phone to take a snap of the photograph. The couple were both in the picture. The bright-red scarf had a blue slash in the middle. The slash contained white initials, presumably of an American university. Robin, considerably taller than his wife, was laughing and holding it above his head while she stretched to grab it. Happier times.

"Is there any chance he took the scarf with him that day, could he have been wearing it?"

Angela looked away. "I'd left before him, but I doubt he would wear it to work. He might have taken it if he had planned—" The words caught in her throat. "Maybe he wanted to surprise me at dinner?" She sobbed then. Deep sobs, almost like gasps. She tried to contain them but gave up and turned away.

You could never predict what might take people over the edge. Andy had spoken to many like Angela over the years, standing at the precipice of loss, unwilling to believe the worst until the ground gave way beneath them. You couldn't fix that kind of grief for someone; he knew that better than most. It just had to be lived through. He told her they would do all they could, and signalled Devlin that it was time to move on.

THE OFFICE BLOCK was a featureless modern build, in keeping with the out-of-town business park location. "You're sure this is it?"

Devlin flicked through his notebook. "According to the council switchboard."

Andy frowned. "So where's the council building?" The wall in front of him bore the self-important acronym of a multinational.

"He was working with a services company that day, apparently."

"Fine. I'm off to see the new pathologist. I'll come back for you in an hour."

"But what am I doing?"

Asking to be spoon-fed was a credible first step on Devlin's long road to distinguishing arse from elbow. "We need to know McKay's movements that day, when he left, where he was going, anyone who left with him. Any office conflicts? Had he said anything curious? Did he drink locally? You know, sniff about a bit."

"No problem." Devlin started towards the reception but then hesitated. "Hang on. What if the switchboard goofed? What if he wasn't here that day after all?"

"Then show some initiative and find out what we need by phone. Or, if you prefer, just gormlessly wander this car park until I return. You choose." Before Devlin's middle finger got the chance to respond, Andy jumped in the car and headed into the city.

ALTHOUGH THE FORENSIC Pathology unit was administratively based on the campus of the Edinburgh Royal Infirmary, postmortems were conducted at the City Mortuary in the Cowgate. Tired of getting the runaround by phone, Andy was here to rattle the cage in person. The last thing he wanted was to develop a reputation for patience with a new pathologist.

At reception he picked up his blue overshoes and surgical cap before heading towards the dissection lab. The previous head of department, Professor Abernethy, had left with little warning. He'd brought a macabre enthusiasm to the role, keeping much of what he'd called the 'juiciest business' to himself. Andy sighed at the memory. The prof's retirement had eliminated a valuable point of contact. In a job that was already a churning sea of missing information, a new pathologist was another unwelcome unknown.

As he entered the chilled lab space, Doctor Yasmeen Nassar glared up from a body on a trolley. She did not seem pleased by his arrival. "Oh, hell's teeth!" Her voice was both plummy and hostile, like a once-jolly hockey stick was now being wielded as a weapon. "And you are?"

"Detective Inspector Lorimar, major investigation into the death of Councillor Joan Wood."

"You're my nuisance caller. Yes?"

"Yes, Dr Nassar, that's me. My chief inspector wonders what you've been prioritising above our high-profile murder."

The pathologist pushed the trolley to one side and moved over to the sink to wash. Without warning, she said, "Move husband and family to Edinburgh! Leave the smog and stress of London behind! Enjoy open air, outdoor living and the charming accent! I imagined dissecting contented corpses who expired on a surplus of short-bread." She pulled on afresh set of gloves. "But it isn't sodding like that." She stared at him.

"I suppose not." What could he say? Unless shortbread was a euphemism for street drugs, she'd been sold a pup.

"The department head left before I arrived, a fact that slipped his mind at my interview. One of my colleagues has gone full-time academic, another is at a two-week conference and we're behind on recruitment. We've too many bodies on trolleys and not enough in sodding surgical scrubs."

"Look, I accept that. I only need an accurate estimate for the postmor—"

She turned on him. "The autopsy? That's done. It's the paperwork I'm neglecting! You think it's easy to type elbow deep in a thoracic cavity? Yes?" She sighed, and her face softened. "I know we're late. I apologise. How about you take what I have verbally and I send a write-up by end of play tomorrow?"

"Works for me, Doc." He opened his notebook.

"The councillor's death resulted from a massive cranial haemorrhage. That barely pipped the extensive thoracic and abdominal trauma to the post, however. It's easier to list the organs that weren't damaged." She caught his eye. "Left kidney was in fine fettle. Full stop." He followed her to the wall of refrigerated drawers. Opening one, she tugged the U-shaped zip on the body bag inside.

Andy had seen a lot of autopsied corpses. The fresh Y-incision on the chest was usually the most obvious mutilation, but not in this case. The medic described the highlights. "Her spine and skull show the initial points of impact. The scarring reveals the vehicle drove over her body on two occasions. This tread pattern on the neck and shoulder differs from that here, for example." She pointed out livid furrows on the crushed belly of the corpse. "These were made by a vehicle in reverse."

"Might the subsequent impacts have been accidental, trying to flee the scene?"

"After the initial impact the victim landed face down. The vehicle could have reversed to flee the scene at that point, but did not. Then, after driving forward over the body, the vehicle could have fled, but instead reversed to inflict additional injury. The attack dragged the body a considerable distance, severing a finger against the edge of the roadside kerb. There was nothing accidental about this death. The driver wanted absolute certainty. Nobody could have survived this."

Andy continued scribbling. "Toxicology?"

"Alcohol. Nicotine. Fluoxetine, that's Prozac. She'd been on long-term antidepressants, high strength, sixty milligrams daily."

"So she'd been drinking that evening, while on antidepressants?"

"Yes, given her background you'd think she'd know better."

Andy frowned. Mixing fags, booze and strong medication was exactly what he'd expect from an elected politician. "Know better?"

"As a doctor. Yes?" She waited for a sign of comprehension that didn't come. "Joan Wood wrote one of the standard texts on haematology before politics lured her up here. I only realised when I pulled her records."

He supposed most councillors would have had a useful job at some point in their lives. "So, she was an ex-doctor with vices."

"I wouldn't get too carried away. Based on blood alcohol, I'd estimate she'd been moderately drunk, but not legless."

He dourly inspected the crushed ruins below the corpse's knees and decided to let the joke lie. "Anything else worth knowing?"

The pathologist's eyes widened. "Ah yes! A hair analysis showed no special finding, except she was naturally brunette. No hair dye."

"That's noteworthy, because?"

"One for the medical geeks, perhaps. We'd expect a fifty-year-old to be around half-grey. Yes? So, lacking all trace of silver at fifty-nine, despite being a smoker? This woman was blessed with singularly impressive genes."

For all the good they did her, he thought. What nature giveth, nurture driveth a van over. But who the hell did it, and why had they wanted her dead?

PULLING INTO THE CAR PARK, he saw Devlin angrily tapping his watch. His colleague wrenched open the door while the vehicle was still moving. "I've been cooling my heels here for twenty minutes! I need to get home. It's pizza night!"

On the drive back to Fettes he brought his colleague up to date with the pathology, then Devlin returned the favour. "On Tuesday, Robin McKay signed out at 18:07. He didn't socialise much with the staff. I picked up a bit of them and us, since he was council and they were the service provider. The receptionist was chatty though, he'd told her he was getting the train into town to meet his wife."

"So it takes, what, fifteen minutes to reach the Gyle train station on foot?"

Devlin nodded. "They thought he was going for the six-thirty train. He should have been in town twenty minutes later."

Andy nodded. He knew what he'd be doing that evening, and it wouldn't involve pizza. "I don't suppose you fancy a trip to the CMF?"

Devlin scoffed. "That's the difference between us Link. I've got a home and a family who love me. You knock yourself out needle hunting if you like. I'll be eating a calzone the size of my head."

Andy pointed at the half-full Tupperware box in the storage bay behind the handbrake. "I'll be fine with my evening sandwiches."

As they turned into Fettes Avenue, Devlin grimaced at the tail-back of vehicles heading towards Stockbridge and the City Centre. "Fun for you." But they parted amicably, with Andy relishing the prospect of his own company. He transferred the scuffed sandwich tub to his lap, popped it open, and rejoined the traffic.

OUTSIDE THE CENTRAL Monitoring Facility in the City Chambers, light was fading. Inside he found an even deeper twilight, the windowless world where council staff operated feeds from the more than two-hundred cameras spread across the city.

The main viewing room was noisy. Some of the older analogue monitors ran hot, and only permanent air conditioning made the room bearable. That background drone, plus the near-constant radio chatter with emergency services, resulted in workers shouting to be heard.

Saj, the backshift supervisor, had an old hand's grasp of the necessary volume. "Inspector Lorimar! Good evening! What do you need?"

Andy produced the photograph of Robin McKay. "This man, perhaps wearing this scarf, might be somewhere between Waverley

Station and Waterloo Place between 18:40 and 20:15 on Tuesday, August 30th. Can we check?"

The supervisor led Andy to a viewing station. "Camera 106 is at the corner of Princes Street and South St David's Street. Camera 110 is on the corner of Princes Street and Waverley Bridge. We've got a chance from each of those, but the crowds can be hellish."

Saj sped wholesale through the video until the corner timestamp read '18:40'. Then the work of tracing one face in an ever-changing slow-motion throng began. In the real world, a painstaking thirty-two minutes elapsed before the video timestamp trickled past '18:53'.

Andy had hoped Robin McKay would be visible by this point. Many people were milling around, but based on Angela McKay's comments, they were searching for someone roughly his own size. He should at least stand out from the crowd.

Suddenly Saj pointed at a frozen video frame. "Sweetie man!" A large figure at the Princes Street exit to Waverley Station held a confectionery bar to his face. Andy checked the image against his photograph. Shorter hair, and no beard, but it was a very plausible match. Saj restarted the footage, only to see the camera swinging to a new orientation.

Andy was crestfallen. "Bugger. Can you find him again?"

Saj shrugged. "If he heads west to Waverley Bridge, we'll catch him on the other camera." They tracked through, and waited, but their target didn't show.

This vanishing person act was an occupational hazard. The vagaries of crowds, camera movements and the targets themselves meant that CCTV was consulted with crossed fingers. Their man could have jumped in a cab, walked back into the station, or pulled on a pantomime horse outfit. But it wasn't over yet. He'd have been an hour early for his dinner date, but Andy asked, "Say he went east?"

Saj, thankfully, had a camera for that. "We've got 105 at the junction of North Bridge and Princes Street." He retrieved the footage, found the time point and soon they were tracking through. "Man with Snickers approaching! There! What do you think?" Saj froze on a clear image of their target. He stood behind a hen party, the strap of a backpack visible on his right shoulder.

The probability was rising, but the identification was not yet definitive. "Follow him." The pursuit lasted all of ten steps before the man halted with his back to Princes Street and examined his watch. A fold of cloth hanging from his left-hand pocket revealed a fragment of bold white lettering, the acronym for a college football team. The scarf he'd received from his wife.

No sooner had they found Robin McKay than he strode into the building ahead of him and disappeared from view. "I need two clear shots from that sequence, full face and side-on." While the printer hummed, Saj tracked forward at high speed for more than an hour. McKay did not re-enter the frame.

Andy left the CMF with his two screen captures and walked down the Royal Mile towards the Bridges. On the evening of his disappearance Robin McKay had an appointment at the Balrannoch Hotel. It was time to find out why.

6

THE BALRANNOCH

FRIDAY 2ND SEPTEMBER, 19:10

Five-star hotels like the Balrannoch didn't welcome police asking questions at reception, so Andy was rapidly escorted to the duty manager's office.

Richard Ellison was the consummate salesman, his smile morphing into solemnity at all the right moments. But his default expression was a sparkling panorama of teeth. His was a celebrity kind of dental perfection, where every grin deserved a whinny as a sound effect. "Of course, Constable! I guarantee every assistance." He inclined his head, mouth instantly serious. "But as the bustling centre of Edinburgh's commercial and cultural life, we have many, many guests passing through here." The smile appeared again, and the man waited.

"I'm a Detective Inspector not a Constable, Mr Ellison. And I'm working the major investigation into the death of Edinburgh councillor Joan Wood. So, let me try again. For the evening of Tuesday 30th August I need to talk to staff on duty in the bar or cafe areas."

Ellison's grin faltered. "Festival evenings are so very busy."

"I'm sure they are. Especially here at the centre of ... what was it again?"

The manager pursed his lips. "Edinburgh's cultural and commercial life."

"Cultural, commercial but not criminal, we hope. Why don't I just wander around, make my presence felt? Perhaps Robin McKay had met some guests? Perhaps he had a room here?"

"No need. I'll fetch our bar manager. One moment." Ellison left pulling the door behind him, but it didn't catch and slowly rebounded. A large laundry trolley trundled past, overflowing with towels and bedding. The sight made Andy's palms itch. That laundry would be cleaned, pressed and given to new guests in fresh rooms. A place like this was always moving; the half-life of evidence was horribly brief.

While waiting he considered the options. Most likely, Robin McKay met someone here. Perhaps a colleague from work, or a buddy from the rugby club. Saj might even find footage of them staggering home. The only certainty was that Robin McKay had not completed the one minute journey to meet his wife that evening, despite being alive and well in this building only an hour before.

Ellison grinned his way back inside with a flustered colleague. "I can confirm Mr McKay had no room with us that evening. Our bar manager, Iain, will look at your photographs."

Iain examined the two CCTV captures, his eyes flicking between the printed images and the face of his boss, who grinned fixedly throughout. The eventual verdict was unconvincing "Maybe. I don't know." He checked back with Richard Ellison who nodded.

Andy rose, closing on the bar manager. "Iain. Don't look at him. Look at me." The man's eyes widened. "The guy in the photographs. He would have been around my height and build. Difficult to miss. Think. Did you see him?"

"I ... I think so. If he was your height."

"Tell me about him."

"He was pished." Ellison frowned at this. Clearly people could find themselves merry, or tipsy, perhaps even tired and emotional.

But never pished, not at the Balrannoch. Iain continued. "His friend carried him out of the gents."

"Who was his friend?"

"Some guy. I couldn't tell you much about him."

This was plausible. A big man staggering around will always pull focus from the supporting cast. It appeared Angela McKay's suspicions had been right; her husband had gone on a bender. "When did you see him getting carried?"

Iain paused. "Well the pianist was starting about then, so no later than eight?"

Then Andy felt it again, the prickling under his skin. Given the scenario described, he'd expected midnight. Something was wrong here. A guy this size shouldn't be staggering drunk in less than an hour.

He examined both faces in front of him. Anxiety on one, frustration on the other. "After the bar where did they go? Did they leave the hotel?"

The bar manager shook his head. "The other guy was supporting him. To the lift I think. I assumed to a room."

"Did they charge the bar tab to a room number?"

"Maybe there was cash on the table, but it was a busy night. We did nothing wrong here. The big guy must have arrived with a skin full."

Andy's phone buzzed with an incoming text message from Saj at the CMF.

SWEETIE MAN NEVER SEEN LEAVING HOTEL.
CHECKED UNTIL 7AM.

"Mr Ellison, if someone didn't leave the hotel where might they be?"

The duty manager scoffed. "We don't keep space for stowaways. We have two-hundred professionally managed rooms over six floors. Housekeeping visits most of them every day." He showed that equine grin of his again, but now it had taken on an edge of desperation.

"What surveillance is available inside the hotel? From Tuesday evening?"

"We don't have many cameras on the guest floors, but public areas are well covered. Our security manager controls viewing. He'll be around tomorrow morning. Pete Cunningham."

That name rang a bell. Top-end hotels often employed ex-police in security roles, so the familiarity was unsurprising. Andy could imagine a worse fate than ending up somewhere like this one day.

Ellison took the brief silence as an opportunity. "So. Shall we reconvene in the morning, say around ten?" His smile struggled to regain its earlier bravado.

He remembered the trolley. Always changing. Always moving. "No thanks, Mr Ellison. Either you work with me now or I return in an hour with twenty uniforms and a search warrant." He knew he'd never get such heavy-handedness approved, but the duty manager nodded mutely and signalled for the bar manager to return to his duties.

When they were alone, Andy asked, "Housekeeping visit *most* rooms. What are the exceptions?"

"Unoccupied rooms aren't serviced daily, but remain locked. And we respect client requests for privacy; housekeeping rarely enter rooms displaying a Do Not Disturb. They keep records of such matters."

"In that case, let's stretch our legs. We'll ask housekeeping whether any rooms are unserviced since Tuesday evening when Robin McKay disappeared."

· · ·

PAST A SET of double doors just outside the main lobby, the duty manager stopped to push a section of the wall. A wallpapered door swung open, revealing a service corridor. They squeezed past a linen trolley and a large refuse barrow to reach a staircase, and proceeded downward. On the lower floor they passed a pair of tall mesh cages. Pristine stacks of plastic-wrapped bathrobes, towels and bedding filled the first. The second contained loose mounds of the same raw materials, but considerably less fresh.

In this private inner sanctum of his temple of hospitality, Ellison had regained some of his former energy. "Our service partner delivers and collects from Fife. There's too much to launder on-site." As an afterthought he added, "Two-hundred thread count luxury cotton." That second cage hadn't smelled like two-hundred thread count luxury, but Andy guessed such was life in the hotel business.

The door of a management office at the end of the corridor stood open, revealing a woman rummaging through a large sack of fluffy dressing gowns. She looked up at their approach. "Guest leave wedding *and* eternity rings in pocket of robe at spa. Two days later, she notice her fingers not worth twenty-four-thousand dollars no more. Crazy, crazy."

"Krysta? Can you help with a police enquiry?" Ellison flashed his world-class gnashers and she jumped to her feet. People probably complied just so he would put them away. "We need to know if any occupied rooms have been DND since Wednesday morning?"

"No, no, no. Not policy Richard. Two mornings, do not disturb. Third time, wakey-wakey."

"I know Krysta, but Detective Lorimar here would prefer we check the records."

The woman sighed but moved to her desk and tapped at a keyboard. "No, no, no. All serviced Wednesday... We have DND on room 510 yesterday and today though." She paused. "Says here 510 due to check out today, but I don't see?"

Ellison joined her at the screen. "That is odd. Can you open the room access log?" Andy sidled behind them. "Door locked and key left room on Tuesday at 21:04. It didn't reopen until room serviced on Wednesday 10:47. DND Thursday. DND Friday." Ellison turned around, cheeks flushing. "This should have been caught earlier, but with conference activities we didn't spot it. I doubt this relates to your enquiry, but room 510 might have gone AWOCO on Tuesday night."

"Pardon?"

"AWOCO. It's a comical little expression of mine. Away Without Checking Out. Fortunately we have a card on file, so billing should be fine."

"But if they left on Tuesday and their room was serviced on Wednesday, who hung the Do Not Disturb covering yesterday and today?" Ellison and Krysta were clearly stumped. "What names are on this room?"

Ellison eyed the housekeeping manager until she began typing. He appeared more comfortable as the tour guide than the driver. "Stop! Thank you Krysta! Names were Tricia Black and John Reynolds. Only Mr Reynolds checked in. Sunday twenty-eighth August. Champagne and chocolates on the Sunday night. Pedicure pre-booked for Tuesday morning, but unused."

Every hotel booking tells a story. Reynolds had probably been jilted and returned home early, but that had to be checked. Andy noted the details. "I'd like to view room 510. Mr Ellison, shall we?"

He followed the duty manager back to the service corridor and the plain steel door of an elevator. From the buttons marked '1' to '7', Ellison punched '5'. Andy felt his pedantic muscle twitch. "You said two-hundred rooms over six floors. What's on seven?"

"Roof access and accommodation for the general manager. The family have been on holiday since mid-August. This weekend was the earliest our GM could down tools to join them."

"When did he leave?"

Ellison glared at his watch as the elevator trundled upwards. "Sunday. A clear two days before your vanishing drunk. Do you need to know more? Will I request he sends you a postcard?"

Andy smiled. "Generous offer. But hold off on the postcard. For the moment at least."

They arrived at room 510 to find the predicted "Do Not Disturb" sign still hanging from the door handle. "Third time means wakey-wakey, Mr Ellison, chop-chop." The duty manager fumbled the keycard, his face flushing. But eventually the door opened to reveal only that housekeeping's last visit had left everything in order. The unit beside the door contained clothes hanging above an empty suit-case: a bulky waxed jacket, two polo shirts, jogging shorts, a cable-knit jumper, a pair of flip-flops. It was a testament to Edinburgh's meteorological diversity that a careful tourist might require all those items in August. A nearby drawer contained socks and boxer briefs, apparently arranged with fresh at the front, crumpled at the back. "Is it normal for a guest to leave in such a hurry?"

Ellison scratched his chin. "Not usually, but it happens. Some wealthier clients place such a high value on travelling unencum-bered they'd rather repurchase items than carry them. Books are common, but also clothes, luggage and even electronics, such as laptops or iPads. The more a guest leaves behind, the less likely they forgot. Often when we follow up it proves to have been deliberate."

On a nearby writing desk they found a Festival program and leaflets for a ragbag of shows: 'Abattoir the musical', 'Silence for Tuskegee', 'Finest Scottish stand-up'. Nothing particularly noteworthy.

Moving into the bathroom Andy saw ordinary bathroom things: toothpaste, toothbrush, mouthwash, an electric razor. An unfamiliar container caught his eye, and a prescription label on the side revealed an ointment for eczema. It was heavy, well over half-full. Andy experienced again that sense of something gone awry. Travel-ling light wouldn't involve abandoning dental hygiene, clean under-wear and treatments for a skin condition. This was surely more than trimming down on hand luggage.

The bedroom window faced out over Princes Street. He looked right, pressing his face to the glass, and saw the doorway to

Martone's restaurant, where Angela McKay had waited to meet her husband. Something had entered Doirin's eyes when they discussed Robin looking down on his wife. Her odd clarification niggled: that down simply meant down. He considered the floors above his head. And the seventh floor, with the general manager's accommodation, empty since the previous weekend. It was a crazy thought. But Robin Mckay arrived here and didn't appear to have left again. Perhaps Doirin was involved? Perhaps she somehow had knowledge he shouldn't ignore? Or perhaps, he had just developed an itch he needed to scratch.

"Mr Ellison, two final requests. First, by all means reach out to this guest as per your usual policy, however, please leave this room untouched for the moment. Second, I want to see floor seven."

The duty manager complained. He complained about his other duties. He complained Andy's impatience was bypassing their security manager. He complained about taking visitors into the passcode secured management accommodation. But he did it all the same.

ONCE ON THE SEVENTH FLOOR, the duty manager hovered at the entrance leaving Andy in the dark. It was a transparent attempt to encourage his annoying guest to take the briefest of looks before turning around.

Instead, Andy pulled a torch from his jacket pocket. The door to their left appeared to lead to the management accommodation, but through the glass door in front Andy could see the slate and metal of the roof space. "Who has access out there?"

"The general manager's family. Occasionally housekeeping or back of house staff where the family need assistance. Every so often we bring a prearranged wedding party up here for photographs, but that's weather dependent." As if underscoring that point, raindrops began bouncing off the glass in front of them. "We sometimes need contractors for maintenance, but because this is a home, we try to minimise footfall. As you can see, there's nothing of interest."

Adjusting the focus of his torch beam, Andy crouched to examine the carpet leading out to the roof. Despite the uniform charcoal colouring, a pattern was apparent. The short pile was flattened in two linear tracks a couple of feet apart. Tracks that led out to the roof. "Those housekeeping trolleys and refuse barrows we passed in the service corridor. Are they ever up here?"

Ellison joined him. "Perhaps when the family have rubbish to clear, but not usually."

Andy was already pressing forward, flashing torchlight ahead as Ellison opened the external door. A chilly evening wind threw needles of rain against their faces. To the west, he looked out over the glass and concrete roof of the Waverley Mall, following the lights of Princes Street towards the black pinnacle of the Scott monument. But that wasn't where his interest lay. He wanted to look the other way, east, down to Martone's. And that meant picking his way over roofing ducts, air conditioning outlets and structures of concrete and steel to reach the front of the building. As he set off, Ellison reacted with horror. "Wait! There's no public access over there!"

Andy glanced back. "In that case, you stay here. If the public arrive, make sure you stop them." He widened the torch beam and headed on.

It wasn't climbing so much as scrambling, negotiating irregular surfaces never built with walking in mind. In the centre of the roof space was a drop straight down to the glasshouse dome of the bistro where Edinburgh's cafe society enjoyed their afternoon tea. Andy had never fully grasped why sandwiches became more expensive as they dwindled in size, but it seemed an accepted law of middle class life.

Ahead on his right, the top of the clock tower marked the midpoint of the front of the building. But his torch caught something incongruous on the roof flashing. In a cranny mostly sheltered from the rain, an organic blob of lumpy wetness. He knelt down, wincing as he drew close. The smell was unmistakable. It was old vomit.

He knew now. Knew he was on the path. Knew something had happened here. He passed the turret on the front leftmost corner and turned towards the clock. Even by torchlight he could see the protruding shoe from some distance away. Grimly he murmured, "Mr McKay."

He'd been a large man, but he'd grown after two days on a roof, his face and abdomen puffy with the gases of decay. His head lolled against the tower, mouth agape, glassy eyes staring beyond the corner of the rightmost turret. One hand stretched out over a wall, the other gripped the fabric of his jacket. It was easy to imagine him there, struggling, trying to stand, trying to look across to where Angela waited, perhaps to glimpse his wife one final time. But that was all it was, Andy knew. Imagination. And it had no place here.

A corner of clear polythene jutted from the dead man's shirt through a gap created by two missing buttons. Andy raised the fabric with the edge of his torch. It was a document, wrapped against the elements. On the uppermost page, he saw a scrawled love heart, and inside that, a handwritten message.

Joan Wood and Robin McKay. Loose talk costs lives.

He stood for a moment, gazing at the city streets below. At all the shoppers and cars and lights and life. Only yesterday this man had been a distraction, someone to find drunk in a bus shelter and drop from the enquiry. "Big man. What did you get yourself into?"

He called in the details before making his way back to Ellison. The duty manager had been cooperative, so Andy led him inside out of the wind and rain before informing him of the other kind of storm about to descend. For once even Ellison couldn't fake a smile.

HE RETURNED to his tenement flat on Ferry Road just after midnight. He had stayed to liaise with the SOCOs, and to establish ground rules for the coming days with the staff at the Balrannoch hotel. It had proved a complex business to retrieve a body from the hotel roof while preserving the evidence, but it was done.

He poured himself a cup of chamomile tea and switched on the television. Someone was being voted out of somewhere and a crowd of idiots was very excited about it. He switched if off again. It was trivia. And life was many things, but not that. Trivia was an anaesthetic. Like drugs or booze. Trivia was an escape. A ploy to distract the child from the reason they hid under the table. He understood the need for that, but he'd left it behind. It didn't matter that life was loss. And regret. And pain. Life was the only game available, so you played it until you were removed from the board.

He thought back to Jimmy, teaching him calisthenics as a method to bring him out of the gloom. It still worked, and he could do with it now. He started with squats, seeing no reason to change a cycle that had served him for decades.

Today had been a breakthrough, but it somehow didn't feel like one. Two people were dead. He had evidence of a link between both victims. He even had the beginnings of a suspect, either in a guest who had absconded, or, and he felt a pang of regret for this, a hapless spiritualist who perhaps knew more than she should. But there remained many unanswered questions, and something felt wrong. A killer leaving a crib sheet about why they did it? That was a career first, and he'd investigated numerous murders before now.

He dropped into his push-ups, aware of a quiet voice in the back of his head. Quiet, but insistent. He'd investigated numerous murders, yes. But maybe none like this.

PART II

THE VORTEX

3RD - 9TH SEPTEMBER

7

MEMENTOS

Thomas stared down at them. And from the desk, they stared back. His twin burdens. The credit card and the phone.

He removed his glasses and rubbed the bridge of his nose. These items were entrusted to him, not merely as mementos, as Max mockingly suggested, but as an opportunity to make amends.

Max blamed him for the situation in Edinburgh, and these items proved it. But their leader possessed a particular relationship with blame, believing its arrow could point only one way. Thomas held different beliefs on responsibility for the current situation.

However, despite their group carrying an increased risk of exposure that weakened them externally, they were strengthened internally. Their leader's grisly events were designed to create a wave of zealotry and fear that washed away all dissent. Thomas was not immune to that fear. But nor was he immune to other feelings. Joan was gone. She had been stolen from them.

Thomas would keep his own counsel for now. Joan's last gift had been to show him the cost of speaking out. Instead, he would hold tight to a fundamental truth: the work remained as important as ever, probably even more so, now Joan was dead. He would visit several facilities over the next few days, including his own appointment with Rene in Bucharest. If protecting the work meant these mementos must travel with him, then so be it.

8

WORKING WEEKEND

SATURDAY 3RD SEPTEMBER, 09:38

The man hurried into the foyer. "Sorry I missed you last night. I'm Pete Cunningham, Security Manager for the Balrannoch." He was older than Andy by about a decade. He walked with a slight limp, but his grip was firm.

"Detective Inspector Lorimar. Andy."

"Pleased to meet you, Andy. We're through here." After a few steps it became obvious the other man was staring. "Sorry. Were you Jimmy McArthur's boy?"

Edinburgh law enforcement was truly a small world. Andy nodded, surprised both by the question and by how it made him feel. If he was anyone's boy, he supposed he was Jimmy's. Cunningham continued. "He was my boss until he joined CID. He mentioned vouching for a lad with recruitment. Big and brainy he said. I can tell he was at least half right!" They approached an office door, already slightly ajar. Papers rustled inside. "We view the imaging from here. Your colleague arrived ten minutes ago."

Devlin winked as they entered, lowering the CMF images of Robin McKay. "DI Lorimar, you finally made it! Take a leaf out of my book. Early to bed, early to rise! And that's with me on public transport too." Iain the bar manager, now out of uniform, watched the exchange sheepishly from the opposite corner of the room.

At least Devlin had shown willing by coming out on a Saturday morning. It hadn't been obvious he would; Andy's messages to keep him in the loop hadn't raised even a basic acknowledgement.

Andy peered over the security manager's shoulder as he deftly sifted through the video streams. Hotel clientele stuttered through the reception area at high speed. A child rode on a suitcase. A woman wheeled a double-bass. A striking gent in a white top hat and tailcoat raced a young woman towards the staircase. Andy commented, "Somebody's lost Ginger Rogers."

Cunningham smiled. "All sorts, but that's the festival for you. Skip another hour or so. OK. We're done. Right." He froze on a frame of Robin McKay standing upright. "Now, our Iain reckoned he saw the victim drunk, but it isn't obvious as he goes to the gents." They watched McKay making his way across the screen. He looked fine, overall, although Andy spotted possible signs of gait distur- bance in his final steps before entering the restroom. "Let me skip forward. He's in there a few minutes. Ah. Out he comes. As you can see, he's hammered."

The bar manager said, "That's the other guy I was talking about." McKay was staggering, but supported by another man whose face was a picture of concern, every inch the good Samaritan. Or, keeping an open mind, every inch the maniacal killer with theatre skills. The pair exchanged words and then set off together.

Andy asked, "So they'd been drinking together? Or they met in the gents? Or what?" The bar manager shrugged his shoulders in response. In the footage though, any question of their intended destination received an answer when the new man pressed the call button for the elevator.

Devlin smirked. "Wouldn't be the first time two blokes met in a toilet and headed upstairs." Andy ignored him. The anxiety on the unknown man's face suggested no kind of hookup. As the lift doors opened, however, a man wearing glasses hurried into the frame. He engaged the pair, seeming to protest, pointing in the opposite direction. McKay was too out of it to provide any input, and the men debated for a few moments before they all stepped inside the elevator.

The interplay between the three fascinated Andy. "Stop here. Go back. OK. Step through slowly." He turned to Devlin and Cunningham. "Do you think these other guys know each other?" The footage advanced through changing expressions on the toilet Samaritan's face. First anxiety and effort, supporting his large companion, but then eyes widening at the arrival of the man with glasses. After that his face softened, but remained questioning, before morphing into disbelief.

Cunningham spoke first. "I'd say he's surprised initially then relaxes as they talk, but he's always unsure of what's going on. If I was a betting man, I'd say they're strangers, but we can't be certain."

Devlin shrugged, although Andy felt sure his colleague would be more opinionated later, recounting this scene in hindsight. "My take is they don't know each other. At first McKay's toilet buddy thinks the man with the glasses wants to take responsibility, so he's relieved. Except glasses guy doesn't want to get in the lift. He's pointing away ... is that towards the front entrance?"

Cunningham nodded.

Andy continued. "It's like he suggested taking McKay outside. So toilet buddy's shocked at that, thinks it's ridiculous. And he's right. Look at the state of McKay." The large man was perilously close to keeling over. "So, he protests to glasses guy, who's now smiling. But this isn't a smiling situation, unless that's about reassurance, maybe even damage limitation. Whatever, they all head upstairs."

Cunningham grinned. "Silent cinema was clearly your era. But a passably convincing interpretation doesn't make it true."

And he was right. They needed more. "Print me screen captures of both men. I'll see if these faces ring any bells." Cunningham manipulated the video to get the best views of the participants. The printer hummed and spat out two sheets. "Pete? Can you restart it from here?".

They watched the footage proceed for a full minute before Andy explained himself. "Look at the floor numbers above the lift door. They stop at the fifth floor. Can any of your video sources follow them when they got out?"

"Not within current policy. I have cameras throughout the public areas, but hardly any on the accommodation floors. We have to balance security with privacy for our guests. So they tell me."

Andy took a different tack. "We need to know who McKay came to meet. Any footage from inside the bar? Do we see him with one, both or neither?" Cunningham clicked through thumbnails on his monitor. After a few moments, he adjusted the screen position for the detectives.

The new video was from an earlier time point. McKay sat at a table exploring his rucksack. When he retrieved a document, a tremulous sensation began in Andy's gut, a suspicion he found those same pages on the man's corpse. Certainty might be impossible; office workers carried documents all the time and one set of A4 sheets looked much like another at this distance.

On screen, fifty seconds ticked by before McKay returned the document to his bag. He gazed around the bar, face serious, nervous even. He also appeared stone-cold sober, so the idea he had arrived at the hotel already drunk was a non-starter. A minute passed before the man wearing glasses joined him at the table and they shook hands. They chatted briefly before the other man left, returning after two minutes with coffee cups. What followed appeared to be a simple conversation until McKay exited the scene to head for the gents.

By now, Devlin had seen enough. "So, our man's whammied in the toilet, either by toilet buddy, or by something he takes himself. I fancy the other guy for this. You don't hug a big stranger unless you're up to no good."

Andy inhaled slowly. It always helped. "Well, Pete thanks for your time. Usual drill. We'll send a tech over to pick up a copy of the footage. Final thing: we'd welcome help identifying either mystery man. They both seem familiar with the hotel. Could they be staff or guests?"

Cunningham frowned, perhaps a slight awkwardness in his expression. "They're not staff, I know that much. But we might identify them as guests by going through the check-in footage for a few days prior. I'll need some time on that though. Perhaps one of them …"

"What?"

Cunningham shook his head. "Nothing. I'm not sure. Let me check the footage. I'll call you."

Devlin handed over his contact details. "DI Lorimar's not always available. Early mornings or what have you, you can always call me."

Cunningham took the card and put it into his desk drawer. "I'll be in touch then. Andy. DS Devlin. Good luck."

DEVLIN GRUMBLED as they parked at Maritime Square. "Couldn't they have sent a uniform for this?"

"I suppose."

"We're not grief counsellors."

"No. But we own this lead. Remember?"

When the buzzer sounded, both men entered the building in silence.

Angela McKay didn't meet their gaze as she showed them inside. Her eyes were puffy and red. She sat rigidly on her armchair so they adopted yesterday's position on her sofa.

Andy was senior, worse luck. "I'm very sorry to tell you that yesterday evening—"

"The Balrannoch. I heard on the radio. Was it Robin?"

"We believe so."

"Are you sure?"

"We might require formal identification. If so, this wouldn't need to involve you. Anyone who knew him—"

"I'll do it. When?"

"That's with the pathologist. Someone will contact you if it's required."

"I want to see him."

Perfectly natural. But her loved one wasn't hers anymore. Not after something like this. Not for a while at least. "Give us time on that." Her jawline clenched, locking her mouth closed. "This leaflet has details of a counselling service we pass on in similar circumstances. Do you have any friends or family nearby?"

"Yes. My sister's just down the road."

"OK. Try to contact her now. We'll wait."

Angela left the room. They heard quiet conversation and louder tears. Andy stared out of the window. She should have someone. Not to prevent her drowning in grief, since that was impossible, but to hold the rope until she was ready to stop sinking. Devlin could check his watch all he wanted.

When she returned he raised the main formalities. "I'm sorry, but as part of our investigation, we'll need any computer equipment or mobile phones Robin kept here."

"He always carried his phone. I'll go fetch his laptop."

When she left again, Andy whispered to his partner. "More work for cyber crime."

"Maybe he had a Portuguese granny?" Devlin at least had the sense to keep his voice down.

Shortly, Angela returned with a black holdall. "There's a laptop and a tablet in here. I checked again, but I don't have his phone."

Andy wasn't ready to leave just yet. "Angela, I'm sorry for more questions. Did Robin ever mention any threats? At work, or anywhere?"

Her eyes welled up again. She was barely holding it together. "The council disciplined him twice over his drinking. He hated it there. Big dreams, I suppose. Exciting at first, but they wore him down in the end. Nobody threatened him though. He said nothing like that."

"You said big dreams? What were they?"

She almost spat the words. "Stupid stuff. Money. So we could see the bloody world." Then she softened. "Actually, it was more than that. He'd been a drunk here. He wanted to live somewhere that didn't see him that way."

A dark thought: Edinburgh would not remember Robin McKay as a drunk. The manner of his death guaranteed it. "Had he mentioned meeting anyone at the Balrannoch?" Andy folded the two screen captures he'd received from the security manager to exclude Robin from the images. "Do you recognise either of these two men?"

Her face paled. "These men? Did they—"

"We only know they had contact with your husband on Tuesday night at the Hotel."

"I don't know them. Robin never mentioned going to the Balrannoch."

"What about work? Did he mention anyone recently? Even positively?"

"He said the new service provider was slightly better than the last lot. But he didn't talk much about work."

"Any drinking pals at the office?"

"Not in the last year. He'd been ... he'd been better."

The buzzer sounded just as the tears overcame her. Andy pressed to allow access, and a few moments later opened the flat door to another woman, taller, but with Angela's eyes. "Thanks for coming. She could do with having you here."

He signalled Devlin to bring the holdall of computer equipment, and together they left, passing through an angry flurry of rain before reaching the refuge of the car.

AFTER LODGING McKay's computer gear in evidence, Andy dropped Devlin at the train station. He had a family waiting for him after all. Andy sometimes wondered what such a life might be like. It was a scenario that could easily turn bad, that much he knew for sure.

He planned to spend the rest of the afternoon reading the document found on Robin McKay's body, but first he needed to action the interesting text message that had arrived earlier that morning.

WHO NEEDS A SODDING WEEKEND. DOING YOUR CORPSE NOW. FAST ENOUGH FOR YOU?

Doctor Nassar was definitely growing on him.

At the City Mortuary, a security guard masquerading as the weekend receptionist let him inside. "What d'you want?"

"DI Lorimar, Police Scotland. Can I see Doctor Nassar?"

"Don't ask me mate. I've not heard the bone saw going for an hour or so. Your call."

"I'll take my chances."

"That's the weekend sign-in book there. I don't have a clue about swim caps or flippers. You can do all that yourself."

Fortunately Andy knew the drill and was soon sashaying into the lab space wearing pristine blue overshoes. He found the pathologist typing notes in a glass office at the rear. "Detective Lorimar. What took you so long?"

"Apologies, Doc. Busy morning."

"Snap! I started at five. However, since clearing my backlog depends on this newfound inability to sleep, perhaps I should thank you for the constant harassment."

"You're welcome." She wasn't entirely serious, he was almost sure about that. "So. Robin McKay?"

"Yes. Your roof murder."

"Then it was a murder? We know that?"

"I'm damn near certain. I found a recent injection site in his neck. Although, we'll need a day for final toxicology."

Andy took notes. He wouldn't see a final report until the tox screen was complete. "I'm grateful for the preview."

Doctor Nassar turned to her screen. "Time of death I'd estimate between around 20:30 and 23:30 on Tuesday 30th August. The SOCOs at the scene found his watch face smashed at 20:28, and we found small scraps of dirt wedged into the exposed mechanism. Similar dirt had aspirated into his airway, but that was not causal."

Andy interrupted. "Would that be consistent with his unconscious body being shoved into a wheeled refuse trolley?"

"Absolutely. I examined a similar trachea in London after a vagrant passed out in a skip. Cement dust may not be healthy but nothing crushes skulls like a discarded toilet bowl." The good doctor's anecdotes weren't particularly chat show friendly. "Your roof man had cirrhotic liver damage. Unusual in someone his age, so a history of alcoholism is likely. Yes?"

"I can corroborate that. Had the liver damage contributed to his death?"

"Not directly, although it can impact how drugs metabolise. The direct cause was extreme respiratory depression leading to coma and death. You may have noticed blue lips and fingernails when you found him, and there was systemic evidence of extreme oxygen depletion. At a guess I'd say opiates, but toxicology will confirm."

"Any chance he injected himself?"

"I'd say no. A neck injection is a risk even when administered by a third party, but as a DIY high in a cramped toilet cubicle you'd need to be sodding insane. There are much safer places to inject all over the human body. And crucially, his veins were pristine. This man simply was not an intravenous drug user. The recent injection site was the only one I found."

"Signs of violence?"

"I would classify lividity on his left shoulder as antemortem. If someone forced him into a refuse trolley while still alive that could easily explain it."

On the drive home Andy considered the footage viewed earlier that morning. Nobody injected Robin McKay in the neck while seated in a public bar. It seemed Devlin's 'toilet whammy' theory was in the ascendant, with a killer who acted the good Samaritan for the camera, but it still didn't feel right.

Whatever. He'd circulate the pathology notes around the team and then spend the rest of the weekend reading what might be the last will and testament of a murder.

SUNDAY MORNING BEGAN the same way Saturday night had ended. Andy retrieved the photocopied document from the bedroom floor and flicked it open. After reading the first line, he reached down again, scrabbling on the carpet for a yellow highlighter he'd brought to bed to mark interesting passages, but had found no reason to use.

He reread from the beginning. And just as eight hours before, he required a conscious effort to relax, his mouth tightening with each turn of a page. If this thing hadn't been found on a murder victim, he'd have classed it irrelevant. After forty minutes he raised his eyes and gazed around the room in silence.

He had little feeling for interior decor, especially not his own. Alternating beige and brown stripes embossed with olive-green islands of bacterial Paisley pattern. A local shopkeeper had once branded this wallpaper contemporary-yet-restful, and two decades of buyer's regret ensured Andy had never forgotten the encounter. The man had a special talent for offloading factory rejects, enthusing over the design with one corner of his mouth while a cigarette waggled in the other, hypnotically closing the deal.

If the memory of that conversation was fresh, the same could not be said of the wallpaper itself. A strip was peeling just above the door. Eventually it would curl around the tangle of cobwebs on the upper-right of the frame, like a house-proud Venus flytrap. At least someone was making an effort.

The document propped open on the pillow beside him wasn't going away. Four pages more until he finished. Could he face it?

The morning sunlight, previously faltering its way up the undressed duvet, stuttered and withdrew. Sunday's Met Office roulette wheel had settled on cloud. Perhaps he would start reading again from the beginning.

Instead, he pushed the document away and stuck the kettle on.

9

LINES OF ENQUIRY
MONDAY 5TH SEPTEMBER, 09:05

The note stuck to Andy's desk read only: *'INTERVIEW ROOM 3'.*

Inside, he found Nesbitt sticking sheets of paper to a whiteboard. Each contained a photograph beside a block of printed text. "I'm linking council interviewees who worked committees with Joan Wood, especially where she was the convener or vice convener." In the middle of a web of marker lines, the face of the murdered councillor regarded the room, her expression more inscrutable than the one she'd worn in the pathology lab.

The chief waved at the board. "I'm unsure I've got much." He sat down at the interview desk and Andy took the seat opposite. "On the plus side, though, your line of enquiry seems like it's going places. Devlin brought me up to speed."

"Good of him."

"So Robin McKay. Attacked in the toilet? Killed by overdose?"

"Possibly. We're not certain about the rest, but the overdose thing looks like a banker."

"And you've got a prime suspect. It's good."

"We've got two suspects. Listen Brian, I'm not sure you've got the full—"

The door crashed open and Devlin announced, "It's sorted. McKay was whammied by John Reynolds, in the hotel toilets, using a syringe in the neck." Just like that real life had become Cluedo.

"I don't see how we can know—"

"Look Link-man, I get that you fancied the other guy from lip-reading the CCTV." Devlin's grin widened as he flipped open his notebook. "But I've just spoken to security at the Balrannoch. Two men got in the lift with McKay at 19:54. One of those left the hotel twelve minutes later. The only man who could still have been with McKay around his estimated time of death has now been identified as their vanishing guest: John Reynolds AKA the cubicle killer AKA the bog butcher AKA—"

Nesbitt interrupted. "We're sure on the ID?"

"Yup. Reynolds' check-in time matched footage of the same guy from reception. It's him."

Devlin wasn't famed for intuition, but this could be a first. And he wasn't finished, brandishing an A4 sheet. "This screen shot DI Lorimar took from the CMF, right when McKay stepped up to the hotel? Look what's parked out front."

There it was. The side of a white van, plate obscured by the vehicle stopped behind it. It was such an everyday sight that Andy hadn't considered it before. But with a hard suspect now in the hotel, they needed to acknowledge the possibility of Joan Wood's murder weapon being parked right outside.

Nesbitt rubbed his hands. "We've placed an alert on Reynolds' credit card. The Balrannoch took their pound of flesh yesterday, so we know it's working. If he gets peckish at a service station, we'll have him, but we need to consider releasing something, bringing the press and public on board."

Devlin's scenario seemed a decent-enough working theory but it was premature to bet everything on a single interpretation of the evidence. If his colleague wanted to take the driving seat, fine, but someone else should kick the tyres before the team road trip. "Chief, this sounds compelling, but let me check the fuses. We can't afford to miss something."

Reluctantly, however, credit was due. "DS Devlin's your best man to dig into Reynolds' motive." He'd be hungry enough to do a thorough job for once. And if he was right, he deserved the chance to join the dots. "And Jamie?" Devlin stepped back, face wary. "If you're planning to build anything around the document from McKay's corpse, you'll need legal input. Find someone dull who knows local government procurement. It's dry as dust."

With Devlin and Nesbitt planning their next move, Andy called Pete Cunningham at the Balrannoch and thanked him for the identification.

"You're welcome Andy. I hope you catch him."

"Well. I want to be sure it is only him we need to catch. Did you get anywhere on the other man? The one with glasses McKay met in the bar?"

A long silence.

"On the CCTV footage I got the impression you recognised something. But you said you needed to check. What was that?"

Another pause, awkwardness palpable. Then Andy heard a phone being placed down, followed by a door slamming shut. "I found nothing definitive on the other guy."

"Nothing *definitive?* What do you mean? What were you looking for?"

Cunningham sighed. "I wanted something on camera, not just an I spy with my little eye."

"Whose little eye are we talking about?"

Cunningham's voice lowered. "I thought I saw the other guy before. But I needed to be certain, and I'm not."

"I understand Pete, but you were in the game long enough to

know we don't need certainty, not yet. Two people are dead. We need lines of enquiry. The certainty comes later."

A long deep exhalation. "Daniel Cochrane. I might have seen the other guy talking to Daniel Cochrane."

That name tickled the back of Andy's mind. Daniel Cochrane was someone he'd read about in the papers. "Is that the businessman?"

"Yeah. That's him. Important client for us too. Uses the hotel for accommodation, commercial meetings, seminars, product launches, everything. And multiple times a year."

Andy now understood the sensitivity. "When did you see them together?"

"Might. I might have seen them together. A month ago. End of July. I was in the lobby and I saw Cochrane outside. I thought he was about to come in. So I straightened up and got my smile ready, you know how it is. But he didn't enter. He stood talking to this person for five minutes. Then they both moved on."

"You saw them together. For a full five minutes?"

"I didn't have a stopwatch. But yes. It lasted a few minutes."

"Any chance it wasn't Cochrane?"

"No. That's not possible. I might not be 100% on the other guy but I know Daniel Cochrane. And he had his stick."

"Stick?"

"He walks with a cane. Recognisable thing. Natural wood, rustic almost, but with a gold handle."

This was a specific, detailed recollection, from a professional observer, based on a visual that had taken place recently. Andy was minded to trust it. "I don't suppose Cochrane had a room with you on the night McKay was murdered?"

A short pained laugh. "Try seven. And a meeting area. He'd had people over for a few days."

"Ah. This is probably just a loose end, but I have to follow it up."

The awkward silence intruded again. "Andy? Can you be gentle with him? I don't want us to lose a key account. The Hotel's in enough shit as it is."

10

HOPPERSOFT
MONDAY 5TH SEPTEMBER, 11:27

I t proved straightforward to get an appointment at Cochrane's offices on Greenside Row. Andy received a callback within fifteen minutes confirming an opening just before midday. There was no sense of a runaround so this might turn out the formality he'd suggested to Cunningham. However, given Cochrane's presence within the hotel around the time of McKay's murder, this meeting needed to happen. Andy used his phone to conduct some preparatory internet research prior to the appointment.

Upon entering the office itself, he almost tripped over the space hoppers. Inflatable aliens, green, blue, red and orange, balanced plump and jolly against foam starting blocks on a huge racetrack-styled play mat. Each lane contained irregularly spaced foam-rubber hurdles. Andy had no career experience outside of the force, but he'd seen enough corporate workplaces to recognise something unusual. A roiling sensation began in his stomach as he realised the tracks ended at the reception desk.

"No need for concern, Inspector Lorimar. Bouncing for your visitor's badge is not mandatory!" The man striding towards him had a cane, exactly as advertised, but he moved at a fair pace.

Andy shook his hand. "Thanks for your time Mr Cochrane. I'm happier not bursting your toys. I doubt they'd take my weight."

Cochrane smiled. "You'd be surprised. We specified these to handle our largest software engineers. It's a career of late nights and chair-bound pizza, so the HopperSoft hoppers have seen heavier backsides than yours and come out smiling." He waved around the play area. "All this stuff, it's fun for the staff, and we look suitably millennial at press-events." Then he raised a conspiratorial hand to his mouth. "But if people spend too much time on it I open the nearest window and ask them to keep bouncing."

Frank and forthright. And unruffled by police questioning. "So that's what you do here, computer software? Do you do much for Edinburgh Council?"

"Straight down to it? Bravo detective! Goal-oriented, much like myself! Come through to the office and we'll chat."

Cochrane swiped Andy through a double door and then into a smaller glass-fronted meeting room. They took opposite seats at a boardroom-style table. A younger man typed at a nearby desk. "Don't mind Nick. He's my technical guru, setting up a demo on my workstation. He's also the only one in my family who understands all our latest stuff."

"So Nick is, what, your son?"

"In here we call him vice president software development. But, yes, he's a silicon chip off the old block. I rarely get to use that joke with somebody new. Forgive me!"

"You don't mind if we discuss these matters in front of him?"

"Not at all! No secrets and nothing to hide. We all heard about the Balrannoch. Bloody awful business. If we can help, we will. What was your question again?"

"Do you write any software for Edinburgh Council?"

"No. Not our line. We're a private software house in the gaming industry."

"Gaming? Like Pac-Man and Space Invaders?" At the desk, Nick smirked. Andy was less out of date than his question suggested, but feigning naivety sometimes prompted greater disclosure.

"Not games, detective, *gaming*. Think licensed gaming, but web and mobile. I started in the bricks-and-mortar world of casinos and betting, but abandoned that sinking ship long ago. Restricting yourself to a few punters walking through a door is a mug's game. Global reach is the prize of going digital. Our software supports online gambling services worldwide. The bricks-and-mortar brigade could only dream of what we've achieved."

Andy had garnered an inkling of a gambling connection from his research, but the digital industry awards and technology leadership profiles had somehow obscured the fact the man's whole business was skimming the wallets of idiots. "So you provide the software, but don't run gambling services yourself?"

"We do both. After we created the HopperSoft toolkit, we launched our own site using our own games. It became our shop window: they passed muster with the regulator, proved attractive to players, and convinced partners and investors we could turn a handsome profit. Fifteen years on, and here we are. Thriving."

"You never worry about the players? Gambling addiction and so on?"

"People can get addicted to hoovering. What're you going to do?" He held up his hands, face faux-sheepish. "No, our job is to create games that give the end user a great experience for their RTP."

"What's RTP?"

"Return-to-player ratio. The UK Gambling Commission require we publish for every game, over the long run, how much of every pound spent the players get to keep. House always wins, of course. Look, why don't we give you our investor pack? It will answer any question you have about our business."

It felt intriguingly tawdry, so Andy accepted the offer. Perhaps he was being overly judgemental, but it wouldn't hurt to dig a little.

Nick left his desk and walked to Andy's side. "Our investor pack is an app. We're HopperSoft, not jotter soft. We don't do paper. Do you have a phone?"

Andy would have preferred a booklet, but he handed over his personal mobile. He'd copy anything relevant into official systems later.

"Nick," Cochrane interrupted, "Install the one that integrates my personal contact details. I want Inspector Lorimar to be able to reach me whenever."

Nick smirked again. "You'll be the only person with this version that doesn't own a yacht."

Andy was about to challenge the assumption, but caught sight of the fraying seam on his right trouser leg and let it lie. "Mr Cochrane? Were you at the Balrannoch on Tuesday August 30th?"

"Me personally? I wasn't, not in the evening. We had a group booking of some rooms there for our guests. We'd been having discussions over several days. My guests arrived on Sunday twenty-eighth August."

"Who were your guests?"

"Ah. That's commercially sensitive. I can't risk disclosing details that might influence an investment. Insider trading accusations? No thanks, I value my freedom."

"Can you say anything about them?"

"Not much. They're all professionals but our dealings are under non-disclosure. I've signed a contract."

Cochrane, previously so keen to disavow bricks and mortar, had thrown up a wall faster than Bob The Builder. "But we've one man wanted in connection to a murder, so we need you to identify him at least." Andy handed over a screen print from the Balrannoch CCTV. It showed John Reynolds supporting Robin McKay, standing beside the as yet unidentified glasses-wearing man.

Cochrane stared at it from various angles. Then shook his head. "I would ask which one you mean, but I don't recognise either of them."

Andy persevered. "What about this shot from the bar area? You see a different view of his face here."

Again Cochrane scrutinised the page, holding it out at different angles. "Nope. Wouldn't know him from Adam. Is he your prime suspect?"

"That's my area of non-disclosure, Mr Cochrane." Andy leaned across and tapped the image. "I have someone who believes they witnessed you and this man in discussion together."

Cochrane was unfazed. "Really? This man? Are they sure?" He shrugged. "I'll happily look at any evidence on that, because I'm unusually good with faces and I don't remember this one."

Nick intervened, returning Andy's phone. "Installed, one HopperSoft Partner Pack. You can guess the icon."

Cochrane stood up. "You have my details now. Just contact me if you need to ask anything else. Any time." He reached for his cane. "Unfortunately I have a lunch appointment. It was good to meet you."

It was obvious to Andy that his audience was now over.

BACK AT FETTES AVENUE, he knew time was running out for him to propose an alternative to Devlin's theory. He took a careful look through the app Nick had installed. It presented a marketeer's dream of a modern business, with real-time updates of company press releases and stock information. The blurb claimed their software was 'instantly skinnable' around 'new properties', such as characters from hit video games, TV shows or superhero movies. The app also contained demonstration versions of the HopperSoft games. Unlike the punters, the wealthy investors got to play as much as they wanted for free.

The HopperSoft Partner Pack was, without question, the most glamorous depiction of theft and robbery he had ever seen. And considering the suggestion of superhero theming, he didn't doubt there was also an element of mugging kids for their lunch money. But these crimes were beyond his jurisdiction, the kind committed without any eye mask, striped jumper or sack for ill-gotten gains. This kind of larceny dressed in polarised Ray-Bans, two-tone cashmere and designer man bags.

But whatever bag you stuffed it into, swag remained swag. And the app's continual flaunting of a moonshot share price suggested substantial amounts of it. He preferred not to even contemplate how much Cochrane was worth.

Despite the plethora of opportunities for direct access to the man himself, he soon realised he would never wish to Skype, WhatsApp, or Google hangout with Daniel Cochrane. Andy recorded just an email address and phone number in the system, then wrote up the interview with some background on the man's business. After that he found instructions online and used them to delete the Hopper-Soft application from his phone.

Not long after, he spotted Nesbitt and Devlin locked in debate with the Assistant Chief Constable for Crime. The seniors would be after a public demonstration of progress. A murder during the Edinburgh Festival made global headlines and risked profound economic consequences. Additional political and civic pressures would drive the usual push for results.

He gazed around the office, watching the bustle of his fellow officers. Resources would soon mobilise around a questionable theory. But six hours effort had brought him no further forward in supporting or refuting Devlin's scenario.

Since he couldn't afford to wait for a formal report, and with a reputation for harassment to maintain, he called the pathologist. "Guess who, Doc?"

"Detective Lorimar! I've put a telephone-pest whistle through expenses, but it hasn't arrived yet. What can I do for you?"

"I'm sorry to jump the gun, but—"

"You'll always jump the sodding gun. Only apologise for behaviour you intend to change, Detective."

"Right. I'm calling on the off-chance you've got toxicology back for Robin McKay."

"I do, and I'm typing up. But don't tell me; tomorrow morning is simply too-too far away, and can you get a preview?"

"You read my mind."

"Toxicology confirmed McKay's death arose from opiates, morphine to be exact, and a large amount of it. We also found trace amounts of something tricky to identify. It appeared related to a benzodiazepine called clonazolam."

He was unfamiliar with that one. "What's that used for?"

"It isn't, at least not officially. In fact, our basic tests don't even look for it, but we caught it on a more detailed screen. The drug isn't approved for medical use in the UK, EU or US. That means we've no medical trials to provide reliable evidence on the effects, but it appears as a designer drug now and then. We know it's strong, acts fast at low doses and given in isolation will act like rohypnol crossed with valium."

"So, it's a sedative?"

"Yes. Also a muscle relaxant. Inhibits anxiety. Amnesic."

"But why give that and morphine together?"

"The most likely reason would be to secure the outcome. There was sufficient morphine for a fatal overdose, no question. However, adding clonazolam or, indeed, any benzodiazepine strengthens the respiratory depression and toxicity. From a murderer's perspective it provides belt and braces."

"So the morphine alone should have been enough to kill him, but he was a big guy and clonazolam was an insurance policy... OK. That's most likely. Is there a less likely reason?"

"Well ... it seems likely these drugs shared a syringe, but based on the bloods and bladder fluids we can't be certain. The clonazolam may have been administered earlier, and lacking another entry point or evidence of a patch, I'd assume orally."

Andy voiced what he'd been thinking since he first saw the hotel CCTV. "Could it have been added to a coffee?"

"Yes, it's possible, This powerful drug requires only tiny amounts. There would be no impact on taste or texture."

The less-likely scenario was becoming interesting. "Let's say it was given orally prior to the morphine. At the amounts found can you imagine what effect someone might have been seeking when they dosed him?"

The doctor fell silent. Requests for speculation were doubtless outside her comfort zone. But he needed her expertise, so waited until an answer was offered. "We don't know the precise quantity given or ingested. The effects of this drug run along a continuum from 'taking the edge off', through 'meek compliance' to 'coma'."

"Would McKay's size have suggested a larger dose to achieve a given state?"

"Yes. Although as we discussed, there are no dosing guidelines for this chemical."

"But your postmortem showed previous cirrhosis. Could liver damage have caused the drug to act more quickly or more power-fully? Might an attacker have set a dose based on his size only to get a shock when McKay ends up totally wasted?"

"The liver is intimately involved with metabolising such compounds, therefore your suggestion is entirely plausible." Before he got too excited, the caveats arrived. "I'd reiterate however, I have no histological evidence of oral administration, but I most assuredly do have an injection site on his neck."

LATER, as he completed the documentation, most of his colleagues were packing up and heading home. Devlin had waved as he cruised past twenty minutes earlier. Lacking any other inspiration he decided to down tools himself. He had a psychic loose end to revisit on the way home.

But passing Devlin's empty desk, the phone rang. Upon answering, he heard a woman's voice. "Hello? Detective Sergeant Devlin?"

"DS Devlin's unavailable. I'm Detective Inspector Lorimar. We're working together so I can help you."

"OK. It's just, when we spoke today, he said I should call him with any developments."

"Good. Can I take your name?"

"Sorry. Yes. It's Tricia. Tricia Black." There was a guilty pause. "I was John Reynolds' partner."

"Thanks for calling Ms Black. We're still trying to understand what happened. Anything you tell us might help."

"Well, I just got a message. From John, that is."

He scrambled for a pad. "So you recognised the phone number or the message claimed to be from him?"

"He's in my contacts. The phone recognised him."

"OK. What was the message?"

"It was weird. It said 'HEY TALLULAH. I'M SORRY BUT I DID IT.' That was all ..." Her voice faltered. They both knew it sounded like a confession.

"We'll follow this up. When did this message arrive?"

"Just ten minutes ago. The time stamp shows 17:54."

He logged her handset details so Petrakis could run checks with the mobile network. Since he hadn't read Devlin's call transcript yet, he decided to avoid having her repeat herself, and kept the focus on this new development. "When you said the message was weird, did you mean just unexpected, or something else?"

"Well. It's not like him to apologise," then she paused awkwardly, perhaps struck by the gravity of what the apology might be for. "Sorry, stupid joke. It was the name he used. He'd called me it only a few times before. We saw an old kids film with my niece a few months back. Bugsy Malone. Gangster thing. Good fun, but daft. Anyway, there's a character called Tallulah. She doesn't remember names, but she remembers faces, and I'm hopeless with names. So for about a week he called me that. But not since. Until now."

Strange, but how people acted under stress wasn't entirely predictable. "Does your phone keep a history of your messages?"

She seemed puzzled by the question, but she answered. "Yes, we both have smartphones."

"If you have your phone now, could you scroll back through the history for me? Do any of his prior messages call you Tallulah? Or does he normally call you Tricia?"

"We hadn't been calling each other anything affectionate lately. But I'm looking. Nope ... nope ... he normally calls me 'T' if he calls me anything. I'm still scrolling ... Ah! On June 26th he sent 'DO YOU REMEMBER THIS FACE TALLULAH?', and then a picture of him girning. That's him. A bit of an idiot." She paused, a slight crack in her voice. "But he's not ... bad. Not violent or anything. Not that I've ever known. What happened up there?"

"We're working to find out. Respond to his message and ask where he is. Contact us if he replies."

She didn't hang up. "Please. Can't you tell me anything? John wasn't involved with drugs. Your colleague also asked about John's job. What does that have to do with it? He'd be back at work if he could. He never missed it."

Tricia Black didn't sound like she had seen any hint of this coming. And the questions raised by Devlin's attempts to construct a motive had left her floundering even more. She was lost. "I'm sorry. I wish we had more to pass on, but we're not there yet. We'll be in touch."

On his way out of the office Andy noticed that Nesbitt's meeting with the top brass had traded Devlin for yet another Assistant Chief Constable. The pressure for progress had turned extreme. The full force of this investigation was about to roll over the reputation of John Reynolds and despite what his gut was telling him, he saw no practical way to stop it.

11

LILIES AND GIN

MONDAY 5TH SEPTEMBER, 17:58

After the tension at Fettes, Andy was glad to reach the comforting impossibilities of the Palmerston Centre. Doirin Chambers was thanking her last few visitors while packing a holdall with her priceless fake flowers.

"Can't leave them overnight Doirin?"

"My silk lilies? It's not stems they've got. It's bloody legs."

"You're not surprised to see me?"

"Not at all, son. Ever since I heard about that roof business I knew you'd be back."

Again with the son. Couldn't she see they were about the same age? He'd ignored colleagues on the force dodging his real name for years, but Doirin's lack of recognition somehow vexed him. "I'm not here to arrest you. You'll be glad to know, the case is moving in another direction."

She made another impeccable job of arching her eyebrow. "Hopefully towards actual criminals."

"I'm here about your job." Specifically, he hoped to reassure himself she'd just struck lucky. "It's a strange career after all." Some evidence for his last statement was sticking from the other end of the holdall. "Not everyone brings a bottle of gin to the office."

"Shh! You'll get me in trouble!" She shoved it back into the bag. "I only need a wee bit of something to get the job done." She smiled for a moment, remembering. "Wee Davie called me Dairy-Milk Doirin. A glass and a half in every reading." Her eyes deepened, smile taking on a hint of melancholy. "He knew me at least."

The confusion must have shown on Andy's face, because she quickly snapped back into the conversation. "Davie was my late husband. Builder. Fell off a tenement roof in the Gorbals five years back. Bloody eejit."

Andy decided it would be insensitive to ask, but she was ahead of him. "And no. I don't get messages from him. Everyone wonders about that. Me most of all." Her expression softened again. "Still. I'll see him soon enough." She put the last of the lilies into her holdall.

An awkwardness grew between them until Andy said, "I only want a few minutes. To ask some final questions. Draw a line under your involvement in this thing."

She checked her watch, then inclined her head slightly, as though listening. "Give me a lift to the waterfront at Lower Granton Road and you can ask whatever you like." It sounded like a fair exchange.

When he closed the car door, Andy scented the perfume he'd first encountered during her interview last week. It wasn't unwelcome. Any vehicle smell not originating from his tupperware lunch box was a step in the right direction.

He set off, heading towards Ravelston. "So. when you make a ... a prediction—"

"Whoa son, let me stop you there. The name's Doirin, not Nostradamus. I'm not a fortune teller."

He tried to remember her terminology. "When you pass on a message? Say, for talking sake, some of it seems, well, accurate. How do you decide if it was real or—" He was on potentially dodgy ground here. "Or a fluke? Not in a bad way, but a coincidence I mean."

Doirin clapped her hands. "You're freaked out. That's a result! Rational big man like you? That's a notch on my crystal ball!"

He realised she was right. He was, at least slightly, freaked out. Would he have explored the roof of the Balrannoch Hotel if not for Doirin's message? Would Robin McKay's body have been found? He couldn't be sure. And that troubled him.

She softened. "Look. I get impressions. I don't know for sure if what I pass on is accurate, I just hope it means something to the right person ..." She smiled. "But fluke? Cheeky midden!" Her expression became pensive. "One thing though. The past week or two has been very ... very noisy. Much more than usual. More voices, pressing in. I even wondered if they'd been trying to get *your* attention."

"Mine? Why?"

"You seem a part of it. There's an intensity around you."

"I have that effect on people."

She snorted, something he could probably have done without. But her face turned solemn. "No. I've never experienced spirit this way. It's like," she grimaced, "a swarm. And that's not a word I would ever use. But there's a purpose to it. It brings things through."

"Brings things? Like the messages from Jimmy?"

She nodded. "I can't even tell if Jimmy wants to. But it's the same now, the swarm just cleared. And he's here."

He stopped on amber, sitting in silence until the light changed to green. As they pulled away, he spoke quietly. "OK. If he's here now, what is he saying?" There was less challenge in his voice than he'd have expected. In fact there was none. Did he want her to fail, or prove herself?

She started with a question. "His wife is still this side. But not here. Abroad? The name I get is Elsie?"

"That's close. Ilsa."

"I wasn't close enough. Jimmy's kicking off. She's special. Exotic. Is that right?"

He cleared a roundabout. "She's Hungarian."

"Right. He says don't blame her. It wasn't her fault."

Andy blushed. This had to be a coincidence. But he did blame Ilsa, in a way. After all, it had been her decision, he was sure of it. Jimmy would never have left Scotland for Spain if Ilsa hadn't wanted to go. But Andy had been a grown man, and they weren't chained to him, even though they'd been close. They had every right to go wherever they liked, but it had knocked him all the same. Still. That wouldn't be what Doirin meant. "Her fault? About what?"

"You're testing me now." She paused. "Remember what she did. She gave you something? A puzzle? Does that mean anything?"

Andy reddened again. She'd given him a few puzzles over the years. But lots of people liked puzzles. "How can I be sure you didn't know them somehow? Or spoke to them before he, you know." Christ. He missed Jimmy still. Nearly seven bloody years later.

"I didn't. But he's hesitating. Pressure, all around." Then she spoke quickly,"Ask Ilsa about the wallpaper box." She exhaled slowly. "But that's bloody odd again. I feel like he wouldn't have. But they forced him, like they need you to know that." She hesitated. "Turn up here. We're looking for Boswall Road."

Andy flicked the indicator, waiting for a break in the traffic. "Are we heading to the hospice?"

She nodded. Her smile was tight. "Just for ten minutes, and then I'd be obliged if you dropped me on London Road. I might not fancy the walk after."

When they parked, Andy was unsure what to do. But Doirin touched his shoulder. "Please," she said, "Just come in. It won't be for long. It's my wee sister."

As they entered, Doirin acknowledged the nurse at the desk and led Andy through double doors. This was an unexpected turn, but it felt natural somehow. Doirin touched his arm again. "We lost wee Flora two years back. Ovarian cancer. Twins can be alike in bad ways."

The interior was unlike that of a hospital ward, the battle for survival being an altogether noisier and more fraught affair than what happened here. The furniture was simple, the decor peaceful. Discreet monitoring equipment and a single IV drip stood off to one side. The woman in the bed lay unmoving, her breathing ragged. Doirin lifted her hand and kissed it softly "Rosie? It's me darling. It's Dodo." She looked over at Andy "It's progressing quickly. I'm not sure if she wants to stay."

Andy stood to the side while Doirin put fresh water in the flowers, tucked sheets and spoke softly. There were no tears, just love expressed in little ways. Like Doirin had suggested, it didn't take long. She promised her sleeping sister she'd return soon and then guided Andy back out to the car. She thanked him as they set off again but they made the rest of the short journey in silence.

When they stopped outside her flat, she touched his hand briefly. "I might get things wrong, but I don't deliberately lie. I respect loss, and I've suffered it." She frowned. "And I'm long past trying to impress folk at my age."

"Careful! That's our age! We're young yet I hope."

She was quiet for a moment, then shook her head. "I met my man at school. We were young together. But when he died our young life died with him. I'm old now, whatever my birth certificate says. Lose enough folk and you've more company on that side of life than this one. It's been a horrible few years. First Davie, then my sister Flora. Rosie will probably go soon. After that? Me. I'm not scared."

Andy remembered Jimmy and Ilsa. "When I was young I believed something similar. But life doesn't stand still. I met people who gave me a reason to think differently."

He doubted he'd convinced her, but she attempted a smile at least. "Well. Maybe spirit will keep me busy a while longer." As she left the car, she turned back for a moment. "With Rosie, I get to say goodbye, but not everyone does. My strange career can sometimes give folk a chance to do that."

The words came without thinking. "Can you contact specific people? See, my mum ..."

She blinked, shaking her head. "It doesn't work like that."

"Well, what's the point of it then?" He swallowed the anger. He should be mad at himself. He was the idiot starting to buy into it.

"Sorry. I hope we talk again soon, Andy." She was inside her doorway before he realised she'd used his actual name for once. But he didn't have much time to ponder the significance; his phone chimed with a message from Brian Nesbitt.

MEET ME AT THE STARBANK 8PM?

Sounded like the chief's grilling was finally over, and he was eager to share.

As THE DOOR of her flat clicked shut behind her, Doirin wondered where this experience was heading. Usually she felt spirit had a plan, a pattern for her to discern and follow. But this time, she'd been thrown into fog, with no certainties except that this detective, Andy Lorimar was somehow important.

In under an hour the doorbell would announce her private sitting, so she needed to prepare. In the kitchenette she popped open a fridge-cooled can of gin and tonic. Bloody man had her marked down as an alcoholic, but she only took what she needed to loosen the ties. She moved to her sitting room, and shuffled yesterday's newspaper back under her coffee table.

She dropped into her armchair, and found herself in a staring contest with a pigeon on the roof opposite. Andy was annoyed with her, she could see that. But the other side was reaching out to him through her, for reasons neither of them fully understood. And these communications weren't always welcome. That had been the first lesson spirit taught her.

THE DENTIST'S surgery loomed down from the top of the stone steps. There had been a bubble-glass door, a brass plate, and the sound of children screaming.

But thankfully the children were just her sisters. "Dodo's getting a tooth out! Dodo's getting a tooth out!"

Doirin loved Rosie and Flo, even though having twin siblings placed her on the outside looking in. But being older had its compensations. After winching wee Davie at last night's school disco her position in the family seemed somehow less important. "I'll have you terrible wee lassies know, my mouth is just like your bedroom. Overcrowded. After this I'll be even more beautiful."

They giggled. Mammy shushed all of them. "Quiet! Girls, leave your sister alone. Doirin, stop talking like a hussy."

Inside, there was a long plastic runner on the carpet. It crackled as they walked on it. Mammy spoke to the receptionist before marching them through to the waiting room.

"I could have come myself. I get the bus to school so I know what I'm doing."

"Quiet." Mammy wasn't much for consensus.

Doirin started to flick through a magazine. When she reached a page about choosing the perfect bikini, she knew it was only a matter of time. One-elephant. Two-elephant. Three—the magazine was slapped from her hand. "Put that filth down!"

Doirin hadn't had a tooth removed or even had a filling before. She was always careful about brushing her teeth. Everyone said she had a good smile. She was still practising it when the snooty voice sounded from the speaker above the waiting-room door: "DOIRIN CHAMBERS, SURGERY TWO PLEASE."

The first room she reached contained an old man holding his false teeth and clacking them like castanets. She quickly decided that must be surgery one.

One door down, her dentist smiled and guided her onto the chair. He'd explained the procedure last time around, but she wasn't looking forward to it. As he pressed the rubber mask to her face, the smell became overwhelming. She felt sick, but she counted backwards just like he asked.

Ten.

Nine. The nausea was fading, replaced by a sense of displacement. Growing. Something growing. Pulling her into

White noise. Whispers struggling to become words.

Eight.

Him. The boy in the quarry.

Seven.

A flash. The thrown firework.

Six.

Bang!

Doirin's ears were ringing. Five.

He tried to catch me.

Four.

The scream. The tumbling rocks.

Three.

An awful, soft, vegetable sound.

Sleep.

She woke to find him wiping her chin. "Bite down on the dressing Doirin. I think we're all done. Take your time. You'll be groggy, maybe a little queasy for a bit. Probably have a headache too."

Doirin felt all those things. And something else as well. Something she had to say, but her mouth wouldn't work. She gagged, spitting a cotton swab into her hand. The pulpy red wetness against skin reminded her of blood on sandstone. "I know. I know you tried ... you tried to catch me."

The dentist smiled, taking her arm. "You're just a bit sleepy."

Doirin felt a strong frustration, and the oddest sensation that it wasn't entirely her own. "No. Not me."

Susan.

"It's Susan. Susan knows you tried to catch her. It was the boy at the old quarry. He threw it at you both."

The dentist dropped her arm and froze. His face trembled slightly. He looked to his assistant, eyes filled with confusion. And then pain. "Please. Get her mother."

No. He needed to know this. Doirin grabbed his arm, and spoke quickly.

"It was the boy. He threw the firework. Susan fell. You tried to catch her."

He tried to shake her away, something like revulsion contorting his features.

Doirin couldn't let go. "Susan says she was falling anyway. She knows you tried to save her. She knows." She remembered when granny lanced a cyst with a heated knife. These words made her think of that knife. Just as sharp, just as hot, but maybe letting a poison of a different type.

His mouth moved before he spoke, his jaw working silently, until the words came. "I ... I pushed her. I didn't mean to but I pushed her. I grabbed for her arm but I missed and I pushed her." He was sobbing now. Tears that became uncontrollable. He tried to pull away.

A whisper in Doirin's head.

First love.

A feeling in her stomach briefly overrode the nausea from the gas. A tremulous, excited heartache.

Susan and Greg carved on a bench.

"Greg. Your name's Greg."

Music.

"That day you'd had a radio. Flowers in the Rain. And she said she loved you and you blushed and kissed her. You didn't say it. But she knows. She knows ... She knows you loved her."

The door to the surgery crashed open and Mammy rushed in, eyes wide, taking stock of the scene in an instant. Absorbing every detail. Recognising it as if she'd waited for it all her life. She slapped Doirin's face hard. Once. Twice. Three times. A spray of blood from the girl's dental wound spattered against the clinically clean mint-green wall.

Doirin, trembling, slumped to the floor, still groggy from the gas. She gazed up, her fuddled mind overrun with questions and shame. She examined the lines on Mammy's face, desperate for answers. Anything to help make sense of what happened. Anything to help her understand.

But as Mammy dragged her from the surgery, Doirin had heard only one whispered word: "Witch."

———

THE BEATEN PIGEON averted its gaze, stretched its wings and flew for a telephone wire. She drained the last of her drink and rose with a sigh. Her gift sometimes brought trouble. And people weren't always grateful. But that didn't mean she could stop trying.

———

AT THE STARBANK INN, Nesbitt swapped an empty pint glass for the full one in front of him. Consciously or not, Andy noticed he'd chosen the same small table they'd sat at ten months ago when he'd confided a relationship with another man had ended his marriage of twenty-two years. His friend had been dealing with the personal fallout ever since, doubtless finding murder and violent crime enquiries an odd kind of sanctuary. Today, their window overlooked the peaceful waters of Newhaven, but his face suggested storms ahead.

As Andy took his seat, Nesbitt tapped the teapot in the middle of the table. "They didn't do chamomile. Peppermint?". There was no hint of a sneer. They'd known each other a long time.

"Thanks. Miguel working tonight?"

"Restaurant owners work most nights. I'll walk down there after this."

Andy could appreciate the irony. His friend's romance with an award-winning chef had left him routinely eating alone. Probably not the magic and stardust he'd hoped for when they started out last year. Then again, since Andy shared dinner with a Tupperware container most nights, he couldn't get too worked up about it. "How are the kids?"

Nesbitt scowled. "I'll see them next weekend." He raised his glass and took another gulp. Andy liked Brian's family, but the affair had put a bomb under it. The dust hadn't settled yet and might not for a while. There was no getting away from it: being true to himself had created an ugly amount of collateral damage.

Andy poured his tea, enjoying the scalding heat radiating through the cup. It was a sensation that almost made pain seem safe. They chatted for a while, and it sounded like things were slowly improving. The kids would be OK and their dad would still be there for them. Other people lost parents in ways there was no coming back from.

But while picking through the detritus of people's lives was occupationally unavoidable, they could both do with being off-duty for a bit. "Thanks for the invitation." Andy looked around the pub. He'd always liked it here. The proximity to the Forth excused the model sailboats and maritime theming.

Nesbitt wiped his lip. "It's not entirely social. I wanted to warn you. The shit-storm just thickened."

"The war council today?"

"Not much of a war. The seniors examined two competing realities. In the first we're in control, knowing the who, the what and most of the why. In the second? We've got Schrödinger's suspect: the same guy being victim and villain depending whether you or Devlin last sniffed the box. You can imagine which reality is going public."

Andy's jaw tightened. He'd known this was coming. "Is there any chance we could—"

"No. John Reynolds is in the frame for a double murder. With immediate effect we dedicate all our resource to hunting him down."

"Motive?"

Nesbitt snorted. "We've worked up a profile. Short version? Mild-mannered accountant. No criminal record. Passion for crosswords." Nesbitt rubbed his chin, tugging at the skin. "But Devlin found something. Reynolds' employer is part of a group of companies, one of whom had a client involved in the Edinburgh Trams project. So it could be a public sector, procurement contract cover-up, rogue employee type deal."

"What kind of deal is that?"

"We've no idea. But every day's a school day."

It wasn't much. But it was something. "The company with the Edinburgh connection? Was that Reynolds' direct employer?"

"No."

"Did Reynolds have a link? A previous assignment? A secondment? Had he worked with them?"

"Not that we know. We're still digging. This is all hot off the fan."

Andy paused to absorb it. "A quick turnaround from Devlin, though."

Nesbitt smiled, but without warmth. "Yeah. If I want something tenuous in a hurry, he's my guy."

Good. If Brian wasn't completely convinced it left room to manoeuvre. "Did you see my write-up from today?"

"Which one? Your soapbox pamphlet on the evils of gambling? The unsubstantiated theory that McKay drank the world's sleepiest espresso? Or the thought experiment that Reynolds' text-message confession might have come from a kidnapped phone? Oh, I read them all right. But we'll need something a lot more bloody concrete than that lot."

We. We'll need. Another good sign. "Let me keep digging then."

"Bet your arse you keep digging. There's too much we don't know here. Way too much." Nesbitt drained his glass before catching Andy's gaze. "But anyone asks, you're not checking fuses, kicking tyres or playing 'Mary, Mary, quite contrary'. You're tracking Reynolds. You're investigating his movements, interactions and possible accomplices. That means the hotel, the unidentified guy, any connections between Reynolds and the victims? They're all fair game. And if you stumble over hard evidence that contradicts our current reality?" The wooden chair scraped in protest as Nesbitt rose. "We're all about hard evidence, right?" He belched, tapping his chest. "Time. I'm off for a slash and a stroll to the Leith Waterfront. And you're meeting Petrakis first thing. I've pulled her back from cyber crime. She's not happy."

On the way home Andy reflected on the good fortune of working with Nesbitt. Uncovering, qualifying and interpreting evidence was something he knew how to do. But when the pressure was on, and political factors complicated an investigation, you needed a different skill set, one he couldn't lay claim to. But one Brian Nesbitt had in spades.

12

GOING PUBLIC

TUESDAY 6TH SEPTEMBER, 9:42

I t was a morning for facial expressions. Facing Andy, Nesbitt's mouth was a grim line. Devlin, beamed like a moggy who'd discovered his own fur was made of buttermilk. Petrakis, opposite Devlin, scowled at her phone.

Nesbitt addressed the group. "Let's get started. DS Petrakis has graciously accepted my invitation to base herself here for a bit."

Petrakis didn't meet his gaze. "You're welcome." Her words dripped sarcasm. "I was eight hours back in London before my boss handed me a train ticket and an ultimatum."

"Sounds like a well-oiled machine." Nesbitt paused, face devilish. "And free Wi-Fi on the East Coast main line now. You must have been in your element!"

Petrakis appeared to be counting her breaths, but said nothing.

Nesbitt continued. "Two murder victims, both Edinburgh Council. First was Joan Wood, a councillor and then Robin McKay, a council employee. John Reynolds is our prime suspect and a fugitive. All resources are now engaged in tracking him down."

Devlin pouted, probably expecting a round of applause. Since it would be better all round if they dropped their rivalry, Andy acknowledged him with a curt nod. Beyond that, he could whistle.

Nesbitt stood. "I'll catch up later. We're going public with a press conference, and since Lenny Burns is finalising the script, I best go and completely rewrite it. I'm sure you experienced officers can take things forward from here."

When the door swung shut, Petrakis pursed her lips. "Before we start, I found a parapsychology professor at the university that'll speak to you if you need it. Seems smart too. In a chasing rainbows kind of way." Andy stuck the business card into his shirt pocket for later. He might have displayed more gratitude if his new colleague hadn't suddenly sneered. "My role in this investigation could and should be handled over videoconference. Do Police Scotland have a problem with the H264 codec?"

Since Andy was unsure quite how to answer her question, he did the sensible thing and answered a different one. "DCI Nesbitt is just concentrating resources, bringing the whole team together. All seniors do it, it's investigative nesting."

"Then I should be at the Gartcosh Crime Campus with the other specialists." Andy and Devlin exchanged a frown; their company was her definition of slumming it. But she didn't stop there. "Edinburgh in September? At least Glasgow has a bit of life about it."

Andy shook his head. "Detective Sergeant. Where are you on the analysis of the computer equipment?"

Petrakis nodded. "Fine. Shout if you don't follow something, I'll try to dumb it down."

Andy shared another glance with Devlin. Petrakis was turning them, however briefly, into kindred spirits. She might just be the genius she imagined herself to be.

"We recovered a Windows 10 machine from the house of Joan Wood. We also had an Android tablet and a Windows 7 laptop from Robin McKay who was an IT specialist."

"Trying to crack an IT specialist's hardware was difficult, presumably?"

"Ought to be. Not in this case. He was a muppet." For Petrakis, respect for the dead seemed contingent on the strength of their digital hygiene. "He based his entire security regime on nobody getting hold of his kit. His wife knew his laptop login, and then after that, his browser and email app stored all his other passwords. They were encrypted, but guess what? He reused his login password as a key for the encryption. I hope it saved him a lot of time because it made my job a cakewalk. Given what he was up to, it was stupidly lax."

Andy guessed the behaviour of most people would fall under her definition of stupidly lax. "Given what he was up to?"

"You guys can define the crime, but I found an amanda-dot-conf file and a bunch of compressed tar files. It looked like he was harvesting."

Devlin stepped up to the plate. "In English?"

"He was storing council backups on his personal machine. He was also keeping notes on the councillors and senior staff. Personal details and press clippings. He was linking public statements back to documents in the backups, trying to find something juicy."

Andy said, "Define juicy?" McKay may have died for the most boring document ever printed.

Petrakis sighed. "I'll do your job for you. I'd say he was looking for blackmail opportunities. Half of that document you found on his body supposedly no longer existed. One of his press clippings announced it lost during the wind-up of the arm's-length trams project management company."

Devlin was now borderline ecstatic. "This all fits Link-man! It all fits!"

Andy could see it did, in a way. It was also consistent with the earlier statement from McKay's wife. He'd had big dreams, all right. So big they crushed him. But the motive of the murderer remained bizarre. Killing someone to shut them up was entirely plausible, but if you don't want someone to complete the jigsaw, why leave a piece on the body? "Any insights into the other half of the document?"

Petrakis shrugged. "That was a list of council procurements. I couldn't tie them to anything specific. Perhaps they were dodgy somehow?"

"We'll need copies of all files. Attach your material to the incident system." Now the question was whether they could connect the other victim to this public-sector espionage scenario. "What did you get from Joan Wood's machine?"

Petrakis cleared her throat. "That was way more interesting. But I haven't got anything off it yet."

More interesting, and yet still an enigma. Andy understood that mindset. Perhaps he shared more common ground with Petrakis than he cared to admit.

She continued, "Wood was more savvy than McKay. She encrypted her system using a pre-boot PIN. McKay's document helped me out. I used lots of variations from his information to find the access number. It was a rearrangement of the digits in her son's birthdate. People are predictable, but at least she shuffled the numbers."

"Her son?" Andy knew nothing about that. Wood had no family locally and they'd had no contact from anyone further afield. He wasn't sure how they'd missed it.

"Yeah. Her son. Marc? Apparently, he'd be in his thirties. If that's news to you, maybe McKay was better at sleuthing than he was at digital security."

"We'll look into it. So once you had the PIN, didn't you have everything?"

"No. That was just the start of it. Then I needed to get past the windows login. My password cracker mixes GPU brute force and rainbow tables. It took a while, but got somewhere in the end."

"Like this story, we hope." Devlin muttered.

Andy asked, "What did you find?"

"Well that was just it. Nothing of interest. But she had another layer of security. Have you heard of RealCrypt?" Petrakis paused meaningfully, then shrugged. "No, of course you haven't. Well, it's an open-source application that makes encrypted file containers. And I found just such a container. It stuck out like a sore thumb, 200 gigabytes in size. I could tell from the entropy it wasn't a normal file."

"By the entropy?"

"It's a measure of randomness, or information. That's how I knew what I'd found. A large file with too much information."

Devlin snorted. "I understand how that file felt."

Andy asked, "Can you explain why she might have used this technology?"

"An encrypted file container appears like a storage drive to your computer, but all contents are packed into a single file. You can store anything in there, all encrypted using one or more ciphers. You know. Ciphers. Like AES and Twofish?" She examined their faces for confirmation of bamboozlement, found it, smirked, and continued. "So, anyway, we need a password or phrase to mount that file as a storage volume to see what's inside it, but so far I haven't been able to brute force the passphrase. That means I can't see what she was hiding."

It was obvious Joan Wood had wanted to keep prying eyes away from something. But what? "Sergeant Petrakis? Did a little-known local politician approaching sixty, with no background in information technology and using domestic computer equipment, create a security scheme to defeat cybercrime's best and brightest?"

Petrakis flushed and looked away. "Not defeated. Not yet. I'm still working on it." But she didn't sound hopeful. Her mouth opened, then closed, before a buzz from her phone saved her blushes. "We've got a transaction on Reynolds' credit card. And it's from a local business. Portobello postcode."

Andy and Devlin were out of their seats in no time. Finally, something concrete to chase.

SPEEDYWASH TURNED out to be a ground floor flat a short walk from Portobello Beach. When police arrived at his door, the proprietor, Mr Alan Speedie, was unimpressed. "What's the story? Phone ringing off the hook? Polis turning up mob-handed? You guys are forgetting I'm the victim here!"

Andy remained calm. "Mr Speedie, we're investigating a murder. Since you're up and about and shouting at us, we're very confident you aren't the victim."

The man grimaced and brought them inside.

When they reached the kitchen table, Andy said, "Apologies for the drama. But your company placed a credit card transaction this morning."

"Ordinary guy tries to get paid for his work, so up screech the panda cars? I was out working late so I put through a few of yesterday's transactions this morning. Including the one that's got your knackers clacking."

"What is it you do?"

"SpeedyWash? I make things dirty. Really, really slowly." He glared around in abject disgust. "Christ's sake! We're a mobile wash and valet! Interior, exterior, wheels, trims, the whole shooting match. We'll wax, polish, shampoo, water or waterless, your choice."

Devlin said, "Skip to the bit about John Reynolds' credit card."

"Hark to Mr Snippy! So I get the call last night. I'm keen to get home, but us self-employed don't get far turning away work."

Andy began taking notes. "This call was from John Reynolds?"

"That's what he said. I didn't get a letter from his mum."

"What did he sound like?"

Speedie rolled his eyes. "He sounded exactly like a punter who wanted his motor washed! What kind of question is that?"

"Sorry Mr Speedie, but people are dead. We need to ask various questions, and they won't all make sense to you. Just try to answer as best you can."

"He sounded human. Male." After a few moments, he continued. "So anyway, he had a van that needed cleaning. Gave me his credit card details. Gave me the address, said just to do as much as I could, and charge my time."

Devlin sat bolt upright. "Definitely a van? He said he had a van?"

"Aye. A white van, heavily soiled, needing a full exterior clean. Wanted me to concentrate on the front; bumper, bonnet, wheels, underside. That was slightly weird I suppose. Most people don't care about the underside."

Devlin's smile collapsed. "Tell me you didn't clean the van." That would be a nightmare, potentially compromising recovery of DNA.

Speedie's lip curled. "You're in luck, officer. I did not clean the van."

Andy was puzzled. "What stopped you?"

Speedie's face purpled at the memory. "There was no van! Halfway across bloody Edinburgh! Roadworks on the bypass! Pissin' rain! You bloody name it. No van." The man paused for a moment. "So this morning I charged him anyway. Time-wasting bastard!"

DEVLIN WAS UNUSUALLY chatty on the road back. How glad he was that people were finally seeing things his way. How happy that his intuition was paying off for the team. How great to have everyone pulling together. But for the whole journey Andy couldn't get one thought out of his head. After vanishing off the grid, it took one police visit to Daniel Cochrane, and John Reynolds rediscovered the joys of communication, not once, but twice in twenty-four hours.

———

THE PRESS CONFERENCE was beginning just as Andy and Devlin returned, so they squeezed in at the back. Senior officers in full uniform occupied a long table strewn with media-branded microphones. Brian Nesbitt took the centre spot, solemnly facing the audience of journalists and photographers.

A wall-mounted screen was visible just to the right of the top table. DC Lenny Burns sat perched at a laptop beneath, blinking in fright with every camera flash.

After a brief introduction by the Assistant Chief Constable, Nesbitt spoke. "One week ago on the morning of the 30th August, Councillor Joan Wood was found dead on Charlotte Square. We now believe this hit-and-run incident to have been a targeted killing. Later that same day, between 20:30 hours and 21:30 hours, council employee Robin McKay was murdered in the Balrannoch Hotel. We have compelling evidence of a connection between these crimes and are pursuing a single suspect. The security team at the Balrannoch have provided invaluable assistance to our investigation, and supplied the following images."

A meaningful glance towards Burns set him fumbling at the keyboard. The screen displayed a still image taken from the hotel CCTV system. Nesbitt continued. "Our suspect is John Reynolds, a resident of Greenwich in London, who arrived in Edinburgh on the twenty-eighth August. We are investigating connections to council activities arising from his employment history. Reynolds and Robin McKay were together prior to his murder, and evidence on McKay's body connects his death to that of Councillor Wood. We appeal to anyone with knowledge of Reynolds' current whereabouts, or the whereabouts of this man." The display changed to the bespectacled man who had met with McKay at the hotel. "We believe this person may have information about Robin McKay's murder, or about Reynolds' activities at the hotel that evening. Any person with information relating to the individuals mentioned or to any other aspect of this case, should contact the police as soon as possible."

Nesbitt then handled questions from the floor. His message was clear: nothing suggested a general threat to the public; the crimes appeared related to esoteric aspects of council business; the suspect had admitted involvement in a recent communication, so there should be public confidence that the net was closing in.

Andy also noted that by flagging the unknown man in glasses as a potential accomplice, Nesbitt had left an important door open.

Should later evidence turn the spotlight on this person, the investigation wouldn't appear wrong-footed. It was a decent result under the circumstances.

As Andy followed the throng out of the conference room, Devlin asked, "Do you think they'll catch him? The CLUDGIE KILLER I mean? You know, the BOG BUTCHER?". Andy gaped. Why was Devlin referring to his own team in the third person? And why was he speaking so loudly? "They should put him inside, right? They must stop the TOILET TERROR. Edinburgh can't remain in the grip of the PRIVY POISONER, surely?"

Then it sank in. Devlin was trying to propel one of his vacuous alliterations into the headlines by sounding off around a crowd of reporters. "You better hope they don't run with that. We didn't describe this as a poisoning."

Devlin smirked. "Oh, I think I've earned some latitude by breaking this case wide open. Anyway, no need for jealousy Linkman. We're on the same page now. I've forgiven you." He beamed towards the departing crowd of journalists as though they'd just been waving lighters at him on stage. But Andy couldn't waste time playing the groupie at Devlin's imaginary theatre door. Instead, he hoped his appointment with the parapsychologist Petrakis had found would alleviate a persistent mental itch he'd been experiencing for days.

THE EDINBURGH UNIVERSITY campus contained numerous examples of grand architecture, and the seat of the parapsychology unit was impressively unexceptional. Inside the building Andy found an ordinary reception area with a regular person at a desk and a conventional switchboard. There was no need to link hands or communicate his arrival on a planchette. When Professor Maxwell arrived to escort him, he eyeballed every space they passed through, but couldn't escape the sense of being in an everyday university department guided by a common-or-garden academic past run-of-the-mill academic offices and lecture rooms.

She smiled. "You're looking for a fire pole, maybe? Or a Ghost-busters logo?"

Rumbled, he blushed. "Sorry. First time here. I don't know what I expected. This is a big space you have."

She laughed. "This isn't all ours. We're part of the psychology department. Parapsychology is a small team here. Small, but gifted." She took another turn. The place was a warren. "We're not a breed apart, however. We use the same scientific toolkit as our colleagues, only to explore a somewhat controversial domain area."

"So you're a believer?"

She frowned. "I don't see belief as helpful to my work. Our field has literature on so-called sheep and goat effects, where belief or the absence of it biases results. What humans believe, why we believe and the effects of those beliefs are additional important research areas for us."

"If you're neither sheep nor goat, then what?"

"I'm on the farmyard fence, Detective Lorimar! I'll believe data, so long as the experimental method behind it was sound. But that data had better show something exceptional — and repeatable — if we're to argue for abilities with no accepted physical mechanism." After one more corridor she stopped and unlocked an office door. "Welcome to the Edinburgh Parapsychology Unit!"

They sat, and he flicked open his notebook. "As I mentioned on the phone, this is about a psychic at the Palmerston Centre. Doirin Chambers? I don't suppose you know her?"

Professor Maxwell nodded. "Yes. We have good relationships with the Palmerston Centre. Often they'll assist in our research. But I've met Doirin, and I doubt she would describe herself as a psychic. She'd say a medium."

He opened his notebook. "What's the difference?"

"Some people would claim to be both, but not Doirin. Psychic abilities include a variety of phenomena, including telepathy, remote viewing, precognition, telekinesis, psychometry and more. Such claims are relatively amenable to laboratory study although the results are mixed. Mediumistic effects deal with spirit communication and proving the existence of an afterlife. These can be trickier to examine."

"Trickier why?"

"Developing a robust methodology to evaluate mediumship is complex, since it won't often translate well to a lab setting. Many mediums feel they need specific conditions to perform." He thought of Doirin's gin, but Professor Maxwell hadn't finished. "A medium expecting a receptive and engaged audience might find white coats and clipboards something of a buzzkill. And while all of our work can be controversial, mediumship studies may be especially emotionally charged."

"Isn't an experiment just an experiment?"

"You must recognise spiritualism is a religion, dealing with life and death, love and loss, belief and the afterlife. Nobody is neutral." She smiled. "To never lose the people that formed us, our most beloved family and friends? To believe those people are still around us and we'll reunite with them one day? These are immensely seductive ideas."

He fell silent for a moment, remembering when Doirin mentioned Jimmy. Seductive was a good word for it.

She continued. "So, for entirely natural reasons, some embrace mediumistic evidence more enthusiastically than others. Impartial assessments are hard to achieve and not always welcomed. Recipients may ignore imprecision around details, around places, around names and so on. They might even supply information inadvertently."

He remembered accepting Elsie for Ilsa. And hadn't he even volunteered Ilsa's Hungarian nationality? But there remained an elephant in the seance room. "Doirin told me the full name, pretty near bang on, of someone who was close to me. She also gave verifiable information to audience members, one of whom was related to an ongoing investigation. So I'm asking myself, should I treat this woman as a suspect, a charlatan, or as a potential resource?"

"I can't answer that for you, but I can make observations. Doirin worked with us on a study attempting to mentally influence random number generators. She decided it was a crazy idea and her results were unremarkable if I recall, but she played by the rules and struck me as honest and forthright."

"I'll second the forthright."

"The honest part is important too. Deception must be considered when dealing with extraordinary claims. My experience with Doirin would suggest that she isn't any kind of faker. Mediums work intuitively, so aspects of their messages can derive from natural rather than supernatural perception but in Doirin's case that's more by accident than design. Her convictions are deeply held. And I'd be flat-out astonished if she were a criminal."

Andy nodded. That was his gut feeling too. "If she isn't faking it, then how do we explain what I experienced?"

Maxwell nodded. "A mathematician, Persi Diaconis, proposed 'the law of truly large numbers', which in a nutshell tells us that in any large enough sample, bizarre occurrences are bound to happen. Somewhere in the world, every single day, people will encounter surprising events like those you experienced with Doirin. And that isn't supernatural, but expected."

"So, it's like the lottery? Umpteen-million to one, but somebody still wins?"

"That's a reasonable way of looking at it. For the person it happens to, it's a lighting bolt, but for a lottery company selling tickets to the entire population, these payouts are regular, business-as-usual events."

"And people like me, knocked for six by a medium? We're just business-as-usual on a global scale?"

She nodded. "We'd be far more surprised if extraordinary communications weren't happening somewhere."

Now Andy had what he needed he wound down the conversation

and left the Parapsychology Unit whistling. Rather than representing the academic branch of the Addams Family, Professor Maxwell had placed his rational worldview back on its axis.

Time to return to the coalface. Andy dared to hope that the phones were ringing off the hook after the press conference. Hard evidence of entirely known origin had always been his favourite kind.

THE PHONE CALLS ARISING from a public appeal were often a hit-and-miss affair. After eliminating the crazies and the merely mistaken, you might stumble over some solid leads. In Andy's experience there were rarely as many in that latter category as you hoped. Often conversations would start optimistically, only to nosedive shortly thereafter.

"I saw him! John Reynolds! I saw him!"

"Great. Could you give me some details?"

"It was at the Balrannoch hotel."

"OK. Could you tell me what he was doing?"

"Checking in. I work reception there."

"Anything else?"

"No, that's it. It was only that one time."

In addition to the calls he fielded himself, Andy made a point of skimming the summaries from other officers. They too, made depressing reading.

A twenty-eight-year-old coffee-shop barista thought she "might have sold John Reynolds a mocha."

A retired mechanic believed the mystery man with glasses was his childhood swimming teacher because "He wore glasses just like that. I heard he'd drowned, though."

An angry street entertainer recognised Reynolds because "He'd watched for ages and given me fuck all. I never forget those bastards."

A housewife called concerned because "her book group was planning to meet at the Balrannoch and would all this murder business be over and done by next Wednesday?"

And so it went. On and on. The details of the callers were recorded, sorted and marked for follow-up. There were a few to consider, but nothing revolutionised the existing lines of enquiry.

One leaped out for another reason: a woman claiming to be John Reynolds' ex-partner wanted to know "why the hell the detective she'd spoken to yesterday hadn't warned her to expect tabloid photographers camping in her garden."

Andy was glad he hadn't fielded that one.

13

NIGHT TRAIN TO BUCHAREST
TUESDAY 6TH SEPTEMBER, 19:42

After Sara's meeting in Vienna she sent a message to Father updating him on their new target. Their hopes had not been in vain, and this new acorn could replace a damaged oak, should that be required. However, although this prospective client had great potential, he remained wary, carrying the emotional and financial scars from earlier dashed hopes. And as with all clients, he was deeply protective of his privacy. However, time and his condition would compel him to action, so Sara believed there was cause for optimism.

Father's reply, when it arrived, was shocking. It made scant reference to her own communication. As instructed, she headed for the Hauptbahnhof and the overnight sleeper to Bucharest.

Upon boarding, a young guard checked her tickets and guided her to a twin-berth compartment. Father had booked both berths to guarantee her privacy. The guard was nervous and friendly; she observed his pupils react whenever he glanced towards her. She doubted she would have a use for him.

The compartment itself was acceptable, the best Father could arrange on this timescale, she didn't doubt. The noise wouldn't bother her. As an adult, she seldom found difficulty sleeping. The night terrors of childhood had proved the short-lived psychological quirk Father had assured her they would be.

She had plenty of research material to read, and this was a perfect opportunity. It wasn't until four hours later, when they passed though the outskirts of Budapest that the gentle swaying of the carriage wove its magic. She returned her tablet to her satchel and closed her eyes, submitting to the hypnotic rhythm of the rails.

AND SHE HEARD THE SONG.

But the experience went beyond hearing. This song was something she floated inside.

This melody was a nurturing cocoon, swaddling her in its protective warmth. It was more than music. It was a chrysalis from a time long past, a chrysalis that might have transformed her.

Even the memory of this song had power. And the memory of this feeling too. But also, the voice.

There was power in that voice most of all.

Mẹ-Mai.

WHEN SARA AWOKE, her couchette pillow was wet with tears.

This had happened before. Rarely, perhaps, but on each occasion it left her deeply unsettled. Weeping was for victims, not leaders. While a facsimile of distress may be a useful manipulation, real tears were supine in a child and contemptible in an adult. She knew these things.

Father had taught her well from her earliest days. The lesson to keep her safe: the strong devour the weak, so be strong. But the song did not strengthen Sara. It made her think only of Mẹ-Mai.

It was the first Vietnamese she had learned, literally, mother-Mai. It became a child's totem, and one she still carried, a word she would never relinquish. Mẹ-Mai sang beautiful songs, but those songs did not keep her safe. She had been frail in body and weak in mind. Father could not reverse her disease or overcome her superstition. He'd spoken of his failure, how she resisted all his attempts to cure her. The work had advanced so much now, perhaps today she could have lived.

Sara lay listening to the metallic thrum of the tracks, hesitant to reattempt sleep. She was unsure about whether she might re-enter the same dream, and even less certain about how that might make her feel.

She sat up, raised the blind on the carriage window, and stared into the blackness. Outside, the night was ceaselessly moving. Shadows streaked toward shadows, collided and were torn apart, leaving empty voids in the darkness.

Too much thought of parents.

She knew the trigger for her weakness. They had both been only ten when she first met Marc.

SHE HAD BEEN in the library at Vaduz, leafing through the research publications.

The papers were hard to absorb, and she frequently needed Father's dictionary. Where that failed to bring clarity he had instructed her to gather questions. He would either provide answers or, better, find additional references for her to pursue. She must learn alone, she understood that. While Father could be a guide, she needed to walk the path herself. And although the path was often boring, her studies were important. These papers contained clues that might have saved her mother.

Father hated sentimentality, but she found his dislike of photographs unsettling. She looked to the skylight for a moment, finding the heavens shrouded in cloud. The world had hidden its face.

It saddened her that she couldn't remember how Mẹ-Mai had looked anymore. Sometimes, at night, she thought she could remember her voice. And it was the strangest sensation; a momentary warmth that filled an empty space, but defined its magnitude at the same time.

The journal papers called her back from the edge.

She would begin with the ones Father had prioritised. Although she wasn't scared of bugs, she didn't want to read about them just now, so she placed 'The role of age in the process of regeneration of hydras' to one side. She decided 'On the immortality of the germ line' would be more bearable. Father described review papers as a road map, directing you towards merit and away from mediocrity. Perhaps one day she could find those routes herself.

She turned at the decompression of the rubber door seal. The open door revealed a boy in a pale-blue surgical gown. He was near her age, perhaps a little younger. "Hello," he said, "am I allowed in here?"

Good. He spoke English, the language she was most capable with. Her German was fine too. Father had started her on Russian, but he wasn't satisfied with her progress.

But the boy.

She should fetch Father, since he forbade patients from wandering around the clinic offices. But that would mean leaving the boy unattended. And it might also mean not finding him again.

Father often chided her for a lack of independent thought, so she decided for herself. This was just a child, and he needed a chaperone. She would stay with him and keep him safe. She held out her hand firmly, just as Father had taught her. "You may come in."

The boy hesitated, before scuffing across the vinyl flooring. His face reddened as their fingers touched. "Hi. I'm Marc. Who are you?"

"I'm Sara. I'm a researcher here." She wasn't, at least not yet. But she would be.

Marc's eyes widened. "You're young for a researcher! Aren't you still at school?"

She pointed around the library. "This is my school, I suppose." She'd heard of ordinary schools, filled with children who wasted time on trivial play. The teachers shoved funnels in ears and poured meaningless facts. Children from those schools grew up with brains stuffed with banalities, joined the herd and achieved nothing.

She'd wondered about experiencing a school like that, but Father said it was out of the question. They weren't places for children of destiny.

The boy gazed wide-eyed at the towering shelves, sagging under the weight of textbooks and old tomes, papers and proceedings. "Have you read all these?"

"Not all." She registered his disappointment, so added, "We've progressed beyond the bulk of it now."

"Hey! If you are a researcher you might have heard of my dad."

"Oh? What does he call himself?"

"Thomas. Thomas Hofler. He's a scientist too."

"Yes! I know him!" She needn't worry about Father being cross after all. "We worked with Mr Hofler before. He's surprisingly competent. Father wants him to join us permanently." She hesitated, considering the boy's surgical clothing. "But why are you here?"

Marc looked down. "I've been really ill and the hospital couldn't fix me, so Dad decided we give this clinic a try. I've been here three days now." He paused before continuing. "The beds are weird. Why are they like that, leaning diagonally against the wall?"

Sara smiled. She knew little bits about the work already. "It's part of the treatment. The platforms are in pairs. Patient on one side of the wall, donor on the other. They're upright because of the flow requirements. We might improve on that in time, but it isn't," she'd heard Father talking about it, "an operational imperative." She'd never visited the other side of the wall. Not yet. Soon she'd do everything. "So. After three days, how are you?"

Marc stared at his hand, spreading and clenching his fingers.

There was livid bruising around the intravenous cannula, but the boy didn't seem to notice. "I'm spaced out when I wake up. But now? I'm OK. Good, in fact. Better than in ages. My dad says it isn't a cure though. It's a therapy. Whatever that means."

"That just means you need regular treatments. We have several patients who keep well that way."

"Then so long as I can keep well I'll stay here... It was scary back home."

Sara wasn't sure why, but she liked that Marc might attend the clinic for a while. "Back home? You mean in Zurich?"

"No, my dad works at the university, but I've never lived there. I'm from London." His lip trembled for a moment, but he continued "I didn't spend much time with Dad. My mum's a doctor back home. She tried a lot of things, but they didn't work. I lived with her until now."

That made her pause. She'd lost a parent, but at least she knew they both loved each other and stayed together until the end. Neither of them would have left her willingly. She wondered how Marc dealt with that abandonment. "Are you coming back tomorrow?"

"Yes. Every day for a fortnight. Then Doctor Vorsky will schedule my long-term plan."

Sara felt more than just pride when Marc used Father's name. She didn't have words to explain how important Father was, but to this boy he was the difference between living and dying, so no explanation was necessary. Marc just understood.

She took his hand and walked him back round to the clinic.

Later that evening when she interrupted Father's reading to ask about the boy, he smiled. "A most unfortunate child. I believe this will motivate his father to work with us exclusively. We may even gain the experience of his mother."

Sara accepted Father's judgement in all things, but this was puzzling. "Why do we need them?"

Father nodded. "It is a reasonable question, Sara. Our task has mighty appetites, but what it craves most of all is time. Time, however, is a commodity I cannot squander." He took off his reading glasses and rubbed his eyes. "Understand, child, I will not be a dead giant providing shoulders for others to mount. We need to proceed faster than I can alone." The glow from the desk lamp glinted on his silver hair. "We need skills and very specific ones. Even among the herd, a researcher may show exceptional promise. Such is Mr Hofler. It transpires the boy's mother may be an even greater prize, although, only time can reveal the truth of that."

"What makes his mother so special?"

"Ms Wood is a haematologist. You remember what that is?"

"Yes Father. A specialist in blood and diseases of the blood."

"Exactly. And blood is significant. You understand why?"

"Blood, and products derived from it, can dilute the toxins of age."

"A generalisation I once used. Tell me more."

Sara tried to remember. "It plays a role. In both ageing and reju-venation."

His eyes were piercing. "More."

She flushed beetroot. "Signalling ... environment?"

"I fear your studies lack depth. But waste no time on shame, spend it instead on reviewing our internal research. And remember, the human animal is a factory of life. Blood is merely one of many exploitable resources. Despite great experience in her own field, the boy's mother would find much to surprise her."

The boy's mother. The question rose unbidden. "Can we talk about Mẹ-Mai?"

Father winced, as she knew he would. "Sara. Please. She is gone."

"I know she is gone. That's why I want a memory." She didn't understand why discussing Mẹ-Mai irritated him, why he took no joy from their past. She supposed the pain was too great.

Father sighed. "Your mother was both beautiful and innocent. But her innocent mind shackled her to the herd. She would not accept our work, and when her illness came, she rejected us. She left me powerless to change her fate, Sara, and that was all her choosing. Stupidity cost you your mother."

His words were like spears. This wasn't what she had wanted from him at all.

Eventually his face softened. "Your mother is part of me as she is of you. I will mention one aspect that still fills me with wonder. Towards the end. Her loyalty, her love, her vigilance around you; it was a marvel. She understood her own predicament, but thought only of her child. She would have sacrificed anything for you. In that, at least, we had a measure of understanding."

When her eyes moistened, Father raised his hand and spoke sternly. "No tears. Child, understand, for us, loss is an opportunity. Each wound forms a scar, and scar tissue is tougher than flesh. It creates a foundation."

But her mother's loss had created nothing but pain. She almost sobbed the words, "I don't understand!"

He nodded. "Each loss is a lesson. For the memory you seek I will tell of my first such lesson." He waited until she had composed herself, then he began. "I was the son of an elderly father. He did not teach me ice hockey or boxing or take me running since he himself had no interest in outdoor pursuits. He read to me on occasion, although always from whichever book he found himself engaged upon. More often he left me alone. He was, in keeping with the time, the lord of our household, and he rationed my mother's attention like miser's gold. I believe he felt it would ruin me. Perhaps it would have."

"Did you lose your father? Your mother?"

"Yes, but later. This is not that lesson. My father's character imposed self-reliance upon me from infancy, and hence, I enjoyed solitary pursuits. But solitude in a child makes some uncomfortable. Such was our Belarusian neighbour, Useslau, who frequently interrupted my wanderings to engage me in conversation. He taught me to swim, shouting instructions from the bank of the lake on his smallholding. He kept geese, and whenever he slaughtered a bird, he rendered some fat so I could grease my skin and swim for longer in the cold waters. I spent hours alone in that lake every day. When not swimming I read voraciously; I would eventually complete every book in our family library, but my neighbour's books were better. For his books brought me conjuring."

Sara enjoyed when Father performed tricks. He would pull a toffee from her ear, or find her chosen card in a sealed box. "Was that the start of your magic?"

"We prefer conjuring, Sara, but yes. That was the start. My neighbour was a great talker. When Uselsau described a performance by Harry Houdini, who toured our country in 1903, I felt I watched the master myself. Tsar Nicolas, our ruler at that time, perhaps came to regret paying insufficient attention to this American wonder worker; escape techniques would soon become of value to the Romanov family. But I digress.

"Ridiculous as it may seem, at the time of the revolution of 1917, I was innocent of politics. One cause of my father's remoteness was the time he expended keeping our family safe from those factions seeking to transform our society. Like any child, I believed politics could not touch me. So I practised exhaustively with Useslau's props, his cards, cups, ropes and rings, while he offered his expertise, his criticism, and occasionally, his applause. He was an enthusiastic conjurer himself, with much to teach."

"Did you like him?"

Father paused. "I expect I did. But Useslau had often boasted there was no knot he couldn't escape. And here is the lesson: I discovered my mentor's fallibility on the morning I arrived at his farm to find him swinging from a tree. His smallholding was not so small they didn't hang him as a wealthy kulak and seize his land. I hardly recognised him: the bloody froth at his nostrils, the blackened stub of his tongue, the drooping head of a broken mannequin."

Sara shrank, but he held her gaze.

"I tell you what you must hear: these memories you seek, the stories of relationships, of people long past, they are talk, and talk is not knowledge. Talk is not rigorous or codified. Talk is not something on which we build." He held up his journal. "I entered that looted house and retrieved the conjuring materials. The ignorant mob saw no value in skills, only in roubles. The Red Terror cost me his companionship, but until his rope rotted, I continued to pursue his art from the upper window of our house. And I learned, Sara. I studied and I learned. A hanged man and his audience of crows witnessed my developing mastery of knives and chains and padlocks. Each sway of that branch was the applause of a teacher whose lesson had been grasped.

"The evening before my enrolment with the Medical Academy in St Petersburg, I prevailed upon my father to purchase tickets for the, as it was called in those days, Leningrad Circus to see the great Emil Kio. Emil *Teodorovich*, you understand, the father, not the son. The famous illusionist was early in his career, but still his performance was magnificent. A simple collection of oddments: hats and handkerchiefs, crates, screens. In his hands the mundane metamorphosed into unforgettable marvels. I told my father we had witnessed a worker of miracles. But he corrected me, branding my hero merely a maker of colourful lies."

His book snapped shut.

"My destiny, so my father insisted, could be to save a life that changed the world. While colourful lies never loosed their grip on my imagination, I knew then that mere fascinations must retreat in the face of destiny. So I dedicated myself to my father's dream and decided that the world-changing life would be my own. But for that, I need help. Yours most of all."

He clasped her hands. His grip was cool and strong. "What lies ahead demands the involvement of others. As you will one day discover, there are ugly details in what we must do, and dealing with such details is expensive. We expose elements of the work to people of means, for their benefit and our own. But clients are time-consuming and we require medically literate colleagues to share that burden. For we, Sara, you and I, we cannot become sidetracked by such matters. We are the centre. Do you understand? We are the axis around which all else pivots. It falls to us to change the world, but maintaining order and focus is a continual challenge. Soon, you will shoulder that challenge with me."

The honour of such a partnership was what Sara wanted most of all. That evening, although the hour was growing late, she sought permission to continue her research, and her request was granted.

And she followed the progress of the boy, careful observation readying her to assist in his treatment. She learnt enough to be his guide through the elements of the process he needed to understand, and later, his protector against the uglier details from which his parents had requested he be shielded.

Sara was not shielded. She experienced the totality.

When she came to understand the other side of the wall, the role of the donors, and their eventual fate, it shocked her. But her research had already guided her into a tangled thicket of questions that only this final revelation could cut.

That was the day Father had explained the necessary and fearful symmetry of the work, how the energy of life could neither be created nor destroyed, but with appropriate intervention, could be transformed and wielded. Since then, she had never forgotten their higher purpose. Progress, too late to save Mẹ-Mai, was now being made. Sara need not lose Marc. He had become her project, her measure of success.

———

OUTSIDE THE WINDOW of her speeding train, shadows still raced and pooled and wrenched apart. Transience was the natural state, permanence a prize that must be fought for. Sara lowered the blind and returned to a dreamless sleep.

. . .

IN THE MORNING, when she woke, Sibiu approached, only three hours from Brașov. The sky was beautiful, but would darken before Bucharest. There would be plenty of time to continue her reading.

She did not anticipate her arrival with eagerness or urgency. Father always told her: we perform some actions we believe to be right, others because we must, but true maturity sees no difference. Her own maturity did not yet pass Father's metric. This task, she performed only because she must.

She had not seen Marc since his last treatment. He never missed an appointment — not that she would let him — but he stuck to the plan and remained stable and well.

She envied him. Not his condition of course, but his ordinary life. It lacked true purpose, but instead contained a kind of lightness, a lightness she could only experience in his company. Things changed when they were together.

Marc's estrangement from his parents was a blessing. She was on his side, and would remain so, whatever. And she was accustomed to protecting him from the ugly details.

14

PHOTOGRAPHS

WEDNESDAY 7TH SEPTEMBER, 10:05

Andy approached Nesbitt at his desk. "Can I ask about your workplace interviews at the council?"

"Shoot."

"When you were digging around, did anyone mention Joan Wood's son?"

"A son?" Nesbitt frowned. "No. Everyone thought she lived alone. Electoral roll said the same. Someone would have mentioned a son if they'd known about one."

"You spoke to friends, then?"

"Colleagues she'd shared the odd drink with after committee meetings and so on. Where d'you get the son thing?"

"Petrakis found it on Robin McKay's laptop. He kept a cache of information on council members. She thinks he was looking for blackmail opportunities." Discovering a close family connection at this stage was strange. Especially because they'd received no approach from any family representative to release Wood's body for a funeral. "Can I revisit her flat?"

"Yeah. Do that. I had a glance around the morning after, but fresh eyes couldn't hurt. Sign out a set of her keys."

"Will do. I've also got an appointment at the Balrannoch. Although ... Devlin?" His partner remained glued to the phone, but it seemed poor form to exclude him without checking. "Should I be taking him along?"

"No. We need substance around the connections with Reynolds' employer. Leave him to it."

Andy headed for the door, tempted to skip.

PETE CUNNINGHAM LAID down his phone as Andy arrived. "Flying solo today?"

"We're stretched thin at the moment, as you might imagine."

"I saw your DCI gave us a credit at the press conference."

"Brian knows you were invaluable on this. He remembers you, believe it or not. Something about a distillery tour?"

"Ouch. I gave up whisky after that. Thought it would be off my record by now!" His expression blended embarrassment and wistfulness. "Anyway, how can I help?"

Andy grimaced. "We need to consider whether Reynolds had an accomplice."

"I see."

"McKay's body got to the roof, so somebody knew the layout."

Cunningham nodded. "I'd been wondering that too. But Reynolds arrived on the twenty-eighth. That gave him two days to prowl around, get the lay of the land."

"What about the passcode on the seventh? Wouldn't somebody have noticed that level of prowling?"

"Probably. But not definitely. The General Manager left on holiday the night Reynolds arrived, so we'd had plenty of back-and-forth up there, with luggage and so on. Maybe the door got wedged open somehow? Wouldn't be the first time."

All possible. "Have any staff with seventh-floor access made a sharp exit?"

Cunningham nodded. "In hand. I'll have a list soon from HR. Around the end of the festival we naturally shed short-term help."

"Presumably seasonal staff wouldn't have the passcode?"

That raised a grimace. "It's *supposedly* a need-to-know thing. But with the GM's family at home, anyone could get a task up there. And nothing stops staff helping each other out and sharing the code. Still—"

A woman in the corridor thrust a printed sheet towards Cunningham before continuing on her way. The security manager shouted "Much obliged!" before examining the list. "We're in luck. Just two deserters fit the profile. Charlene Brose came in 2nd September, due next day but didn't show. Radu Dudnic worked 31st August, also expected 1st September, but didn't arrive."

"Someone killed McKay on the evening of 30th of August. So both showed up after that. Were either here on the night of the murder?"

Cunningham turned to his desktop. A short flurry of typing commenced. "Charlene Brose. Australian passport on file. She worked in hospitality, the bar by the looks of things. But not on the roster for 30th August." He peered at the sheet again while he typed. "Radu Dudnic. Romanian passport. Worked back of house. He *was* on the roster for the 30th."

"Back of house?"

"It's the department for maintenance, janitorial, that kind of thing. You don't see them in public much, but they keep things tidy and moving."

"Janitorial? So he'd have had access to those big garbage trolleys?"

"Yes. But don't get too excited. You'll often find those parked in the service corridors."

"Would back of house staff know the seventh-floor passcode?"

"Some do for sure."

"OK. I need his address and a photograph if you have one."

Cunningham tapped at the keyboard. "Sure. We keep proof of address for every hire. Looks like a guest house."

"A guest house?"

"Not unheard of for back of house. It can be a fairly casual position. People just arrived in the city, not fully settled, not staying long." The man navigated a few more screens. "As for photographs, we've got a passport photocopy, plus the one we took for his hotel pass."

The printer hummed and spat out three sheets. Andy glanced through them. "How long did he work here?"

"Not long. First day 21st August."

"So this guy was here one week, then a murder. He arrives as usual the following day, but no-show since?"

"Seems so. Hold on." More tapping. "Time recording shows he didn't work a full day on the 31st. Swiped in late at midday. Swiped out again an hour later. Maybe he was ill."

Andy's jaw clenched. Maybe ill, or maybe an hour was enough to clean house. But then he spotted something strange. "Hang on, Pete. Do both these photographs look like the same person to you?"

Cunningham examined the sheets. "The passport photocopy isn't great quality. And the photograph is small. But they don't seem a great match. One minute." He interrogated the computer again. "Those photos are the ones we've recorded though. Maybe he bulked up?"

"But the passport date was only last year. In just over eighteen months he'd need to have scarred his cheek, broken his nose and doubled the width of his head."

Cunningham shrugged. "Fighting over too many deep-fried mars bars? Don't know. They're all we have."

CORRYVRECKAN, the guest house listed on Radu Dudnic's proof of address, was on the way to Joan Wood's part of town. Andy hoped to eliminate a loose end before it snowballed into a fully fledged line of enquiry.

This part of Newington lacked any touristic feel, and the building itself was far from welcoming. Perched on a rat run road, only a tiny strip of garden shielded it from the drone of passing traffic. He let the garden gate squeal shut behind him and approached the house. All signs were of a wasted trip: bolted storm doors; grime-streaked windows; lifeless curtains. In the neighbouring house the fabric seemed far more animated, twitching with every move he made.

Balanced against a scraggly privet hedge was a clean 'For Sale' sign. Apart from the freshly stubbed cigarette butts strewn beneath the front window ledge, the place seemed abandoned.

A final few rings at the doorbell and he turned to leave. But a woman stepped out of the neighbour's door. "If you're the environmental health, you can't condemn anything until five. That's when she reopens."

"I'm Police. Detective Inspector Lorimar. So the guest house is closed?"

She tidied the strings of her apron. "Guest house? Hah! She calls it a B&B. Bugs and bloody bacteria. Basically a homeless hostel. Social work don't pay for lunch or dinner, so she kicks them all out on the street. She closes eleven until five every day and pisses off back to Ravelston."

Hanging around that long was out of the question, but perhaps this one-woman neighbourhood watch had a decent memory. "I don't suppose you recognise either of these pictures?" He showed her the two faces of Radu Dudnic he'd picked up at the Balrannoch.

"Big one for sure. Little one, probably. Is she in trouble? Will you be able to close the place?"

"So these are two different people?"

She snorted, pointing at the photo from the hotel pass. "Look at the size of that one. Big brute of a man. I only know the little beanpole because Bluto was always collecting him in that van of his." She leaned closer. "I think the little guy was on..." She mouthed slowly, "*Ill-icit sub-stanc-es.*" She glanced around before continuing. "He was in no state to go anywhere on foot. That van was his taxi service. Took him away bad, brought him back worse."

Andy removed the other image, leaving only the hotel pass. "Just to be clear, you're saying the man in this photograph drove a van? What kind?"

"A white transit. But like everything else to do with this place, it never saw a mop."

"And he worked here?"

"Doubt it. Frequent visitor though."

"When did you see him last?"

"He was here last Wednesday. Had to move his van for the bin lorry. The filth that came out his mouth. Not that I understood it. Polish or something. Anyway. He's not been back since."

The dates aligned with what he'd heard at the Balrannoch, so now he could be confident of an identity theft. But the possibilities ran far deeper. He may have found an accomplice to murder.

AFTER THREE O'CLOCK he reached the gated complex on Salisbury Road where Joan Wood had lived. The concierge buzzed Andy inside and he crunched his way along the red gravel drive, past the grand oval lawn and up sculpted steps guarded by a pair of stone herons. Soon he stood outside the old nursing accommodation block more recently converted into exclusive apartments.

The place was striking, but the desire to put a gate and video-phone between themselves and the rest of the world suggested a lack of confidence in the direction of Edinburgh's crime rate. He couldn't help but take that a little personally, but given the recent fate of their neighbour, he wasn't in a strong position to argue.

A uniformed concierge examined Andy's warrant card. "Detective Inspector Lorimar ... excellent! Let me show you the elevator. You'll need the fourth floor."

He suspected a personal escort wasn't everyday treatment. This man wanted to talk. "I saw the press conference. You know. About Ms Wood? It surprised me. Stunned, in fact. I was sure it was a traffic tragedy. The Edinburgh roads, am I right? The driving! Appalling. I almost lost my toes the other week. I'll bet the drivers keep you busy. Am I right?"

"I focus on major investigations, mainly murder and violent crimes."

"But what causes those? Most of the time, road rage. Am I right?"

Andy offered non-committal noises. They were almost at the lift.

The concierge continued to expound. "People need people around them. They do. A little scrutiny keeps us well behaved. But what are cars? Bubbles of anonymity! Nobody's watching! Brings out the worst! Am I right?"

"It's a theory for sure. Worth thinking about."

The concierge beamed. "You're welcome!" He tapped a button beside the stainless steel door. "I'll get back and keep an eye on things. Like I said, a little scrutiny, you know! Anything you need, I'll be here." The door opened with a muffled clunk. "Good luck, sir!"

Flat 4/2 had an inconspicuous white-painted door. Andy worked through the keyring and in moments was standing inside the victim's home.

He pulled on gloves and wandered from room to room. The place could have been on a lifestyle channel. Not through any innate fashionability, but because of the emptiness. Only two of the three bedrooms contained a bed. Only one of those contained a wardrobe, its contents businesslike and autumnal. The third room was as large as the others, containing a desk, a chair and a bookcase. A single non-bare shelf offered the pristine spines of classic paperbacks, all unread.

Mass-produced prints decorated the walls, but no photographs. The surfaces were clear, or draped with plain beige cloth. Every room was devoid of the knick-knacks and mementos that time scattered around ordinary homes. Here, there was no clutter. No mess. No life.

The environment revealed little of the character of its occupant. Doctor Nassar had discovered Joan Wood was a user of antidepressants, yet in the homes of the depressed, Andy expected to find disordered environments, arising from months and years of avoidance. This was something else. It felt organised and deliberate, the controlled suppression of personality. Even the kitchen tea towels were anodyne. Were these identical sheets of featureless grey linen chosen by a person with nothing to say? Or something to hide?

He opened drawer after drawer only to roll them closed within moments, the sensation growing that this was an environment for someone on life support. It contained everything necessary to exist, but nothing beyond. In fact, moving through these rooms raised uncomfortable thoughts about his own flat. He put some memories on show, at least; the ones he chose not to display were the ones he had no desire to remember, nor any ability to forget.

The dead councillor's kitchen window overlooked the garden. He watched another resident's car enter the gate before trundling to the rear of the property. There was nothing further to find in this place. She had lived here for over five years, yet it felt as if she had never moved in. This couldn't be her whole story. There had to be more.

DOWNSTAIRS ANDY APPROACHED THE CONCIERGE. "Did you know her well?"

The concierge nodded. "It's my job to know all our residents. But it's a professional relationship; approachable but unobtrusive. I don't pry."

"Did she ever mention a son? Or other family?"

He seemed taken aback. "No! I don't believe she had any close family, not that I knew of. Dedicated to the city. Poor Ms Wood."

"You mentioned seeing the press conference. Did you recognise either of the men we flagged as ever visiting here?"

"No. Sorry, sir. Ms Wood was a private person, not one for guests."

Andy took out the crumpled images of the two Radu Dudnics. "What about these pictures? They're not great quality, but would you recognise either of these people?"

"Can't say I do, sir."

"One of them perhaps drove a van?"

At this the concierge's eyes widened. "A van? Well! A van sometimes picked up Ms Wood in the evening. Never came inside, always parked on the road. I assumed it was council business."

"Any council livery?"

"No. The one I saw was a plain white transit. I never thought it looked clean enough for chauffeur duty, mind you."

"How often did this happen? Was it always the same pickup time?"

"It varied. I'm on back shift, and my recollection would be two or three times a month, never later than 9pm? Weekdays, and the odd weekend too. I couldn't say more than that though."

"One final thing. From the windows upstairs I spotted someone drive in. Is there a car park to the rear?" He hadn't considered this earlier when leaving his own car on the main road.

"Visitors can park on the drive itself, but there are garages to the rear."

"Did Councillor Wood have a garage?"

"Oh yes. I'm not sure if she used it much. I don't think she drove."

"How will I find it? Is the key here?" He held up the set he'd signed out of evidence.

The concierge tapped a dirty bronze yale. "That one. The garage doors have the same number as the flat. The accommodation is a horseshoe, and the garage block sits in the middle."

WHEN THE GARAGE door tilted upwards Andy wondered if he might just have found the rest of Joan Wood's life. Could this be her stored history, cryogenically suspended in musty cardboard and black polythene? The stagnant air suggested nothing had been disturbed here for many months, probably years.

The contents and layout, however, seemed the product of an organised mind. Boxes and bags, stacked neatly around the walls, left the centre free for movement or further storage. He gazed around; the place contained far more material than he had bargained for, doubtless most of it irrelevant. And it was getting late, possibly too late; to make sense of this would take hours.

He left the garage door open and flicked a light switch.

As the ceiling tubes blinked into life, he hoisted two boxes from the rear wall to the open space in the middle of the room. Inside, he found papers, lecture notes and transparencies, many marked 'University College London'. From the bottom of one box he lifted a bound thesis dating from 1982 'The regulation of coagulation factors in human plasma'. The contents were beyond him, but he remembered Doctor Nassar's comment about Wood's previous life as a medical consultant.

He opened another box, this time containing albums of photographs, and flicked through the pages. She was young here, her university years or perhaps medical school. Her facial expressions seemed happy. Later came several shots in a hospital setting. In those she seemed more careworn. Robin McKay's research had been correct about one thing: Joan Wood had been visibly pregnant here.

He untied the handles of a nearby polythene bag. It contained clothes, neatly folded, but unmistakably those of a male child. McKay's information also appeared to have been accurate about gender.

More boxes, more notes, most relating to her medical career. He found a large hardback book 'Fundamentals of Haematology by Joan F. Wood'. The cover trailed a foreword by 'Professor H Prosser'. The flyleaf contained a hand-written dedication. 'Dearest Joan. Your magnum opus is our new syllabus text! The pupil has become the teacher, and I couldn't be more impressed. Yours, Harry Prosser.'

A quick web query revealed Professor Harold Prosser still held an emeritus position at UCL. Andy called the faculty reception to leave his details and a brief message to pass on before he continued the search.

Hidden within boxes of clinical research, he would occasionally find more photographs. The absence of personal pictures inside her apartment had not arisen from a habitual dislike of the medium, and it left him with the eeriest sense of spending this afternoon sifting through the details of two different lives. What caused such a schism wasn't clear, but its existence was undeniable.

And the eerie sensation grew until it became personally unsettling. Examining these pictures was proving more difficult than viewing Wood's corpse at the pathology lab or reading the graphic descriptions of her injuries. Each turn of an album page showed a family not unlike his own. Here, Joan Wood swung her baby in a park. There, she tickled him on the sofa. And now, swaddling him at bedtime. It would be ridiculous to imagine he remembered such times from his own life, and yet, the images conjured the ghost of a feeling he was unsure how to process.

The moon was high now, shining through the open garage door. Another reminder it was time to pack up. Another reminder he ignored.

A further few pages and the air froze around him. On one level this was a simple three shot; Mum, Dad and baby in the middle. The baby's vest bore the words "Marc #1 Munchkin". But confirmation of the child's name wasn't what locked the breath in his throat. He unfolded one image from the Balrannoch bar. Robin McKay at a table, fine, but the mystery man handing him coffee? The graininess couldn't hide the uncanny resemblance to the father of Joan Wood's child.

He caught himself. This wasn't definite. It couldn't be. So many years had passed. But look. Look. At his smile. At his hair. This man hadn't even changed his style of glasses. Christ.

A harsh ring shattered the silence. The number was unrecognised, so he opened the call and waited. The voice was male, mature, confident. "Hello. Is that Detective Lorimar? This is Harry Prosser."

"Professor! Thank you for calling back. I thought I'd missed you."

"You did Detective. By about nine years. I'm retired, only do odd bits of research now. But when your message mentioned poor Joan ... I've only got ten minutes, but if I can help you I will. What do you need?"

"Background. From before Edinburgh. Personal life, previous career and so on. How did you know Joan Wood?"

"We met when I taught the haematology aspects of her medical degree. At first I judged her as solid, a hard worker. But as her degree progressed it became obvious she was something special. She had a gift for blood work." There was a pause at the end of the line. "I believed her research could have achieved things. But instead her life took a different turn. She walked an accomplished, but perhaps more prosaic path."

"We only have details on her life at Edinburgh Council. What could you tell me about her medical career?"

"It was star-crossed in some ways. She became a great young researcher for a while, but at a conference she met a young scientist, a Thomas something. Well. She fell pregnant. She needed stability and income, so she left research and took an NHS position in London. The chap was from ... Austria? Switzerland? Somewhere. So. The long distance relationship didn't seem to work out. She had to raise a young son herself, alongside her career. It was hard for her. But she was gifted. Kept at it. Made consultant young, wrote a core text in the field. Amazing, considering everything."

"What do you mean?"

"It was tragic. Horribly ironic given her specialty, too. Her son was well into primary school before his leukaemia diagnosis. The treatments didn't go well, and you can imagine she knew the prognosis better than anyone. My understanding was his father found a local last-ditch clinic or treatment option and the boy moved to live with him. My assumption was the child died, but I wasn't brave enough to make contact. I'm ashamed to say I heard the rest third hand."

That explained why they'd had no reports of her son. "What was the rest?"

"Well. She took on, created almost, a highly responsible role. We had some dreadful problems with contaminated blood in the eighties, you remember? Five thousand or more infected with hepatitis, over one thousand with HIV? Joan brought in new screening and handling protocols. Not just for blood products, clotting factors and so on, but for much of the donated blood in the UK. She was hands-on, applying her new precautionary principles, and it started well, but ended badly. I imagine that is why she left medicine, but I never asked."

"Ended badly how?"

"Her precautionary principles proved flawed. They opened the door to mishandling of some kind. Healthy blood became excluded from the supply chain. Some of it was lost altogether. I don't know what Joan could have done to stop it, but next I'd heard she was in Edinburgh standing for the council."

So, a professional scandal, and a new career in a new city. It made a kind of sense. "Had she shown much interest in politics when you knew her?"

"In all honesty? None. Public health and politics are intertwined, but I wouldn't have pictured Joan ending on a local council. I'm sure she did a good job. Meaning no disrespect to your city, however, it was a waste of her specialised knowledge and experience."

Andy thanked the professor and closed the call. He glanced again at the solitary photograph showing Joan Wood with this 'Thomas Something', the father of her child. There were smiles, but also an awkwardness. They were in an airport. Was he arriving or leaving? And his trip, judging by his absence from the other photograph albums, was rarely repeated.

But the question remained: if the image from the Balrannoch's CCTV was of the same man, why had he met with Robin McKay? An estranged ex-partner in the city at the time Joan Wood was murdered? Such dots were conventionally easy to join, but they were now surrounded by a pointillist snowstorm of potential connections. This case felt bigger than the mere conventional.

Outside the garage door, the moon was swallowed by a thick bank of cloud. The case felt not only bigger, but darker too.

15

REPLENISHMENT

WEDNESDAY 7TH SEPTEMBER, 19:22

The fluorescent lamp beckoned Thomas from sleep. It wavered above him, fading and drifting drowsily as consciousness returned. Through this, he lay unmoving. The procedure itself was routine to him now, but the pseudo-parabiosis had unavoidable consequences. Unconsciousness was short-lived but pacifying agents administered to the donor had residual impacts upon the recipient.

As a scientist it irked him, this lack of polish. But the work was a product of pragmatism where results mattered more than elegance. And the results were beyond question. At some point, he understood, their endeavour had moved from pure science to matters of engineering and logistics. When effect became sufficient, focus had shifted to delivery: raw materials, processing, cleanup.

As his recovery progressed, he noticed her standing to the left of the platform. His voice emerged slurred, but intelligible "Sara? Why are you here? Where's Rene?"

Sara smiled. "I just arrived, and we needed to talk. Rene didn't need to listen. So I took over."

"But I'm almost done. Couldn't it wait?"

She smiled again, and it unnerved him. The warmth on her face was entirely absent from her eyes. "Don't worry. He'd already commenced the purgatives. I do this all the time for Father."

This was true. The number of colleagues Max permitted to oversee his replenishment had dwindled. It had been three years since he trusted anyone other than Sara. Thomas sighed. A cannula in each arm and the lack of power in his legs meant this conversation would be forced upon him. "You have my undivided attention. What are we to discuss?"

"Developments." Sara examined the IV lines on either side of his platform. She was paying attention to the procedure at least, but he'd still have preferred Rene. Rene's exemplary running of the crucial Adana clinic had more than earned him Thomas's trust.

Seemingly satisfied with the state of the equipment, Sara continued. "We have both good and bad news from Edinburgh."

"Mixed news from Edinburgh is a profound improvement. What happened?"

"They've accepted our scenario, so congratulations are due for that. Max would like to control the Reynolds identity now."

Thomas nodded. "I keep the phone and the card in the privacy case. They are outside with my jacket. I'll get them for you when we finish."

"And you were careful in your communications?"

"I did as Cochrane's son instructed. He'd removed the phone's cellular capability. All my communications were over the private network he installed."

"Good." She detached the second of three syringes and loaded his final dose.

He was puzzled. "But if they accepted our narrative, what is the bad news?"

Sara appraised him for a moment, then nodded. "They gave a press conference, making your photograph public. Cochrane's questioning has left him concerned."

That was annoying. Their strategy hoped to shift focus exclusively to Reynolds. "So what next? Do I have to dress differently, change my appearance?"

Sara nodded. "Yes."

Thomas smiled at the thought. He was not a creature of fashion. He had sported the same hairstyle for at least twenty years. Doubtless he had worn similar clothing too. A forced change might be a welcome novelty. "I'll take your advice then. How will I look?"

Sara activated the syringe pump. "Paler," she whispered.

Thomas felt a cold gush, a line of ice entering his arm. He snatched across to wrench out the cannula, but his movements were sluggish, uncoordinated. Grasping empty air, he fell back against the platform.

The ice reached his lungs first. Then his heart. Then everywhere else.

16

RADU DUDNIC

Petrakis reached Andy's desk with a stack of paper. "Robin McKay definitely spotted something your investigation missed. I got this from the register on Joan Wood's son." She slapped down a printed image of a birth certificate.

"Good morning to you too, DS Petrakis."

He lifted the sheet and examined it. Marc Wood had been born 12th March 1981. Last night, the professor had recalled that the father was 'Thomas Something'. That something turned out to be 'Hofler'. The certificate listed Thomas Hofler's occupation as 'Research Assistant'.

She grinned. "I found him in PubMed. He's published a few research papers. Last one was from October 2005 at the University of Zurich." She handed Andy a printout of an abstract, titled '*Possible rejuvenation approaches for hematopoietic stem cells.*' The authors were Dr Dirk Müller and Dr Thomas R Hofler. Both had emails listed.

Andy asked, "D'you think they still work there?"

"I checked, but no. My emails bounced. However,"—she ferreted in her stack of printed sheets—"this report suggests that we won't reach Herr Müller anytime soon."

The printout was from an English language newspaper in Prague, dated April 2016. 'Ten Years On: Whatever happened to Dirk Müller?'. In town for a conference in 2006, Müller informed hotel staff he'd won a ticket for a Black Light Theatre show. He missed a later appointment to join fellow academics at the annual Witches Night parade and had never been seen since. The parallels with John Reynolds were unmissable. Here was another person who vanished after a night at a festival.

Petrakis grinned as he finished reading. "Interesting, right?"

It was more than interesting. "I'd like to speak to this Hofler character."

Petrakis shrugged. "Yeah. Well, good luck. I called the university. They parted ways in 2005, and they don't have any record of his later employment."

He sourly scanned the rest of Marc Wood's birth certificate.

Petrakis said, "If you're wondering about the absence of a mother's occupation, remember it was 1981. In those days when a woman had a kid, her job was mommy dearest, end of." She regarded him frankly, "That's your generation, that is."

"If you mean my generation sorted it three years later," he smiled, "then you're very welcome. Anyway I discovered some of Wood's history myself last night. I was in—"

But Petrakis was already walking away. "No time. I'm tracing that supposed SMS traffic you've told me came from John Reynolds phone. That's looking problematic too, I'm afraid. Later."

Charming.

A quick call arranged an appointment with the council's Housing Options team at Parliament Square. The timing left enough space for him to complete his write-up from the previous day. He was careful to flag the missing Radu Dudnic's impersonator as a potential accomplice, implicated in, but secondary to, the crimes of John Reynolds. He didn't want Devlin to suspect he still harboured impure thoughts. Meanwhile, the golden boy remained glued to the telephone, presumably seeking stronger evidence tying Reynolds to

Edinburgh Council. Devlin appeared less gleeful than when his telethon began yesterday afternoon, but telephone tag with things-to-do types in the City of London would have that effect on anyone.

As he rose to head out for his appointment, Nesbitt caught his attention. "Those CCTV checks you asked for? No sign of any white van parked or driven near the address given to that Speedywash outfit in the 24 hours prior. Maybe Mr Speedie got the address wrong?"

"Maybe." Or perhaps the whole thing was a carefully orchestrated wild goose chase.

A FULL THIRTY minutes trickled past at the Housing Options reception before a woman rushed over. "Sorry to keep you. My meeting ran over."

He outlined the situation on their way to her office. After they seated themselves, she regarded him frankly. "Some expectation setting, Detective. Once we place someone, that's usually the end of the matter. The only reason we have extra documentation on Mr Dudnic is because his qualified person status was under review."

"Qualified person?"

"Eligibility for housing assistance. It's guaranteed for EU migrants who are self-employed or former or current workers, but Mr Dudnic's job offer fell through after he arrived, so his claim became subject to special scrutiny. We might have something of use, but no guarantees. What do you need?"

He unfolded his image printouts. "Can you assist in clarifying which of these images is the real Radu Dudnic? Someone may have misrepresented their identity to get a job at the Balrannoch hotel."

The manager flicked though one of her files. "Well. We have no record of our Mr Dudnic having worked at the Balrannoch, or anywhere in fact. I imagine this job started after we lost contact." She continued flicking and then smiled. "Your passport photograph here is the same as the one we have."

But then, a frown. She squinted at the image from the Balrannoch access badge. "Is this one a mistake? This looks nothing like him."

"That's what we thought. Did you meet him?"

"Not me. It was ..." She flicked again. "Ah. She's on lunch, but usually eats at her desk. Let me check." The team manager stuck her head out of the door. "JULIE! ONE MINUTE! SORRY LOVE!" The manager turned back to Andy. "She could do with pacing herself on that baguette anyway."

When the younger woman arrived, still dabbing at her mouth with a napkin, the manager thrust the paper files into her hands. "Julie, this is Inspector Lorimar, looking into one of your placements. Can I leave you both to it?" Then she closed the door behind her.

Julie squinted at the front of the folder. "Radu. Dudnic. Oh yeah! I remember that face!"

He showed her the image from the access badge. "But do you remember this one? Perhaps he gained a little weight?"

"Ooh. Nope. He's not one of mine. Little thing he was, Mr Dudnic. Needed a good meal or three."

"OK. When did you last meet with him?"

Julie checked her records. "Says here six weeks ago? Seems about right, two weeks after I first placed him."

"How did he end up at Corryvreckan?"

"In a B&B you mean? We've got a few options for a temporary like this. Single young man won't need a furnished flat. No complex needs at first, so didn't need supported accommodation. Bed and breakfast was a suitable placement."

"No complex needs, at first?"

She confirmed from her files. "Yeah. I recorded probable substance misuse on a second meeting. Drugs rather than alcohol, it says in my write up. Alcohol looks and smells different, you know? I'd recognise pissed any day of the week."

"But no sign of that at the initial meeting?"

More referring to notes. Radu Dudnic might be his primary focus, but for this unit, he'd just been one of a long procession of people they'd needed to help off the streets. "He was clean at the first meeting. He was just here for work." She closed the folder. "Actually, you know what? I think I do remember something. He said his girl-friend was pregnant back in Romania. He planned to get work and send money home. Optimistic, he was. Upbeat. Good sign, that."

"But two weeks later he was drugged up to his eyeballs?"

She nodded. "I'd gone to Corryvreckan on another matter, but I spotted he was out of it. He looked terrible, whatever he'd been taking. He said something about doing medical research. That's one way of describing it I suppose. Later, we got word from the propri-etor that Mr Dudnic had taken his things and left. We've had no contact since." She frowned and shrugged her shoulders. "It's a shame, yeah, but it happens."

"Did this happen at Corryvreckan before? A service user vanishing?"

She seemed mildly surprised by the question. "Sometimes users drop out of the system. But it was short-term housing placement, not a prison cell. We wouldn't escalate anything unless there was an obvious cause for concern. And yeah, this has happened before, but I wouldn't single out Corryvreckan. Maybe he heard there were jobs going somewhere, but who knows? Being homeless is a chaotic exis-tence. It frees up a place for someone else. We get used to it."

His grip tightened on the arms of the chair. Didn't Dudnic's vanishing deserve a less blasé response? But he knew how it worked. Distance yourself from a victim to avoid having to feel. Relax every-one, he was homeless. Don't worry, they were an addict. Who cares? She was just a whore. And everyone whispers, stares and shrugs to themselves, knowing these things don't happen to normal people.

It made him angry.

But he caught himself.

His personal baggage was getting in the way, and the workers here obviously faced huge demands with limited resources. But the fact a young man's disappearance went unreported wasn't something he could easily make peace with.

He took the contact details for the proprietor of Corryvreckan and headed out into cleaner air.

MARION AND NIGEL GREYBURN'S impressive Ravelston Gardens address was a few steps up from their Newington guest house. It looked across to what might even be an embassy, complete with a flag fluttering proudly in the wind.

When the door opened, the proprietor's demeanour was less than gracious. "Who on earth gave you this address? Is that harpy at number six going through my mail?"

"I got your details from the council. I'm sorry if that's a problem."

It was absolutely a problem. She checked nobody was watching, ushered him inside, then closed the outer and inner doors immediately after. This was a discussion for the vestibule, and she wouldn't sully her home with it. "You can't expect me to know anything about what those people get up to."

"In that case, this shouldn't take long. We are looking for one person who was in your care."

Her face flushed. "It's a business, and they aren't even my responsibility. The council organise everything and pay me for room and breakfast."

"So, who mainly runs it? You or your husband? Who's over there cooking breakfast of a morning?"

"Nigel has his own business interests. Corryvreckan was my project. And I've optimised around the cooking." She smiled at her own cleverness. "I budget for a carton of milk per head and a choice of cereals. They help themselves."

"You say it *was* your project?"

"I thought you'd been around already. Didn't you see the for-sale sign? I decided last week. I'm sick of it. I want out."

"Do you remember this man?" He held out the passport photograph, but she barely looked at it.

"No."

"He would have been with you for nearly three-weeks. Could you please check again? This is Radu Dudnic."

She stared at the photograph, her face tightening. "They all look very much alike."

"He may have mentioned his girlfriend was expecting a child? He was trying to send money home?"

Her cheeks coloured again, but she said nothing.

He was sure she recognised Dudnic. "After one visit to your establishment, the housing team recorded this man was misusing drugs. It seems unlikely you missed something over many days that was obvious to them inside an hour."

And her stonewalling crumbled. "I suppose I know the one you mean. After the first few days, he was on something."

"Constantly? Continuously under the influence?"

"After the first few days. I suppose so."

Andy showed her the photograph of the other Radu Dudnic. "Was he ever with this man? This person appears to have stolen Mr Dudnic's identity."

Marion Greyburn tensed her fingers. She turned her face to the side.

He pressed on. "As well as stealing a passport, this person may be involved in a murder. Perhaps more than one." A slight tremor in her lip. "A neighbour beside Corryvreckan believes she witnessed Mr Dudnic and this other man together near your establishment."

The woman snatched the other photograph from the detective's hands. "That vile woman sees so much through her curtains it's hard to keep up!" But despite the grabbing, she didn't re-examine the image. Instead her eyes cast around the vestibule as though searching for a hiding place. "I've seen this man. He's been friendly with a few of them. They called him Uri as far as I remember. Perhaps he's someone in their community."

"Which community?"

"We've had several immigrants, that's all I mean. He did them favours, took them places if they needed it. His van put him in demand."

"The first time you saw Radu Dudnic 'on something' as you described it, had he recently met this other man?"

She didn't look at Andy as she spoke, but something about that recollection unnerved her. "It ... It's possible."

"What about the last time you saw Radu Dudnic, was he in the company of this other man?"

She stared at Andy, although her voice was quiet. "Could he be dead? Do you know that? Is he dead?"

"Please. Just think. The last time. Were they together? Was he with this other man?"

Her voice was now barely more than a whisper. "I think ... I think so. Yes."

"You said his van put him in demand. Was this man ever seen with anyone else who left Corryvreckan unexpectedly?"

She was silent again. Then, "What are you suggesting? Are you saying ... are you saying he killed them?" She raised her hand to cover her mouth, twisting at her lips.

"Perhaps you had concerns. Perhaps you passed them on to the housing unit?"

"They asked if he had packed before he left. And he had. He'd taken a bag with him that day, most of his things were in it, so they decided there was no need for follow-up."

"Most of his things?"

"Apart from some scraps and bits and pieces left in his room. But he took his clothes and his bag." She paused. "Same as nine months ago. A young man from the Netherlands. Ed. Ed De Graff."

"This Mr De Graff took his things and vanished the same way?" She nodded. "Was he ever seen with this man, this Uri?" She nodded again. "You mentioned Mr Dudnic took everything but scraps. Did you keep them? The bits and pieces?"

"Not the first time. But after what happened with the other young man I hoped Mr Dudnic would come back. I hoped so. So I do have them. At Corryvreckan."

THEIR DRIVE to the guest house was silent. The proprietor sat with her hands entwined, fingers clenched, knuckles pale. On arrival she guided Andy into a locked office and retrieved a plastic shopping bag from a drawer. "Those are Mr Dudnic's. I kept nothing from the time before."

She'd been right. The bag held scraps: A foreign book, *Jocurile Foamei*; a telephone charger; a plastic comb; a bag of licorice sweets; a woollen hat; some cables; various forms, unfilled; two foreign newspapers; a photograph of a young woman; a pizza delivery menu and a pair of gloves. But looking closer, the menu had a name and telephone number written in the margin. He turned to Marion Greyburn. "This man, the one with the van, could his name have been 'Yurik'?"

She nodded. "Yurik. That's him. That's what they called him."

Andy radioed Petrakis. She agreed to run a reverse lookup on the phone number and get an address. He wouldn't call until he knew a little more about who might answer.

Later, after dropping Marion Greyburn back home, he sat outside in the car examining the contents of the polythene bag once more. As he did so, his thoughts returned to John Reynolds' hotel room. His clothes, toiletries, and abandoned belongings might be no different to the forlorn contents of this little polythene sack, both simply the remnants of a stolen life.

His radio crackled to announce Petrakis had completed her work. The mystery of whether Reynolds killed with an accomplice or was a victim himself remained open for now. But part of the answer might lie at an engineering workshop in the South Queensferry Marina.

17

CAGE OF WATER

THURSDAY 8TH SEPTEMBER, 14:42

Andy arrived at the Queensferry Marina and parked in the shadow of the Forth Road Bridge. The sky was grey, with a spit in the air. It felt colder than it should for this time of year, but Scotland could practically put that on a tourist brochure.

He turned up his collar, but started as Petrakis detached herself from the bonnet of a nearby vehicle. "Nesbitt's stuck at the council offices with Devlin and Burns, he sent me as backup. And..." Her smile had an edge. "Tricia Black's in Edinburgh. She's out for blood. Yours."

Tricia Black. John Reynolds' partner. Great. "Mine? Why not Devlin?"

"You told her you'd be in touch, but next thing she saw the press conference. Suddenly she was beating photographers away from her door. She's going apeshit."

He remembered her call-in sheet after the press conference. It was ugly, but it would have to wait. "Anything else?"

Petrakis shook her head and pointed towards the marina. "The chief said you think this guy might be more than just a sideshow?"

Good old Brian. Never met two lines he couldn't read between.

"Yeah, maybe. Might just be an opportunist who stole a passport, or an accessory who knows something. But it might go even deeper." As deep as murder. "Anyway, thanks for coming."

"No problem." She pointed at the bridges, the water, the nearby cars, "This isn't my skill set, but it's interesting to see a pavement pounder at work now and again."

He didn't know quite how to take that so said nothing. Recent developments were unsettling, so he was glad of the company, even if it came with an attitude.

They walked along a row of corrugated iron buildings, passing a yacht club, a sales reception, a Royal Naval Sailing Association office, but no obvious engineer's workshop. Skippers Kitchen was distinguishable only by the blackboard menu beside the door. When they went inside to ask for directions, a pained sigh rose from behind them. "Can't a guy catch a cup of tea?"

A world-weary older man sat at the corner table. His sagging mouth and tired, rheumy eyes gave him the look of Droopy the cartoon dog after a shave and fresh blue overalls. Andy spoke quickly before Petrakis said something sarcastic to alienate him further. "We're sorry to disturb you, but are you one of the engineering team?"

The man stared at his hands. He spoke slowly, each word launched with minimal enthusiasm into the void somewhere between them. "Yes. I'm chief engineer. Frank Galbraith."

Andy showed his badge. "I'm Detective Inspector Lorimar and this is my colleague Detective Sergeant Petrakis."

The man rattled his cup against the saucer. He looked up, straightening himself, perhaps not panicked, but wary. "What d'you need me for?"

Andy handed him the photographs from the Balrannoch. "Do you know either of these men?"

The engineer took glasses from his overall pocket and inspected the images. He tapped the one from the hotel access badge. "Him. But they've got his name wrong. This is Yurik."

Andy took out his notebook."Yurik who?"

"Yurik Sokov. He's a contractor who works for me. What's the problem?"

"We're not sure yet, but we do need to find Mr Sokov and speak to him. He works here full-time?"

"We've been using him a lot for the last couple of years. I've not been in great form, health-wise, I mean, and Yurik knows boats. Was a merchant seaman, I think."

"Is he around?"

"He's out on a job. A yacht club member stranded their RIB on the sands at Cramond, damaged the outboard. It was a task for someone with biceps."

"Does he work regular hours?"

"He keeps his own schedule, but he puts the time in. If he wants to do his maintenance work late at night, that's his business. I don't mind so long as he gets the job done."

"Might he be working other jobs?"

"Could be. He's a contractor not an employee. Not my business."

Petrakis said, "So long as he gets the job done?" The man nodded.

Andy asked, "Did he have a phone or an office here? Do you recognise this number?" He held out the note he'd transcribed from the pizza menu.

"That's the phone in the workshop. I've been ill, so he's been the main hand on the tiller." The man gave a long sigh. "Anyway. I'm match fit as of this week. So they tell me."

"Do you provide him with a van?"

"No. He's always had his own transit. He's like a snail with that thing. Takes it everywhere."

"What colour is it?"

"Gunmetal grey now. He had a white one before I signed off sick. I imagine he fancied a change." Andy noted that down. Fancied a change, indeed. Then the old engineer chuckled. "I said his new one looked like a stealth bomber but he called me a Yankee Imperialist."

His relationship with their suspect certainly sounded friendly enough. "Can we see the workshop?"

Galbraith's involuntary groan drowned out the scrape of his chair. "Ach, aye. I knew that was coming."

He took them down a lane leading towards a large concrete hangar. Inside they found racks of industrial tools, various hydraulic hoists and a mobile crane. They walked between stacked sleepers lifting two small yachts to waist height, the scent of brine battling fresh paint.

The workshop had entrances at both ends. The door on the far wall opened to reveal a bank of pressure hoses and a long jetty stretching into the water. Some way out, the jetty split like a fork with clusters of boats moored along each of the four tines. "We bring vessels that need attention inside."

Petrakis said, "Forgive the ignorance, but what exactly goes on here?"

"Routine maintenance mostly. Once a year most clients take a full inspection with cleaning, fungicidal repaint, service as necessary. It changes with time. The new biofuels can be prone to bacterial over-growth for example. We get emergency jobs too; Yurik's trip today was out of the blue, for instance. You can't account for the eejit factor."

She nodded at that. Detectives were intimately familiar with the eejit factor. It helped close a lot of cases. "So, it's hard work?"

"Too much for me on my own, that's for sure." The engineer threw them both a look, half condemning, half pleading. He lapsed into silence, but the unspoken message was clear. This place needed Yurik Sokov. Andy wondered how much flexibility Sokov had conjured from Galbraith's frailty. By the sound of things, every bit as much as he'd wanted.

Andy said, "The boat was beached at Cramond you said? Any idea where specifically?"

"No, Yurik took down the details. But you should see his transit van parked near the sands. It looks like—"

"A stealth bomber. You told us already." Petrakis tapped her watch.

Andy nodded. "The crime we are investigating is serious Mr Galbraith. It is imperative you don't contact Mr Sokov and warn him. You'll implicate yourself if you do."

When Petrakis added, "Message in haste, repent at leisure," it sounded like a cyber crime unit motto.

On the way back to the Marina car-park, Petrakis said, "We'll travel together. You drive."

THE JOURNEY DIDN'T TAKE LONG. They drove past the few opportunities for parking along the seafront until a dark grey van outside the Cramond Gallery Bistro caught their eye. They double-parked in front of it, blocking its exit.

The yachts moored just over the sea wall were in no obvious disarray. There was no sign of Sokov in any direction.

Andy walked to the grey van and took a penknife from his pocket. He levered a corner of the black plastic surround on the rear door handle. White paint beneath. He was sure now. They'd just found Joan Wood's murder weapon. Most likely, they'd also identified her murderer.

Petrakis returned from the bistro carrying a borrowed pair of binoculars. "Gotta love birdwatchers." She scanned the beach front.

"Check out the water too. He might be mobile."

She cast around. "Yup. I spy with my telescopically enhanced eye."

"What?"

"Looks like an orange inflatable?"

"Could be. Galbraith said a RIB. I'm no expert, but I think that's a rigid inflatable."

"Pan left." She handed Andy the binoculars and pointed over the long causeway to Cramond Island. He scanned along a stone and concrete path that bisected the wet sandy surface for well over a kilometre. When the brick-built wartime fortifications came into view, he pivoted left.

There. On the beach. A figure crouched over an orange bodied boat, a bag, probably containing tools, open beside him.

They could wait for Sokov's return, but his vessel repair would provide him a means of escape by sea. At any moment he might spot police activity back on the shore, and by waiting they risked losing him altogether. But now they had the van in their possession, they needed to protect it.

Andy threw Petrakis his keys. "Get on the radio. We need uniforms and forensics, plus a tow truck. Don't leave this van until we've got people on site. Then get me some backup." He ran for the causeway.

HE WAS deep into the crossing before he began to question his strategy. There had been a board at the start of the causeway, but he understood why he hadn't stopped at it: adrenaline, excitement at finding the van, the chance to interrogate Sokov. Next to all that, what was such a finicky little technical detail? It was only a tide table.

But that information mattered. When you should cross, when you *absolutely* shouldn't. He had no idea how fast the water came in. In Morecambe Bay he'd heard the tide moved faster than a person could run, but that place was extreme. Presumably, here, if he kept running, he should be fine. A thought niggled at him: he wasn't running away from the tide. He was running parallel to its advance and daring it to catch him.

If the tide table was the expectation, the visible landscape was the reality. Why hadn't he paid more attention to that? He was almost sure open sand had stretched beyond the dragon's teeth, the line of tall concrete pylons to his right. Almost sure he'd checked the full length of the causeway. Almost sure he hadn't simply seen the first section clear of water and recklessly gone for it. Now, approaching halfway, those looming pillars stared down reproachfully; they deterred enemy boats, but couldn't save him from the tide. He'd be submerged long before they were.

He halted, considering retreat. Behind him, weakening light showed previously isolated puddles had become large, growing pools, eagerly lapping across the path he'd just travelled. The exposed sea-bed had lost its grip on the landscape, was being overcome by the ocean. Soon, he might be too. It was safest to return to Petrakis.

But if his suspicions were right, Sokov hadn't just killed Joan Wood. He'd taken Radu Dudnic, a soon-to-be parent, he'd plied him with drugs and made him disappear. So Sokov had destroyed a family too, and unless caught, that family would never move on. Turning back ensured Sokov's escape in a repaired boat. Sea breached the pylons all the way to the island, but he could still make it.

With a few hundred metres to go, he was sprinting through deepening water. When he was younger he'd read about the spring tides, how extreme they could become. What lunar-phase was this anyway? His memory from yesterday evening at the garage provided the answer: and it was big and round and wide, like the face of an idiot.

Forget that.Waxing, waning, full or new, the prescription remained the same.

Run!

His airways were stripped raw, an unfamiliar wheeze sounding deep in his chest. He continued to push for the land, legs leadening with each passing moment. Perhaps Petrakis would call in the Marine unit? But they were based in Aberdeen, too far to be useful for anything other than retrieving a body. Years from now, would she remember him as the pavement-pounder who ran out of pavement?

Move!

The Queensferry Lifeboat Station could probably get a vessel out quickly. But Petrakis didn't know the area or the local services. In fact hadn't she recently declared the entire physical world outside her sphere of expertise? He would send her some direction by radio, if he weren't knee-deep in water and raising plumes with every step. With each splash he tasted brine, the unwelcome appetiser for a main course that would sate him to extinction.

In his mind's eye he saw the clinical blue light of the pathology lab as someone unzipped his body-bag. Devlin. Smiling. That would not be his final image. No. Way.

Closer now. If he didn't stop, he could make it. So don't stop. Even if your legs turn to jelly and your arse falls off. Don't stop moving.

Don't stop.

Don't stop.

Don't stop.

The mantra circled his mind and water sucked at his thighs as he waded the last steps to safety. He collapsed face-first onto cold stone, coughing, choking, desperate to catch his breath. How much oxygen did he need? More. Much more than he was getting.

Rolling onto his back, Andy wheezed towards the darkening sky. He'd won the race, and claimed first prize: lungs filled with air rather than water. But Sokov better remain busy for a while longer; there was no way he could confront him in this condition.

WHEN HE FINALLY RAISED HIS head to look across to the mainland, the causeway was submerged along its entire length. But in the distance, was that the blue-yellow chequerboard of a police vehicle? Perhaps, but he couldn't be sure. He reached towards his coat pocket, hoping his radio had survived the water, but his hand froze mid-motion.

Just a flicker. In the corner of his eye. Movement out on the sand to his right.

Andy sat up and peered closer. There. Rising above a mound of grass.

Yurik Sokov, walking towards him.

Perhaps he'd been spotted or maybe he'd been heard, but it was no huge surprise either way. That causeway crossing wouldn't qualify for anyone's top-ten stealthiest approaches.

He stood, picking his way down the steps, legs trembling with fatigue. His worst fears concerning this suspect might be misplaced. Perhaps Sokov would be cautious enough to not risk starting any trouble, choose to brazen out an interrogation.

Cause for hope. As the man came closer, he smiled. And he held up a hand, in welcome or recognition. Andy held up his warrant card and shouted across the divide, "Yurik Sokov?"

Sokov smiled again. And nodded.

It was a strange smile, although it had a familiar quality to it. Sokov was an imposing figure, nearly as tall as Andy himself, but more muscular. He moved across the ground, not with a boxer's swagger, but with a powerful directness that drew attention all the more by not seeking it.

"I'm Detective Inspector Lorimar."

Within moments they reached each other, and both men stopped. When Sokov replied his English was clear, his accent Slavic. "I know who you are." He smiled again, although close up, it was best described as a grin, exposing all his teeth. That was the moment Andy realised what it meant.

Being a larger man usually warded off certain kinds of trouble. But for particular individuals, it qualified you as a challenge. Individuals who felt this way, who regarded another human being as some kind of Everest of violence, these individuals needed careful handling, preferably by multiple officers.

He'd last seen a similar smile in the Central Bar on Leith Walk. That evening he'd paid for the arrest with twelve stitches on his arm. But when that ruckus had started, Nesbitt had been nearby to help.

Andy scanned the water. The coastguard cavalry were nowhere in sight. Sokov's grin grew hungrier.

The detective held up a hand, palm first. "Wait. I'm only here to—"

But Sokov charged.

Despite Andy's greater reach, Sokov was inside his defences before he even moved. He felt a blow to his midriff. Once. The air exploded from his lungs. Twice. A snap of bone. He went down onto the sand. Sokov squatted on his chest, amplifying the lancing pain in his ribcage. Andy screamed, raising his arms to protect his face, so Sokov lashed out at the side of his head instead. The strike landed with a flash of blackness.

He regained his senses just as Sokov completed binding his hands. Then his attacker stood, moved out of sight, and returned holding a rock. It was the size of a house brick, perhaps a little larger, but the Russian wielded it as though it were a feather. His grin was gone; Everest, now scaled, had proved disappointing. Sokov scanned the sea. He appeared to be calculating something, perhaps how much time he had, or his best next move.

With every breath a piercing spasm, Andy gritted his teeth. "Please. This is crazy. For fuck's sake, it was just a stolen passport!" A serviceable cover story, but no more than that. Perhaps Sokov would be stupid enough to believe it.

Sokov knelt in the sand. He rubbed the stone against Andy's forehead. The ragged edge snagged and scraped the skin, releasing clumps of dirt to drop into the detective's eyes. He spoke quietly, almost reverently. "I need this to stop, so I stop it today. You see?"

Then he raised the rock and bared his teeth, muscles tightening for the descent.

―――――――――

AT A BUS STOP on Princes Street, Doirin Chambers jerked violently, dropping her coins to the pavement. She couldn't risk stooping to fetch them. The voices had jostled her off balance. And they continued, crowding around her, noisy, hectoring, uncontrolled.

A teenage boy retrieved her money, face taut with concern. He asked her something, but she couldn't hear him. "Sorry. Sorry, son. Thank you." She staggered towards the crossing.

Get away.

The street thronged with people, all of them loved, all of them magnets for spirit. The crossing turned green. Perhaps it was beeping, but she couldn't hear it over the tumult in her head. She crossed the road and ran into the gardens. Here, should be calm this late in the day. But what time was it? She didn't know. She couldn't think over the noise. They wanted her to understand something, and she couldn't silence them.

She grabbed at the empty bench like a raft in the flood. It would subside now. There was no one. No one to draw them near. No one to spur the urgency of this contact.

But it didn't subside.

It grew.

And it wasn't one voice, one message.

It was many.

But this was wrong. To be alone, and face this noise, this cacophony of sound and symbol. It was impenetrable.

Nearly.

She grasped for fragments.

Drawing her coat around herself, she tried to swaddle the squalling. The physical sensation allowed her to focus. To sift and filter. To extract meaning. And the onslaught stopped as suddenly as it began. She knew what to do. Perhaps not why, but what.

Doirin headed out of the gardens and along to the taxi rank outside the Caledonian Hotel. She climbed into the leading cab and relayed their instructions. This was what they wanted from her. She was going to the hospital.

18

UNCLE BILLY

Interference. A choppy, whirring, slapping sound. A static hiss. Slowly resolving into music, and a sense of clarity. Andy had been trying to read, but the song on the radio reminded him of Granda.

When he'd been younger, seven or eight, Mum had serenaded Andy about the first time she saw his face. Granda had interrupted, horrified. "Don't sing him that, Marie. God's sake! He'll be thinking he's bonny! He's a great kid. But we don't want him thinking he's bonny!"

But Mum had just stroked Andy's cheek and looked into his eyes and replied. "No, we don't. We want him *knowing* he's bonny."

But that was back then. Now he was an older boy. And he needed to return to his book. "Hey Mum! Do you know what they called the world's first atomic submarine?" Andy brandished his tattered annual: *Look and Learn 1972*. It was two years out of date now, but perhaps he'd get a new one for his birthday. The weekly magazine was too expensive, although he sometimes read it at the library. "C'mon Mum! I'll give you a clue. It was a name used by Jules Verne? In '20,000 Leagues Under The Sea'?"

But mum was busy poring through the job adverts in the evening newspaper, twin plumes of steam and cigarette smoke rising from the saucer beside her. They'd both hoped she'd get that job at the Electricity Board, but it hadn't happened.

Andy had an idea. "What about the library? They must need people." Imagine Mum could end up there? She would order in the books he wanted, and he'd join her straight after school. He'd introduce her to Mr Gallagher who was teaching Andy chess in the Periodicals room.

She laughed. "Libraries need O grades and Highers! Stick to your schoolwork, and maybe you'll be the librarian." Mum was keen on his schoolwork because she regretted what happened with her own. Granda didn't believe school mattered much for girls, and by the time Mum found out he talked through his bahookie she was already on the cigarette counter at John Menzies.

Her smile wavered for a second. "I've got a wee surprise for you. Guess who's visiting for your birthday tonight?"

"Granda?" It would be the first time since his funny turn. It would be great. So great.

"Oh Andy-bear, Granda's still not well." She fell quiet. He knew she was worried, but she never admitted things like that. "It's a good surprise though! It's Uncle Billy!"

"I thought he'd gone away." Hoped. Hoped he'd gone away.

"Well, he's back now."

Andy said nothing. He remembered Granda getting so angry at Billy. It was weird because Granda always hated a scene, but he made the biggest one the close had ever heard. He apologised afterwards, but Andy was pleased when Billy stopped coming around. Mum said Granda shouldn't have stuck his oar in, but to Andy it proved he didn't always talk through his bahookie.

Mum wouldn't want to hear that though. So Andy didn't say it.

· · ·

AFTER SCHOOL he noticed it immediately. Not the large '10 TODAY' cut out of newsprint and taped above their door, although he noticed that soon after, and not the music from Mum's yellow Neil Young LP that she always put on when people were round. What he noticed first was Billy's voice echoing in the stairwell. Most adults didn't want to be so loud, and to swear and to make a show of themselves. But Billy didn't care. He did what he liked.

When the door opened it was his mum. "Happy birthday Andy!" She gave him a big hug, but he was glad she didn't call him Andybear. Not in front of Billy. Not after that last time.

In the living room, Billy was sprawled in the good chair, basking in the twin smells of fried food and the dust burning off the bars of the little electric fire. "What? No hug for your Uncle Billy?" Andy hung back, unsure. "Hey Marie! The wee bugger's learning at last!" Billy took a swipe, clipping his shoulder.

"Stop teasing him you!" Mum smiled again, but not in her normal, comfortable way. He'd forgotten that. How even her smiles changed. "Uncle Billy bought us fish suppers for your birthday. What do you say?"

"Thanks."

Billy was suddenly angry. "You? Thanking me?"

Confusion. Billy never acted like people were supposed to. "Yeah?"

"What about Baillie's Comet? A tenner at four to one! It's him you should be thanking." Granda said Billy spent a lot of money at the bookies, considering nobody ever saw him earning it. Andy didn't follow that exactly, but he understood enough. Granda didn't like Billy for lots of reasons.

A whole fish supper to himself should have been a rare treat, but Andy couldn't enjoy it. He would rather have had tea and toast, just him and Mum. He could feel Billy watching him the whole time.

"So wee man. Let me tell you how you win big." Andy was hardly ever called wee man nowadays. He had just started in primary six, but he was easily taller than the kids a year above him. "When you pick a bitch, pick the best." He'd smiled at Mum then, but she rolled her eyes. "And for racing, always pick the dog with the longest leg." He'd looked Andy up and down. "You're lanky enough to make a decent dog. Hey Marie? Where's his basket? It's bedtime!"

Billy pulled Mum onto his lap. Then he leaned over and increased the volume on the record player.

That was the end of Andy's tenth birthday.

The period that followed was a slide into darkness.

BILLY LED Andy into the darkened room containing Granda's body. Mum left weeping, and Andy wanted to follow, but thought perhaps it was his duty now, to somehow say goodbye. He didn't know what to do, so he stood beside the open casket for a few seconds of silence, and wondered if that would be enough.

But Billy had other ideas. "Touch him."

"I don't want to."

"Do it. Touch him."

Billy grabbed the boy's wrist and thrust it into the casket.

The flesh of Granda's face was cold. Strange. Not like he remembered him at all. He tried to pull away, but Billy held him firmly in place and whispered. "To think. This old clown said *he* would bury *me*."

THE FOLLOWING morning was bleak and cold as they shouldered the coffin. There was just Billy, the men from the funeral directors, and Andy giving token support at the back, pretending his face had been caught in the drizzle. He didn't show emotion to Billy if he could avoid it.

Not many had turned up at the church, but that was for the best. It meant people wouldn't see how Billy smirked his way through the service. Andy swallowed his anger to avoid causing a disruption. Granda hadn't been right about everything, but he'd loved them and they'd loved him back. He'd been the last family they had left, and he would have hated an argument at his funeral.

Andy had no real memories of his Gran, but Granda had often spoken about her, so it felt right as they laid him down beside her. But when Billy had sneered and kicked gravel onto the lowered coffin, Andy couldn't stop himself. He moved beside Billy and whispered. "Why did you do that?"

Billy winked. "You're right. That isn't what I should've done. But it's rude to piss in public." Andy didn't dare respond. And he hated himself for it.

Later, as Billy guided Mum towards the car, Andy hung back as a kind of apology.

He thought about how different things might be if Granda had stayed well. They used to see him all the time. He'd been a serious man in some ways but he loved to sing. Those were the happy memories Andy wanted. Not the ones from the last few months, when he couldn't speak or walk. And certainly not those from yesterday's darkened room, the awful feel of cold, empty flesh. He tried hard to remember one of Granda's happy songs, but it was impossible, so he rejoined his mum and Billy.

It took an age to exit the cemetery, sitting in the line of posh cars from better attended burials. But Andy was glad for that extra time, and he spent it staring back towards the plot. Soon the men with shovels would arrive and cover him over, then he'd be gone for good. As they finally drove away, the boy's last view was of the worsening rain, as it darkened Granda's headstone and turned the graveside dirt to mud.

IN THE DAYS after the burial his mum grew more distant, continuing the downward path she'd been walking for weeks. In his S.R.A cards at school Andy had read about wartime shell shock. He wondered if this was similar. He'd heard some neighbours whisper she "wasn't coping", but they'd changed the subject when they noticed Andy on the stair behind them.

Whatever it was, she seemed lost in a maze of grief. For days, she'd been crying uncontrollably, impossible to reach. It was like the mum he knew was inside a cocoon. He hoped she'd emerge soon. One morning when she appeared slightly brighter he tried to speak to her about it, but she said they had no one but Billy now, and they needed him more than ever.

You need him, Andy thought. I'm just stuck with him.

THE FOLLOWING week at the Library, Andy talked over recent events with Mr Gallagher. It passed the time at least, while he scratched his head over the old man's latest challenge, a plastic Towers of Hanoi puzzle. "What makes Billy do these things?"

The old man wiped his glasses and thought for a moment. There was a lot of silence with the old man, but when he did speak, it was usually worth hearing. "Well, Andrew my boy, I've done a bit of travelling in my time." He pointed and tutted as Andy placed a larger disk on top of a smaller one, then paused until it was corrected. "I've met a small number of fellas, not many, but some, who behaved in a similar way to this Billy chap. I must say, considering the thing, now you've raised it, I think they all shared one common trait."

Andy was fascinated. He might learn something that could help the situation. He dropped another disk into place, then leaned over the library table. "What? What did they all have in common?"

The old man replaced his glasses and nodded. "Without exception. To a man. All of them. Total pricks."

A woman clattered her leather-bound folder against the tabletop and scowled. Mr Gallagher smiled and waved, before whispering "The natives are restless. Best mind our manners."

Andy tried not to laugh. He heard bad language all the time from Billy, but liked the entirely different way Mr Gallagher employed the same words. There was no aggression in it, just mischief.

The old man continued. "I will say though. He sounds like a piece of work. I'd stay careful around him. Hopefully your mum will find someone better."

Andy hoped so too, but doubted it. His mum only really went out now when Billy needed her to sign something. Billy handled the money and brought in the messages. Her job, for now, he said, was just to keep everyone fed. Andy didn't know what was going on, but Mum seemed to have stopped looking for work.

He saw them in the kitchenette one day just before he left for school.

"Please, Billy."

"Later."

"Now. Please!"

"OK."

When Billy had handed her something, she'd swallowed it.

On hearing that, Mr Gallagher glowered darkly and swore without mischief. "Bastard."

WHEN MUM and Billy started going out in the evening, they locked Andy inside with instructions to do his homework and put himself to bed. He didn't mind much at first; anything was better than having Billy hanging around. But he wondered why Mum still couldn't smile.

She'd sometimes said that she missed her social life, but now she had one again, it wasn't making her any happier. She barely looked at Andy anymore, and never laughed like she used to. Something seemed to have stolen the real person away, like the fairies did in that big book of folk tales he'd once borrowed from the library. He was living now with someone who looked like his mum, but didn't seem to actually *be* her. Something had happened, but it wasn't quite what he'd read. Those stories would describe a parent horrified by an odd creature placed in the crib. But not this time. Now it was the child who woke up one day and found themselves living with a changeling.

But what had changed her?

Granda's death, of course.

Andy still felt that sadness as well. But this was bigger even than that. Her favourite phrase. "Oh Andy-bear don't be such a pessimist!" She had always been the one who bounced back, who saw the bright side, who *was* the bright side. But something was stopping her. Something was blotting out her light and locking the darkness in. And nothing could fix it.

Or perhaps it was a puzzle? A serious one, deadly serious, but a puzzle for sure. And puzzles could be solved. Andy had always been interested in puzzles. And he was good at them, according to Mr Gallagher. And the old man should know. He'd been crowned Edinburgh's King of Crosswords once, or so he claimed. Maybe there was something Andy could do. But to solve anything, you had to learn the rules.

He'd noticed that when his mum and Billy left, it was always Billy who locked up. So he took a chance, after school one day, to steal the keys from his mother's bag. When they left that night, near eight o'clock, he pulled on his coat and waited until he heard the stair door bang shut. Then he sneaked out and began to follow.

His first fear was that they would be taking Billy's car somewhere. He would have to run, and even then he would probably lose sight of them. Thankfully though, as he carefully left the close he saw them walking down Ferry Road towards Leith. It was dark, and it was cold, and Mum wasn't dressed for the weather, so hopefully they wouldn't be walking far.

Andy followed at a distance, occasionally ducking out of sight, as they made their way past the library, across the road into Coburg Street and then down towards the docks.

Before long they reached a pub and went inside. Andy walked closer until he could read the sign: The Ship's Bell. He didn't like how it looked. There were some people hanging around outside so he walked on for a bit before dropping between two parked cars. If the people outside went away, he might try to look in a window. If he saw Mum happy, if she was smiling, then he would go home.

Just as Andy was planning his next move, Billy and an older man came out of the pub. The man gave Billy something from his wallet, probably money, before walking down a lane at the side of the building. Billy went back inside the pub and brought Mum out. Then she walked down the side of the building too. Billy stayed at the front, leaning against the wall.

About five minutes later, the bigger man reappeared, scurrying past Billy without looking back and heading down towards the harbour.

When Mum appeared soon after, she didn't look right. She said something to Billy and started crying. So he handed her something and she swallowed it. Then he sent her back down the lane and out of sight.

Andy's skin started to prickle. Something bad was happening, and he wondered if it was part of the puzzle of his mum's sadness. He needed to find out more.

Outside The Ship's Bell, two other men approached Billy. They chatted briefly and exchanged money. The men, and Billy, turned to go down the lane.

Andy's heart hammered in his chest.

He ran from his hiding place and over to the pub, then crept down the dark lane. Slowly, so slowly, following the line of damp brickwork beneath his fingers, stopping before the passage opened out into a muddy area at the back of the building.

He heard the noises first. And the swearing. And his mum. Pleading.

Hoping not to be seen, he glanced around the corner. It was confusing. And horrible. They were hurting her in a strange way and he wanted it to stop. But Billy, keeping lookout, must have spotted something and moved to investigate. "Nosey, nosey. Looking costs money."

Andy jerked back, but Billy continued round the corner. His eyes widened as he saw the boy, and he pushed him further down the lane, hissing "Fuck you doing?"

"Uncle Billy. Please. Get her away from them." Andy's voice wavered, on the edge of tears.

"Interfering with a man's business?" Billy swiped and caught him on the side of the face. Andy's head struck the wall to his left. A smash of stone. A flash of blackness. A static hiss. The choppy, whirring, slapping sound and a rush of air on his face. Wind in the lane?

The boy looked up from where he had fallen. Billy crouched down and whispered, "You make trouble about this, you make trouble for her. Serious trouble. Understand?" Billy punched at the boys legs, but Andy pulled away, sustaining a glancing blow. "Now fuck off home and keep your mouth shut."

Andy ran, his sobs a broken counterpoint to the slap of his school shoes on the pavement. When he reached home, he locked the door and went to bed. He vowed to never follow Billy ever again. He vowed to never mention it to Mum. He vowed to forget what he saw.

Even as a boy, in his heart, he knew the last of those vows would be impossible to keep. And some months later, not long before Andy Lorimar turned twelve years old, his mother went out and never came back.

19

THE HOSPITAL

THURSDAY 8TH SEPTEMBER, 18:53

She was back with him now. Stroking the inside of his wrist. It was a tender touch, pulling him out of the darkness. "Mum?" His speech was hoarse and uncertain, unable to rise above the sound of trundling wheels.

When his hand was released, he heard her voice, but strangely muffled. "Pulzsteddy. Getim traydoljy."

Awareness was a tide, and he didn't know which way it was turning.

He tried to force open his eyes, but the light hurt. And not just the light. The movement itself. His left eye, glued shut; his right eye, unfocussed. Cold oxygen hissed against his nose and mouth.

His head couldn't move to either side. So he looked at the ceiling.

And each bar of strip lighting became a rung on a ladder. A ladder offering him only one direction. Each rung graduated the descent. Back down, down to unconsciousness.

———

THE BOARD DIDN'T LOOK good, that was for sure.

"Give up Andrew. It's gone pear-shaped." The old man plucked the white queen off the magnetic surface and placed it alongside his other captives. They'd exchanged a lot of pieces, but Mr Gallagher was up a bishop and two pawns. "A king with only four wee pawns? Time to topple him."

"No thanks." Andy knew he was a beginner. Learning how to attack, and how to defend. But tactics for when things were pear-shaped seemed worth learning too. Endgame strategies, one book had said. He needed to queen one of his pawns. But how to break past Mr Gallagher? Maybe tempt him with a sacrifice?

The old man yawned as he played his moves. "Don't make me do this Andrew. Chase you all round the houses. It's demeaning. We know how it ends. That guy." He pointed to the beleaguered white king. "He needs to kiss the tarmac."

"No thanks." This was interesting. His opponent was in such a strong position, his play had changed. He seemed to have lost focus, his moves almost automatic, as though victory was certain. "I'm sorry. You just need to chase me all round the houses."

Mr Gallagher nonchalantly advanced his bishop then opened his Evening News. "Radio Rentals are fair pushing those colour TV's. Bet you'd like one of them."

"I prefer books. They're always in colour." Andy focused on keeping his king out of trouble. His pawns advanced too, mainly, but not solely to protect their king.

"Come now Andrew. It's getting late. What time d'you need to be home anyway?"

"I'm OK." Mum knew tonight was library night. "Nice try though. You can resign if you're in a hurry."

The man snorted, and returned to his paper. Andy took one of the black pawns and his opponent barely noticed. Nearly time for the sacrifice.

"How's school going Andrew? Still enjoying it?"

"Mostly." This next exchange would cost Andy a pawn but get rid of two of his opponent's.

The old man reappraised the board. "You're doing a bit of damage with those pawns." And you're practically ignoring yours. Treating your bishop like a rock star.

The pawn was offered. And Mr Gallagher's bishop swooped to take it. Then Andy's other pawn broke for the back rank.

The rock-star bishop was blocked by his own pieces on one side and by the threat of Andy's king on the other. If Andy was right, it wouldn't be possible to stop the promotion. It sounded as if Mr Gallagher agreed. "Andrew, you sleekit wee rogue!"

When Andy had the queen, he played carefully, alternating between mopping up and protecting his king from reprisals. It didn't take too long, but he enjoyed every second. And then it was over. He'd done it. His first victory. And against the odds too.

And now, finally, he could spare time for small talk. "So, Mr Gallagher. Do you know what your mistake was?" He wanted to hear an admission. Too much confidence, too little attention, underestimating the brilliance of his opponent. But he got something different.

Mr Gallagher tapped his nose. "Oh I know what I did wrong all right." He pointed at the promoted pawn now sitting on the library table. "My big mistake," he sighed heavily, "was leaving that annoying little bugger on the board."

———

BANGING INSIDE A WHITE TUNNEL. It shrank to a loud tapping, then he could hear music. Muffled on one side, but on the other, recognisable. "Raindrops keep falling on my head". It wasn't raindrops that did the damage. He remembered that much. He could see the rock, suspended above him. Then a noise. A growing, whirring sound. And the look on his attacker's face. Momentarily startled, as the rock began to plunge.

A voice asked him to touch his fingers with his thumb. He did what he could, but he didn't fully understand. The voice asked other questions. And told him to be still when he kept moving his fingers. They needed to make up their mind, whoever they were. It would be easier to sleep. Someone would take him out of the tunnel eventually.

———————

THE HEAD'S office didn't seem so scary on the inside, but nobody ever wanted to end up here. The most frightening thing was the clock. It ticked loudly. Really loudly. So loudly it made you want to confess to something. "Well, young man. Do you know why you were sent here?"

Andy nodded.

The headmistress leaned forward. She didn't look angry. "Well? What's going on?"

"I was crying in class."

"We know that part, Andrew. You need to tell us *why.*"

He shouldn't do this. She'd get in trouble.

"Are you being bullied?"

Maybe she was already in trouble.

"No. I'm not being bullied." He felt the tears welling up again. Then they escaped, and so did the words behind them. "It's mum. She's gone. Two days ago. I don't know where she is."

The headmistress pursed her lips, then sighed. "Surprise, surprise." She reached for her phone.

But something was wrong. When she turned the dial, there was no rotational sound. Just an electronic chirping.

———————

FIRST, the beeping, a regular digital pulse. And then a conversation in whispers. Now, light.

One sticky eyelid responded. And, eventually, opened.

His blurred vision cleared slowly.

Someone above him, peering down.

"Detective? It's Doctor Nassar." The shock must have shown on his face. "Don't worry, I'm just visiting. You're at the Edinburgh Royal. Can you understand me?"

His voice was hoarse and gritty, and his jaw ached. "Mostly."

She looked to one side. Something around his neck prevented him following her gaze. "Elisia? Could you fetch Detective Lorimar some water?" She leaned over him again. "You've got a fractured skull. The fracture is linear and well behaved, though, so, silver lining. A winning combination - a hard skull being bashed into soft sand. You're on strong pain relief, but you'll still feel sodding awful from the concussion."

Understatement. His head throbbed. He felt like puking. And it was difficult to focus.

"You had a lumbar puncture to monitor your cranial pressure, and they drained off a little CSF. That's another headache I'm afraid. You're still in a support collar. The paramedic was worried about your spine when he reached you, but the scans show only soft tissue damage. You have a broken rib."

Another voice, too muffled to understand. "E I Lomar? Ndy?"

Nassar registered his confusion. "Come closer, and around to his right. There's been damage to the tympanic membrane on that side." When the other woman came into view, she was very familiar. He struggled for her name.

"DI Lorimar, Andy? It's me, Petrakis." She held a glass with a long straw down around mouth height. Andy tried to latch on as best as the support collar would allow. Petrakis pressed a button to raise the back of the bed, then continued. "I had the binoculars. Remember? I saw you collapse after running to the island. "

Cramond. He remembered. Sokov.

"Anyway, I panicked. I called the air ambulance."

That was the noise. A helicopter. And Sokov had heard it too. Just before he brought down the rock. Andy realised he had something to say that was worth the jaw pain. "I think you saved my life."

"Well, it didn't look that way. I thought you were dead. I couldn't see everything but he ran for his boat when the helicopter approached."

Andy wanted to ask more about that, but couldn't quite face any long speeches. The deep ache at the top of his jaw, same side as his dodgy hearing, grew sharp when he spoke. That was where Sokov had struck when he was on the ground. Most of what mattered was coming back now, reassembling in his mind, like a jumble-sale jigsaw; he'd just have to live with a few missing pieces. "Did you catch him?"

Petrakis shook her head. "They've found the boat abandoned near Dalgety Bay. But there's no sign of Sokov."

More words worth the jaw pain. "Shit! Fuck!"

She continued brightly. "Early days. But some good news. We think Sokov basically lived in his van. He had a lot of stuff in there. Including ..." She paused for a drum roll, but Andy didn't have his sticks on him. "Including his *laptop*. I'll take a run at it after the forensics are finished. He'd cleaned the van up pretty well, but not perfectly. Nesbitt thinks they'll find something for sure." She held up her phone. "Don't worry, I'm still in the loop!"

Better that than in traction.

Still, it was unlucky for her to be left minding the invalid while everyone else chased the villain. "How long will I be stuck here?" There was a note of petulance in his question, but he couldn't help it.

Petrakis shrugged, but Dr Nassar said, "Be patient, patient! Your neurologist knows best. You've had a serious injury. Right now it appears you've been lucky. But they'll keep you under observation until they're sure."

Lucky. Among the tiny subset of people who'd ever been trapped on an island with a homicidal maniac, that was probably true, but it was hard to feel blessed. He recalled the attack itself. The hammer-blow strikes to his midriff, his collapse, the punch to his head. His memories ended with the rock, of course.

But, it did look like he'd walk away from this. He would take comfort from that, because it meant he could ensure this case didn't go unsolved. Sokov and his accomplices probably didn't realise it, but they had made a significant mistake. Since childhood he'd known how the endgame played out. He was the annoying bugger. And they'd left him on the board.

20

VISITING TIMES

THURSDAY 8TH SEPTEMBER, 10:35

After the pathologist had left with Petrakis to buy coffee, Andy spent five minutes trying to get comfortable before giving up. Instead he lay back, face frozen in a collar-assisted scowl, letting the incessant digital pulse lull him back to sleep.

He had just started to drift when the nurse entered. "Mr Lorimar? I've found a visitor for you, wandering the corridors. A lady."

Andy doubted anyone would get away with calling Petrakis a lady unchallenged. "Any name?"

"She said Doirin Chambers. She's been here a while, she said, but now you're ready to see her? She shouldn't be here this late, so I can ask her to come back tomorrow?"

"No. Send her in." When Doirin eventually entered his line of sight, she stared, frowned and then went to fetch a chair. "Stay on this side Doirin, I'm deaf in one ear."

She dragged a plastic seat around. "Show me a man who isn't."

So much for sympathy. He was going to have to suffer his jaw and just talk. "How did you know I was here?"

"Will it annoy you if I tell you the truth?"

"Probably. But do it anyway."

"That earpiece you think I'm wearing went ballistic. I knew I had to come here, and when I arrived I knew I had to wait. Eventually I knew it was you I needed to find." She squinted. "You look a right picture by the way."

"Thanks."

"What happened?"

"Didn't your earpiece tell you?"

She scowled. "I know you think it's weird anyway. But this isn't how things usually go. Normally I'm with someone and I open up and I receive some bits and bobs to pass on."

"Don't you also have to be pissed?"

"Cheeky beggar! No shame in drinking professionally. Anyway, this isn't normal." She leaned forward. "I don't know what you're involved with." She pulled her coat around her. "So many ..." She waved a hand at her ear, as though swatting flies. When she spoke again she was strident. "Look! Spirit that communicates about you, should be yours. These aren't yours. When they started you weren't even there! They're not your connections. But they're watching you." She paused, puzzled.

"Are they saying anything specific?"

"Too much." She paused and then spoke loudly, as if in rebuke. "And all shouting over the top of each other!" She frowned in confusion. "It is hard to make out. But part of it is definitely about you. You met one."

"I met one? One what?"

She thought for a second more. "One. Of the ... thieves? The takers? I don't know exactly. But you've met one now."

"One of the takers. Do you mean the guy who put me in here?"

"Maybe." Suddenly she flinched. "No, hold that result. That's a definite. The guy who put you in here. He's one."

"Anything else?"

She shook her head, frustrated. "It's like being chased by an army of town criers with megaphones." She closed her eyes. "You. You're similar. To one of them. One of the takers. And that's important. Somehow"

"Christ, Doirin. That's bloody useless."

"Well it's not meant to be profound *now*, but it might be eventually." Her eyes widened in surprise. "Oh. Now I've got one of your people pushing through." She took his hand. "That's more like it. An older gentleman. A relative. He knows you were thinking about him."

Andy eyed her warily. "Who?"

Doirin shrugged. "He still doesn't want you thinking you're bonny." She cocked her eyebrow, examining his swollen face, bandaged forehead and single functioning eye. "Statement of the bloody obvious. Not sure what he was getting at."

Andy fell silent. His focus drifted: To the regular beep from a monitor in the ward next door, the rolling trundle of a nearby trolley, a passing conversation in the corridor outside. He knew those things were real, they could be heard, they could be seen. That was how it was. He believed in things he could hold in his hand.

Doirin squeezed his fingers.

Petrakis sidled hesitantly back into the room. "Ah. Awkward. Sorry. I didn't know your wife-stroke-girlfriend was coming."

Andy blushed. "She's not ... wife-stroke-girlfriend? No! I mean ... well ... she's a friend who's a girl."

Doirin smiled at the notion. "I'm sure he means woman. But you catching us has got him all flustered." She leaned in conspiratorially to Andy and whispered, "She looks a fierce sceptic. I'll best be off."

Petrakis's expression betrayed growing panic. "This is my bad. I was delayed at the coffee shop. But if your visitor isn't family, don't tell DCI Nesbitt. I said I'd keep people out until we had uniforms guarding the room. "

Andy rolled his one visible eye. "Guarding the room? Every spare officer should be on a bloody manhunt!"

But Doirin flinched again, and then rose to her feet. "No. She's right. They recommend guarding the room."

Petrakis stared. "Who does?"
But Doirin was already leaving.

———————

IN THE MIDDLE of the night Andy sat up for the third time. The hospital was too bright and too noisy for deep sleep, but the worst problem was a fixation upon the moment Sokov hoisted the rock. It wasn't only the image, but the feeling in his throat and his chest, the urgent certainty of his own imminent death. It was much more than a memory. A memory could be taken out, examined and then placed back in its box. No. This was a stain in his mind, an experience that bled through and infected every other thought he had.

It was warm on the ward, but he shivered as he reached blindly to the bedside unit where Petrakis had left his phone. He was done with feeling powerless. He couldn't call anyone so late, but instead he sent a text message to the security manager at the Balrannoch.

PETE - IN HOSPITAL AFTER RUN-IN WITH EX-JANI-TOR. COULD YOU CHECK TAPES AND ASK AROUND. DID HE HAVE ANY CONTACTS IN-HOUSE?

Sokov remained at large so they needed every scrap of information on his background. Even then, he couldn't shake a creeping fear that Sokov might remain a cipher. A bogeyman with a rock.

Sleep was slow to return.

———————

THE FOLLOWING morning he woke to the sound of Devlin and Nesbitt shuffling into the room. As far as his collar permitted, he followed their movements, noting their glum expressions. Perhaps they felt guilty they hadn't visited on the day of his attack. If so, that was silly. It was bad enough his injury had wasted a day for two officers. They couldn't justify losing the whole team.

He was uncertain of the time, and still slightly groggy, but the depth of his colleagues' gloom was unmistakable. "Just say it."

Nesbitt grimaced. "He's bloody vanished. Sorry Andy. We've got bodies out in force though."

Devlin stared at the floor. "Yeah. Sorry, Link-man."

With each passing hour their chance of catching Sokov dwindled, and they all knew it.

Nesbitt broke the growing silence. "We always thought you were a hard-headed bastard. At least now you've given us some proof." He didn't appear able to smile at his own joke. Having three officers conducting routine interviews in safe council offices while one detective had his skull smashed on a remote beach might be considered poor resource management. It wasn't Nesbitt's fault, although Andy had known him for long enough to understand his thinking. "Fucking hell! I just thought you were following your nose a bit, and we'd throw bodies at it when you turned up something solid."

Andy's smile, never the most expressive, was further restricted by his neck brace. "The rock felt solid enough. Does that count?" Nesbitt flinched. "Anyway, chief, you sent Petrakis. If I'd been alone I'd be dead."

Devlin raised his head. "And now we know Reynolds was working with some serious muscle." It was a definitive statement. Perhaps even a challenge.

Andy rose to it. "That's one possibility."

"What d'you mean? His hands are all over it! He admitted it! "

Nesbitt said nothing. Good. Andy decided to throw a bun at the invisible pachyderm. "Correction, Jamie. Somebody using Reynolds' phone admitted it."

"But I linked Reynolds' company to the council! C'mon!"

Nesbitt's contribution was pleasingly equivocal. "That's only a link of sorts. A big group of companies has a lot of tentacles. A direct connection to his employer would be more solid, but we didn't find that, did we?" But the DCI received the look Julius Caesar showed Brutus. As Devlin's face purpled, the senior officer relented, but only a little. "So, we don't rule Reynolds out. But this Sokov character is ruled *in*, that's for damn sure."

Simultaneous neck and jaw pain told Andy he was both nodding and smiling. Things were moving the way he wanted them to, and he'd only had to get brained to achieve it. Result. Sort of. "Did Petrakis ever trace the source of those phone messages to Tricia Black?"

Nesbitt grimaced. "Where is she anyway?"

"She spoke last night about visiting the Gartcosh Crime Campus. Sounded worth doing."

The DCI scowled. "At least she cleared it with you. Bloody free spirits those computer bods. How have you found her?"

Andy touched his bandaged scalp. "She's definitely growing on me."

Nesbitt nodded. "She said the messages from Reynolds phone weren't SMS at all, they were Viber messages or some such thing—"

Devlin broke in smugly. "And Viber is sent over the data network, but he used a private one routed through a Malaysian VPL."

Andy's smirk was at least fifty-percent wince but he enjoyed it anyway. "Routed through a visible panty line? Really? I think you mean VPN, Jamie. Virtual private network." Hanging around with Petrakis was rubbing off.

Devlin blushed. "Whatever! Who cares? She can't find where they bloody came from!"

Suddenly, Nesbitt stared towards the door. Andy wished he could turn to look. Devlin snapped to attention as well. "Sir!" he said.

The Assistant Chief Constable for Major and Local Crime moved to the head of the bed. Anthony Flynn's scouse accent had been unaffected by his transfer up to Scotland. He was known for impressive enthusiasm despite a daily grind of mainly brickbats and rotten tomatoes. "So this is the famous Inspector Lorimar I've heard so much about!"

"All good I hope," Andy offered, while very much doubting it.

"Great that a man in your position keeps his optimism! But look, as an officer injured in the line of duty, I want you to know how much we appreciate what you've done." He turned to Nesbitt. "What did he do again?"

Nesbitt blushed. "Erm. Attacked on Cramond beach by Yurki Sokov, a susp—"

Flynn punched his arm. "I knew that Chief Inspector! I'm joking! But seriously Lorimar, we'll catch the bastard." Again, he turned to Nesbitt. "Where are we on catching the bastard?" He saw Nesbitt's hesitation and continued. "That's a real question this time, you can answer."

Nesbitt nodded. "We're following multiple lines of enquiry, sir. We've got his van, his prints and his computer equipment. DS Petrakis is at Gartcosh right now working with the specialists on some promising leads."

"Good. But how does this attack fit in with Reynolds?"

Andy was pleased whenever a senior demonstrated a basic grasp of the case. But just as he prepared to respond, Devlin leapt in. "We're looking at an accomplice sir. We believe Reynolds, motivated by a business-related grudge, recruited Sokov at the Balrannoch. So the attacker was the monkey to Reynolds' organ grinder. Sir."

Andy added, "Alternatively, my attacker was King Kong to Reynolds' hapless World War II biplane."

Nesbitt intervened. "Sergeant Devlin articulated our primary working theory. But we've got a second hare running, sir. Inspector Lorimar refers to the possibility Sokov may have disposed of Reynolds and used his phone for the purposes of misdirection."

"Motive?"

All men looked to the invalid, whose attempt at a shrug foundered at his support collar. "I don't know that yet. But Sokov's stolen identity may now be another victim. There may be others."

Flynn frowned. "How do the documents on McKay's body figure in this?"

Oh well. He did ask. "McKay brought those documents to the Balrannoch, possibly on the promise of monetary reward. My fear is they were displayed on his corpse to send us off chasing our tail. And by tail, I mean the primary theory sir."

"Shite and onions!" Flynn walked away from the hospital bed, and Andy heard the door close. When the ACC returned his face was grave. "Keep this second hare discreet for Christ's sake. If that line of thinking reaches the media we're deep in the brown stuff." He pointed to the younger detective. "Bottom line, DS Devlin, I'm rooting for your theory. Two murderers commit two murders, both relating to political and commercial corruption, giving a manageable amount of public concern." Devlin nodded, face glowing, as if he'd somehow planned the whole thing for maximum convenience.

The ACC then turned to Andy, shaking his head. "But you, DI Lorimar? You see Devlin's two corpses and raise him at least two missing bodies, a lone-wolf foreign psychopath and no clue about why or who next. Am I right?"

Andy hesitated. "I accept it needs fleshing out a bit."

"No shit, Sherlock." Flynn turned back towards Nesbitt. "Well, Chief Inspector good luck with those hares. I hope the right one wins." He headed for the exit. "And catch Sokov for fuck's sake!" The door slammed, but before the three colleagues could react, it opened again and another shout echoed across the room. "Get well soon, Lorimar. You've got a shitload of bloody spadework to finish."

After they were sure their morale-boost was complete, Andy raised the point bothering him most. "When can I get back on the case?"

He regretted the question as soon as Nesbitt's gaze began its voyage of scrutiny, lingering on his neck brace, the seepage on the pad at his left ear, his bandaged skull, and just showing beneath his hospital gown the mottled black and crimson of his ribs. "Ask me again when you can turn your bloody head!" He included Devlin in his next statement. "This is a state of emergency. We need people firing on all cylinders, physically and mentally." Nesbitt stopped, rubbing his eyes. "But we can't afford to lose your input, Andy. So, do what the doctors say and get out of here. But until that time, Petrakis will work with you."

"You can't make a specialist officer a bloody babysitter!"

"Lose the attitude. We wouldn't have known about Sokov if it wasn't for your digging. Petrakis maintains her specialist role, and she won't be here all the time, but she'll visit daily to take direction from you. Meanwhile Jamie and Lenny will work with me to try and trap our primary hare."

Devlin was enthusiastic. "We'll do it, chief." He turned to his wounded colleague. "Our bunny's toast. Count on it, Link-man."

Nesbitt scowled. "We need a breakthrough, wherever it comes from. We've got a serious maniac on the loose. Take a look at Andy if you need a reminder."

PETRAKIS ARRIVED BACK in the early evening clutching a cinema-sized beaker of coffee. "This stuff tastes strangely good here. I think it's an olfactory thing. Maybe it mingles with the disinfectant or something."

"I'll stick to my water." Andy reached across to his bedside and grabbed the bottle Petrakis had left him yesterday. His head wasn't the clearest, but his mobility was improving. He knew he'd be counting the minutes until he got out of here.

She was in a chatty mood. "How did you get on with Lee?"

"Lee?"

"The officer on the door that I just sent on his break."

"Oh. I haven't spoken to anyone. I think they've been leaving the old cripple in peace."

"Or maybe they took a glance, caught that scowl of yours and thought better of it. I can relate, I guess. I'm not the most sociable myself." She checked her phone before continuing. "Apparently we're now special forces deep undercover on a black-ops mission?"

"Come again?"

"You and me."

"Ah. Nesbitt's idea. Sorry. I don't want to be a burden."

"It sounds like a blast. Improving on that Ass-wipe Assassin theory of Devlin's?"

"I'm not sure he called it that exactly, and we probably shouldn't personalise it." Petrakis smirked at that idea. Then Andy joined her. He couldn't help it.

She said, "The international assistance unit at Gartcosh, they're following up on Radu Dudnic, checking if he's back home. Between you and me I doubt it. The lab rats are trying to match DNA from some old blood inside the van to that comb you got from the guest house." She paused for a second, her face thoughtful. "D'you know, Sokov's laptop is strangely similar to Joan Wood's? Nothing much to see outwardly, but a huge encrypted file container that I can't crack."

Weird discoveries were nothing new on this investigation as far as Andy was concerned, but he was glad to be sharing the burden. "Is that kind of encryption used a lot?"

"Commercial tools are used by businesses, and some people use features built into their operating system. But everyday drones wouldn't install and configure something like this."

Drones. Muggles. People like him and most of society. Petrakis swam in waters where ordinary folk feared to paddle. "How similar were the setups, on Wood's and Sokov's laptops I mean?"

Petrakis grinned. "Very different, superficially. Councillor Wood's was a newer device, more expensive brand. But for me, both machines contained identical soul-crushing disappointment after I hacked past the initial login prompt. D'you know? On Sokov's machine I needed a parallel password cracker and a Russian dictionary?"

He frowned, hoping she'd skip to the good bit, or at least the bit he could understand. She took the hint. "Anyway, when I got in, same as Wood's PC, there wasn't evidence of much historical activity at the operating-system level. I'd guess neither machine was really used that way. There was probably another operating environment inside the encrypted file container." She paused again, shaking her head. "I'm not one for hunches, but I got a feeling looking at this. Different machines, one older, one newer, different versions of the operating system. But it felt as if they were setup deliberately in the same way, just a couple of years apart. Same techniques."

He just about followed that. A strongbox you cracked open only to find Fort Knox inside it. Why would this double-security strategy be shared by a victim and a potential murderer? "Any ideas what it means?"

"That's your job. But maybe the same person was involved in setting them up? It would be a really extreme coincidence otherwise. Bad news is, that's all we'll get from his laptop." Then she paused. "Actually I tell a lie, I did get one more thing. Fingerprints, good clear ones. They're being checked on the UK national database, and I've also shared them with the International Assistance Unit at the Crime Campus in case we don't find anything locally." That seemed worth a punt. Someone like Sokov could easily have a record overseas. Petrakis now held a stylus above the screen of her phone. "OK, Inspector. This is the part where I take direction."

He had considered the action plan. All he could do here was think. "OK. Sokov was a contractor for the Queensferry Marina. We need statements from everyone who worked with him."

She wrote directly onto the screen. "Gotcha."

"Also, check out Sokov's bank accounts. Did he just receive payments from the marina, or did he earn money some other way? And what did he spend his money on? Any employees or subcontractors we need to have on our radar?"

"I'll get the bank details from the Marina and apply for a production order. Anything else?"

"One thing. Drop into the Balrannoch. I messaged the security manager to look into contacts Sokov might have made while posing as Radu Dudnic. Maybe he let something slip. We need to double-check."

Petrakis smiled, clipping her stylus back into her phone. "Wow. Real detective work, With humans and talking and everything?"

"Looks like it. I'm jealous."

Her face became serious. "I don't blame you. I'll rock at this, but I'll try not to show you up too much."

He nearly laughed. But noise from the corridor interrupted them. Petrakis turned around and stiffened as someone crashed through the door. Then came a shout. "MCGLINCHEY! LORIMAR ROBBED MCGLINCHEY!"

Andy strained his neck to see. A thin man, unshaven, in a dirty blue suit.

Holding a knife.

Shit.

As the man staggered forward, Andy attempted to stand, but his rib pain flared, leaving him helplessly clutching the side of the bed.

Petrakis, however, was already in motion, placing herself between Andy and the intruder. And fiddling, inexplicably, with her beaker.

The man was wild-eyed and angry. "MOVE YA CUNT! IT'S HIM AHM WANTIN! FUCKIN MOVE!"

She did move, but not how he'd intended. A cascade of steaming coffee hit him square in the face and he howled, knife clattering from his hand as he attempted to wipe scalding liquid from his eyes. Petrakis manoeuvred behind him, pushing and kicking simultaneously, sending him crashing face first to the floor. Once he was down she threw herself heavily onto his back. His lungs emptied in a gasping wheeze, a wheeze that climbed to a squeal as she wrenched his arms up towards his shoulder blades, cuffing his hands together.

The scuffle was over in under a minute. Then while holding him down with her body weight, Petrakis radioed for assistance. She struggled to make herself heard above the ranting beneath her. "GET AFF ME! FUCK'S SAKE! MCGLINCHEY WANTS HIM DEAD! FUCK OFF! FUCK OFF!"

Questions to the intruder produced more heat than light. "Who are you?"

"MCGLINCHEY! LORIMAR ROBBED HIS SMACK!"

"Who sent you?"

"LORIMAR ROBBED MCGLINCHEY!"

And so it continued for a further eight minutes until officers turned up to take the intruder into custody.

When they were alone again, trying to make sense of it, Andy said, "You're a dark horse. What was that? Aikido, Judo?"

"Macchiato. You owe me a new coffee."

He smiled. "I owe you more than that. But you know what's really bothering me now?"

"What?"

"Who the bloody hell is McGlinchey?"

21

CONTROL

FRIDAY 9TH SEPTEMBER, 18:08

Outside Ridotto Lodge, a mansion in the Grange conservation area of Edinburgh, the pink draped branches of a hardy fuchsia swayed serenely in the evening breeze. But inside, the Victorian tiles echoed with pacing footsteps.

Daniel Cochrane stopped for a moment and listened. Was that a car?

It must be. It *was* a car. Stopping.

The heavy thunk of the boot. It sounded ... like the Audi?

If so that meant Nick. It had to be Nick.

Steps on the path.

His heart hammered in his chest. A key in the lock. Thank God.

Cochrane held back until his son was fully inside and the door closed behind him. Then he pulled him into a tight embrace. Cochrane knew he was breathing too fast, the words spilling out of him. "Nick! Thank God! Are you OK? Is it done? How did it go?"

Nick pulled back after a moment and looked him square in the eye. "It's done, Dad. It's dealt with. We're fine." A simple reassurance, but hard to accept. Was he too confident? Cocky, even? Nick had been placed front and centre in last month's subterfuge, and despite the continuing backlash, he feared his son had learned the wrong lesson. He seemed to have developed a taste for it.

But Cochrane's mind teemed with questions "The first pub you tried?"

"Yeah. The one we thought. It was all OK."

"You didn't park nearby did you?"

"Walking a mile through Prestonpans in a bloody grey and white balaclava's not my usual definition of good sense, but today was the exception that proves the rule."

Cochrane knotted his fingers. "Was the guy reliable?"

Nick snorted. "We didn't need reliable. We needed do-anything-for-the-price-of-a-score."

"The cab? Any awkward questions?"

"None the extra cash didn't answer. Look. Our guy will have reached the hospital, made plenty of noise, and might even have got lucky."

Cochrane felt a churn in his gut. "This was a huge bloody risk."

Nick shrugged. "Maybe, maybe not. But anyway. No time meant no choice. You saw the message Lorimar sent the same as I did. He's still pushing, still digging. It's like Max said, we either put him down or his reputation. Either play works."

Cochrane's breathing slowed. "I hope so. But what about—"

Nick grinned and raised his hand. "Forget it! It's done! We've taken the reins again." He dropped his holdall onto the hallway floor. "I'm going for a shower. Get the stink off me. You can relax now."

Despite his son's confidence Cochrane couldn't relax. He had one more thing to do. He fired up the secure calling app on his handset and dialled. The line opened at the other end. "Hello Max? It's Daniel."

"This is Sara. Father is in replenishment."

Annoying. Some things were best discussed man to man. "Again?" It seemed like only last week.

"He sets his own schedule according to his needs. What should I pass on?"

"Just tell him it's done. He'll know what I'm talking about."

"Daniel. I also know what you are talking about. Father and I have no secrets. Did you find an appropriate narrative?"

Impassive and yet judgemental. Bloody typical. "Yes. Of course." He hoped the narrative was good, but his doubts were none of her business.

"When will you know the outcome?"

"It depends. Worst case Monday. We give it the weekend." But enough responding to her questions. He deserved some answers of his own. "Who replaces Joan?"

"That hasn't been decided."

"When will it be decided?"

"Soon, I expect. You will be contacted when Father has reached a conclusion." One minute ago they shared everything, now she hides behind him. "Until this is resolved, you must travel to meet your replenishment schedule."

She enjoyed these displays of power. He'd never have to accept her oversight in any other sphere. "Look. If it wasn't for my money you'd have nothing! Why should I travel?"

The pause on the line became a lengthy, frosty, silence. "You travel because to continue operations in Edinburgh at this time risks exposing us all. This should be obvious even to a powerful man such as yourself Daniel. Accept it. You cannot have what you want."

"Tell Max I must speak to him."

"I will. But one final thing."

There always was. "What?"

"The facility you use to track Lorimar and intercept his communications. We would also like access to this."

"I'm sure you would. But at our own risk we installed a phone exploit and it feeds information to Nick. That bloody detective is an Edinburgh threat, so the exploit remains under Edinburgh control."

"But duplicating the feed, is there a technical solution?"

An irresistible opportunity. "Accept it. You cannot have what you want."

"I understand. Good day Daniel."

After disconnecting the call, he unstoppered his Italian crystal decanter and poured a generous measure of Dalmore 1978. He leavened it with a trickle of water from the matching jug, and raised the glass to take in the aroma. As he drank, the searing alcohol obliterated the acid taint of fear that had been clinging to the back of his throat.

Upstairs, he heard Nick singing in the shower.

His son was right.

They had made their move. They were now back in control.

PART III

FALLOUT

10TH - 17TH SEPTEMBER

22

REBEL ALLIANCE

SATURDAY 10TH SEPTEMBER, 10:32

When Petrakis arrived Andy was tentatively rocking and turning his head. "Trial run without a collar! Freedom!"

But his colleague's smile was strained. "One step forward, two steps back."

"Ah. Fallout from yesterday."

"Yup. I helped question our blue-suited knifeman, Ricky. No second name yet; I think he's forgotten it."

"Impressive witness, then?"

"Impressively out of his face. Although he was pretty lucid about suing me for, and I quote, 'leaving him pure reeking of the Starbucks'. The main thing is, the attack wasn't his idea. Somebody sent him. "

"Do we know who?"

"No. But we discovered what ninety quid will buy you in the right kind of pub. Cash in hand to come here, stab you, and shout out that stuff about McGlinchey while he did it."

"Only ninety-quid? To stab a cop?"

"Gig economy depresses wages I guess. But he insisted he didn't know you were police. Apparently he 'just widnae dae that, man'"

She had a good ear for the accent, and he allowed himself a dark laugh. "But as an ordinary citizen I was fair game?"

"Not the clearest thinker. Incidentally, the ninety-quid was upfront, with the same again when the job was done."

He shrugged. Imagining a £180 price tag on his carcass didn't sugar the pill. "Don't tell me. Nobody turned up to pay the balance?"

"We found the pub and the taxi, but we got diddly-squat. Take your pick of the dead ends: Ricky was delivered to the hospital by a cab ordered from a pub phone; The cabbie kept eyes-front because he thought it was a gang-related injury and didn't want any trouble; The fare was paid in advance and in cash by some guy wearing a grey and white balaclava. Fifty quid to shut-up and drive. According to Ricky it was balaclava-boy who gave him his instructions."

"Any description?"

"Our photo-fit begins and ends at the two-tone balaclava. From his voice, the cabbie guessed late-twenties or early thirties, with a slightly weird accent, East Lothian-ish"

"Ish?"

"He thought it sounded put on. But like I say, he didn't try to see the guy's face, and Ricky wasn't much for fine detail. But they both agreed the balaclava didn't have a Russian accent. And he was around five-foot-ten. That's too small for Sokov."

Andy gingerly shook his collar-free head. He was worried about what he'd find in the centre of this particular labyrinth. "Did Ricky say who McGlinchey is?"

"He had no clue. Just that Lorimar stole his smack. Basically, the stuff he shouted yesterday was the full extent of his knowledge."

"Shit. Perfect."

Petrakis said, "Oh, it gets even more shit-perfect than that." Free-floating anxiety settled into a knot in his gut. "See, Nesbitt took a call from *The Weasel*."

"That's the website, right? Investigative journalists?"

"Yeah. They'd had a tip-off that one of Nesbitt's team had been moonlighting for a dealer and that a drug transaction went very wrong on a beach in Cramond."

"For fuck's sake!"

Petrakis nodded. "We all know where this is going. McGlinchey, according to *The Weasel*, is a mid-level heroin dealer who was acquitted in Edinburgh three months back after alleged evidence irregularities. There was a piece in *The Scotsman* at the time apparently."

Now Andy felt properly sick. "Has this been published?"

"Not yet. But they were told you'd been working for him constantly since his acquittal. Their piece had 'Detective Andrew Lorimar: McGlinchey's Pet Detective', with your face superimposed over a Jim Carrey movie poster. Nesbitt went ballistic. It stalled them because the tip-off was anonymous. They don't have anyone to go on the record. Yet."

"I'm off the case, right? Pending an investigation?"

"We talked about that. Since you're in here you're already off the case. You've to rest up over the weekend and follow doctors orders," then she winked, "and I'll continue bringing you grapes every day."

For a moment he fell silent. Then he said, "But you know, though, right?"

"That this is utter bullshit? Totally. More importantly, Nesbitt knows it's bullshit too. But it's a messy kind of bullshit."

He could see that. And he could see something else as well. He was being attacked. Directly and personally attacked. For the second time in days. Surely it meant he was onto something.

Petrakis interrupted his thought. "Let's imagine for a second that Devlin's narrative is mistaken. If so, then call me a conspiracy theorist, but I see a pattern here."

By now he'd forgotten why he'd ever found Petrakis annoying. "I'm listening ..."

"Wood is killed, and material appears online linking her with some dodgy dossier from the trams project. McKay is killed, and they plant said document on his body, annotated to explicitly connect his death with Wood's. Then phone messages arrive claiming Reynolds is the killer. And after Sokov fails to murder you, a piece of public theatre connects you to a drug dealer. It feels like they're telling us what to think, trying to control the agenda."

"You're saying they?"

"Because this extends beyond Sokov. Balaclava-boy means two's company at least."

Andy stood and gingerly shuffled to the window. "You are a conspiracy theorist. But then, I'm one too. You said this McGlinchey court case had been in the local news? Well a cop in the pocket of a criminal is a useful stereotype. The tram debacle bubbles in and out of the media. And council procurement scandals happen whenever they buy a new photocopier." He ran his fingers through his hair, avoiding the shrinking, but still prominent dressing. "Someone is offering highly plausible, in fact, tempting answers to all of our questions." He pulled open a vent in the UPVC window, and a sliver of cool air caressed his face. It felt good. His headache was clearing, for the first time since he got here. "It's like a magician. They'll invite us to inspect the hat, or the cup, or the sleeve or the handkerchief. But they don't want us to look behind the hand."

Petrakis was solemn. "You got too close to the hand?"

He closed the window and limped back to the bed. He carefully touched the bruising on his ribs, thinking about the lancing pains with every breathing exercise the nurses made him perform. Then he grinned, fiercely. "I think I got too close to the hand."

THAT AFTERNOON STARTED BADLY when a group of medical students crowded into his room. Andy regretted granting consent upon the consultant's calm announcement that two-thirds of those experiencing similar head trauma suffered 'long-term neurological impairments'. The students were then given a flashlight and asked to pronounce on the abnormality or otherwise of his pupil dilation. Finally they trooped out to view a collection of formaldehyde-preserved brain specimens, each of which had suffered similar concussive injury.

But things improved.

The support collar was taken away altogether. And his hourly breathing exercises, although still a peculiar form of torture, were becoming more bearable. Whenever his injuries received a routine inspection the expressed medical opinions had moved from cautious to encouraging.

Best of all, beyond a short and fairly opaque reference to an injured detective transported by air ambulance in Saturday's Scotsman, Andy found nothing in the papers mentioning him or, more importantly, anyone called McGlinchey.

On Saturday evening, when Petrakis dropped off the previously promised grapes, she mentioned Nesbitt was behind the continued media silence. Andy believed it. The chief was no stranger to the ways of the press, and the investigative team at *The Weasel*, although pains in the arse by chosen occupation, had a reputation for being professional about it. They wouldn't create a stink until they were sure they'd done the homework.

That night he slept pretty well.

ON SUNDAY AFTERNOON he was standing by the window when he heard Doctor Nassar's voice. "How excellent to see you out of bed, Detective."

Given the pathologist's daily struggle against rigor mortis, he supposed moving flesh in a hospital gown was a welcome novelty. Or maybe a nightmare. He'd shoot for the former. "Hey Doc. Good to see you. It's nice to be up and about."

"How's your head?"

"Good, I think, considering. My hearing doesn't seem so bad either, at least now they've taken the padding away. My ribs are the main problem. And the staff keep forcing me to take deep breaths."

"The very definition of evil, but it keeps your lungs clear, so do as you're told!" She moved to the end of his bed and glanced at his notes before continuing. "They're certain now. You dodged a bullet. So I expect they'll let you leave soon. To be honest after that business with the junkie knifeman, I think they want rid of you."

Andy tried not to dwell too much on the injustice; on top of being attacked, he becomes a pariah. Still, since he was climbing the walls, the hospital wanting shot of him was a result. "I'll be glad to get back to the case."

The pathologist glanced back at the doorway. "But ... will you be safe?"

He'd wondered that himself. "Safer than here, probably. The junkie you mentioned wasn't exactly a seasoned hitman. His attack seemed designed to discredit me. A public location and a police guard advertising my presence just invites more trouble."

Nassar nodded. "I hear you're partnering Elisia now?"

Always something juicy on the grapevine. "Seems so, at least for the moment."

"She says the two of you are the rebel alliance, whatever that means."

He smiled. Trust Petrakis with a geek reference. His lack of faith certainly disturbed Devlin enough to make the image halfway appropriate. "We're not exactly rebels. But we're certainly under-dogs. One thing that would help is finding Reynolds, our current prime suspect. I think you or your colleagues are as likely to stumble across him as I am. Can you keep your ear to the ground?"

"You believe he's destined for a slab somewhere?"

"I strongly suspect he's already dead. I don't know if his body will be found or if it would even be recognisable anymore. But anything unidentified, anything that might plausibly be connected to him, I'd be grateful to know."

The pathologist nodded. "Understood. I'll ask around. For what it's worth."

"Anything. Any time. Day or night. You have my number."

She stood back for a moment, observing him. "My, my, Detective Lorimar! You're truly starting to feel yourself again, aren't you?"

He didn't attempt to deny it. His ribs were painful, but his head was clear. And the certainty he'd burrowed under the skin of his adversaries felt like progress.

Tomorrow started a new week. He'd get a taxi home tonight and then consider the best way to approach Brian Nesbitt. All he needed was a quiet corner with a desk and a phone. In fact, the desk was negotiable. It was time to get back to work, and this time he'd be the one lifting rocks. See how the bastards liked that.

23

FIFE

MONDAY 12TH SEPTEMBER, 08:23

As Andy climbed into Nesbitt's car, he thought he'd get his explanation in early. "Thanks for this Brian. But I only called you for a heads-up. I didn't expect a chauffeur service. I've been feeling fine. The painkillers are working. I was planning to get a bus."

The Chief Inspector's features hardened into mockery. "A bus? A bloody bus? Any other exposed public situations you want to place yourself in? Two murder attempts in under a week! You going for a hat-trick?"

"Steady on Brian. Don't exaggerate. Only one of those murder attempts was serious."

"I'll serious you, mister! And forget the 'Steady on Brian' business. This is your boss speaking now. The boss that almost lost the same detective twice in four bloody days. That boss doesn't want you home alone. You should have contacted me last night!"

In the face of this onslaught, Andy raised his hands. "See how you are right now? That's why I didn't contact you last night." A plastic shopping bag hit him on the shoulder and fell to his lap. "Wh— What's this?"

"It's a toothbrush. And a bar of soap. And a box of chamomile bloody teabags. If you expect to waltz your injured arse back onto the case I have conditions." At least, Andy supposed, returning to the case remained on the dance card. "You'll stay at my flat until I say otherwise. No ifs. No buts. I'm at Miguel's some nights but nobody will be looking for you at my address. Anything you need from back here can be fetched by car, and you'll have another officer with you when you do it. Are we on the same page?"

It didn't sound too bad. In fact, this was probably the most touching strip he'd had torn off him during his whole working career. It would be at most a few days before everyone relaxed and he could head home. Besides, if he refused, the situation would play by the book. And medics who'd set ten deep breaths per hour as a metric for safe exertion were unlikely to give their blessing. "Yes. Fine. I agree. Now come on. Let's get back to work."

Nesbitt relaxed as he pushed the car into gear and started along Ferry Road. "On that note," he switched on the radio, landing in the middle of a weather report, "She's been beavering away all weekend."

"Who?"

"Petrakis. Really got the bit between her teeth. He has family in Fife."

"Listen, Brian. Imagine for a moment I was, say, recovering from a head injury. What are we talking about?"

"McGlinchey has family in Fife."

Nesbitt headed straight through the Crewe Toll roundabout before Andy protested. "Why didn't we turn left towards Fettes?"

"McGlinchey doesn't have family in Fettes." The weather report gave way to music and Nesbitt cranked up the volume. "Now whisht." The car accelerated past the Telford fire station, towards the Forth Road Bridge and the Kingdom of Fife.

By the time they'd parked outside the block of flats in Hayfield, Andy was conflicted. Given the suggestion of criminal complicity with their family member, somebody might conclude he'd been brought to intimidate the rest of the family into silence. "Brian, I'm not sure I should—"

"Smile!" Nesbitt's phone clicked once. Twice. Three times. "Right big man. Wait here. I'm meeting Kirkcaldy Community Policing inside."

And so he waited in the car, relieved that Nesbitt was handling what might be an awkward encounter. But that relief soon shifted, passing through vague concern to land at strong misgiving. At this very moment, two officers were inside taking a statement about the degree to which his own likeness was recognisable as a member of McGlinchey's criminal entourage. He prayed nobody in there had an axe to grind. Imagine they'd been got at? This could be a really bad move.

After an agonising ten minutes Nesbitt returned, his face solemn. As he opened the door, a wide smile escaped before being fiercely suppressed. "Right. C'mon up. But stay quiet and respectful for Christ's sake."

The first-floor flat was well kept. Three bedrooms. Photos on the wall of two school-age children. In the kitchen they passed a uniformed officer before stopping in front of a young woman. She sat on a stool beside an uncluttered worktop.

Nesbitt made the introductions "Detective Lorimar, this is Officer Ross and Mrs Colleen Miller, Edward McGlinchey's half-sister."

The woman looked Andy up and down. "I don't recognise him in the flesh either. And let's be honest. No offence. But he's not a bloke you'd forget in a hurry."

Andy decided to give that statement the benefit of the doubt.

Nesbitt continued. "Now, Mrs Miller just passed on some sad information. Apparently her brother went to Wolverhampton after the court case and—"

"Dozy fucker OD'd." Her mouth was set. "Ten weeks gone now. His cousins in Wolverhampton registered the death, or so I was told."

Andy asked, "If he was using his own product, how did he get to be a mid-level dealer?"

The woman rounded on him. "That mid-level shit was just the papers trying to big up their story. He paid two daft laddies and suddenly he's a fucking kingpin?"

Andy was chastened. "Sorry. Mrs Miller. Sometimes the papers ... you're angry ... I understa—"

"Don't tell me you understand! Fuck the papers! I'm angry at him! At him!" She rose from her stool, a five-foot ball of fury barrelling towards him. Andy reflexively backed away, and she stopped with only inches to spare. "That case collapsed on a bloody technicality. He got lucky. It was a chance. Another chance. But like every chance he ever had, he shot it up his fucking arm!" Her eyes glistened, but she didn't weep. She showed them to the door in silence.

Back in the car Nesbitt sighed. "That ended on a bit of a downer."

Andy said, "Bet you feel bad about smiling earlier."

"That wasn't really a smile. That was a ... a facial spasm. Stress of the case."

"You'll want to get that seen to."

"Hark to you, with your ribs, skull and general bad attitude." Nesbitt turned on the radio. By the time they reached Fettes the facial spasm was playing up again, in fact, if anything it had proven infectious.

THE CASE MEETING started with a round of applause for Andy's return, but Nesbitt quickly brought things to order. "OK as you've noticed, DI Lorimar has requested to come back in. I've accepted that request, if only to keep him out of trouble. No car as yet, and he's banned from flying solo on anything. Except maybe the toilet. If you spot him sneaking out, and he doesn't have his legs crossed, report it to teacher, got it?"

Devlin stabbed two fingers at his own eyes before reversing them to point at Andy. As usual Burns nearly ended himself. God save his spleen if Devlin ever cracked a real joke.

Nesbitt calmed the hilarity. "Until I organise our returning colleague's occupational assessment, I want us all to be very, very, gentle. Got that?" He appraised the room until everyone, including Andy, had nodded in agreement.

"To business. You've all heard the accusation that the Link-man was moonlighting for a heroin dealer called McGlinchey over the previous three months. This morning we took a statement that Mr McGlinchey hadn't even been here, in fact, he overdosed and died in Wolverhampton ten weeks ago. Bonus biscuits go to DS Petrakis for toiling all weekend to unearth the half-sister who provided that information. Brilliant work, Sergeant." She bowed to the group, before Nesbitt continued. "Could you, personally, break the news to our friends at *The Weasel*? Make sure they don't waste any more time on this nonsense. They can best serve the public interest by snuffling that inquisitive nose of theirs someplace else." Petrakis nodded. "What this does mean of course, is that someone targeted our team with a malicious lie. We can't, as yet, be sure why. However, everyone needs to watch their backs. Find anything fishy, bring it to me."

Alternatively, Andy thought, find anything fish-free and throw a hat in the air. The scent of red herring was everywhere. But at least the investigators were now primed for deliberate misinformation.

Nesbitt slapped a paper report. "We now have definitive lab confirmation that DNA remains found in the left wheel arch of Sokov's van came from Joan Wood. So we have the murder weapon. We came up inconclusive on his laptop, but DS Petrakis, anything from the Gartcosh Crime Campus?"

Petrakis flipped open the wallet of her handset. "Nothing yet on Radu Dudnic, but the International Assistance Unit came through on Sokov's fingerprints. They matched a set taken from the leader of a gang of suspected people traffickers arrested in Albania in the late nineties. After a short-term incarceration in 1998 the trial didn't happen and no reason was recorded for his release. A different alias, but the techs at the IAU described the match as beyond doubt. Sokov has a thin scar running across his ring and index finger, present and recognisable in both sets of prints. It was him."

Nesbitt frowned. "Criminal record tracing back to Albania? Any thoughts?"

Devlin strode forward. "Past criminal convictions mean four things." He dramatically extended his fist. "One." He unclenched his thumb. "In the big house he did a lot of press-ups and became comfortable around violence. Ideal training for hired muscle. Two." The index finger popped out. Andy had almost forgotten Devlin's strange theatre of the inane. It was good to be back. "Pursued by the law, Sokov had to keep moving. First Albania, then, you know, other places. Until finally, Edinburgh. Three." The middle finger stabbed forward. "No clean documentation banjaxed his employability, and a succession of low-paid positions left him receptive to murderous payoffs like those offered by John Reynolds. Four." His ring finger uncurled awkwardly, only fully extending when he decided to unlock his pinkie as well. But then Devlin's voice faltered, presumably finding the flat-pack shelving of his mental warehouse devoid of fresh ideas. "Four ..." He stalled again, searching for inspiration on the faces of his colleagues. His panicked gaze lingered for a moment on the bruising above Andy's right eye and then he smiled. "Four. After life on the lam, the unexpected sight of a detective rising above the sand dunes was a red rag to a rhino." Devlin stepped back, relieved and apparently satisfied.

Andy noted the way Devlin continued to walk a line between plausible and preposterous. It was almost a superpower.

Nesbitt arched an eyebrow. "Aye. Maybe. We'll stick with our two-pronged approach. Specifically, myself, DS Devlin and DC Burns will work the theory that both McKay and Wood were murdered by John Reynolds as part of a commercial grudge against the council. In this scenario Sokov was his accomplice. DI Lorimar and DS Petrakis will pursue the alternative possibility that Yurik Sokov orchestrated these and possibly other killings for reasons unknown. However, we remain *one team*. So we work together and share resources whenever required. Any additional progress to report?"

Petrakis said, "We expect something from the Balrannoch today. The security manager has been checking tapes and interviewing staff all weekend trying to dig up information on Sokov. He should get it finished this morning at some point."

When Lenny Burns raised his hand, even he followed its upward progress with an expression close to disbelief. "Just a wee thing chief. When you were out in Kirkcaldy today? Sokov's bank uploaded statements for the account he used with the Queensferry Marina. They're on the incident system."

"That sounds like work for a desk jockey," Andy said, "I'll pick those up. But there is another thing nagging me that I'd like to place on the schedule."

Nesbitt frowned. "Which is?"

"I'd like to go back to Corryvreckan, the guest house where Radu Dudnic stayed. Maybe another resident knew something about his connection with Sokov."

Nesbitt nodded. "OK. Point noted. I'm not committing you'll be involved personally though. I'll think about it." He addressed the team. "Anything else?"

Devlin raised a hand. "Tricia Black called in. Her phone received another message *purportedly* from John Reynolds." He turned to Andy. "Did you like the 'purportedly'? I put that in especially for you Link-man. Love and peace."

Nesbitt suppressed a chuckle. "Is she still up here?"

Devlin nodded. "With relatives in Melrose. She's has a couple of John's things with her too. Might be handy if the lab-boys need anything. Anyway, she's avoiding going home because of the media circus. She blames DI Lorimar for that, but she'll talk fine to me"

"OK. DS Devlin, get to the Borders and meet with her on those new messages. It's time she gave us her phone I'm afraid, so persuade her. Bottom out the technology aspects of the messages with DS Petrakis when you get back. DC Burns, you're with me. We have to get through the remaining statements out at the Marina. DI Lorimar, as discussed, you're confined to your desk, so hold the fort and run through those bank statements. I expect regular contact from everyone. Nobody, I repeat, *nobody*, is allowed onto any bloody islands this week. I will check your shoes for sand, I kid you not. Stay safe. Dismissed."

24

CLEANING HOUSE

MONDAY 12TH SEPTEMBER, 09:26

They saw him board the train, but they didn't see *him*. They saw only what he wanted them to. A smiling man in boyish clothes: the long shorts with too many pockets, the garish T shirt, the baggy cardigan. He wore a baseball cap with long hair falling from the back. That hair was not his own, but the heavy stubble he'd grown naturally. He would get used to the itch of a beard.

Every eye falling upon Yurik Sokov found just another tourist. Nothing worth distracting them from their crossword or their coffee or their telephone. Nobody worth remembering. This was, after all, the purpose of camouflage. He knew very well how to match the terrain.

In a city, to be invisible was to seem harmless; harmlessness was reassuring and quickly forgotten. If anyone caught his eye, he smiled. If anyone talked, he nodded and smiled some more. When they arrived at Waverley Station, nobody noticed him at all.

Even invisible, this was not a city he had planned to visit again. Not after leaving the detective on the island. That was a failure, but one he understood. The helicopter changed his priorities at the point of the kill. Because of that failure, today's task was even more important, and he would allow nothing to get in his way.

A businessman jostled past, hurrying to somewhere unimportant. His status was pinned to the cuffs of his shirt, little glints of gold undercut by the desperate sheen of sweat. So like Cochrane.

On the South Bridge, throngs of people squeezed past, rushing like ants. He wondered how they lived this pretence every day? But their fake urgency made his task more real.

Cochrane was one of their tribe. Always a film-set man, all shine at the front and no substance behind. Yurik no longer worked on his production. He no longer pointed his lights or carried his equipment or brought him his cast. And he no longer spoke from Cochrane's script. He'd performed for Cochrane before, but always, his loyalty belonged to Maxim.

The bus to Gilmerton crawled, struggling down the arteries of a city narrowing daily through disease. This place was infected by the meaningless lives of the parasite herd.

He disembarked and strode past the clinic, ignoring the boarded windows, taking the lane behind and unlocking the first gate. In the shed, the holdall was ready. It contained the coal and the paint, the slates and newspaper, the petrol can and the hatchet. All prepared three years ago, waiting patiently for this day, its purpose finally arrived.

On the back door of the clinic he sprayed the words, then smashed the lock. When inside he sprayed some more.

In the rear room he built a hearth with the slates, carefully arranging twists of newspaper, then piling some coal and wood on top. This he lit naturally. Whether it established or not was unimportant. But now, he must hurry.

The installation must be destroyed.

He opened the under-vault of the donor platform, and crammed in fist after fist of coal and kindling. This he doused with petrol, trailing the liquid line back into the hallway. Crossing to the front room he repeated for the client platform on the other side of the wall. From there he drizzled another line of petrol and joined it with the first, splashing the remainder by kicking the can around the clinic floor.

When he threw the match it caught immediately.

He left and did not look back. His task today was only half-complete. He must now renew his acquaintance with an old friend.

AFTER NEARLY A WEEK out of action, Andy was more enthusiastic about bank statements and telephone calls than he'd ever have thought possible. He had his sandwiches. He had his cup of tea. He had the statement in the system ready to wade through.

But first he called the Balrannoch to check on Pete Cunningham's investigations. The security manager sounded relieved to hear from him. "Andy! Thank God you're OK! I heard you took a bit of a beating?"

"What doesn't kill you makes you stronger. Except for two thirds of the time, according to my consultant. But I'm the lucky one third. So, I'm back."

"Glad to hear it. I felt bloody awful, given I handed you the vicious bastard's photograph to begin with."

"Ach, forget that. You've been nothing but helpful. I'll admit I'm keen on meeting Mr Sokov again. With more backup next time. But DS Petrakis mentioned you might have something for us?"

"Yup. So I've personally interviewed everyone who worked with him. He was known only as Radu Dudnic, he kept himself to himself, didn't chat much, didn't socialise. He wasn't here very long, and his cover remained completely intact."

"So far, so bollocks then."

"The news doesn't improve much I'm afraid. While I did the interviews, one of my lads finished going through the footage, and he reported no significant conversations involving Sokov."

Andy's interest was piqued. "How did your lad define significant?"

A long sigh. "I knew this was coming. I told him." His voice was resigned. "He'd decided off his own bat that he was only interested in conversations longer than a minute or so."

"But there were conversations? Short ones?"

The sigh again. "I knew you were going to ask that too."

"Did he give you any details on what those short conversations were? Who they were with?"

"OK Andy, I hear you. Give me a bit more time. I think my guy made some bookmarks in the system. I'll go back through things myself."

After the call concluded, Andy felt guilty about sending the security manager chasing his tail, but something in that footage might help find a killer. Anyway, Cunningham was ex-police. He knew the ropes.

All of which meant the time had arrived to wade through those bank statements. He brought them on-screen and examined a more than three-year history of Yurik Sokov's monetary transactions. They were mostly mundane: regular deposits from the marina, small withdrawals here and there. But an early transaction with a reference of *MMSLTD* caught his eye, due to the substantial payment amount of fifty-five thousand pounds. That transaction needed to be traced and identified, so he began a follow-up request to the bank referencing the existing warrant. It would likely take twenty-four hours or more to get a response, with the potential outcome that they'd need to approach a different bank. Still, a payment of that size was a stone you didn't leave unturned.

When the phone rang on Petrakis's desk, Andy tried the pickup code twice before rising with an involuntary grunt and walking past two banks of desks to take the call the old-fashioned way. "Detective Lorimar, Edinburgh CID?"

"Hello. This is Marie Schmidt from the International Assistance Unit. I'm looking for Detective Petrakis?"

"She's out right now. We're working the same case. Are you calling about the fingerprint match or Radu Dudnic?"

"About Mr Dudnic. He meets the definition of a misused identity under Schengen Information System rules. We passed your enquiry to the Romanian Police and they checked with his family. We have the translated report from them, and it looks reasonably comprehensive."

"Could you give me the headlines?"

"They spoke to his mother and his girlfriend. Mr Dudnic hasn't been home for seven months. But they had a contact from him on the 8th August, when he sent across money for them. They thought everything was fine. Until the police visit, that is."

"What kind of contact did he make?"

"An email arrived telling them to expect the money."

"How much money did he send, and how did he do it?"

"Eleven thousand Romanian Leu, so more than two-thousand pounds. It was an international money transfer straight to his girlfriend's bank account."

"As far as we were aware Mr Dudnic was homeless, and a drug user. Does the report indicate where he got the money?"

"His email said he was working in medical research and was sending his wages that they should use to look after the baby."

Andy paused, trying to process the idea. He'd given a medical research line to the Housing Options team. "Wages? He said wages?"

"According to the report. Politia Romana conclude with a statement that the family are very concerned. His child will be born next month. They have sent recent photographs of him to assist with the search. They want Mr Dudnic to contact them as soon as possible, and for your team to send an update as soon as you have one. You can liaise via our department."

Andy made arrangements to have the report transferred to the incident system. Then he tried to make sense of things, but it wasn't easy. A little over six weeks ago, a case worker at the Housing team had found Radu Dudnic on drugs. She'd disregarded his 'medical research' claim as a cover for substance abuse. People do lie about such things, but it seemed he'd repeated the same claim to his family, and sent them a not-insignificant amount of money. Had Dudnic been selling drugs? Even if so, why write to his family with such an outlandish employment story when any other job would have been more believable?

What they could prove was that one week after the email to Romania, Yurik Sokov joined staff at the Balrannoch using Dudnic's passport. Sometime in the week between the 8th and 15th of August, Radu Dudnic had simply vanished. His family wanted an update, and they would get one, but the signs were not good.

LATER, Petrakis returned grinning triumphantly. "I showed their journo the death certificate and *The Weasel* squeaked and fell over. They'd had another phone call on Sunday evening urging them to publish, so they're very relieved they didn't."

"That goes double for me. Do we have a source for Sunday's phone call?"

"Coin-operated payphone in Gillespie Crescent. No live CCTV nearby. It's a dead end."

"We'll add that to our growing collection."

Petrakis shrugged, before frowning. "I contacted the chief to ask what next. And I got a weird message back." She read off the screen, "The scowl and the pussycat fetched his clothes, in a beautiful pea green car."

Andy smiled. "He's been chirpy since Kirkcaldy. That's his idea of whimsy. He wants you to accompany me back to my place to pick up my stuff. He's forcing me to relocate to his flat for a few days."

"Fair enough. And I suppose I am driving a green car. But why am I the pussycat?"

"You get off lightly. I'm the scowl for God's sake!"

She appeared genuinely upset. "But ... scowls are cool. I scowl too you know."

And she was right. She demonstrated it all the way down to the car.

INSIDE HIS FLAT, Andy ushered his colleague past the mess of a cupboard he'd searched on his return from the hospital. In his bedroom he grabbed a duffel bag and began cramming clothes inside. Petrakis briefly patrolled the windows to check if the flat was being observed, but she spent most time eyeballing the interior decor. This made him feel distinctly uncomfortable, since it wasn't a place he ever intended to entertain guests.

The austere nature of his bedroom appeared to bother her. "I pegged you as a reader. But where are your books?"

"At the public library down the road mostly. Works for me."

"When did you move in here?"

"Twenty-five years ago, roughly."

She was quiet for a moment. "I thought it might have been more recent. Your flat's rocking a not-yet-fully-unpacked look."

"Sorry. I just don't have that much stuff." Hopefully they could leave it at that.

"Did you actually choose this wallpaper? With the stripes and that weird pattern thing, your bedroom is basically a satanic barcode."

Nobody would ever accuse Petrakis of not calling it as she saw it. He considered the peeling wallpaper above the door. Try as they might, these walls were unlikely to ever strip themselves. "Not one of my better choices. I might change it eventually." He doubted it, though. She sat on the bed while he packed, snooping apparently complete.

But she scuffed something on the floor "Oh. Sorry. I stood on this." She picked it up. "Were you looking at photos?"

Shit.

He'd only brought the album out last night. He didn't have many photographs of his mother, and the ones he did have had gathered dust. They'd always reminded him of the newspapers after she vanished. Lurid headlines had stared back at him whenever he saw her face, so he'd stopped looking.

Then, after the hospital, he'd thought maybe he could see her clearly again. But that didn't mean he wanted to get into the whole thing with Petrakis. "That's just some old stuff lying about. I'll get it out of your way."

She flicked a page. "Is this your Mum and Dad?"

"No. That's my old boss Jimmy. And his wife Ilsa."

"Ooh. Boss in the photo album." It was a weak attempt at humour. She didn't realise she was walking on razor blades.

"I stayed with them for a bit. After ..." But his mouth simply stopped, like a horse refusing a fence. Funny how he still struggled to get the words out, forty years later.

"After what?"

"After ..." He always assumed everyone he worked with knew. That was ridiculous of course, to suppose folk still talked about it, but that was how he felt. For him, it was an event too huge to get past, so he'd simply turned away. But that didn't deal with it. It had always remained, a looming presence at his shoulder.

Her expression suggested she was finally reading the signals; she'd turned over a bigger rock than she'd intended. "Look. Sorry. We don't have to talk about... unless it's something I should know?"

"I don't know if you should or shouldn't. It is what it is. My mum vanished when I was young. I don't normally look at photographs. I was in care for a while, and Jimmy and Ilsa kept an eye on me, took me in eventually. Jimmy got me started in the police. Long time ago."

She was shocked. "Vanished? Did you ever—"

"No." He looked towards the window, surprised to find himself swallowing, forcing down the catch in his throat. The sky was darkening, dirty clouds trying to extinguish the light. "Please, Elisia ... can I have the album back?"

She closed the book and returned it. "Sorry."

Andy took it and threw it under the bed again, this time making sure no edges were visible. Then he zipped up his duffel bag and hoisted it off the bed. Not a lot of weight, considering it was everything he needed.

Petrakis broke the silence. "I suppose we better get you to the chief's flat."

Outside Nesbitt's place in Newington, they parked between a large communal bin and a mound of rubble from ongoing road maintenance. Petrakis unclipped her seat belt, but Andy said, "For God's sake! I can drag a bag up a flight of stairs!" The photo album discussion had left him raw. She seemed to understand and returned his wave before driving away.

The walls of Nesbitt's block were a freshly painted two-tone, burgundy below and cream above. Coordinating maintenance in his own communal stair was a challenge Andy had never been able to face, so he'd left it to someone else. Unfortunately, so had they.

Two floors up, he rang the bell. When the door opened, Miguel stood smiling, as tall and slim as ever. His spare frame went against Andy's preconceptions for a chef; Nesbitt had once said his partner lived off sips and spoonfuls. "Andy! Ay-ay-ay!" Miguel stepped back, regarding the bruising on Andy's face. "You been through wars, huh?"

"I'm on the mend. Good to see you, Miguel." He extended his hand, but his host had already moved in for the hug leaving Andy no option but to open his arms and thank God for strong painkillers.

Miguel led him through to the living room. "Brian's not home yet, but I got oven on. You like cod? I do it simple, wrap with Serrano ham, with aubergine, garlic stuffed olives, capers, tomatoes." Andy didn't like causing a fuss, but it seemed Miguel misinterpreted his expression. "Oh no! Don't worry! Proper tomatoes, from Andalusia. Flavoured by Spanish sun, not Fife drizzle. You love them. You like flavour, huh?"

It was a question with only one answer, so Andy nodded meekly. "Sounds lovely."

Miguel grinned and slapped his shoulder. "You deserve something lovely. Someone tries to kill you, then what? Hospital food? A bad joke, huh?"

"People don't bed-block for the haute cuisine, that's for sure."

"Haute? Hot cuisine would be a start! My surgery for broken ankle. Brian tell you?" He hadn't, so Andy shrugged. "In overnight, and they serve this strange gazpacho. Except it was cock-a-leekie. Huh? Cock-a-leekie? Cold? I Spanish. I know this very wrong. Insult both our traditions at same time, huh?" A timer sounded next door and he left the room.

The sounds of Miguel pottering about in the kitchen made Andy slightly ashamed. Firstly, that he was the cause of this disruption and secondly that his complete understanding of award-winning culinary skill could fit inside the words 'pottering about'. He shouted through, "You've got the night off?"

"Not all night! My sous-chef handle early sittings. But we got important booking that I attend later." The walls reverberated with an impressively loud slurp. "Aah! *Muy sabroso!*"

Andy was relieved when, eventually, Nesbitt arrived home. Miguel was great, but they didn't know each other well enough for the conversation to transcend small talk unaided. "Hi Brian, I'm being well looked after here."

"Good for you." Nesbitt scowled. "What a bloody day. Every person at that marina thought Sokov was a great guy. All of them, completely scoobied. Waste of bloody time." Aromas wafted temptingly from the kitchen. "Did Miguel put his toys down long enough to show you the spare room?"

The shout of protest was good natured. "Hey! I'm making a masterpiece!" Pans and spoons continued to clatter.

Nesbitt sighed. "I'll take that as a no." Andy followed his friend to the other end of the hallway, where he was given a set of keys and a run-through of his new accommodation.

DINNER WAS BETTER, by far, than anything Andy could ever have created for himself. For him, food was just fuel, important for sustenance but no more than that. He enjoyed this reminder that there was another way to exist. Seeing the effort, care and precision that had gone onto his plate, he knew he'd received a gift. "This is absolutely stunning, Miguel. You're a genius."

Nesbitt frowned and pushed away his plate. "Well. It could have been worse. But I'd have used haddock rather than cod."

Miguel responded with mock outrage. "I rescue you from La Cabina and I get these thanks?"

Andy saw the look that passed between them and reckoned he'd cracked their code. "La Cabina? I take it that's Spanish for closet?"

Nesbitt nodded. "Weird and surreal Spanish for closet, maybe. It's this guy's favourite film. Bizarre thing from the seventies. Sick puppy."

Miguel pulled an imploring face. "But you fell for my sick-puppy eyes, didn't you?"

Nesbitt threw his napkin, scoring a direct hit. "I did. God help me."

Seeing them together was an education. His friend seemed lighter somehow, freed, for a time, from the dark context of a criminal investigation. Andy had known him at home before his break-up but this was different. He sparked off Miguel in a playful way that Andy struggled to keep up with. They talked about books, television, music, cinema, flitting prolifically from one topic to the next, following associations visible only to themselves. Apparently, even a lumbering house guest couldn't put a downer on things. He was happy for them.

After coffee, Miguel tapped his watch and stood. "Well, gents, I got my booking. Glad you feel better Andy. Maybe next time you come over to mine?"

Andy shook Miguel's hand. "I'd like that. I can't imagine what you could achieve if you weren't stuck with Brian's stone-age kitchen."

"Andy! Andy! You so right. I tell him. These pots are for banging at nursery, not for feeding people."

Nesbitt smiled and stood. "I'll nursery you two in a minute!" He leaned over into an embrace. "Good luck tonight Migs. How you fixed for the rest of the week?"

"Tomorrow another big night, but if Andy's settled, you could come over to mine Wednesday after nine?"

"Deal." They kissed briefly and Miguel left.

After a final lick of his spoon, Andy stood. "I'll get these washed."

The chief began to protest, but then shrugged. "OK. I'll dry."

while Andy mopped he realised Nesbitt's Newington flat was even less peaceful than his own on Ferry Road. Their conversation struggled to compete with fire sirens streaking past in the street outside. "The water fairies are out in force tonight."

Nesbitt frowned. "Some poor bugger's chip pan probably. You were right about the marina by the way; Sokov had the run of that place. He turned up at all hours, did what he liked. Whenever he took out a boat it was assumed to be maintenance. One person even saw him painting his own van and thought nothing of it."

Andy nodded. "Someone else paid him money, you know. There's a big transaction in his bank statement from three years back. I'm trying to identify the source. Could be something or nothing."

Nesbitt put the dishcloth over his shoulder and yawned. "Anything from the Balrannoch?"

"Sokov didn't have connections among the staff, but there's possibly some interaction with guests. I'm waiting for details." Andy racked a salad bowl before continuing. "And I heard from IAU. The

Romanian Police interviewed Radu Dudnic's family. He didn't make it home." He rinsed some cups and glasses then decided to venture a suggestion. "You've drawn a line under the marina now. But we're not far from Corryvreckan here. How about, tomorrow morning, you and I sniff around the guest house, draw a line there too?"

Brian gave him a firm stare. "That's your idea of desk duty, is it?"

"Ah. C'mon. I'll have a big brave minder with me."

The DCI dried the last of the dishes before answering. "OK. You've talked me into it. Time for a last cuppa?"

In the living room they reviewed the progress on Devlin's theory, but Nesbitt scowled. "The truth is we've plateaued. We've not proved or disproved anything, and we're exactly where we were."

"Maybe this new message to Tricia Black will—"

"I wish. More claiming responsibility, but nothing to prove it was from Reynolds. We've got her phone now, so we made a move."

Andy frowned. "Started a dialogue? Pretended to be his wife?"

"Not quite. He's been ignoring her messages. He contacts only when he wants to. So, we've tried to shake him up a bit. We replied, clearly identified ourselves, just to see the effect. If any."

The attempt made sense to Andy. Whoever had the phone would know the police were involved. "Worth trying." He paused for a minute. "Is that another siren? What the hell's going on out there?"

The chief was already dialling. "I'll ask dispatch what they know." He spoke for a few minutes then hung up. "Where is this guest house exactly?"

Andy felt a chill. "Prestonfield Grove."

"I'm regretting that wine now." Nesbitt sighed. "I think we've got ourselves an evening stroll."

IT DIDN'T TAKE LONG. They just followed the flashing lights and the sound of sirens. Two uniformed officers stood at the head of the road behind a line of yellow hazard tape, while curious onlookers clustered at the boundary. This was the same street Andy had visited, but reimagined by a surrealist. Water-spray rainbows hung in smoky twilight, while fire suits shuttled between glowing street lamps and the urgent flashing of emergency vehicles.

He knew before they arrived that the blaze would be at Corryvreckan. His gut told him, and he trusted his gut. It reliably cried 'horse' whenever a stable door smacked his face.

Stepping inside the taped perimeter, he steered Nesbitt away from an angry voice behind them shouting "I told you! You should have condemned the place!" The words echoed as they moved on.

At the guest house itself, the hoses still blasted through an open door on the right of the building. Most of the windows were flung open too, and one was smashed. Black clouds billowed from every opening.

If this was a clean-up job, then what had he missed? And could he have stopped it? After the attack on Cramond Island, events had followed in waves. Was this fire just another crashing swell from the failed attempt to kill him? Or perhaps he was self-obsessed, and this was all just pure coincidence. But to see the last address of Radu Dudnic transformed to a smoking ruin did not feel like coincidence.

When a firefighter approached the nearest engine, the detectives identified themselves. The man unlatched his breathing apparatus. "Two of your guys are over there." He pointed towards the officers at the perimeter. "We filled them in." He sighed and rubbed his face, leaving a streak of grime in the sweat.

Andy said, "We're working a specific case involving this guest house, so we needed to speak to someone who'd been inside. Could you give us a summary?"

"Sure. Looks like a gas explosion. A leak concentrates over time. Someone lights a match or whatever. Bang."

"But does anything look suspicious? Any deliberate tampering?"

"Couldn't say for sure. The kitchen is totalled, and we think it started there, probably at the oven. The house is unsafe now. You can't go in."

Nesbitt said, "What about the outside of the building. Any sign of a break-in?"

"Not obviously. Plenty of signs of a break-out though." He nodded at a huddle of the Corryvreckan residents, standing in a nearby garden while paramedics moved among them. Nesbitt left to speak to the survivors, so Andy continued the questioning. "Any serious casualties?"

"One guy. His window was open but looks like he stumbled trying to reach it. We fetched him on a stretcher and put him in the ambulance. Caretaker, we think."

A caretaker. Marion Greyburn hadn't mentioned she had one, but then, in a second swipe from that stable door, Andy realised he hadn't asked. A caretaker would be a useful person for Sokov know if he wanted to access all areas, but also the kind of person who might eventually become a loose end. "When you sent him away, was he conscious? Talking?"

"No chance... he was in a bad way. The paramedics didn't call it though. He'll be at the Royal by now. He could have been lucky, you never know."

Andy was about to join Nesbitt, but turned back with a final thought. It was possible, if someone was setting fires to cover their tracks, that there might have been a blaze or two elsewhere. "Did your squad spot any unusual incidents over the last day or two? Anything that could have been deliberate?"

But beyond dropped fags and faulty wiring the man's best offering was a fire in a storage unit at the Jenners Depository on Balgreen Road. It started as a bit of a locked room mystery, but even he admitted it was probably just shifting weight in a box containing a camping stove. He shouted a colleague over who might have something more promising. "Rab, can you tell this detective about that old dentist's?"

The man nodded. "Oh aye, it was up just off Gilmerton Road. The place was boarded up, but looked like kids had broken in. Ransacked a shed. They left graffiti. GYT? Gilmerton Young Team? Is that a thing?".

Andy shrugged. "Probably." In a my-first-gang-name kind of way. "So a break-in by kids who start a fire? Sure of that?"

The firefighter turned slightly spiky at being forced to clarify. But the only details he had were circumstantial, and he couldn't know who did it, or even whether the burglar and fire-raiser were connected. His face hardened. "Two of your guys from Howdenhall Road attended and wrote this up. They even took some photographs. I'm surprised you don't know this already."

Because we're all a big hive mind, of course. But Andy bit his tongue and kept writing. The story of the fire was odd. Someone had made a hearth out of roof slates sitting on the floorboards. When the firefighter revealed that spilled petrol had contributed to the blaze, Andy balked. "Petrol? That's from an arsonist's toolbox, surely?"

"There was a petrol mower in the shed they broke into, which explains the petrol can. So arson or arseing about? The idiots had kicked it like a bloody football all over the shop."

It was halfway plausible. You don't spend time in the emergency services without adjusting your low-water mark for human intelligence. He could imagine someone who made the hearth getting more than they bargained for when they tried to light it. But then again, he could also imagine this was all bullshit to cover the place being torched for other reasons entirely. "Was there anything else unusual there?"

"Aye. They'd been keeping coal inside a couple of aluminium units. They went up too."

"So like storage boxes? Or shelf units?"

"Not like that at all. Unusual things. They were back to back either side of a wall. Looked like they'd been around two metres tall, by less than half that wide. Leaning against the wall like a ramp, so the storage was all at the bottom."

"Any clue what they were used for?"

"Nah. They were badly melted by the time I saw them. I assume they'd been some kind of dental equipment? You could see the holes in the wall where both sides had been connected."

Andy resolved to pull further details from the police report. He thanked the men and they headed back to rejoin the rest of their squad.

Since Nesbitt was busy speaking to the residents, Andy introduced himself to a paramedic administering oxygen to people sitting on the grass. "How goes it?"

"Better than it could have been. Another ambulance is coming to take two more away for tests. Carbon monoxide, but I think they'll be OK. They got out. Unlike the night manager, or whatever he was."

"So he's in bad shape?"

The paramedic frowned and stepped away from his patients. He spoke quietly. "I wouldn't expect to interview him, put it that way. Looks like he slipped climbing out of the window, cracked his head, his nose was smashed. He was in there unconscious for a long time." He paused, looking around again. "Carbon monoxide does a lot of damage fast."

"So maybe he panicked, fumbled his escape attempt. But based on the injuries, could there have been an assault?"

"It's possible. I've seen this kind of thing more than once though, and the firefighters said there was blood on the window surround. It seems consistent with a slip."

Andy wanted to check for physical evidence in the caretaker's room. But the open fire hoses had precisely zero respect for investigative protocols. The chances of finding anything definitive in there were now slim. He had to hope the caretaker pulled through, because a statement might be the only way to get to the bottom of what happened here.

He turned to find Nesbitt scowling at his back. "I've nothing much to report, I'm afraid. They heard the bang, smelled the smoke, panicked and fled the house. They were all in their rooms when it happened. Only the caretaker had access to the kitchen. But he's dead."

Andy froze. "I heard he'd been taken to the hospital."

"Me too. So I called the Royal. DOA."

That put paid to the idea of getting a statement. "He could have been assaulted."

"I knew you'd think that. But apparently the cooker was old. This could be just as it seems. A coincidence."

He couldn't tell if Nesbitt really believed that or just wanted to. Adding more strands to this spider's web wasn't something anyone would relish. But either way, belief didn't matter. They needed hard evidence, and their best chance of that was cooling on a slab.

25

FORMAL STATEMENTS

TUESDAY 13TH SEPTEMBER, 12:05

Depressed after a morning chasing down details relating to the Corryvreckan fire, Andy was relieved when Pete Cunningham called in from the Balrannoch. "I finished my second sweep through the security footage, and I found Sokov a few times. There were no long conversations, and nothing obviously meaningful."

"Your guy wasn't too far off base then?"

"Not too far. I found some conversations with the back of house manager, but he didn't spend any time speaking to other staff. However ..."

"I'm listening."

"On two occasions he talked to a guest."

"The same guest each time, or different?"

"The same. Now bear in mind, a second conversation might just be a 'hello again' thing."

"Who was the guest?"

"Right. D'you remember the old guy in the white top hat and tail-coat? We saw him checking the Robin McKay footage. You said he was desperately seeking Ginger Rogers or something?"

Bells were ringing. It wasn't an image he'd tried to commit to memory, but it was in there all the same. "Yeah. I remember." So a strong silent type whose job was to remain away from the public was captured twice speaking to the same guest. "Do we have a name?"

A sigh. "So we've been here before. I matched check-in time-stamps against reception footage, and that guest was in suite 552, one of the rooms block-booked by Daniel Cochrane."

"But you've no names for those occupants, right?"

"Correct. There was some commercial non-disclosure thing."

"Were these long conversations you captured?"

"Short. They might be nothing at all. But given the situation, I thought you'd want to add it to the circumstantial pile in case you find a use for it later."

After replacing the handset, Andy considered what he'd heard. He disliked Daniel Cochrane, so needed to avoid exercising any personal bias, but the anonymity of those block-booked rooms continued to grate. If the conversations captured had been lengthy, they might have represented sufficient reason to tangle Cochrane in the Sokov net. But with Sokov still on the run it was critical to focus their efforts and avoid distraction. Diverting resource to Cochrane right now just didn't seem justified.

Shortly after, when the previous evening's fire recaptured his thoughts, he called Doctor Nassar. She sounded spritely. "Good Morning DI Lorimar! I received that unexpected corpse you sent me."

"Ah. Good. Have you—"

"I have. I imagine you're wondering whether the chap was killed by something more than a stumble leaving a burning building."

"That's about the size of it. Opinion?"

"It's possible, but I can't be definitive."

Nothing was ever definitive in this bloody maze. "OK. What do you have?"

"Firstly, carbon-monoxide poisoning was the direct cause of death, no doubt. But he took a serious crack to the front of his head, more than we'd normally expect from a simple fall."

"How much more?"

"He suffered a severe fracture of the lateral orbital margin. That's a strong bone which usually withstands common or garden injuries. He also had a nasal fracture, which was the source of most of the bleeding reported at the scene. A broken nose is a painful mess, but the orbital fracture is the real story here. It speaks to considerable force. Such an injury will easily render a victim unconscious. And a burning building is the wrong place to pass out."

"Is it possible, say, that the head injury was caused by a third party? Could our caretaker have been a victim of assault?"

"Based on my examination, his face impacted an unyielding surface, probably not a fist but a windowsill or frame would fit. Could he have been forcibly rammed against such a surface? Absolutely. An assault is certainly possible. Lividity on the back of his head plus visible bruising on an arm suggests he may have been grabbed and pushed. However, he was found on his back and manhandled by the fire service to extract him from the building, so we also have innocent explanations for those marks. And I found no obvious defensive wounds. If there was an assault it was brief and brutally efficient."

A momentary flashback to the beach. If Sokov were involved, brutal efficiency was guaranteed. But he had to avoid simply painting his own nemesis into the shadow and smoke of Corryvreckan. He needed to remember what was being said here; these injuries didn't require any assault to have taken place at all. He needed to remember that a window was flung wide but left unused, and a simple panicked stumble could turn a dash for safety into a fatal head injury. He needed to remember these things, because he couldn't believe them. To stumble with such force? So close to safety? When survival instinct was in control of your body?

He couldn't believe it, but that didn't mean he could disprove it.

LATER, the blink of an incoming notification drew him to check the incident system. Sokov's bank had returned with welcome news. They were also responsible for the account which had remitted Sokov's fifty-five-thousand pound windfall, so there was no need to serve the warrant elsewhere.

Opening the supplied report revealed the organisation behind the payment was *Marine Maintenance Services Limited*. Companies House data revealed the entity had been incorporated four years previously. It had one active director, listed as Archibald Roker.

Then Andy leaned back in his chair and whistled. This company also had a previous director who had resigned in the first year of business. Why the hell had Cochrane been bankrolling a psychopath like Yurik Sokov?

Strangely enough, despite all of Daniel Cochrane's previous Martini-like admonitions to get in touch any time, any place, anywhere, he now appeared oddly unreachable.

On Andy's third call he decided to play hardball. But the receptionist was implacable. "He's still out of the office and I've no idea when he'll be back. Perhaps if you explained why you need to speak to him?"

"I doubt Mr Cochrane would wish a police matter to become the subject of office gossip."

The woman was supremely unfazed. "You needn't worry about gossip. I'm his personal assistant. I schedule all of his availability."

Andy quipped, "I guess you know where all the bodies are buried?" When telephonic tumbleweed rolled in judgemental silence he tried another approach. "If you schedule all of his availability why don't you know where he is now or when he'll be back?"

"He's an independent man which makes my job challenging. If

you can't clarify your requirement, I could perhaps give you thirty minutes sometime towards the end of next month?"

Fortunately, with what he could now prove, there was no need to be coy. "You need to understand the gravity of this. If I don't hear back from Mr Cochrane within the next twenty-four hours I'll make our interest in him formal. Then it won't be office gossip he's worried about, but newspaper headlines. Am I being clear enough now?"

That dealt with, he grabbed a chamomile teabag and rose to fetch hot water. He had taken only two steps before his mobile phone buzzed against the desk surface. Since he'd called Cochrane from his desk number and left the extension with the receptionist, he picked up intrigued as to who might be calling.

"Hello! Detective Inspector! Daniel Cochrane! I hope you don't mind me calling your mobile. Direct relationships are everything. You've been trying to reach me?" An over-eager tension lay beneath his words. A callback within five minutes suggested he may have been in the office the whole time.

"Mr Cochrane. Didn't reception pass on my details? We should use my professional number for case-related discussion."

"Oh. She'll have written that somewhere I'll never find it. But we exchanged numbers before, and man to man's always best." Andy didn't remember sharing his mobile number, but had given them his handset, so made nothing of it. "Anyway, Inspector, how can I help? Always keen to help, as I said."

"Good, because you'll need to, I'm afraid. We've found something odd involving you that we need to make sense of. When can you come in to make a statement?"

Cochrane's reply was quieter, drained of all bonhomie. "A statement? About what?"

He considered simply demanding Cochrane's attendance, but, curiosity prompted him to fish a little. "We're pursuing a suspect in connection with at least one murder. He recently evaded arrest by brutally attacking a police officer."

Cochrane filled the silence, speaking rapidly. "No. Good God. How awful. Really horrendous. Well. I hope y-your officer is fully recovered."

"He's getting there, Mr Cochrane, but he won't be his happy-go-lucky self until that suspect and his accomplices have been apprehended."

"Yes. Yes. Of course. But how can I help?"

"Bank records reveal one of your companies made a substantial payment to this violent individual."

A long pause. "Are you sure?"

"We're sure."

"When was this payment made?"

"Three years ago."

"That's going back a bit ... but this is bizarre. Is your suspect in the software business? Office services? What did HopperSoft pay him for?"

"Not HopperSoft, Mr Cochrane. Your company 'Marine Maintenance Services'. Ring any bells?"

"Aha!" It was either relief or an approximation of it. "Then it isn't me you need to speak to. Archie Roker works out of the marina at Inverkip. MMS is his baby, not mine. I just provided seed capital and launched the thing."

"Why did you do that?"

Cochrane's voice lightened. "Do you know the dictionary definition for yacht, Detective Inspector? A yacht is 'a hole in the water into which you throw money'. With two of the buggers I found that to be doubly true, so MMS existed to ring fence a potential hemorrhage of capital. To stanch the bleeding, if you will."

"That's perhaps not the best image considering what your employee Sokov has been getting up to."

Cochrane's voice tightened. "No. Quite right. Bad business. The main thing was to offload responsibilities. I didn't want to micromanage the administration. Archie took all that off my hands. Including recruitment decisions."

"In that case, perhaps you could bring Mr Roker down to Fettes? We need to get to the bottom of this."

"We will. I'm sure this is all a horrible coincidence. Archie will set us straight."

"Can you both attend tomorrow morning? Say 10am?"

"Yes."

"Don't need to check with Mr Roker?"

"No. He'll be there. Something like this needs to be dealt with."

After the call, Andy pondered whether Cochrane's certainty around Roker's availability painted the man as something less than a fully independent business owner. It was also curious that Cochrane hadn't asked for more detail on the payment or the suspect. Perhaps the entrepreneur had the confidence of innocence, but a more cynical conclusion would be Cochrane hadn't bothered asking about things he was already fully aware of.

26

EXTRACTION

WEDNESDAY 14TH SEPTEMBER, 09:43

Petrakis tapped the side of Andy's monitor. "Our guy's in reception."

Andy stood. "The interview plan looked OK?"

"Straightforward enough. A standard why-did-you-drop-fifty-grand-on-a-murderous-nutjob dealio."

"That's it in a nutshell. Take the folder to interview room three and I'll bring him through."

The man in reception seemed smaller somehow than his body. He shrank into his waxed jacket as Andy approached, his weather-worn face squirming beneath the imperfect mask of a seaman's beard.

"Mr Roker?" The man's grip was clammy. "I'm DI Lorimar. Is Mr Cochrane with you?"

"Naw. I mean, not yet. He's making his own way here." The man hesitated, staring for a moment. "Sorry. That's some shiner you've got."

"Ach. Life as part of the thin black-and-blue line. Anyway. Let's get started."

Roker peered through the glass doors to the car park. "Can we no just wait? I'd rather wait for Mr Cochrane."

"No need. He suggested that you were the person I should speak to."

"Oh ... well. Aye ... I suppose. But him too. And he'll no be a minute."

"Don't worry, my colleagues DCI Nesbitt and DS Devlin will make sure he's looked after. You're with me and DS Petrakis."

Shock played over the man's features. He'd obviously hoped for moral support. But it was time to break with Cochrane's imagined personal relationship, and formal police interviews were solitary experiences for good reason. He guided his nervous guest towards the interview room.

Roker was silent as they walked, ignoring all attempts at small talk, his hands opening and closing reflexively with each step. It was too early to read into this anxiety. In any investigation, the truth was hidden in an undergrowth of hearsay and unknown connections; nobody enjoyed being part of the thicket.

Petrakis introduced herself as they entered, only to have Roker flinch mid-greeting when the door thunked shut behind him. Evidently, the man was primed for fight or flight. Petrakis calmed things by discussing Roker's journey to Edinburgh, while Andy fetched water for three.

Eventually they got down to business. "We'll be recording our discussion so if I could remind everyone to speak clearly." Andy began the formalities. "DI Andy Lorimar and DS Elisia Petrakis with Mr Archibald Roker. Police Scotland, Fettes Avenue. Commences 10:01. Mr Roker, thank you for attending to make your statement this morning."

The bearded man said nothing.

"We asked you to attend today because a company set up by Mr Daniel Cochrane and yourself, Marine Maintenance Services Limited, made a substantial payment of fifty-five thousand pounds in August 2013 to Yurik Sokov, a suspect in an ongoing murder investigation. Are you clear on why you are here to make this statement?" After a short pause Andy continued. "For the recording, Mr Roker, please respond verbally."

The man's voice quavered as he answered. "Aye. Y-Yes. I know what this is about."

"Did Mr Cochrane give you some background?" Roker looked hunted. "There's no trick in the question Mr Roker, and no restriction on conversations you might have had about this. I'm merely asking what was discussed and how much you know."

"Eh. Right. So we spoke a couple of times by phone last night and then again this morning. Mr Cochrane filled me in on everything."

It was natural they would talk, but three separate calls might suggest an element of coaching. "In that case let's just start on your relationship to Yurik Sokov."

Roker glanced towards the door, swallowing. "We needed someone to look after our boats in Edinburgh because I'm mainly based at Inverkip Marina on the west coast, so it wasn't practical to have me dealing with both. Anyway, Yurik Sokov was the person we found."

"Ok, when you say, *we* found, could you specify which 'we' you refer to?"

"Well ... I found him. But for Mr Cochrane's maintenance."

"What did you hope to get from Yurik Sokov?"

"Eh ... we needed someone to look after the Edinburgh boats because I'm mainly based at Inverkip Marina on the west coast."

The reworded question had received an almost identical answer. It might suggest some rote learning. "Can you describe the circumstances of your first meeting?"

"I'm not sure I remember that."

"You've no idea at all? Was it you who met him first or Mr Cochrane?"

"Me. It was me."

"Where did you meet him?"

"I can't remember. I think he'd been looking for work."

"Work. So Yurik Sokov applied to you in writing? Or he'd spoken to you verbally? What happened?"

Roker paused. "It was verbal, I think. Just a casual approach."

"So Sokov came through the Inverkip Marina while you were working and asked you about a vacancy? Did he also ask others there?"

Again Roker hesitated. "I think I did meet him at the marina, but I think he only spoke to me. I'm not sure anybody else met him."

"Mr Roker. We need to hear what actually happened. Instead you are telling us what you *think* happened. This was not so very long ago. And Mr Sokov is more memorable than you give him credit for." Andy touched his black eye meaningfully and Roker flinched. Memories were imperfect, but this man's responses might be an attempt to eliminate Cochrane from the picture while tying himself to nothing especially concrete.

Petrakis said, "You wanted someone to look after your boats, but were any boats owned by MMS limited?"

"Eh, no. It was just Mr Cochrane's boats. He has a CX-45 sailing yacht in Queensferry, plus a Solseeker-75 motor yacht and tender in Inverkip. MMS was the company we set up to manage them and have them ready when he needed them."

"Do you see MMS as your company, a joint venture or Mr Cochrane's company?"

"No, no. Mr Cochrane just helped set it up. After that he just wanted the job, the maintenance, done. So it was my company, providing services to Mr Cochrane as our sole client."

Andy asked, "So it was Mr Cochrane's money for the setup, and it was Mr Cochrane's money that paid Yurik Sokov?"

Again, a hunted expression. "It was MMS Limited's money. Mr Cochrane provided the initial investment, y'know, the seed capital, but I had complete control of the finances and staff recruitment."

"Did Mr Cochrane meet Yurik Sokov before or after you selected him to perform maintenance?"

"I can't ... can't really remember."

This was hard work. Harder than it ought to be for someone describing their own recruitment decision. "Is it possible that you found Sokov, but Mr Cochrane was the one who decided to hire him?"

"No. All hiring-and-firing was my decision."

"But you can't remember when Mr Cochrane met him, or if he approved of your choice?"

"Not really, but he trusted my judgement. That was what he wanted, to offload the responsibility. He didn't want to micromanage it."

"What's your own relationship to Mr Cochrane?"

The man's shoulders dropped, visibly relaxing, perhaps because the question had no angle on Sokov. "I'd been working at Inverkip when he first started thinking about buying a yacht. We spoke a bit and got on OK, so he hired me to come round the boat-shows to keep him right on his purchases."

Petrakis said, "He trusted you to the point of funding a business and installing you as the managing director. Why did he feel you were qualified?"

Roker bristled, but only as much as his nervousness would allow. "I've been in sailing and boating all my life. Solo, small crew and piloting leisure vessels. I've got an engineering background, so upgrades and maintenance are second nature. I had a sales job with Inverkip Marina, but I did a bit of everything. I know my stuff."

Petrakis nodded. "I understand. It's your specialism. And your reputation. So how did you ensure Yurik Sokov was up to standard? He was a stranger and you had an important client to impress. How did you check this guy wouldn't embarrass you?"

Roker's face flushed slightly. "I ... eh ... I think I asked him, y'know, about his background. And probably his experience."

"And what did he tell you? What did you learn?"

"I ... I don't remember."

Andy asked, "When you hired Sokov, who set the fee for the work? Fifty-five grand is a hefty sum."

Roker looked down. "That was an upfront lump sum. We'd bought his services for a year with that."

"And what did he do that year? You know he was also working for the Queensferry Marina? And since you moored there, presumably you were paying them too?"

"I think so. I'd have to check the dates. I can't remember."

Andy shook his head. "For heaven's sake, Mr Roker! I'm wondering why your responses seem so evasive."

Roker shouted. "See this?" He pointed around the interview room. "I'm finding it bloody stressful! I didn't do anything wrong!"

"I hope that's true, Mr Roker. Because coming in here and not being honest with us, that would be doing something wrong. Obstructing a murder investigation is a serious matter. Are you doing that right now?"

The man answered quietly. "No. I'm nothing to do with anything."

"But Sokov is plenty to do with things. And you employed him. You managed him, presumably. And you definitely paid him. But, curiously, you seem to have virtually nothing to say about him."

"I didn't ... I didn't know him that well. It was all so busy at the time. I was leaving a job I'd been in for years ... The whole MMS thing, I'd never been a director before. It was scary."

"So you needed advice and guidance presumably?"

"Yes, of course."

"And you took a lot of advice from Mr Cochrane?"

Roker froze. "Only ... only about certain things. I made the decisions about hiring and firing."

Andy opened a folder. "I'm going to show you some pictures. Tell us what you know about each one." He placed a photograph on the desk. "This is location A." Roker stared at the exterior of Corryvreckan guest house, before it had been consumed by fire.

His answer was confident. "I don't recognise it."

Andy covered it with an interior shot of the burned-out dentist's surgery in Gilmerton. "This is location B."

Again, no hesitation. "I don't recognise that either."

Andy showed him a shot of the fire-damaged storage unit at the Jenners Depository on Balgreen Road. "Location C?"

"Nope. I can't help with that."

Andy put up a photograph of Radu Dudnic. "Individual D."

"No. Sorry."

Then a Prestonpans CCTV image of a figure in a grey and white balaclava, perhaps on his way to arrange an attack in a hospital. "This is Individual E."

"Again, I can't help you."

Next a still from the Balrannoch showing Sokov in discussion with the unidentified guest. "Individual F."

Roker hesitated. "Well ... that's Yurik."

Andy said, "We know Yurik Sokov. The other man."

"Look, I can't talk about some people. Mr Cochrane has a non-disclosure agreement."

Petrakis frowned and tapped the photograph. "Did you sign it then, this NDA? Are you legally bound by it?"

The man's face reddened. "I don't even know him! I only saw him a couple of times when they were having a yacht party at Inverkip."

"Were you a guest at these yacht parties?"

"No. I just set things up and left them to it."

"Did Sokov attend the parties?"

Roker looked away. "Maybe... I can't really remember."

Andy stood, and signalled Petrakis to do likewise. "Just in case you know something, but you don't want to get in trouble with Mr Cochrane, a couple of points to ponder. Point 1, Mr Cochrane's NDA is a civil contract, but this is a criminal investigation. We couldn't care less about it. Point 2, if you're willing to risk a criminal record, make sure you're protecting people who at least offered you a seat at the buffet."

Roker stared at the officers, panic in his eyes.

Andy leaned forward, putting his weight on the table. "You must have heard someone call this man something. A nickname, a title even. You aren't bound by this non-disclosure stuff. Don't go to the barricades over it."

Roker looked away. "Max. I think they called him Max. But that's all I know."

It wasn't much. But it might be something. "Thank you Mr Roker. Someone will come back to you in a few minutes."

WHILE PETRAKIS WAITED in the corridor, Andy knocked gently on the door. Nesbitt poked his head out. "Goody! Let's compare notes." He signalled to Devlin, who joined them outside.

Andy started. "My opinion is that our guy's holding back. He's too nervous and his answers seem coached. DS Petrakis?"

She nodded vigorously. "Something's wrong. Whether you're an expert in yachts, software or chocolate, you wouldn't make an important hire without performing a technical validation. He doesn't remember enough about that. I don't believe Roker made the hiring decision."

Nesbitt nodded. "Cochrane's full of it too, but in a different way. Plays bullish confidence—"

Devlin interrupted. "But deep, deep, down, his pants are brown. And his reaction to those pictures!" Devlin gaped at Nesbitt, who gaped back.

Andy said, "Well? What about the pictures?"

Nesbitt whistled softly. "He denied knowing Corryvreckan, which seemed kosher. Then Individual E? I'd swear he stiffened before the denial. But most of all, I know you took a punt with that burned out dentist's, but Cochrane lied. He recognised it, and he didn't like seeing it. Not one bit."

"Did he say anything?"

Devlin smirked. "He went grey. The atmosphere in the room changed. The *smell* in the room changed. He shook his head, but his brain had melted."

This was interesting. Roker hadn't reacted at all to the same photograph, and he'd imagined it would draw a blank with Cochrane too. "What about the photographs of the other people?"

"He identified Individual F as a commercial guest covered by non-disclosure, and that he probably bumped into Sokov by accident at the hotel."

Andy nodded. "Snap. Mr F chatting with Sokov was the only photograph Roker recognised. He'd been a guest on Cochrane's yacht apparently. We know he was part of Cochrane's group booking at the Balrannoch, but the NDA means they didn't have a name." Andy turned to Nesbitt. "Any objections to compelling disclosure?"

"No problem. We'll need a warrant to go after the physical contract. In all fairness, a warrant gives Cochrane a *force majeure* that should put him in the clear contractually. The problem is, how certain are we that this old guy is relevant? The sheriff will need a decent justification."

That was the nub of it. Andy wasn't certain. But he was increasingly exasperated at Cochrane swanning through the middle of a murder case protected by a commercial document nobody had even seen. "Can we swap? If you conclude things with Roker, I'd like to ask our Mr Cochrane a couple of questions?"

Nesbitt nodded, although Devlin said, "Now that we've softened him up you mean?" but he stepped aside anyway. Petrakis followed Andy inside.

Cochrane's expression, broken when they first stepped in, quickly assembled itself into a plausible smile. "Detective Lorimar! Nice shiner! But seriously, I'm glad it's you." The man leaned conspiratorially towards them. "So far, with your colleagues, I've been finding this whole business rather heavy-handed!"

"Have you? Apologies. Everyone is tense at the moment. With what's been going on you can probably understand."

Cochrane's face turned peevish. "Yes, of course. But innocent people shouldn't bear the brunt."

Andy nodded agreement. "No. You're correct. Innocent people

shouldn't." He paused meaningfully. "My colleagues mentioned you recognised one of the location photographs. Why was that?"

"I told them I didn't recognise it."

"Yes. They know what you told them. But your reaction revealed otherwise."

Cochrane shifted awkwardly in his seat. "I don't know what you mean. Have we finished? I have business to attend to."

"Just one final point to cover. We saw a person talking to Sokov at the Balrannoch. What can you tell us about Max?"

Cochrane froze. His mouth tightened, but the anger quickly loosened into fear. "But how did you—" He halted, re-establishing control. His eyes narrowed. "I can't discuss any of my guests at the Balrannoch. That was a business conference covered by commercial non-disclosure."

Andy examined the businessman carefully. "Fine. We want to see that non-disclosure agreement." Colour bloomed in Cochrane's cheeks. "Plus a corroborating statement from whoever witnessed it affirming it was signed prior to your meeting at the Balrannoch."

The businessman's right eye twitched. "But I can't show you the agreement. You'll know who I was meeting based on the signatories!"

"That's the point Mr Cochrane. If you don't comply voluntarily within two days, we get a warrant to search your premises."

"I just can't believe this." Cochrane's shoulders slumped.

"You have until Friday close of play, Mr Cochrane. We'll be waiting."

FATHER TURNED his chair to face her. "I hope this is important, Sara. My time for reviewing external research is already so limited." He held up a journal paper. "It transpires Joan may have had a point of sorts. While the herd have no stomach for the countless live trials we needed to resolve graft versus host issues, they make their own kind of progress, some of it striking." The document fell to the desk with a slap. "I have yet to understand the relevance for us however. We start from such a different place."

The technical point Father made came as no surprise. Sara maintained a watching brief on discoveries within Marc's area, and recognised the research. However, she was shocked to hear him acknowledge something only Thomas Hofler had been foolhardy enough to openly state: that Joan Wood's plea to withdraw Marc, to place his fate with emerging conventional treatments, might in fact have worked.

Was he admitting a possible error of judgement? It was an uncomfortable thought, not least because she'd harboured similar misgivings herself. Father's shock decision to eliminate Joan was almost certainly behind Hofler's blunders with McKay: the location of their meeting, the errors over dosing, the messy entanglement with Reynolds. Grief had consequences, although Father seemed blind to that. She let her silence solidify into a change of topic.

When she spoke again, she maintained a neutral tone. Father did not welcome sensationalism. "Cochrane tried to reach you. He has been formally interviewed by the police. He, perhaps in a sign of his state of mind, called us from his car outside their offices." She paused. "He asked why we didn't inform him of the fire at the replenishment clinic. The police had photographs, apparently."

"Then wasn't it wise that we destroyed it? That location has been neutralised. They'll get nothing from there."

She paused again, this time truly unsure of how he would react. "He says Lorimar used your first name."

"My first name?" Father sipped a glass of pure water between pinched lips. Ice chinked at the rim. He swallowed slowly before continuing. "That they know my first name is perhaps less than a crisis. But it is more than I am prepared to overlook."

"They threatened Cochrane with a search warrant for a non-disclosure agreement that does not exist. He wants to be extracted."

"Extracted?" His smile was devoid of mirth. "What is one more global man-hunt between friends?" He exhaled deeply. "I fear our mighty oak has fallen." He opened a drawer in his antique desk. "Reassure him. You will visit to perform this extraction. The letter we prepared will be left at his residence." Sara took the plastic-wrapped letter, folded it carefully and placed it into her satchel. "We have a short-term need of funds until our new prospect in Vienna comes on-stream."

Sara nodded. "I'm sure Cochrane will cooperate."

"Yes. But also his son. He has the channel to Lorimar."

"You wish to maintain that channel?"

"It seems safest. Get the next available flight. Contact Yurik. Arrange for his return when this matter is concluded."

"I will." She turned to go.

"Sara. These are dangerous times for us. We cannot afford to be sentimental."

"I understand. Sentiment is not part of my makeup."

His lips tightened. "I know that to be mostly true. But now." He rapped the surface of the desk. "It is time to dispose of your pet."

"My pet?"

His retort was cold. "Don't be obtuse."

His displeasure was hard to bear. "Marc is not a threat. He was upset about his mother, yes, but he has been estranged from his parents for years."

"Eventually he will ask after his father's absence."

"Perhaps. And then I will sympathise."

Father shook his head. "Hiding your complicity in the man's death? A pet may know its owner better than you realise. The risk is unacceptable."

Sara said nothing. Instead, she controlled her breathing and focused on standing upright. She was ashamed of the feelings his command had unleashed. Father had built the scaffolding that supported the entire structure of her life. She followed his lead. And his mind was set.

He reached across and patted her hand. "Relationships must sometimes be sacrificed for the continuance of the work."

"I see that."

"Good. Then I await a successful conclusion."

AFTER DISEMBARKING AT BAHNHOF STETTBACH, she reached the door of Marc's small flat in a matter of minutes. The apartment was a gift from his parents, bought when he began his university degree. But his life had never progressed as they had hoped, and Sara had secretly feared. All those years, he'd remained, seemingly trapped in her orbit. And she, oddly, and in a way she never fully acknowledged, was trapped herself, unwilling to lose the distant companionship of her solitary satellite.

She hesitated at the door, even though there was no room for delay. She knew she had to do this. Father had given her no choice. It should be simple, but it wasn't.

She rang the bell.

And waited.

When the door opened, Marc was holding his nylon-strung guitar. He doodled with it a lot, writing songs he was too scared to play in public.

His eyes widened. "Sara, hey!" She moved past him and shut the door.

She tried to smile. "Sorry to land on you."

"No, I love it when you ... I mean, it's great to see you."

She hesitated, looking at him for a long moment. Her mouth was dry. "I—I've been thinking about what you said."

His eyes responded, but the rest of his face remained wary. "What I said? About?"

"About us."

He said nothing, holding her gaze. She recognised that uncertainty on his face, because she'd seen it before, many times. Once again, they found themselves balanced on the edge of a question she'd been skirting for years.

Nervously, she filled the silence. "I hoped ... I wanted ... to check the details of your compassionate leave?" Marc was a caretaker at a student housing cooperative. It wasn't too demanding, and it paid his bills. "So ... Wh—When do you return to work?"

His reply was quiet. "Wednesday next. If I can face it. Why?"

Breathe.

Say the words.

Just say them. "I ... I bought you a ticket. Bergen. And ... I've got us a hotel."

"Bergen? Norway?"

She handed him a folder. "You go first, today, get the lie of the land, I'll be there in two days."

He stared at her. Then he looked at the ticket, examined the hotel details. Then he stared at her again. He was surprised. No. Worse. He was shocked into silence.

Her stomach knotted. She never felt this way and it frightened her. And suddenly she knew she shouldn't have done this. That it was irresponsible. That it was folly and it was sentiment and it was defiance. She couldn't do what Father asked, so instead she'd done a crazy, stupid, childish thing. And it was failing.

But Marc kissed her. "Norway! You mean it? For how long?"

Her breath escaped suddenly, a gasp of relief. And then she was laughing and holding and kissing him back. "I'm not sure of every-thing, but I know we need to do this." She couldn't leave him here, alone. Not after Father had made his decision. Father hadn't waited with Joan. How had he put it? 'An unsheathed blade must never rust.' His decisive leadership had brought them through many crises. But this was different. This was Marc.

"You're totally mad. And amazing! I'll pack some things."

She picked up his rucksack and handed it to him. "Quickly! Your flight's in two hours!"

He crammed in some clothes. "You can't come with me now?"

She frowned. "I will, but only as far as departures. I'm flying elsewhere for business. But I'll join you."

He smiled. "Two days? Promise?"

"Two days. Wait for me."

THE FLIGHT to Edinburgh was turbulent but no worse than others Sara had experienced. She idly registered that high winds might even prove beneficial later.

She took a cab to Marchmont Road. From there the short walk to Cochrane's home gave her time to make some preparatory calls. Marc had already landed in Norway and he sounded excited, but she quickly drew the conversation to a close. His warmth was not what she needed; she had a job to do. And it was a job that needed rationality, that needed ice. It was impossible to be that person with Marc in her head.

Despite the winds, the extravagantly named Ridotto Lodge seemed almost peaceful in the evening twilight. But that atmosphere did not extend to its owner. He opened the door barely a crack, scanning the leafy street in both directions before letting Sara enter. Cochrane's whisky was doubtless expensive, but its power as a status symbol plummeted on the way from bottle to breath. He regarded Sara sourly, and then turned away, heading for the living room. She heard the decanter clinking as she followed him.

She decided to play the role he expected of her. "Is it wise, Daniel, this drinking to excess?"

But his defiance, as usual, was underpinned by petulance. "Well? I'm leaving it all behind aren't I? You want me to waste bloody good whisky as well as everything else?" He drained his glass. "What's the plan?"

She sat down. "We're going to Norway. You, me, and Nick."

Cochrane stiffened. "Nick? Who'll run the business?"

The man was a bullying child, without even a basic appreciation of consequences. "If we leave Nick, then after you disappear he'll be arrested. Don't doubt that they will find something. Is he at home?"

"Not yet. He isn't far."

"Then get him here. And call the marina. Tell them a party of three will be taking out your yacht this evening. I will drive. We cannot risk being intercepted on a triviality."

When Cochrane returned he sheepishly handed her a set of car keys. "We'll take the Range Rover, the number plate is already registered at the marina. And Nick's on his way." The man turned to sneer at the wall, the alcohol washing away any final vestiges of propriety. "Hours cooped up in a boat with you? Silver fucking lining for him." He refilled his glass and sagged into a leather armchair. "Who let this fucking shit happen?"

The question was worthless. The fucking shit had happened and they had all played their part. "You should assume that you will have no access to your funds after this evening."

His neck reddened, his anger and disbelief once more inspired by hearing the patently obvious. "No access? None?"

"You are fleeing a murder investigation. So, Daniel Cochrane, software entrepreneur, he ceases to exist this evening. Transfer whatever you can to Zurich now."

Scowling, Cochrane retrieved a laptop from his bookshelves. He hunched over it, muttering as he stabbed at the keyboard. After ten minutes he looked up. "It's done. I've used multiple sheltered accounts. Only Nick and I are signatories. We're not fucking fools." He slammed the screen shut. "All my liquid assets..." Then he smiled grimly. "Well. Not quite all." He let the laptop fall to the floor and headed back to his whisky.

Sara chose to ignore his acting out. "We are almost finished Daniel. It makes sense to pack a bag with some things, plus any small valuables that you can exchange for cash."

He scoffed. "Done already. The bag is on the staircase."

"Then I'll pack the car. Can I advise a shower or a change of clothes?"

"Advise all you fucking want. I'm not leaving one drop of this fucking nectar for the fucking vultures." His pouring was so imprecise, the vultures would find plenty, despite his posturing. "Anyway, my clothes are perfect. The fucking Norwegians appreciate the smell of good booze. Skol!"

Sara pulled on latex gloves and retrieved his fallen laptop. "What technology should we take? We need to dispose of anything that might implicate us." But Cochrane was back in his armchair, past taking advice.

She scouted around the house, retrieving a phone, a secure router and a further two laptops. She crammed them into Cochrane's bag and went out to the garage. A newly bearded Sokov was waiting for her in his cap with the fake hair. "Good evening Yurik. You look suitably ridiculous."

"Thank you. I try."

She handed him the bag and the keys. "These are for the Range Rover. Do you have ...?"

He reached into a pocket of his cargo shorts, and handed her a slim black case. "Is same from hotel, plus extra magic. You need help inside?"

"No. Nick will be here soon."

Back in the living room, Cochrane was slumped in his seat. Moving him to the car would have been problematic, but thankfully, wasn't necessary. Sara decided to make do and began to roll up his left sleeve.

He slurred something unintelligible, before snapping briefly into a facsimile of consciousness. "What? Fuck! Go away!" His glare faded as quickly as it appeared, his eyes drooping. "Let me fucking sleep a bit." He'd made it so easy for her. But then, he'd always been weaker than he supposed. Arrogant, and softened by success.

"Sleep, Daniel. Don't worry." She opened up the black syringe case before tapping at the crook of his left arm. "This makes the extraction more comfortable."

Shortly after the needle broke skin, his head lolled backwards and his breathing slowed. She emptied every drop, leaving the syringe still protruding from his arm. Then, opening her satchel and tearing the letter from its plastic wrap, she pressed Cochrane's unresponsive fingers against the page before placing the sheet on his lap. Finally she moved his hand to grasp the barrel of the syringe. After a final visit to Cochrane's bedroom she decided there was no more to be done. It was time to move.

When she reached the garage, Nick was already unconscious, lying prone across the back seat. She covered him with a blanket, before taking the wheel. She didn't anticipate questions, but if so he'd need to pass for his father. It wasn't unusual for night sailors to catnap before they hit the water. Yurik smiled at her, as excited as a child. "Now. We all go on summer holiday? Yes?"

She said nothing until the garage door closed behind them and the car was idling quietly on the driveway. "You've made this crossing before?"

"No! I've done parts. But now we join parts together." He grinned fiercely. "North Sea. Big fun at this time of year."

Sara knew Yurik's idea of fun would be the wrong side of challenging. As they were undermanned, she would be clipped to the deck alongside him. In Nick's soporific state he'd cause them no trouble down in the cabin.

Trees gusted all around. The winds were wild but Cochrane's yacht was sound and they both knew what they were doing. Speed would be good. She allowed herself a moment to think of their destination and who was waiting for her. She would keep her promise. Two days.

She pressed the accelerator.

27

THE WARRANT

FRIDAY 16TH SEPTEMBER, 17:03

F ive p.m. came and went. Cochrane had been given until the
end of the week to produce his infamous non-disclosure
agreement. And he had failed. What's more he'd been dodging calls.
His office was told on Wednesday afternoon, just after his interview,
that he would be working from home.

Perhaps he'd concluded the threatened warrant was a bluff and
simply decided to call it. But this was a murder investigation, not a
card game. Cochrane had gotten into something his wallet couldn't
buy him out of.

Andy had been cleared to drive by occupational health earlier
that morning, and that ability was about to come in handy. The
Procurator Fiscal's office had arranged they could approach the
recently appointed Sheriff Hoxton directly at his home in Inverleith
before 8pm. This was unusual, but if they wanted to serve the
warrant at Cochrane's house tomorrow morning (and it spoke
volumes that every detective who had spoken to the man *did*), then
they needed judicial sign-off tonight.

Hoxton lived in a semi-detached Victorian villa overlooking the
Botanic Gardens. It was a beautiful part of the city, only twenty

minutes walk but a world away from his own flat on Ferry Road. Not that Nesbitt was ready to let him return home. This was as close as he was likely to get for a few more days yet.

Sheriff Hoxton opened his door while tugging at a black bow tie. Andy had encountered Hoxton only once before, but doubted he'd made much of an impression, and the situation left him uncertain of the protocol. "Evening My Lord. Going somewhere nice?"

Hoxton's response was somewhat harassed. "Cut the crap, Detective, we're not in court now. After hours I'm called James." He extended his hand, and Andy took it.

"Andy Lorimar. Thanks for this, James. Apologies for disrupting your evening."

Hoxton tied the bow again, succeeding only in making his throat look like a lopsided Shirley Temple. "We're off to a charity dinner. But I only just discovered it's a black-tie affair. I can never get these little bastards to sit straight. Can you stick a finger here for a second?"

"No problem." Anything to get on the right side of the man. "Sorry I can't advise on the technique though. I've only ever worn a clip on."

"Quite bloody right. My wife thinks the sensible ones are a breach of etiquette." He raised his voice. "But I'll tell you what's a breach of etiquette … wanting people's money and expecting them to dress like bloody penguins!"

Andy stepped back as Hoxton made some adjustments. "Right. How does it look now?"

"Very smart."

"Excellent. Follow me through to the library and we'll get your business seen to."

It was an impressive room. The walls displayed row upon row of grand legal tomes, plus one incongruous shelf of recipe books. Hoxton seated himself at an antique table, and motioned Andy to do likewise. "Now. The Fiscal's office told me the basics, but as a matter of form assume I know very little. What's this about?"

Andy handed over the application and pulled out his written notes. He shouldn't need them, but since he was disturbing the man at night they at least demonstrated suitable preparation. "The warrant is to search the home and commercial premises of Daniel Cochrane, with a view to retrieving a contract we believe names individuals with information on Yurik Sokov, our prime suspect in the murders of Robin McKay and Joan Wood."

Hoxton frowned. "So why pursue Cochrane? He's a prominent businessman. This is a significant imposition on his privacy."

"Mr Cochrane has been interviewed by four different detectives now. All are of the opinion that his answers were evasive and his reaction to photographs related to the investigation suggest his involvement."

"Suggest? Not strong enough. I like trout as much as the next man, but I don't issue warrants for fishing expeditions. Give me something concrete."

"Yurik Sokov is an ex-employee of Cochrane's. We have reason to believe their relationship was ongoing. Sokov was temporarily placed within the Balrannoch's staff in time for an event Cochrane held at the hotel. For this placement Sokov used the identity of another missing man, Radu Dudnic, who may also be a victim."

"You're getting warmer. Keep going."

"Sokov left the hotel just before the discovery of McKay's body. During his time there he'd remained conspicuously private, however, we have footage showing Sokov in discussion with one of Cochrane's guests, a person he refuses to identify as a result of the non-disclosure agreement we are seeking under warrant."

The sheriff nodded. "I'm satisfied on the link to Cochrane, but what's your best evidence that Sokov was involved in these murders?"

"We found Councillor Wood's DNA in the wheel arch of his van. And when I raised the investigation with Sokov he tried to crush my skull with a rock." Andy pointed to the bruising around his left eye and forehead.

Hoxton was shocked. "Good God, man! Were you the airlift from Cramond Island?"

"Yes, James, that was me."

"Bloody glad you're back on your feet." He signed the papers. "You have your warrant, Andy. I hope you get a more satisfactory response to your questions this time around."

28

REUNION
FRIDAY 16TH SEPTEMBER, 14:40

I t was deep into the afternoon of the second day before Sara sighted land near Ferkingstad. The North Sea crossing had been fraught, and they were running on adrenaline.

Yurik scanned the coast, checking for moorings. "This is good vessel Sara. Shame to waste it."

Sara sighed and shook her head. He would be disappointed. They couldn't risk leaving a trail. Better Cochrane's yacht was found abandoned mid-ocean than have it provide certainty of their destination. Especially since she planned to visit here frequently now that Marc would be staying in Norway. That, however, was a conversation for later.

She tied off the wheel, fixed the rudder towards open sea, and engaged the engines before joining Nick and Yurik in the life raft. As they paddled to shore, she watched their home of the last thirty-eight hours drift out towards the horizon and its likely destiny as a Marie Celeste mystery for the oilfields.

Reaching land, they punctured the raft and waited until the last sign of it disappeared below the water.

The stretch of rocky sand gave way to fields. Soon they would reach a road, and the short bus ride into Haugesund. While they walked Sara outlined the next stage to her colleague. "This bag contains identity documents and cash. Your job is to get Nick to Zurich."

Nick interrupted, grinning sheepishly. "Oh yeah! Zurich. Will Dad be there?"

Sara smiled. "We hope so Nick. But he's using another route. If you arrive first just make the bank transfers so we get everything set up for him when he arrives."

Nick grinned again. "I can do that." He looked back across the grey, restless waters. "I feel happy."

"You should. You're safe from the investigation. But your name is Tom Bryden now."

"Tom Bryden. T-O-M. Like a cat. Meow!"

"Meow Nick!" To anyone who knew him, he was obviously high, but the compound was working well and he was fully compliant. Yurik would simply have to do most of the talking. "You go with Yurik, OK?"

Nick laughed, wagging his finger. "No more hitting, Yurik!"

Yurik raised his hands in apology. "That was big accident, Nick, from behind I thought you were police." Then the Russian turned to Sara. "What about you?"

"I'm making contact with a biomedical researcher at the University of Bergen. We'll see what comes of it."

They remained quiet during the bus journey, and upon reaching Haugesund they hired cars and went their separate ways.

NORWEGIAN WAS NOT one of Sara's languages, but the music stations helped three hours in the hired car to pass uneventfully. It was dark when she drew up outside the luxury hotel.

Marc met her at the door of their room. "Hey! I was worried. I expected you this morning."

She entered the room and kissed him. "I was held up."

His expression was concerned. "Your hair smells kind of briny?"

"Your idiot girlfriend was walking on a seawall and tripped."

He smiled broadly. "My idiot girlfriend? Let me savour that. On a couple of levels." He looked her up and down. "Are you OK though?"

She was suddenly exhausted. "I will be, after a shower and a sleep. Can the fun stuff start in a few hours?"

He pulled her close. "We've waited twenty years. A few more hours is a cakewalk." Gently, he kissed her forehead. "I'm so happy about this, you know. Whatever you want, I want. We only have a few days here before we're back to Zurich."

Sara sighed. Although the fun stuff could wait, expectation management could not. "We might be here a bit longer."

His smile was tinged with puzzlement. "I'm not necessarily upset, but what's going on?"

Truth was like water. Enough was survival, too much, a deluge that destroyed everything. Marc couldn't return and, with Father's decision, his therapy was terminated. "There could be something else here, Marc. Something that your mother wanted for you. Something that I want for you."

His eyes darkened at the mention of his mother, with the warring emotions of their estrangement and her loss. "What?"

She took his hand. "Maybe. Just maybe ..." Her eyes moistened, and she wondered briefly at how natural and unbidden it felt. The words caught in her throat. "Finally, a cure."

29

MEA CULPA

SATURDAY 17TH SEPTEMBER, 09:32

I do not want to be defined by the circumstances of my death. I want to record my other achievements. I want to remind you of what I have built: my businesses, my family, the respect of my clients, the wealth and influence that rightly accrue to talent and success.

I want to do these things but I know that in this document such claims will seem hollow and tarnished. And that is my greatest shame: through my stupidity and weakness I have cast a taint on all I had previously accomplished.

The weight of my lies and evasions has become too heavy for me to bear, so I will bear it no longer. Here is the truth.

I am a man with certain desires. Those desires occasionally got out of hand, and some of the young men who helped me slake my lusts paid the price. To protect my reputation, I did not allow these young men to tell their stories. Their bodies are unlikely to be found, nor do I want them to be, since the shameful details of my physical misdeeds will not advance your understanding of actions that I cannot fully comprehend myself.

Poor Joan. Her entanglement began when I became a donor to a housing charity where she served as director. Robin McKay, a council worker attempted to blackmail her based on material he believed he had uncovered about my wrongdoings. She brought this to me, and in her integrity and honesty, she sealed her own fate and that of her blackmailer.

John Reynolds was another innocent, one who saw more than he should have. I am sorry for the distress my pretence around him has caused his family.

Yurik Sokov is exactly as he seems in this. A strong man too trusting to realise he was being manipulated into a situation beyond his understanding. His actions were committed at my direction and out of loyalty to me.

Finally, my son Nick is innocent of everything save devotion to his father. He instructed me in the technologies I needed to misdirect the investigation, without understanding what I was doing. He believed he was helping me protect our business. I hope he can one day understand that his father's flaws never negated his father's love.

This is my confession. I wish I could undo the awful damage I have caused, but I know I cannot. I am riven with regret for the whole appalling mess. I cannot forgive myself and expect no forgiveness from others. My small hope is that those suffering as a result of my sins can take a shred of comfort from the price I now willingly pay for my commission of them.

DANIEL COCHRANE.

30

TAKE THE WIN

SATURDAY 17TH SEPTEMBER, 09:39

Devlin was unusually upbeat given the mingled stench of human wastes and decay. "Well! At least we know why he wasn't returning your calls!"

Cochrane's head slumped against the back of the armchair, his fat, purple tongue lolling from blue-tinged lips. A hand reached across the distended belly, grasping at the syringe protruding from the left arm. A finger extended along the barrel, pointing the way to the target vein.

Five detectives, wearing latex gloves and overshoes, carrying cardboard boxes, clustered in the tiled hallway, staring at the last thing they'd expected to find that morning. Nesbitt said, "I've called it in, and I've taken responsibility for bagging the confession, but that entire room is now off limits." He nodded towards the front door. "SOCOs will be here any minute, so I'll head outside for the initial briefing." He turned to Petrakis. "They didn't have anyone available with digital experience, so you're up. Take a box and collect any evidence." Then he addressed Burns. "You'll go with her and check the rooms. Make sure no one else is on the premises."

Devlin asked, "What d'you need us to do, chief?"

"You two burly boys make sure nobody crosses the threshold unless they're in a SOCO suit." His next comment was addressed to everyone. "None of us enter that room again!" The outside door swung shut behind him.

But they didn't need to re-enter the room to get the idea. Cochrane was very, very dead. Andy struggled to make sense of it. He'd known the formal interview had upset the businessman, and he'd intended it to. But he hadn't expected things to unravel quite so dramatically.

Devlin had no such misgivings. "I'll give you something, Linkman. I told you Reynolds was involved, but I overplayed his role a wee bit. And you kinda, late in the day, suggested Cochrane was in the mix. Obviously I interrogated Cochrane, but your photographs had him cacking himself. So, all in all, fair's fair. We'll share the glory."

Andy raised his eyebrows, but grunted affirmation. If this really was the end, after such an unmitigated shitshow he didn't want to be the only one taking a bow. A forensic photographer entered, nodding as they let him pass.

Andy said, "It was certainly quite a confession."

"Wasn't it?" Devlin grinned. "Dirty bastard!" Camera flashes flared against the whisky tumbler discarded by Cochrane's feet. Every picture tells a story, and this one had no happy ending.

Andy couldn't help himself. "Is there something about it, the confession I mean, that feels a bit off?"

Devlin's stare was withering. "No. No. Don't start this. Not now."

Andy tried to placate him. "Look, Daniel Cochrane is in the frame here. No argument. But that suicide note. Perhaps a bit wrapped up in a bow?"

"How d'you prefer them? Done as a tongue twister?"

"C'mon. You know what I'm getting at."

Devlin shook his head in disbelief. "There was a bad bastard called Danny. He preferred rough-trade penis to fann-"

"That's a limerick. Not a tongue twister. My point is, would you write 'the young men who helped me slake my lusts', no excuses, no blaming? Or even, say he wanted to take full responsibility, are those quite the last words he'd leave behind, in the final hours of his final day? Take 'riven with regret'. Is the prose not a wee bit purple?"

Devlin slapped his forehead. "I'll tell you what's purple Link-man. The veins in my bloody neck. Take the win."

Petrakis walked back into the hallway holding her box like a trophy. "I found a shielded case in Cochrane's bedroom. It contained a phone matching the description for John Reynolds'. Looks like it was modded to block GSM connections, which might explain why the mobile network couldn't trace it."

Devlin pointed at her. "See? See? That's a smart cookie right there. Please. DS Petrakis, tell him to take the win."

"Certainly DS Devlin." Petrakis smiled at Andy. "God yes! Take the win."

Andy raised his hands. "I'm taking it. I'm taking it."

Behind them a forensics officer entered with a stack of evidence bags. Andy turned to her at once. "We'll need a full workup on the glass, the decanter, the syringe, the bookshelves, his clothes—"

The woman was disgruntled. "What d'you think I'm doing? Bagging stuff for a jumble sale?"

Nesbitt returned in time to catch the interaction. "Is he not taking the win?"

Petrakis and Devlin spoke in unison. "No, chief."

"I am! It's just—"

Nesbitt patted him on the back and spoke gently. "It's just, it's just. Look, when you've been working a case really hard, and it's been a doozy like this one, it can be hard to distinguish the big dark tunnel ..." he tapped Andy on the forehead, "... from the light at the end of it." He pointed definitively at Cochrane's corpse.

Lenny Burns walked down the hallway stairs wearing something over his face. "Look what I found in a laundry basket!"

Petrakis was aghast. "Is that a grey and white balaclava?"

Nesbitt shouted, "Bag that you muppet!" Then he grinned. "See? Good omens abound! Even Lenny's finding evidence!"

PART IV

LOOSE ENDS

18TH - 22ND SEPTEMBER

31

RECONNECTING

SUNDAY 18TH SEPTEMBER, 07:56

After breakfast Andy sat in Nesbitt's kitchen staring at his telephone.

He'd been avoiding this for days. Actually, by tomorrow he'd have been avoiding it for exactly a fortnight. He needed to phone Ilsa.

They hadn't spoken much since Jimmy died, and he knew that was on him. He wasn't proud of it, but he wasn't quite ready to apologise for it either. He took a deep breath and dialled.

"Hola." Spanish greeting, Hungarian accent. At least he knew he'd keyed the right number.

"Hi Ilsa."

"Andrew?" He could tell she was surprised. But then again, when you hadn't communicated for over five years, surprise was a given, and recognition a bonus.

"Yeah, it's me. How are you?" But if he'd really cared, shouldn't he have called long before now? In the growing silence he felt the stupidity of the situation he'd created. He did care, and a lot. He just hadn't wanted her to know it.

"I'm OK Andrew." He heard a long exhale. "Not same without Jimmy, but some good friends here."

It hit him hard then. He was a daft bastard. Avoiding a person he'd shared something so important with. "I miss him too." But he struggled with what to say next.

Ilsa did what she always used to, and came at the problem head-on. "So. Andrew. Why today? Why call today?"

Again, he struggled to respond. He was trying to re-establish their relationship, but with dishonesty. "It ... it's something Jimmy said to me, in a call. Just before he ... he died." He wished he could be like Doirin. Think of Jimmy as still around him. Just passed over. Moved on. Transformed. But the loss had always felt more irrevocable than that.

"He called? What did he say?"

That was his cue. For the lie more plausible than the truth. "He told me about the wallpaper box." Then he waited. He was scared to admit he'd had a message from a medium; she would simply have denied it, and then he'd never know. If she was clueless now, he'd be sure it meant nothing, because Ilsa would never lie over something she thought Jimmy wanted.

"I ... but ... what?" When she paused, he knew. She was stalling for time. Evidence of something real, and more proof of Doirin's weird insight. So he simply repeated his statement, and waited once more, leaving the pressure on her to elaborate. He was unsettled that his attempt to salvage his relationship with Ilsa had moved from lying to employing interrogation techniques, but something in him needed to get to the bottom of this.

When she eventually answered, she did so quietly. "I didn't know he'd told you about that. I didn't think he wanted to burden you with it."

"He must eventually have decided to leave that up to me."

He could hear her indecision, unsure how much to say. Finally, she said "But what did he tell you?"

In this tangled web, he knew so little, so he needed to keep things vague. "Only that this box existed. That it related to me. That I could see it when I felt ready. So I waited. And I feel ready now, I think."

Ilsa sounded upset. "I must adjust to this. I just didn't know." The emotion in her voice was deep, and Andy realised how dangerous the game had become. He'd pretended her dead husband had kept a secret from her, and, by the sound of things, a big one. Could he convince himself that Jimmy's spirit had given permission for this? Even accepting the reality of Doirin's messages, something he continued to struggle with, hadn't Doirin suggested the revelation had been somehow forced? And now here he was attempting to strong-arm Ilsa in turn. "I'm sorry. I should have stayed in touch, mentioned it earlier."

"I wish you had. I wish someone had." By someone she meant Jimmy, and he felt that pang of wrongness again. "You see, that was part of why." She stopped uncertain.

"What?"

"Why things went ... the way they did between us."

"Come on. Things went downhill because of the way you guys just left." He wanted to say they abandoned him. He'd been an adult, so that wasn't fair, but even though it was ridiculous, it had always felt that way. "I mean, you never warned me. And you never explained. You just went."

"That's what I mean."

He thought about that. She was claiming that it had never been some kind of whim. But they'd always laughed it off, making it seem that way. It didn't add up. "But you guys never kept in touch either, you know. And we'd always been close. Almost like..." He stalled there. This was becoming too emotional. The only point was to verify Doirin's information. He had to remember that.

Ilsa was calm. "We weren't *almost like*, Andrew. *We were*. Family."

"So why then? What happened?" But queasily, he suspected he knew where the answer lay. With this bloody wallpaper box.

She avoided his question. "I think ... can you come over? I don't fly so good no more."

Fair enough. "We have an investigation right now, but we might be past the worst of it. Can I check your mobile number? I sent a text to your old number last week but I knew I was taking a chance."

"Oh that one is gone. Long time. My friend Carmen-Teresa got me new handset from Movistar. Has your number changed?"

"No ... I don't much do change. You know that." She did know him. More than anyone left. He'd been a real fool.

His pondering was interrupted by a buzz. "Your message just arrived Ilsa, so I'll come back to you with some dates."

And with that, they closed the call.

His dominant emotion was shame. This proposed reconciliation was built around misrepresenting Jimmy's wishes. He struggled to remember why he'd ever felt this approach was the best way forward. Perhaps his isolation from Ilsa had made it seem acceptable, but that wall had now been breached.

He remained beside the telephone in silence, already finding it hard to live with what he had done.

32

POST-MORTEM
MONDAY 19TH SEPTEMBER, 08:42

W hen Doctor Nassar arrived at the City Morgue he waved, but she examined her watch. "You're taking a chance Detective, camping at pathology at this hour." She sighed. "Don't worry. I worked the weekend on your Mr Cochrane. I've completed his autopsy."

"Thank you."

She frowned. "I had rather expected a morning with people who didn't talk back. I should have known better."

"Sorry." He paused, for what he hoped was a decent interval. "So? What do you think?"

"I think patience is a virtue." She shook her head. "You can come through while I get my coat off."

The pathologist fetched a coffee and powered up her computer and carefully arranged her desk. Meanwhile he tried not to pace, but failed. What would she tell him? He needed something. Something that could either solidify or disperse the growing concern he had experienced since they first found Cochrane's corpse.

When Nassar eventually finished with her email she spoke. "So. Daniel Cochrane. It seems like only yesterday. Evening to be precise." She started to tap at her keyboard. "The good news is the toxicology came through. We're all racing like blue-bottomed fleas for this case. I hope you appreciate it." He nodded briskly, since it seemed like the right thing to do. "I'll finalise his report while we discuss."

He was happy to take what he could get. "Knock yourself out, Doc."

"Right. Estimated time of death, sometime on the evening of the 14th. It's hard to be precise, but between 6pm and midnight."

"That was the day we interviewed him."

"So I understood. Anyway. You found a syringe in his arm, so steel yourself for the shock. Cause of death was respiratory depression leading to coma and death, courtesy of a massive overdose. Almost identical to Robin McKay in fact. Morphine mixed with clonazolam."

"You barely picked up the clonazolam last time, and you thought your trace was perhaps only related to that drug. Was this the same story?"

She checked something on her system then shook her head. "No ambiguity this time. Definitively clonazolam, and a higher concentration this time around. Found in the muscle at the injection site, ruling out oral administration." She waited a moment before filling the silence. "Perhaps Mr Cochrane had some of the drug left over from the previous murder?"

He scowled. "That's certainly a tempting conclusion." Cochrane's suicide note claimed responsibility for McKay, so maybe he used the leftovers on himself. Or maybe someone had wanted to create that impression. "Anything else?"

"He'd been drinking heavily, which compounds the respiratory depression. Bit of a slate wiper, mixing opiates, benzodiazepines and booze."

"But was he held down? What about signs of force?"

"None."

"Physical injury?"

"Nothing."

"Indications of violence?"

"There were none." She stopped typing for a moment, and held his gaze. "I want to be clear; I have nothing in that area. This man didn't have a sodding bruise on his body." She frowned. "Do you think I should recheck? Perhaps I missed cuticle damage from a botched manicure?"

"General health? Was he an alcoholic, say?"

She nodded. "General health. Let's make some notes." She scrolled through her report and started typing. "His liver was in great shape for a man of his age and background. I certainly wouldn't infer alcoholism in this case. Other organs too. In particular his cardiovascular system was clean as a whistle. If he hadn't killed himself he'd likely have lived to a ripe old age." She tabbed down. "But since you are so persnickety today, I'll include one other historical finding. There were signs of muscle atrophy in his right leg. My understanding was he walked with a stick?"

"Yes."

"My guess would be a prior spinal or neurological cause of some kind, but his records contain no indication. Otherwise I found no fault with his general physical health. "

He looked through the glass partition to the laboratory wall of refrigerated cabinets. "Are we genuinely saying Daniel Cochrane just sat down and administered his own overdose?"

"I found zero evidence to the contrary. Presumably you got prints from the syringe?"

"Yes." The sigh was involuntary. "They're his."

"What about the note where he claimed responsibility?"

"We lifted latent fingerprints and a palm print from that too. Also his."

"Right." She frowned. "Isn't this a huge breakthrough? Why aren't you smiling?"

He trudged towards the door. "I wish I knew, Doc. I wish I bloody knew."

ON THE WAY into the case meeting he requested time for a long weekend to visit Ilsa in Spain. Nesbitt seemed strangely pleased "Great! But hold that result until I check something." Then he added opaquely, "When I call Migs this afternoon I'll have a better idea." By that time the throng had gathered, so the conversation was over.

From the volume of chatter it was obvious morale had greatly improved since the discovery of Cochrane's suicide. Nesbitt raised a hand to bring things to order. "OK, people. We've had a result, but we're not finished. For one thing, I'm not sure whether DI Lorimar is smiling yet!"

The expectant staring from his colleagues left Andy nonplussed, since his own emotional state was hardly relevant. But when Devlin and Burns fell to their knees pleading he eventually caved, if only slightly, to popular demand. Nesbitt pointed. "A grin from Mister Misery? Wonders will never cease!"

An impromptu round of applause began, which Nesbitt allowed for a moment before waving it down. "What a difference a few days make. Daniel Cochrane's suicide note claimed responsibility for the murders of Joan Wood and Robin McKay. That same note also claims responsibility for the disappearances of John Reynolds and Radu Dudnic. However, do we have any reason to doubt the suicide narrative? The pathology on Daniel Cochrane's body ... DI Lorimar, please update us."

Andy watched their smiles broaden with every sentence he spoke.

Devlin couldn't resist his own summary. "They found the same drugs that murdered McKay, no signs of violence, and it looks like he injected himself? That's tremendous! Everything backs up the suicide note!"

"Maybe the pathology does, but the note itself doesn't look so clever. It was printed on plain 80gsm paper, but Cochrane's printer was loaded with 100gsm headed paper and used different ink. No matching paper or ink was found on-site."

Nesbitt nodded. "Meaning he printed it elsewhere?"

Andy replied darkly. "Meaning *someone* printed it elsewhere."

Petrakis shook her head. "Without signs of violence or coercion, and Cochrane's own fingerprints, everything suggests he administered his own overdose. Why do we care where he printed the note?"

He was surprised at her. "It could be the difference between something happening, and something appearing *as if* it happened."

Devlin sneered. "You mean like the difference between a duck, and something that looks, walks and quacks like one?"

Nesbitt brought the room to order. "Remember our role. We assemble a sufficiency of evidence, bring appropriate charges, and make our report to the Procurator Fiscal. I'm senior on this case, so no one but me need worry about the definition of *sufficiency*. Are we clear?"

It was obvious who that remark was aimed at. Andy was nearing a place he'd been before with Nesbitt. The point where the adult called time and made him hand in his work. "We're clear, chief. But Sokov is still at large. And what about Cochrane's son, Nick? A car was driven from that garage. We're not buying that the son was innocent just because Daddy's suicide note said so?"

Nesbitt nodded. "Agreed. Next up, DS Petrakis. The old dental surgery that gave Cochrane the heebie-jeebies. What did you find?"

Petrakis pulled out her phone. "Spoiler alert. This one is juicy. The burned-out surgery in Gilmerton was leased to a charitable housing organisation known as Roofover Edinburgh. But I couldn't find anyone there who had heard of the lease or the surgery."

Nesbitt's eyes widened. "I've heard of Roofover Edinburgh from the register of memberships when we were investigating the council. Was that one of Joan Wood's?"

Petrakis nodded. "Oh yes. She was a director there. She signed the lease agreement for this place. But it doesn't seem as if anybody else in the organisation was in the loop."

Devlin was grinning again. "Remember the suicide note? Didn't he claim to meet Joan Wood as a donor to a charity she was involved with?" Andy knew exactly where his colleague was heading. And he arrived there quickly, snapping his fingers. "It fits. It all fits."

Nesbitt caught sight of Andy's scowl and said. "*Sufficiency.*"

Andy protested. "I went back through McKay's blackmail notes. There was no mention of Cochrane. There was plenty on Joan Wood though, and he raised questions about mysterious extracurricular activities. Doesn't this lease indicate she was involved in something suspicious? It's likely this place had a role, so shouldn't we establish that role?"

Devlin said, "Let's settle for a working theory. Cochrane was banging a rent boy there and Joan Wood walked in on him."

"But how? How does that even happen?"

Devlin shrugged. "Get me a couple of Ken dolls and I'll show you."

"No! If that place belonged to Joan Wood's charity, he wouldn't have free run of it, would he? Not unless there's something else we don't know about."

But the particulars of the thing didn't interest Devlin. "You're overthinking, as usual. He was a big donor. Open a wallet, open a door."

Andy tried another gambit. "The fire at Corryvreckan, Radu Dudnic's housing placement. That wasn't a coincidence. Our fire investigator, when she finally got access, found one oven control knob was damaged internally in a specific way. The gas appeared to be off, but was actually on. I think there was tampering."

Devlin nodded. "So? Cochrane tampered with Dudnic, then sent someone to fiddle with the appliances too."

Andy had walked into that one. He had to accept the Cochrane suicide note tied a lot of this up with a bow. And he could see from the faces around him, Devlin's position was broadly shared. Reluctantly, he understood why. This case had been horribly confusing. The investigators had been wrong-footed and personally attacked.

They'd been pressurised by the expectations of the higher-ups, the media and the public wanting answers. A door now stood open to a resolution, and the team desperately wanted to walk through it. His attempt to stop them, to suggest they still didn't know what the hell was going on? It was an impossible sell.

His best hope was to roll over, but buy time to back up his doubts. "OK. I'm in. But we've got a substantial mopping-up job, and it isn't just finding Cochrane's son and Yurik Sokov." He looked around the room ensuring he had their attention. A critical aspect of the investigation was outstanding, and he didn't want it displaced by a victory lap. "The victims have families who need answers. Remember John Reynolds, whose reputation was trashed and whose partner was put through hell."

Devlin spoke quietly. "She blames you for that, Link-man."

Andy ignored him. "And we know of two missing from the Corryvreckan guest house. Radu Dudnic from Romania and Ed De Graff from the Netherlands were both last seen in the company of Yurik Sokov. Both vanished in similar circumstances."

Nesbitt smiled. "That summary my friends, sounds like a basis for consensus. If we find Sokov and Nick Cochrane, then we find answers." He paused to survey the room. "Thing is, everybody thinks we're up to our ears in shit. But we know courtesy of Cochrane giving himself the needle, that the brown stuff has drained below our hips and we'll see our knees again any day now. So the top brass want to go public with this. And I agree with them." He gazed around the group. "Any objections, speak now."

Andy couldn't think of a single one. Cochrane's death changed everything. The claims in the suicide note were credible and would exonerate an innocent victim previously trailed as the prime suspect. They couldn't sit on it. Whether he liked it or not, the case was moving into a new phase. He had just one request. "Before we make the announcement, could I speak to Tricia Black, John Reynolds' partner? I feel we owe her some advance warning after leaving her in the lurch last time. How long before we release this to the press?"

Nesbitt shrugged. "I've still to draft something, and then put it through approvals. Realistically it won't be out until the late news tonight."

The meeting was called to a halt and they each went on their way. Andy left with a clenching in his gut. They didn't have the full story, and the way things were moving, they might never have it.

33

THE COFFEE SHOP
MONDAY 19TH SEPTEMBER, 12:05

Andy didn't fully understand his own motivations.

First, he'd had some good news: by luck Tricia Black was in Edinburgh already, so he could avoid a trip to Melrose. She'd agreed to meet him in a cafe on George Street. It was the call he made next that he was starting to regret. Still. What was done was done. Nothing might come of it.

The cafe was nearly empty when she arrived. Her lips were pursed as Andy stood to greet her. No surprise there; he knew he was the focus for her anger at the handling so far. On top of that, he had no idea how she would take what he was about to tell her, but it needed to be done.

"Hello Ms Black. I'm Detective Inspector Andy Lorimar."

She took his hand, a flicker of concern puncturing her disapproval. "Oh. Your eye. Are you ...?"

He smiled, shaking his head. "Not as bad as it looks."

That settled, the disapproval returned. "I've been wondering if you would ever deign to contact me again. Sergeant Devlin suggested you weren't much of a people person, and I have to say based on my experience ..."

Devlin. Cheeky bastard. "Well, I certainly owe you an apology. The case has been moving fast. I was overtaken by events, but it's no excuse. I should have warned you before the press conference naming your husband."

She stopped him. "We weren't married. Actually we were ending things. It sounds horrible, but I wish we'd split up months ago. I might not have been dragged into this nightmare."

"Anyone would feel the same way. Nightmare is the right word for this. And I didn't make things any easier for you. For which, again, sorry."

She breathed deeply. "OK. Apology accepted. Do you have an update?"

Out of the corner of his eye, Andy saw Doirin Chambers approaching with a steaming mug and a chocolate muffin. When she winked, he felt his cheeks redden, and looked away hurriedly. "Right... sorry?"

Tricia Black's eyes narrowed. "An update? Do you have one?"

"Yes. Things have moved on substantially."

He tried to ignore the scraping of the chair against the opposite wall. Doirin managed to position herself directly in their line of sight, which was a bloody strange interpretation of unobtrusive.

He dragged his attention back to Tricia Black. "We're about to release information that suggests Mr Reynolds was a victim rather than a perpetrator. A victim of another individual." Doirin began liberally dosing her coffee mug from a metal hip flask. "That ..." She necked a slug for good luck, making a disconcerting gargling sound. He forced himself to focus squarely on the person opposite, whose expression was growing more puzzled by the moment. "Sorry ... that individual appears to have committed suicide, but they were found in possession of Mr Reynolds phone."

The woman's face was a mask. She spoke quietly. "Are you saying he was murdered?"

He hesitated, but there was no getting away from it. "That was the claim made in this individual's suicide note. Certainly, the discovery of the phone suggests the recent messages to you did not come from Mr Reynolds, and the previous claims of responsibility were entirely bogus. We don't as yet know what happened but—"

Suddenly, Doirin's head appeared between them. "I'm awful sorry, hen. My muffin is that right sweet way, but my tea isn't. And they just don't go together. Could you give me some of your sugar?"

Tricia's eyes widened. "Yes, of course." She handed the little plastic tub of sachets to Doirin, who took it with one hand, and grasped Tricia's fingers with the other. "So kind of you, darling." Doirin's face froze for a second. "Oh. My. Oh."

Tricia reacted with concern. "Are you OK?"

But Doirin's eyes grew distant. "Oh. No. Oh. Your hands." She rubbed Tricia's fingers again, then closed her eyes. She trembled slightly before recovering herself. "S-sorry... So sorry... I'm havering here. Cold hands, warm heart, darling." She smiled unconvincingly, and left the table, taking the sugar dispenser with her. Andy cringed to notice an identical stack of brightly coloured sugar sachets had been present on Doirin's own table the whole time. "I'm sorry about that. I don't know what she was thinking."

Tricia shook her head. "D'you reckon she's all right?"

He swallowed his self-loathing. "Now her tea's compatible with her muffin, I'm sure she'll be fine... More to the point, how are you?"

The woman's eyes were confused. "I... I just don't know. This morning, John was a murderer. I've struggled with that, so much. I haven't really been able to process it since I first heard. But now... what? Am I relieved he's innocent?" She stopped for a second, fishing inside her purse for a tissue. "I can't be, can I? Because that means he's dead." She dabbed in an unfocused way at her face. "Will you find him? Wherever he is? Will you at least bring him back?"

Hobson's choice: false hope or none at all? But he found himself saying, "I'll try. I really will." And when he said it, it felt like a promise. Looking at Tricia Black's face, he could see just beyond the resilience, this was someone fighting to stay upright. It was the worst kind of emotional roller coaster, a horrible plunge from one misery to the next. "Look, can I give you a lift anywhere?"

"No. I want to walk. I'm catching a train back to Melrose. I could do with the air." She stood up. "Thank you, though. For meeting me. And for letting me know." She glanced strangely towards Doirin, and then left the cafe.

Andy sat in silence with his drink for a minute before walking across to join Doirin. "That was you being discreet?"

But Doirin didn't seem her usual rambunctious self. "Sorry. I just needed... I mean... He just needed. To touch. And then when he did, the floodgates opened."

Andy didn't know quite what to say about that. His enthusiasm about the possibility of fresh information turned distinctly luke-warm in the face of the strangeness Doirin brought with her. "You felt someone, then, a he?"

Doirin nodded. "Yes. John. And he's with Eddie, or Teddy."

"John is right," She might have got the name from the news reports, but tying him to Tricia Black was certainly accurate. "Who was Eddie?"

"Or Teddy. I couldn't be sure. He was their dog. He's in spirit too."

Andy was about to tell her pets weren't a pressing line of enquiry, but stopped himself. She'd done the favour of responding to his odd request, so the least he could do was listen openly to what she had to say. "You're certain that John is dead?"

"Oh yes. They made sure of that."

None of this was admissible anywhere, and he couldn't imagine sharing it with his colleagues. But it was starting to sound interest-ing. "They? Do you know who they are?"

Doirin shook her head. And then shivered. "The takers, thieves ... the audience."

"The audience?" Andy remembered the leaflets from Reynolds' hotel room at the Balrannoch. "He was here for the festival. He'd probably been to some shows, allowing for a moment that any of this is possible, couldn't you just be picking up a bit of that?"

Doirin's face was solemn, her voice subdued. "Oh Andy. He was at a show. And they killed him. All of them." She was deeply upset.

He saw now that to gain these impressions she had to experience something, and in this case, something horribly painful. She was trembling, and he touched her hand. "I'm sorry I put you in this position."

"No, Andy. I think this is what's been around us. Both of us. I'm not usually like this, feeling things so strongly, receiving so vividly. But spirit's pressing in on me. And it's all to do with this... thing... What you're working on." She rubbed her palms, flexing her fingers. "They hurt his hands. They hurt them so badly. I can still feel it."

This was very specific. Might she have something he could use? "Did you pick up what anyone looked like? Or the surroundings?"

"Underground? It felt like they'd covered his eyes. But I did see some things. Sitting near him... a man with a stick?"

Cochrane had a stick. It was hard to see how Doirin could know anything of the dead businessman's connection to this by conventional means. But she wasn't finished. "And a chair. They locked him to a chair."

"So with handcuffs? Rope? A chain?"

"I don't know. But I felt it. The restriction. He couldn't move... And there was a woman. He liked her. But she was part of it. There's something more there, but I couldn't get to it."

"Anything else?"

"The older man. The one in charge. He was dressed in white. Like he was going to a wedding."

Andy let out a whistle and sat back in the coffee shop chair. It sounded like the person Archie Roker had called Max. One of the mystery bookings at the Balrannoch caught on their CCTV. Little wonder Cochrane hadn't wanted to release details of his guests.

"Any more names?"

"No. Sorry... Maybe if I spoke to her again?"

Andy shook his head. That wouldn't be possible, not without being open about what was going on, something no good would come of. He needed evidence, real evidence that would allow him to push the investigation in this direction. But how the hell would he get it?

"Did he tell you where his body was? Please say yes."

Doirin was regaining her composure a little, her sceptical eyebrow suddenly asserting itself. "Now, Andy, what was your first car?"

"An Austin Allegro. Why?"

"Where's that car now?"

He couldn't see where this was going. "I've no idea. Why should I?"

She nodded. "That's it exactly. When John passed, he was with this... audience... at the show. Then he crossed to spirit. What happened to his old vehicle after that, I'm not sure he knows or cares. He didn't show me." Her hands were still trembling as she spoke.

Feeling the vibration of his radio in his coat pocket, Andy stood and touched her shoulder. "Well, Doirin, I'll need to head back in. But really, thanks for doing this. I didn't realise how distressing it would be."

She laid her own hand on his. "Me neither, but I was happy to help. We're in this together Andy. Whatever the hell it is."

A familiar voice sounded behind them "Andy! Hey! Is this lovely lady your secret friend Brian mentioned?"

Andy cringed. Petrakis must have blabbed about Doirin's visit to the hospital, and now everyone was talking about it. "Oh, hi Migs..." There was, sadly, no escaping the introduction. "This is Doirin. Doirin, meet my friend Miguel." Doirin beamed at the new arrival. Miguel, for his part, grinned in the disconcerting way people will when they believe they've stumbled into something juicy. Time to nip this in the bud. "Unfortunately, folks, my radio ... I need to head back in."

But Miguel's buds were impervious to nipping. "Busy, busy! Brian just same. Well Doirin, may I join you? Coffee alone, is a sad thing, no? I get you another?"

Andy started to shake his head, but heard Doirin say "Very kind Miguel. Americano, hot milk on the side." Not good. He'd have to leave them here. Together. Talking. Life wasn't meant to be this way. It was meant to be at least moderately controlled. Compartmentalised. Too many people around and suddenly you were herding cats.

He half-heartedly waved to them as he left the cafe, hoping the discomfort didn't show on his face.

34

EAST-COAST MAIN LINE
MONDAY 19TH SEPTEMBER, 14:04

Petrakis intercepted as he headed back to his desk. "I tracked down Nick Cochrane's mother. She's alive. And she's in London."

"What's the plan?"

"Someone needs to check her out before Daniel Cochrane's suicide hits the news at ten. I baggsied it so I can make an NCCU meeting in the morning. But I'm looking for someone to share my doughnuts."

Andy frowned. "I'd love to, but I'm not sure the chief will let me travel yet."

Petrakis nodded. "He wasn't exactly keen, but he's doing the press release and Devlin has a family thing. So that means you or DC Burns, and we're all worried Lenny'd get lost in the underground."

"I'm there. Are we flying?"

Petrakis wrinkled her nose. "Train. I've got a cab coming to take us to Waverley." Then she smiled. "Still. Like the bossman says, free WiFi and all that." He grabbed his things and they headed down to the car park.

The roads were relatively forgiving, and after the rush to the platform they were happy to find a table to themselves. The train departed five-minutes later, giving them a little over four hours to occupy themselves. Petrakis took the chance to fill in some detail. "Sherry-Anne Jensen split from Daniel Cochrane fourteen years back. She has a terraced house on Oakley Street."

"Where's that?"

"Chelsea. It's a seriously nice address. We can get off at Sloan Square or South Kensington, but either way we'll smell money."

The same smell that clung to nearly everything in Cochrane's orbit. "D'you think Nick ran home to mummy?"

Petrakis shrugged. "It's a definite option, but he'd know it's the first place we'd look. Even so, he might have been in touch. Do we know much about him?"

Andy recalled the meeting at HopperSoft's offices. His father's presence was dominant, reducing Nick to a vague, slightly smug presence behind a monitor. However, it spoke volumes that Cochrane senior kept him around during a discussion with the police. "He was a trusted confidante, and a senior player in the company."

"According to the suicide note, he trained Daddy on digital camouflage. Sound plausible?"

Andy nodded. "Yes. Technology was his area."

"Could he have been behind the encryption on Sokov's laptop?"

Andy had wondered about that very point. And since Petrakis raised it, he thought he'd push a little. "But I remember you said the setup on Sokov's machine was quite unusual, and similar to that on Joan Wood's?"

She nodded. "That's what I thought."

"So much so, that you suggested the same person was responsible for both."

"You've got a good memory. But yes, I did suggest that."

Andy shook his head. "See if that were the case, it speaks to a deeper relationship between Nick Cochrane and Joan Wood than the fact his dad once donated to a charity. Wouldn't you agree?"

Petrakis frowned, opening the screen of her laptop. "Hmm. Enough already." She began typing.

"And then there's why a lookalike for Joan Wood's ex-husband met one of our victims on the evening he died, and hasn't surfaced since." She grimaced at that, but still wouldn't meet his gaze. He couldn't help grinning. "Welcome back to conspiracy country DS Petrakis. We've missed you."

Because he made sure to wink meaningfully each time she raised her head, she absorbed herself in her email.

ABOUT THIRTY MINUTES outside Kings Cross, Andy's phone rang. "It's Brian. I spoke to Migs. About that trip to Spain."

It still wasn't clear where Migs came into this. "What have you decided?"

"So." Nesbitt hesitated. "I'm going over as well. Next weekend. There's a thing? I'm meeting his family. They're in Baldona, just outside Barcelona. Ilsa's not too far is she? In the Costa Brava some- where, right?"

"Right. Palamos."

"So, why don't you do that weekend, combine it with your visit to Ilsa. Migs has invited you as well."

"Me?"

"I suggested it, to be honest. I'd welcome the moral support."

"Oh."

"It's on the Saturday night, so you could do your own thing, meeting Ilsa on the Friday or Saturday morning. And you'd stay with Migs' family so you just need to get flights."

"I couldn't do that."

"Of course you could. He'd be offended if you didn't." Probably true, since Migs was generous to a fault. But it still felt like an imposition. Nesbitt sensed the delay and misconstrued it. "Obviously you'd have a plus-one."

"A what?"

"When I'd called him he'd just met you and Doirin in the coffee shop. He likes her, by the way."

Andy glowered across the carriage table at Petrakis. Her blabbing at the hospital had a lot to answer for. "But me and Doirin, we're not—"

"Yeah, yeah. I know. Early days and all that. But the flights are cheap and a Scottish contingent for me to take a breather with now and again would be ideal."

Andy was about to quash the idea when something stopped him. Doirin's presence could allow him to be honest with Ilsa. He could apologise for the lie, and explain why it happened. He could admit to an unconventional source of information if he presented Doirin as evidence. It felt workable. He'd screwed up something important and perhaps Doirin's presence could help fix it. The answer came before he had time to properly consider it. "OK. Let me ask her."

Nesbitt's earthy chuckle at the other end of the line was unwelcome, but he (and Migs, and Petrakis) could all think what they liked. He'd invite Doirin for other reasons entirely. The main question was whether she would even want to go? She was her own woman and they didn't know each other all that well.

But even in the midst of his denial he recognised that he did feel closer to her than he would have expected. She wasn't the easiest person, but she was genuine and well meaning. And she seemed to have a very puzzling talent; if she accepted, he'd be intrigued to introduce her to Ilsa.

When he came off the phone Petrakis looked up from her email, said nothing, but winked. That made it his turn to look away, but he sent a text message to Ilsa asking if the proposed date would fit. Then he watched the density of London take shape around them as the train made for Kings Cross.

PETRAKIS WAS in high spirits as she guided him through the crowds towards the underground. "Can't you feel it?"

"What? The humidity?"

"No. The energy! London! Centre of the world! This is why I was pissed when Nesbitt poached me."

"I remember."

"Ah, but now you understand. Because you feel it too."

"Let's just say I'm happy you feel it."

Petrakis had the underground map in her head. "We'll take the Circle line towards Edgeware Road coming off at Sloane Square. Sound OK?"

"I'm in your hands. This place is too big for me."

"Only until you expand your mind. Then suddenly, you're a Londoner." She flung her hands wide. He indulged himself with an eye roll. But she was happy to be home, which was a normal enough reaction if you were that way inclined.

He followed her down seemingly never-ending steps then found himself sprinting as she zipped left onto a platform. The train doors were opening just as they arrived and she jumped on board. "This one's ours!" Transport often did that down here in his experience, either anticipating your arrival or turning up damn near instantly thereafter. Yet he still heard many a gripe about it. The residents of this great city had forgotten the simple joys of waiting forty minutes for a bus in a blizzard.

But Petrakis hadn't finished. "I was maybe a bit hard on Edinburgh, but y'know it's a different thing. Small. Cosy. Filled with unfocused little otters."

"And the odd murderer. Don't forget them."

"Throwing shade on your own city? That's my job."

She was entertaining enough company he supposed. Certainly better than travelling with Devlin.

One Night Only

SHERRY-ANNE JENSEN CHECKED their warrant cards then brought them inside with no hint of evasion. Andy scanned the hallway for signs of a new lodger, but found nothing.

Their host was a striking woman with a substantial mane of blond hair. Andy reckoned she was in her mid-forties today, suggesting Cochrane was her elder by about fifteen years when they got together. She was American, with a soft southern accent. "Well I heard the doorbell and I thought Sherry-Anne, you got yourself visitors! But to see y'all were police. Goodness!" She tossed her hair, in a kind of instinctive adornment to her speech.

He suspected she viewed their visit as some kind of adventure. He was sorry they were about to burst that bubble. "Ms Jensen. I'm sorry to have to tell you that your ex-husband, Daniel Cochrane is dead. He committed suicide after falling under suspicion in a murder investigation."

"Oh my!" She raised a hand to her face, but recovered quickly. "Well I gotta say, you won't see me crying, officers. That man, pardon my French, that man? Well. He was a motherfrickin' polecat."

Andy traded glances with his colleague. It wasn't quite the reaction they'd expected. Petrakis broke the silence. "You weren't on good terms?"

"Honey, we weren't on no terms! I served my time, and Lord knows I did not skimp, but once I ditched him, I wasn't going to waste no more of my life on that man. I ain't seen him for more'n a decade now."

"What about your son?"

The woman shrugged. "Nicholas? I ain't seen him in years neither. Every winter I visit my folks in Florida, and first year after the divorce I sent him a ticket. But no. That boy made his choice. There was too much of his father in him."

She was unusually sanguine. Andy wondered if it was an act. "Would you mind telling us how you and Daniel Cochrane met?"

"Well, that's ancient history. But I guess I met him the same way he met most of his conquests at that time. Danny was a partner in the Golden Cutlass casino in Atlantic City. It ain't there no more. But Danny? He got his money out in time, of course, left everyone else holding plastic dubloons." She shook her head. "Back in the day I had a croupier job, just for the summer. There were a few of us girls dealing cards there, all dressed up as pirate wenches and whatnot. Danny saw every one of us as a personal treasure chest, though I did not know that at the time."

Petrakis was puzzled. "How did you end up married to him?"

"I was young, he got me pregnant. I dropped out of college and my folks threatened him with a paternity suit. He must'a figured marriage was the right thing for his career. Everything was a calculation with that man."

"And during your marriage you suspected unfaithfulness?"

"Suspected!" She laughed. "In our first year I caught him butt-naked on the craps table with a cocktail waitress. He promised it wouldn't happen again." She examined her fingernails for a moment. "I think he meant catching him wouldn't happen again. But that weren't true neither. See, after Nicholas was born, I was the catfish in the keepnet. And that man liked fresh snapper!"

Cochrane's promiscuity potentially supported his suicide note. Andy asked, "Did you ever know your husband to be unfaithful with another man?"

Sherry-Anne laughed. "Oh dear me no! That wasn't his thing at all. Oh no! No, sir!"

Andy knew a wife's opinion on this wasn't necessarily definitive. But perhaps the strength of her reaction hinted at something else. "You sound surprised. Could he have been described as homophobic?" A streak of self-hatred might have become a motivation in later crimes.

"Homophobic? Oh no. He didn't mind gays none. After it was over between us, and we was just keeping up appearances, he had a phrase he would use. You know, whenever he found out a man was that way? He'd smile and say 'more pussy for me!' He was a charmer like that."

"We're sorry to say some uncomfortable things will come to light over the next few hours and days."

She shrugged. "Well. Whatever. It don't affect me none. Nobody knows he was part of my history here. If you've had a long bout of something shameful you don't exactly advertise it. I won't be on the news I hope?"

"Not at all, no."

"Well good. Y'all do what you need to do."

"Nevertheless, some of the details may be upsetting. At the scene of his suicide he left a note confessing to certain crimes. People have died and your son Nicholas is being sought to help with the enquiry."

She look modestly surprised at that, but only modestly. "He didn't have much human feeling. But," she shook her head, puzzled. "But, died by his hand? If so, that ain't like him. I could imagine him maybe short-changin' someone else to do it."

Interesting marriage. Perhaps she knew him pretty well. Andy said, "The main thing Ms. Jensen, if your son gets in touch, please contact us as soon as possible." Both detectives offered their cards.

"I doubt he'll contact me. But if he does you'll know about it. I told him cleaving to his old man was a serious mistake, and that was his chance. I'm done with the Cochrane bad seed."

Petrakis said, "So your relationship with Nick wasn't one of unconditional love then?"

Sherry-Anne Jensen's face turned steely for a second. "Oh, honey. All love has conditions. But they're like landmines. Don't know 'til you step on 'em." She sighed and examined their contact details. "Lorimar and Petrakis. Gotcha. I'll watch the news with more'n my usual interest."

As they stood, he remembered one final thing she might have

insight into. "Ms Jensen? A point our pathologist raised. Your ex-husband's leg? Do you know how he came by that injury?"

Her eyes narrowed for a moment. "Well, I ain't supposed to talk about that. Condition of the divorce settlement. That man was paranoid about his competition thinkin' he was weak or some-such."

"But under the circumstances?"

She relented. "I guess he ain't gonna sue my ass, not now. When we was in the States, he started having a problem with his leg. It got kinda weak, then stiffened up. Sometimes it took a sorta spasm? We thought he'd pulled something or maybe damaged a nerve. When he went to the specialist, we got a shock. They said it was Lou Gehrig's disease."

Petrakis froze. "When did this happen?"

"Maybe 15 years past now? No more'n a year before we divorced."

"But Lou Gehrig's? Isn't that motor neurone disease? That's degenerative."

"That's right honey. Gave me the push I needed to drop him. I had other plans for my life besides wipin' ass and listen'n to his bullshit through a synthesiser. Pardon my French."

Andy shook his head. "But that isn't what happened, fifteen years later he was still living an independent life. Can you shed any light on that?"

Sherry-Anne shrugged. "Ain't it obvious? The specialist was full of horseshit. Danny said it were a misdiagnosis and the divorce settlement was conditional on me keepin' my mouth shut. I was happy to. Talking about any part of him was not in my game plan."

"Did he get another diagnosis?"

"I don't know nothin' about that. I just know Doctor Fancy-Pants with all his scans and tests and letters after his name, he was just plum wrong!"

AFTER FEEDING him at a trendy fusion restaurant, Petrakis accompanied Andy to Euston station and waited until his overnight train pulled away. The babying was annoying, but apparently Nesbitt still had him on twenty-four hour accident watch.

The in-carriage sleep kit was a nice touch, but a seat was still a seat, and his legs weren't getting any shorter. He stuck on the eye-mask and tucked the little pillow between his head and the window glass. It would have to do.

While waiting to nod-off he mulled over their encounter with Sherry-Anne Jensen. He found the relationship with her son believable. The lack of maternal connection and concern had been palpable. He believed she anticipated no contact from Nick Cochrane, and he expected she would be true to her word and report any should it occur. He was modestly surprised that his own reaction to such an unconventional mother-son relationship wasn't more judgemental; he knew himself well enough to understand his sensitivities in that area.

But overall it was gratifying that someone originally ensnared by Cochrane had found their way out. Whatever the full story was, others crossing the businessman's path hadn't always been so lucky. Ms Jensen might be doing very nicely nowadays on the back of the divorce settlement, but as she said, she'd served her time.

Working out where it put the investigation was more depressing, since they still had no leads on Nick Cochrane. He pushed the eye-mask up onto his forehead and pulled out his phone. He could at least update the pathologist on the mystery of Cochrane senior's leg. His message was carefully worded to avoid disclosing anything identifiable over the public network.

SUBJECT'S LEG: EX-WIFE SUGGESTS INITIAL (MIS)DIAGNOSIS OF LOU GEHRIG'S

Details of the suicide and Cochrane's claims of responsibility would have headlined both evening and breakfast news by the time this train pulled into Edinburgh Waverley. Perhaps that disclosure would scare out some information they could use. He wouldn't be there to handle any calls tonight, but he guessed most of the fallout would land tomorrow. He put his head back against the window, pulled down the mask and tried to get some sleep.

35

FRESH INFORMATION
TUESDAY 20TH SEPTEMBER, 08:45

Devlin and Nesbitt were already in deep discussion when Andy turned up unshaved and in yesterday's clothes. Neither man noticed; they just waved him over.

Devlin said, "Call from the Marina. On the night of Cochrane's death he'd asked them to fuel his yacht. He and two others were taking the boat out."

Andy shook his head. "But he never went anywhere."

Devlin looked at the carpet. "No. But three others did."

"Christ's sake! They let somebody else take his boat?"

Nesbitt raised his hands. "Be fair. They had no cause for suspicion. Nobody knew of Cochrane's role in anything dodgy until late last night."

Devlin nodded. "And, more importantly, the three arrived in Cochrane's car. The security barrier is controlled by numberplate recognition."

Andy inhaled deeply. "What do we know about the three?"

Devlin shrugged. "Not much. The CCTV is limited, but they reckon it was two guys and a woman. Big guy appeared to be supporting the smaller guy. For my money, just before he offed himself, Cochrane organised an escape cruise for his son, possibly also for Sokov."

Nesbitt scowled. "His note tried to convince us to go easy on them. Looks like he wanted extra insurance."

Andy wasn't sure it was quite so simple. "If that's the scenario, why was Nick being supported?"

Devlin shrugged. "Upset? Pissed on his dad's whisky? How would you feel if your old man just coughed to being a murderer? How would you feel leaving him behind thinking he could top himself? I'd say he had reasons to be a bit shook up."

Annoyingly plausible, but it didn't make complete sense. "If Cochrane had a solid escape option, why kill himself? Why not be on that boat?"

The two men shrugged, lacking any pat answer. Eventually Devlin spoke up. "Maybe it was guilt. Maybe he knew their best chance was that he stayed and took the heat."

Andy scowled. "Or maybe someone else decided to make Daniel Cochrane the sacrificial lamb. Could this be another murder?"

Nesbitt said, "The marina recognised Cochrane's voice. That's evidence he organised a getaway for his accomplice and his son. Sometimes it is how it looks."

Andy couldn't deny that. "What about the woman? Any theories?"

Devlin said, "Obvious. Nick's bird." The fact he could declare anything about this case obvious, put him on an investigative plane far removed from the one Andy occupied.

But Nesbitt silenced the retort before it started. "Let's get serious here. How far could they have gone? What's the fuel capacity of the boat and what maximum range does that give? Fife? Felixstow?"

Andy rubbed his eyes. "Archie Roker said Cochrane kept a sailing yacht in Queensferry, so it wasn't reliant on fuel. It's been pretty blowy for the last few days. They could have travelled under sail power as well."

Gloomy silence descended. Eventually Nesbitt said, "So. They're literally in the wind? They could be absolutely bloody anywhere?" Face grim, he left to spread the joy upstairs.

WITH NESBITT OTHERWISE ENGAGED, and the phones not exactly channelling a tsunami of information on Nick Cochrane or Yurik Sokov, Andy gathered his courage and made a call of his own. "Hey Doirin, it's me."

"Andy. Good to hear from you. Unless I'm a suspect for some other bloody thing."

"No need to worry. It's a personal call. How's your sister?"

"She's rallied a bit. Her schoolfriend is visiting for a few days so that's something." Then she paused. "But did you say personal call? Ooh la la."

"Don't you start. I've had enough of that off Brian, Migs and everyone else."

She brightened."Oh. Miguel. Lovely chap. Nice bit of height about him. I like a man with a bit of height about him."

"So, when you called your late-husband 'Wee Davie', was that one of those sarcastic nicknames?"

"No, but he was the exception that proves the rule. We got together at a school disco. What a dancer that man was! I miss dancing you know. I haven't done any since..." She was silent for a moment. "You don't dance yourself?"

The honesty escaped his mouth unedited. "God no! That's my idea of hell!"

Doirin sighed. "Your loss, Andy. You only live once."

Small talk over. Time to pop the question. "With regards to only living once... This will seem odd, but hear me out."

"I'm listening."

"Migs has invited ... well, I was going to—" He paused, trying to collect his thoughts. "Look. Ilsa lives in Spain. Costa Brava. I'd like to try and explain this ... message from Jimmy thing. To her I mean. But it's awkward. We've not spoken for a while and I've, well, messed up a bit when I called her. Bad start ... wanted to repair things? And—"

"Stop! Go back to the bit about being invited."

"Migs has invited us both to Spain this weekend for a party he's having. But I think he thinks that we're ... which is mad. But anyway, despite that, I was thinking that maybe it would be a chance for you to meet Ilsa. Because that's important to me. But I don't want you to think—or that I think ... it'll be all above board. I'll buy the flights. Leave Friday lunchtime. Migs puts us up. You take the room and I'll take a sofa or whatever."

Doirin gasped. "Really? I've been invited to Spain?"

"We both have. Brian—"

"He's Miguel's man, right?"

"Right. And he's my friend. And my boss. But anyway, he's after some home support when he meets the in-laws. He's nervous."

Doirin laughed. "This story's full of nervous policemen."

She was making fun. Bad sign. "I said it would seem odd. It's fine. You don't need to—"

"I'd love to. I'll dig out my flamenco gear tonight."

"You will?"

"You're buying? A big party in Spain? No monkey business? Of course I'm coming. This is my first sniff of a social life in years." She hesitated. "Plus, I feel like ... like I should be there somehow. Maybe I'm meant to meet Ilsa."

After he put down the phone he wondered about that. Was Doirin *meant* to meet Ilsa? He certainly wanted that meeting, but predestination was a concept he couldn't accept. He'd spent his career believing the difference between outcomes could be as simple as how many hours you put in, and he didn't propose to change now. Still. Doirin had her own take on the world. It was one of the things he found refreshing about her.

When his phone rang a minute or two later, his first thought was of her calling back to cancel. But it was nothing so predictable. First, he heard a ruckus at the end of the line. Then, he recognised the voice of the desk sergeant, "Sir, did you say mime?" An angry retort followed in the background. "DI Lorimar? We appear to have a clown in reception. Asking for DCI Nesbitt. Can you deal with it?"

EVEN THE MIRTH makers on the gauntlet run between the reception and the interview room didn't know quite how to react to their latest guest. Lenny Burns' slack-jawed surprise was cut short by a mouth full of hooped fabric from the clown's enormous trousers. Even Devlin made do with a bug-eyed stare.

Andy wondered if the clown's fearsome expression, mouth set like sharpened flint inside a fooling-nobody greasepaint grin, had put his colleagues slightly on the defensive. This guy wasn't made up as a deliberately scary clown, but he owned the part anyway.

After the interview room door closed, they had barely taken their seats when the previously taciturn jester let loose. "So where's Brian Nesbitt? He's on TV asking me to phone in, I phone in, and nothing. He's on TV again, asking me to contact him at Fettes Avenue, I come in, and he's nowhere to be found?" The powder-white face glared around the interview room in disgust. "I'm seeing a fucking pattern here."

They'd hooked a live one. "DCI Nesbitt is coordinating this investigation, but it's complex, and he has a very busy timetable. He relies on me and other members of the team to handle interviews, screen calls and prioritise follow-up."

The clown's stare was unblinking. "So it's all your fault?"

He was a walk-in, but time to ditch the informality and get a second body in the room for backup. "I'm sorry you feel you've been badly handled. Let's put that right. One second, sir." Andy walked over and reopened the door, shouting across the space. "DS Devlin? Could you bring in the press conference phone-in sheets?"

When Devlin arrived, Andy resumed proceedings. "Can we take

your name sir? You told reception," He looked at the slip of paper "Coco The Clown?"

The man's grip tightened on the edge of the table. "Co-co? Co-fuckin-Co?" He shook his head. "Are you guys from the dark ages? I'm Cacao the clown. CACK-OW. Modern clowning in the raw. CACK, as in your handling of this case! OW, as in what it's doing to my bloody head!"

The detectives shared a frown. "Message received. We'll correct that. But we need your real name, rather than your stage name."

The man rolled his eyes. "Frederick Orr." Then he fixed them with a narrow stare. "But I go by Cacao The Clown."

While Andy updated the notes, Devlin ventured a question. "Mr Orr, I mean, Cacao, are you here in response to the press coverage of Daniel Cochrane's suicide?"

"Give that man a gonk."

Andy said, "I'll record that as a yes."

"You do that. But here's another question. Did the news that you're still trying to trace the movements of John Reynolds make me angry? Record that as a fucking yes too!"

Andy turned to Devlin "Mr Cacao phoned in after the first press conference."

Devlin flicked through the sheets. "We've got call summaries here ... hang on ... were you the street entertainer who felt that John Reynolds had spent a long time looking at you without paying?"

"So you do bloody have it! Why no callback?"

Clearly this witness thought he had more to give, but nobody followed up, presumably because the sheet suggested he was a nutjob. Looking across the table at his fiery glare and tense white knuckles, Andy understood that evaluation. However, since the man was here, they should listen to him. "I'm sorry. We fell down on this. Tell us what you saw and we'll start afresh."

Somewhat mollified, the entertainer nodded. "So festival time, I do an outdoor show in the Pleasance or George Square, or wherever there's an outdoor bar. You might have heard of it? Beers of a

Clown?" The detectives exchanged a mutual shrug and received a glare in return. "Well, you've missed yourself because it's bloody genius! People buy me pints, and I knock them back, fast, down-in-one mostly. And the crowd throw money in my suitcase to show appreciation."

Devlin scoffed. "A sponsored piss-up?"

"It's hard bloody work, mate! Especially when pricks like Reynolds take up eyeball room and pay bugger all."

Bizarre. But worth exploring. "When did you first see Reynolds?"

"So, he came out, face tripping him, at the end of this stupid song and dance show. The one about paper animals getting chibbed."

Andy dimly remembered a pamphlet from Reynolds hotel room, so ventured a guess. "Abattoir the Musical?"

"Aye. That was it. Total crap. Smaller audiences every day. Opposite of my show. But then I've done my research." He leaned across conspiratorially. "Beers of a Clown is precisely calibrated for the late-night Edinburgh audience."

Andy didn't necessarily disagree, but it wasn't a marketing seminar. "So, Reynolds comes out of his show."

"Right. He comes out and he gawks a bit. And I'm drinking, so I can't shout him to toss us a few coins, but I'm thinking it. I'm really thinking it. It's stressing me out in fact." Muscles tightened in the clown's neck at the recollection. "But then, this wanker with a satchel breezes over and tries to poach him. After a minute a woman joins in."

Andy felt the need to challenge. "This is an impressive amount of detail for a man who was basically mainlining alcohol."

"What can I say? If I was the kind who drank to forget, it wouldn't bloody work. Anyway. A T-Rex in cargo pants lingers in the mind, right?"

Devlin spoke for both of them. "Come again?"

"Short arms, long deep pockets. Those arseholes."

Fair enough. "So, then what — he leaves with them?"

"Aye, but he throws some paper into my case, so I'm thinking, fair play. Until I check it later on. Cheeky. Tight-fisted. Bastard!" The clown dug around inside the hoop of his trousers, then threw a grubby flyer on the desk.

Andy read the headline aloud. "Wonderground, Niddry Street. Max the Magnificent, Illusionist Underground." That name again. Max. "You're sure this was from John Reynolds?"

"It was from him all right. Almost everybody else was flinging me coins. I thought he'd bunged us a fiver until I saw that. I pinned it to my wheel of hate."

The mind boggled. Devlin lifted the leaflet, muttering quietly, "Now we know where he went."

Andy nipped outside, returning with some photographs. "Do you recognise anyone else from that evening?"

An outpouring of X-rated vitriol identified Reynolds immediately, but was followed by a series of angry blanks until they reached the white-suited gent and younger female companion from the Balrannoch. "That could have been the woman, but I don't know the bloke in white. What the hell's he dressed like that for? Fucking weirdo." The clown waved his arm dismissively, and his silk shirt fluttered like a battle pennant. They thought it safest to ignore the irony.

Cacao didn't recognise Daniel Cochrane either, but when Andy showed a picture of Nick they had liberated from Cochrane's library, they got strong confirmation. "Satchelly, poaching bastard! That's him! Smarmy fucker!"

Devlin whispered. "Cochrane junior fetched him and Daddy did him over." Andy wasn't certain it was quite as simple as that. Devlin continued, "I'll bet he never made any show."

The clown regained their attention by slapping the table. "Whispering? Rude! Where's your fucking manners?" When he had their attention, he softened again "Right... So, can you guys get your arse in gear and wrap this all up?"

Devlin reassured him "That's the plan. As you know from the news, we're on the home straight." Andy wasn't entirely certain about that either, but this wasn't the time for debate. They were moving forward.

When the clown stood, his hoop caught the back of his chair and sent it crashing to one side. He didn't seem bothered in the slightest. "Good. And I've done my bit. Right?"

"You've been very helpful."

"Next year's festival, I'll have a review on my poster. 'Clown who caught a Killer — Police Scotland' Any problems with that?"

Neither of them wanted to argue with this guy in an enclosed space, so they shrugged. Devlin tried to make light as they reached the door. "Off for a few more beers then?"

"Steaming? For a children's party? Fuck's sake! What world do you live in?" He glared at Devlin for a long moment, until, seemingly as an afterthought, he extended a couple of business cards. "Know anyone with kids? I'll do you mate's rates." They took the cards hurriedly, but couldn't find the words to reply.

36

THE SHORT LEASH

TUESDAY 20TH SEPTEMBER, 13:52

Cold sweat prickled on Nick's forehead. His stomach roiled. Even with the afternoon sun blazing through the passenger window, he began to shiver. Not long ago, he had felt good on the road; happy and childlike and tactile. Yurik had been friendly. The journey was an adventure.

But after they crossed the border to Switzerland, a bleakness descended, and he knew why; the effects of the pills had begun to wear off. Yurik had dispensed pills freely on the trip. For seasickness on the crossing, for the stress of the escape, for peaceful sleep. On some level he'd known it was wrong. They'd shared stressful situations without medication before after all, but by then the sensation was hard to relinquish, an overwhelming feeling of connectedness and calm. Thinking back, the idea that Yurik had misidentified him as police while choking him unconscious was unrealistic, but he'd accepted it wholeheartedly. He must have been drugged while he was out cold.

But now the intentionality behind all of it had become clear. A single call on the road between Yurik and Max, and the pills were no longer forthcoming. Yurik claimed his supply was exhausted, but there had been no suggestion of scarcity earlier. It hadn't taken long before the pains began.

He almost heaved as the car stopped outside the clinic, his throat burning with acid. In the last hour the possibility of threat had solidified into certainty. But even that growing fear was dwarfed by need. He knew the identity of that need. He'd heard Max talk about it in the past: the short leash. A chemical cocktail providing a joy so far from the vicious misery of its withdrawal that it guaranteed compliance in even the most truculent subject.

But now he was finally at Riesbach, he prayed for a more positive alternative. Perhaps they *had* simply run out of pills on the road. Perhaps everything *would* be explained.

Max met them at the door of the clinic, smiling indulgently. "Nicholas, Nicholas. Such a pleasure."

Yurik squeezed past and walked ahead of them. Nick could only think of one response. "Help me."

Max nodded. "I will. Come in."

In the office, an open laptop was waiting. Max motioned him to sit. "Now, Nicholas, your father said you would conclude some bank transfers?"

In the sweating haze, hope bloomed. "He's here?"

Max simply smiled, and pointed to the keyboard.

Nick's fingers trembled. "I can't. N-Not like this. Can you give me something first?"

"No, Nicholas, not before. But afterwards, we will."

The funds needed to be consolidated from multiple offshore accounts. He could initiate that. Despite the nausea, his mind was clear. He remembered the procedures and access details, things that he hadn't thought about for days. His typing was haphazard and it took twenty minutes to complete. But he did it.

He raised his clammy face to Max, gorge threatening to rise. His words were thick, desperate, pleading. "Now ... please?"

The old man's lips tightened. "No. You will be comfortable soon.

But first, you must show us how you track Lorimar." Max turned to Yurik. "Fetch him a bucket."

When Yurik left the room, the thought rose unbidden. Last chance. Rush the old man. But as Nick tensed his muscles, he realised he could barely stand. And Max, while old, was neither frail, nor stupid. Secreted around his person he would likely have a cosh, or a knife. And their leader was skilled with knives. Nick had cheered those skills more than once.

Max seemed sensitive to his thoughts. "Be wary Nicholas. Now is when I decide whether I can trust you again."

"You can ... please."

"You must know your father sealed his own fate with clumsy lies, lies that proved vulnerable to a police warrant. We need truth between us now. Do you understand?"

Nick nodded, too sick to waste words.

"If your father's lies were uncovered, so would we be. Not just me, but you Nicholas, and Sara and Yurik and our whole project. Do you know this? Speak."

His jaw shivered, his arms prickled with goosebumps. Say what he needs to hear. Get the words out. "You had to ... to ... kill him. I know ... it."

Yurik re-entered with a bucket and the bag from the car. He placed a handset on the desk. "His phone is linked to Lorimar's somehow."

"Show us, Nicholas. Show us we can trust you. Explain this mechanism."

How much could he afford to say? His knowledge might be all that was keeping him alive. But he had no option. He needed to prove his worth. The looming spectre of his own execution adrenalised him enough to overcome the nausea and communicate.

So, he showed them.

He showed them how to access the software and use it to track Lorimar's location. How the application received text messages the detective sent, and could permit, block or reroute them. How it could browse messages on Lorimar's phone and send to him posing as anyone in his contact book.

Max pointed to the screen. "So this text here, mentioning Lou Gehrig's disease. That is a message that Lorimar sent?"

"Yes. But I haven't actioned it, so it hasn't reached its destination. We can send, delete or reroute it."

Max frowned darkly. "The man troubles me. Delete that message. It is best that it should never arrive. Hopefully it will be forgotten." Nick did as he was asked. But Max had more questions. "Tell me about the software you installed on Lorimar's phone to facilitate this surveillance."

Nick saw a slim chance and snatched at it. "It was a Trojan, a piece of malware installed as part of The HopperSoft Investor Pack. I could develop a similar Trojan, but based around marketing materials for the clinic network. We could install it for valuable clients and keep an eye on them."

Max nodded. He signalled to Yurik who stepped forward holding a small pill. Nick snatched it, swallowing desperately. It would take a while for the chemical effects to begin, but relief was immediate. For now, he would live.

37

OVERBOARD

WEDNESDAY 21ST SEPTEMBER, 06:52

T he call had come in before five in the morning, but on balance, she'd given Andy an excellent reason. "Meet me in Arbroath, the hand still has some sodding skin on it." On the plus side, at least the roads had been quiet.

When Andy pulled into the car park at the harbour he squinted to see the pathologist approaching. The sun had crested the horizon, and he shielded his eyes as he slammed the door behind him. Like most Scots he had an ambivalent relationship with proper sunlight. He complained about the lack of it all year, but when it arrived in any meaningful capacity it was too bloody bright, like a long-lost friend poking thumbs into your eyes and expecting you to be happy about it.

"Good morning Detective. You appear to have left home in a hurry. That's quite a salt-and-pepper beard you have there."

"What can I say Doc? I'm a man for all seasonings." It was the best he could manage.

She frowned. "On closer inspection I fear you may be running out of pepper." They walked together past the RNLI building and towards the harbour wall.

"But we're not here to discuss my facial grooming."

"No." She scanned the water. "In London I dealt with a number of incidents on the Thames, so I brought with me some experience with submerged remains. When I received this call I thought of your case."

"What are we waiting for, exactly?"

"Maritime archaeologists were shipwreck hunting using a remotely operated vehicle. They found a body, contacted the coast-guard, who in turn contacted me."

"You think it might be Reynolds?"

"Perhaps. Not skeletonised, at least not completely, which suggests it is relatively recent."

The sea had always been an attractive way to dispose of bodies. Appropriately weighted, they should never be seen again. But whoever wrote those rules hadn't counted on passing drone vehicles with cameras. "When are the boats due back?"

"Ten minutes ago, but it will have proven tricky to retrieve the body."

While they waited, he asked. "What did you make of my message about Cochrane's leg?"

The pathologist seemed puzzled. "Your message? I don't recall receiving that. Did you find something out?"

So much for technology. "His ex-wife reported a diagnosis for Lou Gehrig's disease fifteen years ago."

She scoffed. "No sodding way. That condition is unmissable. I'd have found it on the table, and you'd have seen it at interview. Only ten-percent survive more than ten years from onset, most die in three to five."

This was more or less the reaction he'd expected. "Probably a misdiagnosis then."

She nodded. "Must have been." She continued scanning the water. "Hang on. Look there." Two craft were headed their way. "One coast-guard vessel, one archaeology vessel. I'd say our guests are about to arrive."

After the coastguard vessel tied up, a crewman retrieved a small harbour crane from a nearby locker. Nassar turned to Andy. "The worst aspect of a maritime retrieval is the potential for damage to the evidence. Of course, that pales in comparison with what will have been done by the water and wildlife. But," she smiled at the thought, "we might find less deterioration than usual, since by all accounts this one was well wrapped."

The pathologist rejoined the crane operator and began guiding the procedure. Andy turned at the sound of a trolley, and a young man shook his hand. "I'm Tommy, from the City Mortuary." Andy was disturbed to withdraw from the handshake with a sticky red smear on his fingers. "Oops. Sorry mate! Don't worry. It's only the final remains of a bacon roll."

After long minutes of preparation and positioning, the hoist cables finally tautened and slowly, a cylinder of slimy white plastic rose from the archaeology vessel. At first, Andy was unsure he was looking at a human body at all. Then he traced a dangling streamer of seaweed to where it merged with a greenish black arm lolling from one end of the roll. The flesh of the arm appeared blistered, and had a strange sheen. Doctor Nassar stared inside the cylinder and shouted towards him. "We could be in the right ballpark. So far, I'm thinking two to four weeks."

That was, indeed, in the ballpark, but he had no idea how she could arrive at any kind of sensible conclusion while dodging fronds of kelp. He'd leave his chickens uncounted until the lab work was done.

As the body was lowered and secured to the trolley, Andy signalled the captain of the archaeology boat. "What did you guys see out there?"

The man took off his cap. "We'd been noodling about a bit, training near the Isle of May, then we pushed out to open sea. One of our trainees was practising manoeuvring the ROV, and she called me to the console to get my opinion on an object on the sea bed. When we saw the arm we radioed the authorities."

Dumb luck, and a body is found. "How long might it take to get to the location from Edinburgh? Not a noisy speed boat, something a little more refined. Perhaps a leisure yacht?"

"Finger in the air, but, going direct, two to three hours?"

"How did you bring the body to the surface?"

The captain frowned. "It was uncomfortably deep for human divers and lifting bags. So the coastguard allowed us to use the ROV. We attached a line, and used the cutting tools to snip the sandbags weighing it down. It more or less floated up by itself after that."

"You operate in the area often?"

"We take projects worldwide. But yeah, sure, for training. St Andrews is our home base."

Andy pressed a card into the captain's hand. "If you see anything else strange—"

"You mean, like more human body parts?"

"That's what I mean. Any more of those, you have my number."

The man grimaced, but shoved the card in his pocket.

After the body was loaded, the mortuary van left. Andy headed back towards Edinburgh wondering what they had found.

AFTER ORGANISING the last pieces of admin for the trip to Spain and completing his outstanding paperwork at the station Andy couldn't wait any longer, so headed down to the Cowgate. He arrived in time to find Doctor Nassar zipping up the body bag. "Did you miss me?"

"No, Detective, but I have high hopes for when this case is over."

"Sorry. I'll get out of your way as soon as possible. I just needed to know ..."

"The identity of our catch of the day?"

"Yes. Please."

"Well, here's what I can say." She unzipped again. The salty mineral smell of the ocean was still faintly present. One hand and forearm were nearly stripped of skin and muscle. The rest of the body was better preserved, but bloated. The skin shone strangely in patches, while in other places hung loose. "I'd say this gentleman spent between twenty and twenty-three days in the ocean. The sheen you're seeing is the beginnings of adipocere, or grave wax. It can form in water, due to the absence of bacteria to fuel conventional putrefaction." Grave wax, in a corpse that had never been buried. Every day was a school day. "But saponification only reached the initial stages. In other places the skin had begun to slip. Imagine being in the bath too long. In this case, three weeks too long."

"Did this person drown?"

"No. None of the classical indicators are present. From the condition of their lungs, they were killed elsewhere and then dumped."

"Cause of death?"

The pathologist frowned. "Certainty can be difficult in submerged bodies. But everything here points to blood loss."

"Could it have been accidental?"

She grimaced. "No. This person was tortured, perhaps ritualistically. Not only are certain deep scars still visible," she indicated blackish lines on the discoloured torso, "but see also," she gently lifted the stripped arm by the wrist. "Look at the metacarpal bones. This damage here. A blade of some kind was stabbed through this hand."

He tried not to think about what Doirin said in the coffee shop. He didn't want to be influenced by it. "Why ritualistic?"

"We find a near-identical injury on the other side. That happened by design, although we don't know why."

Both hands, punctured ritualistically. Perhaps for an audience? Doirin's words were unavoidable, the tie-in too strong to be suppressed. "Identity?"

"A number of aspects are strongly indicative of our Mr Reynolds. My estimate here would have been of a male late thirties or early forties. Reynolds was thirty-nine. Reynolds had a dental implant, located in LR45. I find an implant in the same position in our victim. Sadly the implant has no batch number, but it is the same type as

Reynolds' dental records describe. Finally, Reynolds had apparently suffered a shin fracture as a child. I find some evidence of one here. Even without a definitive DNA match, if this isn't Reynolds I'd be very surprised."

"Any thoughts on the white plastic sheet?"

She shrugged. "It is easier to move a body when wrapped, I suppose. Beyond that vague generality, I have nothing to offer."

So they'd found him. He'd been dumped at sea after being tortured to death. Cochrane's note suggested a clinical silencing of a witness. But the injuries to the man's hands suggested something more elaborate.

"Anything to indicate where his injuries occurred?"

"The condition of the body is a guide to the duration of post-mortem exposure above and below water: aerobic processes above in contrast to the anaerobic processes below. That answer is hours not days, and although I can't be definitive, my best guess is that death occurred on land less than six hours before he was dumped."

Andy performed a quick mental calculation. "The marine archaeologists reckoned perhaps three hours to reach the dumping site by boat. So let's say three hours on land, three hours by boat. But concluding any ritual or display, then cleaning and evacuating the murder scene would eat into that onshore time window. As would any rigmarole around reaching and then preparing the vessel for the journey. It seems unlikely this body had time to travel far."

"I'd agree. The likelihood is this person was killed locally. East Coast, Edinburgh, Fife. I believe we found your victim, Detective."

BACK AT HIS DESK, Andy called the number he held for Tricia Black. He'd made a promise after all.

He explained their belief that John Reynolds had been found. She agreed to take a visit from a forensics officer regarding whatever she had of John's; some hair or some skin cells would be enough to close all discussion, but even without that, the physical correspondences already logged were enough to make it a formality.

When Andy closed the call, he reflected that they might be nearing the end of her nightmare. He hoped so. Nothing could ever make up for what had happened, but Reynolds had been proved innocent and he'd been found.

To round off the day, he leafed through festival brochures searching for a precise address for the 'Wonderground' venue from the clown's leaflet. It proved elusive, so he noted phone numbers for venues and companies around Niddry Street that might be able to help. If he couldn't find anything on paper or the Internet, he'd have to play telephone tag in the morning. He wanted to bottom it out before his weekend away, and he was running out of time.

38

WONDERGROUND

THURSDAY 22ND SEPTEMBER, 13:15

At quarter-past one, Niddry Street was a rat run for lunchtime pedestrians heading down to the Cowgate or up to the Royal Mile. Andy hovered outside the tour company offices behind a coachload of tourists. He hoped he hadn't misunderstood, and that someone here was actually expecting him. He waved at a belea-guered employee through the window, but she couldn't see him past a skeleton that crouched inside the glass.

"Detective Lorimar?"

The young man stood behind him, burnished copper hair poked beneath the hood of a Doctor Who sweatshirt. "I'm Sam. We spoke on the phone?" Although it wasn't raining, Sam held aloft a golf umbrella; the words *Undercity Tours* arched around a grinning skull. He closed the brolly hurriedly. "Force of habit. Helps the punters spot me. Anyway, sorry I'm late. I was delayed with the midday group. One of them was freaking out a bit."

Andy recognised the voice. Sam had shown interest in the enquiry, and his offer to meet had been welcome, but the call had been cut short. "So. You had thoughts. About Wondergound?"

"That name doesn't exist officially. But we're the only properly underground venue on Niddry Street, so my money's definitely on us. C'mon. I'll show you."

They walked to a nondescript entrance, which Sam unlocked. A damp stone staircase stretched down into the darkness. "It was the dates you mentioned." He let the door shut behind them, leaving them in half-lit gloom. "We run tours all evening during the festival, but we'd had to finish by 6pm on the 30th, because of some council thing."

As they proceeded downwards, Andy took some snaps with his phone. He had no idea why people would spend good money to come here. "I don't suppose you know what the council needed the place for?"

"No, sorry. But we're built into the South Bridge, and we always accommodate the council. Possibly a structural survey or mainte-nance maybe, or it might even have been a research group or some-thing like that."

"Research group?"

They walked through a couple of chambers. Small and bare, and neither the kind of thing Andy had in mind. The tour guide contin-ued. "We get psychic investigators, scientists and all sorts, debating infrasound versus spectral manifestation versus stone tapes. The reputation of the place draws them in. This room's supposedly haunted by an angry little man called Mr Boots, but I haven't seen him myself. Some people do get a vibe here."

Chilly certainly, but being underground with no heating will do that. They passed a small room with a stone circle and kept walking.

"So. The day after, on the thirty-first, the tours carried on as normal?"

"Yeah."

"Didn't spot anything weird?"

"Not visibly, but ..." The young man guided them into to a larger vault. Andy recalled Doirin's impressions from the coffee shop. This one was certainly suitable for a small audience. "In here, a few of us picked up a chemical smell. Bleach or something? It didn't last though. Everything down here reverts to damp and musty within a day or two."

"Where was that chemical smell strongest?"

The tour guide pointed to the right side of the room, and Andy removed a couple of plastic containers from his pocket before mixing the contents. Having brought the luminol, he might as well use it. "Can you switch the lights off in here? Just for a minute?"

Sam went outside and a few moments later the room was plunged into darkness, with only a faint residual glow leaking through from other chambers. Quickly, Andy sprayed the right hand wall and floor in wide passes. A blue luminescence formed a clear spatter arc beginning about one metre up, continuing to around head height. Blood had spilled here, and the hurried cleanup had been less than perfect.

The tour guide returned just as Andy placed the spray back in his pocket. "Detective Lorimar, how much time d'you think you'll need? I've got a group at three p.m."

Andy reached for his phone. "Sorry, Sam. Your three p.m. just got cancelled."

———

AFTER UNLEASHING the dogs of forensic science onto the South Bridge vaults, Andy eked a small amount of extra information from the council. All they knew was that their reservation on the evening of the 30th August had been made by Joan Wood. The lack of further detail was unsurprising. If she'd been preparing for the ritualistic murder of a blackmailer (preparations Reynold's bungled into), he doubted they'd have an agenda item at a committee meeting. Of course, the same secrecy might apply to a backdoor favour for Cochrane, so the suicide note faced no serious challenge.

Still, another face of the cube had come together, another piece of the puzzle had been placed. But now a further piece was calling him.

He tried repeatedly to contact Joan Wood's old Professor, Harry Prosser using the details provided during their first conversation. But he wasn't at UCL and his mobile phone was not being answered.

But Andy couldn't let it go. There had been a show. There had been a venue. Someone disappeared and it emerged they had been murdered. The incident Petrakis had found in the Prague newspaper was now an itch he needed to scratch. He sent a message to Prosser's number.

PROF - COULD YOU FIND ME A CONTACT WHO KNEW DR DIRK MÜLLER? HE WAS A RESEARCHER IN YOUR FIELD UNTIL 2006.

It was a long shot, but he might get something to work on when he returned from Spain on Monday.

As he powered down the workstation he let himself relax. This felt like a decent breakpoint for his long weekend away. It would be a genuine relief to park the case for a few days.

PART V

VINYA ENVERINADA

FRIDAY 23RD SEPTEMBER

39

THE WALLPAPER BOX
FRIDAY 23RD SEPTEMBER, 10:07

Ilsa had become surprisingly digitally savvy. Numerous text messages over the course of the week had confirmed whether Andy's eating and drinking preferences were as she remembered and whether Doirin shared them. She was evidently planning to make a bit of a fuss whether he liked it or not. She also supplied the address and links to maps in case he had forgotten where he was going.

But he was confident he wouldn't have become completely lost; the place was burned into his mind from the time of Jimmy's burial. He recalled a mild sense of incongruity about that funeral in the blazing sunshine, but mostly he remembered an awkward mixture of grief and suppressed anger that held him remote from Ilsa throughout.

At the gate in Edinburgh, finding that their flight to Barcelona would depart on time, he sent her a final message confirming when they ought to reach her in Palamos.

During boarding it was obvious the flight was busy, possibly even full. Approaching their row he became anxious to ensure Doirin, doing him a favour after all, would be comfortable, even if it meant subjecting himself to a two-hour knee press. "I'm not fussed," he lied. "D'you prefer the aisle or the window?"

Doirin smiled at the notion. "Davie always insisted the wee person got the window. So I think I'm due the view for once."

During the journey, Andy read the in-flight magazine. Then he read the in-flight shopping guide. Then he went back to the magazine to make sure he hadn't missed anything. But mostly, he thought about Ilsa and how the afternoon might go.

When they landed, Barcelona airport proved even more hectic than Edinburgh. Andy was glad he'd booked a taxi transfer to Palamos. Ilsa's car was being serviced, and he'd wanted to avoid stitching together multiple legs of public transport. It wasn't cheap, but it would save them hours of messing about, and should help them get back to Miguel's tonight at a halfway respectable hour.

Doirin, embraced the experience with the enthusiasm of a child in a sweetshop. "He's got a card! Lorimar and Chambers! Look! That's us!" She had the driver teaching them Spanish and Catalan for most of the journey. Andy hadn't laughed so much in years. It didn't seem long before they pulled up outside Ilsa's door.

ILSA FINISHED POURING and placed the pot on the table. "Carmen-Teresa go wrong on your herbal tea Andrew. She get me mango fruit tea. Yack. Never mind. You take normal, but I pour yours weak." Ilsa wasn't much changed from the time of the funeral as far as he could tell. She moved a little more slowly, thanks to her knees, but her personality remained as direct as ever.

She narrowed her eyes as she looked at him. "So Andrew? What you do to your face?"

"Nothing to worry about. Just a wee bump."

"Hmm. And Doirin. You know Andrew, how?"

Doirin's cup rattled as she returned it to her saucer. "We got friendly after he interviewed me for—" she turned to Andy, "What was it you thought again? Was I a murderer or an accomplice?"

Good god. That was all he needed. Two alpha females batting him around like a doomed mouse. "C'mon. You gave a voluntary statement. I get hundreds of those from ordinary folk every year."

"You hear that Ilsa? I'm ordinary now. Charming."

Ilsa smiled. "You must forgive him Doirin. He not very social. I blame, well, I blame him nowadays. He stupid and big enough to know better."

Interesting as this might be, Andy couldn't abide spending an age on chit-chat when they needed something dealt with. "Actually Ilsa, I need to apologise." He glanced towards Doirin, who tightened her lips, but gave a small nod. "When I told you about Jimmy and the box, I wasn't being honest. I actually got that information from Doirin, and I pretended he'd told me."

Ilsa spoke quietly. "Why you lie?"

Doirin reached across and touched her hand. "He's embarrassed to tell you. I'm a medium."

Ilsa clenched her fingers and withdrew.

Andy intervened. "Doirin passed on a message to me, about a wallpaper box. I couldn't say it came from ... well ... I've never believed that's possible. And I knew you wouldn't. But I needed to find out if it was true, by telling you in a way you couldn't dismiss ... I'm sorry." He was unsure he could make this sound acceptable, even to himself. "Look, the main thing is, somehow Doirin told me something specific, and it turns out she was right."

Ilsa rose and splashed her tea into the sink. "Yack. Too weak." As she walked back towards the pot on the table her eyes were hard. "So, Mrs Spooky-wooky. What my dead husband tell you, huh?"

He knew Ilsa had mentally reclassified Doirin from house guest to heartless trickster, and she was letting it show.

Doirin said, "This happened multiple times before I told Andy. And the main impression I got was concern. Jimmy didn't want to reveal the information about the box. There might even have been fear about Andy finding out. Jimmy didn't seem to want him to know."

Ilsa was silent for a moment. "A true thing." The cup dropped from her hands, shattering against the stone floor into shards of ceramic. "So why? Why you tell him?"

Doirin knotted and pulled at her fingers as she answered. "I'm sorry. Spirit wanted him to know. There were ... others ... involved, they brought Jimmy forward and he delivered the message because of them. I don't understand. It isn't usual."

Andy retrieved the remnants of Ilsa's cup and put them in her bin. He touched the older woman's shoulder. "Ilsa. Maybe they just wanted me here, with you, now? Whatever, I know now. And I keep wondering if ... if this is what changed our relationship before Jimmy's retirement. Was it?"

Ilsa was silent. Ten seconds. She looked into his eyes. "What you mean?"

Andy sighed. She knew. They both did. "You never talked about leaving before. You always joked about opening a B&B in Portobello. Then suddenly, out of nowhere, Spain, and you and Jimmy couldn't get away quick enough." Ilsa shook her head, but said nothing. "Jimmy said he was looking for better weather, but that wasn't true. You liked it warm, sure, but he'd always burned like toast. So I didn't buy it." Ilsa opened her mouth to speak, but Andy continued. "Don't mention a change of scene. That's all I've ever heard. It wasn't just the scene that changed, it was everything. That's why we're both feeling awkward about this. The way we are now would have been impossible back when you guys were in Edinburgh."

Ilsa sighed, and gave Doirin a hard stare. Then she simply said, "Wait." She left the room.

Andy turned towards Doirin. "I'm sorry you're taking grief over this."

She shrugged. "It's a lot for her to handle, but this is a conversation you two needed. If me being the baddie helps, fine. But you better be nice to me at Miguel's party."

Ilsa returned, struggling with the weight of a large box. Despite expectation, it wasn't quite big enough to hold rolls of wallpaper, but was wrapped externally in the wall covering from Andy's own bedroom. Jimmy must have salvaged some from when he'd helped decorate. Andy approached Ilsa to help, but she only reluctantly surrendered her burden.

As he placed it on the floor, she spoke. "He never give up, you know."

"What?"

"He ... always try ... to find what happened. Your mother."

Andy didn't understand. Jimmy had never even talked about Mum, except when it was unavoidable. Andy sometimes trapped himself wandering the bleak labyrinth of that loss. And it had always been Jimmy and Ilsa who'd pulled him out.

"He always wonder, you see, if it help. To know, I mean, for you. To have peace?" She crouched down beside him. "This box. It contain his investigation."

Dropping the lid, Andy rose. He staggered backwards. It felt like a physical blow to the stomach. This was his own history. And they'd kept it from him. They hadn't trusted him with it.

But, then, could he be trusted? Even now? If he could handle this rationally, then why was his head against the window, quickening breaths steaming the cold glass? Sweat crawled from his neck to his back, down his arms, onto the palms of his hands.

That box had taken them away from him, so what the hell had they discovered? What could have made the people who were his protectors suddenly feel themselves a threat?

He tried to keep his voice even. "What's in there? Do you know what... what happened to her?"

"Oh Andrew. We didn't find out everything. But we found him. Or someone who knew him."

He froze. "Billy."

Ilsa grunted. "Jimmy interviewed an old cellmate. His real name wasn't Billy or William. It was Eric Kidd. He'd spent time in Aberdeen. Craiginches."

It didn't surprise him that Billy had done jail time, even if only a fraction of what he'd deserved. Craiginches was gone now, closed a few years back after decades of overcrowding. "What did they say, this cellmate?"

Ilsa paused. "Eric Kidd went to Spain after leaving Scotland. So now you know only reason Jimmy wanted to be here." She hesitated. "His cellmate say other thing too. We don't know if true."

"Just tell me."

"He boast to cellmate that an Edinburgh detective—"

"Was looking for him? Knew he was a murderer?"

Ilsa spoke quietly. "No. He said an Edinburgh detective was his son."

The first wave to crash was confusion.

It was ridiculous. Impossible. Billy entered the scene way too late. Andy's birth certificate was blank and Mum had only ever mentioned a fling with someone from abroad. Whatever Billy's angle, he'd been talking through his arse. "No," he said.

Ilsa said, "May not be so. Here we might prove or disprove."

Then the second wave was ice, razor shards penetrating his skin, worming deeper, cutting loose old mysteries. Why Granda had known Billy when he first showed up. Why he'd reacted against him so quickly. Why Mum, normally so cautious with her son, had opened their life to a newcomer, letting him treat their flat as his own. The way she'd persisted, against her child's resistance, a perseverance that probably sealed her fate.

A lurch in his gut.

What he'd believed as a child, the toxic anti-logic that somehow what happened was his fault? All along, that poison had coated the simple truth. She stayed with Billy, she tried to make it work, she'd snared herself in his trap, all to give her son a father.

For him.

It all happened for him.

"No," he said again, moving towards the door. "You should have told me. Jimmy should have told me."

Doirin rose and Ilsa reached for his arm, but he waved them away. "No. I'll be back. I need time."

He let the door swing shut behind him and made his way into the air.

40

STRANGERS ON A BENCH

FRIDAY 23RD SEPTEMBER, 16:07

He walked for a while in the warm drizzle. His skin registered the sensation, but inside he was numb.

He barely noticed as Avenida Païssos Catalans became Avinguda de la Mediterrania, as the residential gave way to the commercial. Soon he would reach the sea, and he wanted the vastness right then. He needed it, to render him insignificant, to deny his power to have so perfectly crafted the destruction of the woman who gave him life.

He found a bench, and stared out at the Mediterranean. The wind blew warm rain, bringing the ocean salt into his eyes. He rubbed them, but they wouldn't dry, not properly.

The whole thing was stupid. Jimmy should have known he could tell him, and they would have talked together about the difference between a father and a sperm supply, in that frank, sensible way Jimmy always did. He'd always shown Andy ways of sanitising the unthinkable, given him the tools needed to safely fit things into his head. But Jimmy hadn't done that with this. And that fact hurt almost as much as what Jimmy had found.

Andy closed his eyes for a moment, feeling the breeze against his face. He had to keep this in some kind of context. Jimmy and Ilsa were good people, but after all, just people. People get scared, and relationships, at least ones that matter, are never entirely rational.

He'd already known everything important about Billy, and at the core of it, nothing had changed. He knew himself too, and he couldn't let anything change there either. But, one thing was certain: he'd have to put a face on for the party tonight.

Paper rustled and snapped as a map became caught by the breeze. The man holding it stopped in front of Andy's bench. "Hablas español?"

Andy shook his head. "Sorry, I'm Scottish. Just visiting."

The stranger's face broke into a grin "Scottish? Hey! I've been! Cold! Wet! Good!" He reached out and shook Andy's hand. "I'm Rene, and I'm lost. May I share your bench while I get my bearings?"

"No problem, Rene, I'm Andy." The man spoke English well, but with a slight French accent. Andy budged over, giving him space to spread the map across his knees. "So you're not a local then?"

Rene reached into his rucksack and brought out a flask. "No, Andy, no! I'm from Martinque originally but live mostly in Turkey now." He shook his head ruefully. "Lost in a small place like this? Shameful. I found the sea but not Santa Maria. I'm looking for the church. Do you know it?"

Andy shook his head, and Rene was downcast. "Ah well! It's a day for mysteries. For instance ..." He poured a cup of steaming liquid. "My wife, she's stopped my caffeine, but what is this?" He handed over the lid of the flask filled to the brim.

Andy sniffed warily and then broke into a smile. "Now this, I can help you with. That's chamomile tea. I know this very well."

Rene's jaw dropped. "You drink it? Then do! I have another cup in here somewhere for me." The man rooted around in his bag while Andy sipped. The tea was delicious. Hot, but not scalding, the chamomile rich with a honey sweetness he'd grown to love. Rene held up a lunch box. "You like Hummus? Crackers?" It was amazing, really, how Rene's packed lunch included so many of Andy's favourites. But he passed on the food in favour of savouring the tea, finding some peace in watching small white waves riding the blue towards the shore.

It took a while before he realised his companion had never fetched that spare cup after all, and hadn't eaten any of his own food. Andy felt strange.

Woozy.

He dropped the flask cup and tried to apologise, but his lips and tongue couldn't coordinate the words.

Rene stretched an arm across as he began to slump. Then, dimly, another presence drew alongside, and suddenly he was hauled to his feet.

A voice in his ear. "Hello again, Detective." His last thought as they pulled him staggering towards a waiting vehicle was that he recognised the accent.

It sounded alarmingly like Yurik Sokov.

WHEN ANDY WOKE, he was confined in a strange wooden chair.

His head throbbed queasily, a dull echo of the mickey they'd slipped him. The room was dark, but faint light trickled through a vent on the opposite wall. He pushed up with his feet. The chair was fixed inside some kind of box.

Here, there was no soundscape beyond the one he created himself. Could he be underground? From the lack of external noise, he was either somewhere deep or somewhere remote. Possibly both.

He couldn't turn around. Wooden panels front and rear held his upper body in place, and straps fixed his arms inside curved armrests. The blocks underneath his palms felt ragged and punctured. In front of him, three benches rested on white plastic sheeting. The sheeting extended beneath his own chair.

He didn't want to think about what any of that meant right now. He especially didn't want to consider what Doirin had said in the coffee shop after her meeting with Tricia Black. Or what Reynolds' body had been wrapped in.

He began to shout. "Hey! I'm awake!"

No answer.

"Who brought me here?"

Nothing.

"Who did this?"

He stamped his feet, creating a series of hollow thunks.

"Who are you?"

He wrenched against the straps securing his arms, threw himself against the panel at his chest. A tiny amount of give, but the restraints were solid.

"Who the hell are you?"

The sound of footsteps behind him. Someone approached.

"Who's here? Who are you?"

A momentary touch on his hair, and then a cloth gag pulled tight, biting the corners of his mouth.

But someone spoke.

The voice was accented. Confident. Redolent with grim humour. "Who am I, Detective Lorimar? I am the one you have foolishly pursued. You will have your answers, and shall pay the price for them."

A blindfold was drawn over his eyes and he considered the darkness.

41

FEELINGS

The feelings had been weak at first. Doirin experienced them as a sense of dislocation, a kind of awkwardness. She originally dismissed this, because there were many reasons to feel awkward.

Ilsa remained upset. She was suspicious of Doirin's motives and rejected the supernatural aspects of the story she'd been told. When Ilsa had probed for messages from her husband or other relatives, Doirin's mind answered only with silence. A simple question of whether there was any gin in the house had raised the kind of scornful eyebrow Doirin normally specialised in herself.

When it became clear the spirit cavalry would fail to deliver anything at all, never mind something remotely approaching proof, the conversation shrivelled into stilted small talk. Eventually discussion lapsed altogether, and Ilsa switched on her radio. When even that wasn't enough of a barrier from her unwanted guest, the older woman began to flick through a newspaper.

Doirin drained the last of her tea before fetching an airport paperback from her suitcase. Her attention flitted between the book, the happy pointlessness of the radio and wondering how she could have handled this better. She would be glad when Andy returned from his walk and they could leave for the friendlier climes of tonight's party.

But the feelings continued to grow, building into a crawling sensation that was impossible to ignore. Doirin remembered the evening Andy had been taken to hospital, but there, she had quickly achieved a clear sense of purpose. This time the sensation was amorphous, unfocused. "Ilsa, I'm getting a bad feeling about Andy."

The older woman glanced up from her newspaper. "Is this a spooky-wooky bad feeling, or a he's-not-here-but-I-want-party bad feeling?"

Relations had not thawed, but this couldn't be dropped. "The last time I experienced something like this, he'd been attacked."

Ilsa frowned. "So the bruising around his eye? Not just wee bump?"

Doirin nodded. "Someone tried to kill him. I felt like this. Then I found him in hospital. Please, can we search for him?"

Uncertainty played over Ilsa's features. "We can't leave so sudden. He will return to locked door. Hold on." The woman made a call from the hallway. Moments later she returned with a decision. "Mecánico bring my car in an hour. We give Andrew time to return. If not here by then, we go look. OK?"

Doirin had no choice. But the wait was torture. The crawling sensation swelled, impossible to ignore, grating and tugging at her, like the sound of crying children.

When the doorbell rang, Ilsa grew excited, but Doirin ignored it. She concentrated, trying to distill meaning from a squall of pleading voices in her mind. Spirit wanted her to move. NOW. But where should she go?

When Ilsa returned, the waiting at least, was over. "OK, so my car here. But Andrew is not." Her frown was tight. "I put note on door asking he phone us." Doirin had called him an hour ago, but was now certain no response would arrive. "We drive to waterfront. He probably staring at the sea, so we bring him home."

Although it didn't take long to reach the front, Doirin was only dimly aware of their movements. The first stage of this trip was for Ilsa, but Doirin's journey was different, an internal one, tracing threads of meaning across a web of mental noise.

When Ilsa parked, leaving the car to look around, Doirin remained inside, her eyes drifting out of focus.

She was startled to awareness by the opening door. Ilsa said, "Plenty ordinary people, but no tall, pale men dressed as if for funeral. You want to come and check?"

Doirin shook her head. "Not here. We need to head out of the city. He's in the hills."

42

MAXIM'S STORY

FRIDAY 23RD SEPTEMBER, 17:28

Andy did not move. With his captor pacing nearby, visibly testing the restraints might only win him more of them. He was gagged and bound. It was time to listen.

"Before my tale begins, Detective Lorimar, I will commend you. Throughout our games you have demonstrated persistence and determination. But I, too, am a determined man, and one with something of great value to protect. Something that you, in your ignorance, sought to endanger. I will not tolerate that, and you will finally appreciate who you have challenged. There is no escape from this room my friend. Indeed, that is the only reason you hear these words. For me, this is an exercise in nostalgia. For you, it is a last request."

It was difficult to estimate the age of the speaker. He was mature certainly, but his voice was strong. And horribly triumphant.

"So. Who am I? I am Maxim Vorsky. I suspect you want more, and since we have time before our performance, more you shall have. My father, a practical man and maritime engineer, pushed me academically, towards the medical career he felt I was capable of, and that he would have doubtless loved for himself. He grew to be much impressed by the works of Bogdanov and his acolytes Shamov and Yudin, all pioneers in the emerging science of blood. Indeed, those men were true innovators, the first to demonstrate transfusion from cadavers—"

As the man continued, Andy wondered whether to bother committing these names to memory. Blood from corpses? The gothic nightmare of a mad scientist. He was hearing a fairy-tale.

But uncomfortable recollections intruded: Joan Wood's scandal of misplaced NHS blood supplies, Dudnic's claims around medical research. And Dirk Müller, the academic involved with Wood's husband who vanished. But he could ponder that later. Even if this man proved an unreliable witness, this was a statement and he should give it his attention.

"To my father, the great men of Russian science were leading the world. The fact that Bogdanov's self-experimentation eventually doomed him would, in my father's eyes, only serve to magnify that heroism. That opinion, however, was not one I could ever share.

"Dreams of scientific utopia were hard to sustain in those troubled times. Brutal purges, border conflicts with Japan, involvements in China, Spain and Finland; all ugly preludes to the madness of a world at war. While I trained as a surgeon, my professors, unsurprisingly, had an eye on the battlefield. They gave us this edict to live by: save those you can, learn from the rest. I remember still, my feeling in the classroom as I heard those words. My sense was of a marching piper suddenly falling out of step with the drums. But I had realised a truth about myself. I preferred the learning.

"In the summer of 1941, Stalin's obsession with the enemy within blinded him to invaders without. My parents were blockaded, along with many others, in the Reich's siege of Leningrad. The transport ship *Armenia* had been adopted by the Soviet Navy as a hospital ship, and I would be its surgeon. My surgical cabin, although hastily constructed, was outfitted well. It bested the captain's quarters in both physical dimensions and the expansive window views. While my scalpel might need to overcome the unsteady vexations of the sea, my patients would suffer no deficiency of light or air."

Andy clenched his fists. This timeline established the story false, or the teller insane. A medic practising in 1941 would be in a rocking chair admiring his postcard from the queen, not stalking around a kidnap victim.

"I assumed none would begrudge small comforts to those requiring the sharp ministrations of a surgeon. Until I encountered the lumbering jealousy of Senior Lieutenant Bagrev, a man whose rank had set a flame beneath his outsize ego. He was temperamentally ill-suited to even his small seniority, which he had gained *po blatu*, as a result of the party connections of his father.

"He disliked me, for reasons I could not initially fathom, since I had no interest in him whatsoever, beyond perhaps, the mystery of such bulk sustained by wartime rations in a country of enforced equality. He tried on two separate occasions to wrest my surgical cabin from me, claiming his own accommodation did not match his status. He would have succeeded, if not for the effort required to relocate a floor-welded operating table. Not even Bagrev could elevate his desire for creature comfort above naval mission imperatives while Nazi U-boats patrolled the Black Sea.

"Our paths crossed again when his routine medical results placed him far behind the other crew. He was revealed unfit for his own post, or indeed, any other. When I shared this with our captain, he ordered my results be suppressed.

"The most compelling aspect to Bagrev was that I judged him biologically, measure for measure, decades older than his years. My thoughts turned to adipose tissue. I refer of course to human fat."

Thin fingers were drawn across Andy's bare forearm, pinching at the flesh near his elbow. He clenched his teeth, biting down hard on the cloth gag, unsure of what would follow. But it was another game, and his tormentor resumed his story. "Was such tissue metabolically active? Influencing ageing? The possibility intrigued me."

A footstep. The voice paused. "Ah! But I detect frustration, in the frown lines on your brow, in the whites of your knuckles. Perhaps you feel I labour these early years? No matter. This is my tale, and I tell it how I please. In any case, believe me; you should welcome every added minute of my digressions." The sound of his laughter churned Andy's gut.

"Now. It is the 7th November 1941 and *Armenia*'s mission is one of rescue. Thousands from besieged Sevastopol had already boarded, and nearby Yalta would provide thousands more. The ship was over-laden, the passengers in a state of panic, the crew, barely coping. Bagrev began a screaming battle with the captain, demanding we take our leave while darkness might shield us from Nazi reprisals, but our orders were to await military escort. When our Senior Lieutenant found himself thwarted once more by military imperatives, beset upon all sides by throngs of the traumatised, he behaved to his type, dropping dead on the main deck.

"I knew what must be done.

"After dealing with the wounded among our passengers I delegated minor injuries to others. Our escorts arrived with the dawn and the ship finally limped out of port. That was my chance to grant Lieutenant Bagrev's wish, giving him finally full use of the cabin he had craved. At least, until his dissection was complete. I marvelled at the improvement death brought to his personality. He let my work proceed without the least sneer or complaint, and at last I came to know the only aspects of the man that had any value.

"It was a memorable exploration.

"No matter my years, I have never lost my sense of wonder. Have you seen the inside of a human body, Mr Lorimar? Of course, a detective has familiarity with the great menu of mortality. Butter-flied corpses, their organs laid out in an evidentiary buffet for you to probe and sample and build your case around. I accept you've seen the viscera, but did you understand it? Did you appreciate that beau-tiful complexity, those mechanisms remaining somehow miraculous even in failure?

"Bagrev, that most corpulent of sailors, carried an internal sea of yellow, all the energy he had consumed but never expended. I explored its makeup, classified the types and filled my sample jars: the lumps of subcutaneous fat hanging like plump leeches to the underside of his flesh, the thick visceral fat that pooled around his organs, the epicardial fats that coddled his heart. You will not be surprised by my determination on his death. Those coronary arteries were the most sclerotic I have ever seen to this day. And I have seen many. His innards, in service only thirty-seven years, were those of a man approaching his seventh decade. This apparent malleability of age fascinated me. This was not Bogdanov's dream of rejuvenation. No. Spread before me, writ in cream and crimson was his nightmare: accelerated decrepitude.

"But my enjoyment was rudely disturbed. The siren's wail announced enemies approached, but I was not overly concerned. As a hospital ship, and marked as such, the laws of war should have kept us safe from assault. But that delusion of the herd was destroyed by a torpedo strike. War has no law, beyond to kill your enemy and prolong your own survival. Bagrev had been correct: we should have fled Yalta at night. However, on this occasion no one would suffer his gloating.

"In such a situation, they say time slows. But as you may learn shortly, perception merely narrows, drawing information directed only towards survival. That day, the listing of my ship told me instantly that we were sinking.

"Had I been a good Soviet, like those others on-board, my comrades and those unlucky refugees, I might have chosen that we cleave together and die in our thousands, in a great and final demonstration of collectivism.

"But I was not a good Soviet.

"Childhood swims in Baltic lakes suggested an alternative. Open water makes a cold grave, and unlike in my youth I had no neighbour proffering the insulation of rendered goose fat. So I adapted, looking to my sample jars. The thickest visceral fat was a flawed substitute, adulterated with blood and other tissues, but I shed the constriction of my clothing and smeared those remnants of Lieutenant Bagrev on my naked skin. I slid open my cabin window and leapt into the ice-cold waters of the black sea.

"That dive is burned into my memory to this very day. My arms outstretched in supplication, ready to receive the water's embrace. Behind me, the smell of burning, the shriek of the siren, the low rumble of the mighty *Armenia* groaning and breaking, a counterpoint to the powerless screams from the thousands on-board.

"Plunging beneath the sea brought a roaring silence and instant clarity, a sudden shield against the madness. Then I did what I had trained to do as a lonely child. I struck out as fast and as far as I could, lest the doomed vessel create a sink hole that sealed my fate.

"More than seven thousand perished that morning. You, I imagine, considered Titanic the mightiest of sea disasters, since the fifteen-hundred who perished on that vessel were Westerners, your own tribe, and so worthy of your memory. Our species values our own kinfolk more highly than the anonymous other; it is an inescapable part of who we are. The difference between myself and the herd, Mr Lorimar, is that my kin are of my choosing and I embrace my true nature. Most refuse to acknowledge any truth that brings discomfort. Extending games of childish pretend into adulthood is easier; I understand.

"The escort boats found only me and a further eight survivors. I remember well that voyage back to land. The others, both rescuers and rescued, held themselves apart. But pulled from the water naked, my body smeared and glistening with the red sheen of Bagrev's death, I was reborn, and cared nothing for the distaste of the herd. The great men had played their games and thousands had died, but I had chosen not to be one of their corpses.

"I had chosen.

"Such a choice you must realise, cannot be unmade. You asked who I am? Contemplate that choice.

"But those others who died that day did not pass quickly from my mind, for I am not without emotion. I felt not pain, you understand, but rage. Seven thousand drowned. For nothing. Even today I bear the burden of that appalling waste. I could have learnt from each and every one of them.

"I sought no further naval commission, but my details came to Grigory Mairanovsky. You know him?"

Was this to be a conversation now? Perhaps the gag would be removed if Andy played along. He shook his head.

"No. Of course not. He is not from your tribe, but was a man of significance in his day. Mairanovsky needed medical researchers for his laboratory in Moscow. It was an excellent role for me. Screening fatal chemicals against enemies of the state was undemanding work; it left sufficient space for the conduct of my parallel research into compliance. The deaths demanded by Stalin were of no use in my plan. What worth has a carcass? Meat rots quickly, whichever beast is culled. The miracle of life however, that was a goal worthy of my interest, and only the compliant living could help me with my studies."

Compliance. This wild story created another echo it was impossible to ignore. Radu Dudnic was rendered compliant. Presumably his predecessor at Corryvreckan was too. And Doctor Nassar had used the word when describing the possible action of a compound found in Robin McKay's tox screen. If not for his liver damage would McKay have been compliant? Would he have walked into the van parked outside the Balrannoch and to his own death? Did Reynolds die just for getting in the way?

"Again I read something in the muscles of your face. Feigned horror? Or genuine ignorance of the world in which you live? No matter. I am beyond such things. A mighty state had ruled my subjects should die. I gifted them extra weeks of life, and more; I gave them meaning. They helped me breach the boundaries of human knowledge.

"Eventually I left my country and travelled. These great games of war and wealth afforded me an opportunity. The herd would continue to die but I resolved those deaths needn't lack purpose. This is the trade I continue to offer. It is my life's work.

"Your world lays on a bounty of such opportunities, too many for one man, so my project has gathered supporters over the years. Whenever the veneer of civilisation begins to peel, as it always does, when lives lose value and the masses are displaced? That is where our efforts find greatest purchase. I have grown my own society, but it is different to your own. To us, each life has significance, each death contributes to greatness. We work for the survival of myself and my colleagues, purely since that is necessary for the continuance of our project."

Silence, without footsteps. Twenty seconds.

"But in certain cases an individual threatens the work or our stewardship of it. You, Mr Lorimar, along with Reynolds, McKay and my once-colleagues Wood and Hofler, all blundered into that category. I take no pleasure in such outcomes, but ensure the blood spilt becomes glue, binding our society in common endeavour. While I abhorred the barbarity of Stalin, he had one lesson to teach. When a message must be understood, do not deliver it with a wagging finger. No one is schooled by a wagging finger. Use an ice pick. Whether those who receive it, or those who witness it, all are schooled by an ice pick.

"Such deaths protect our work, so might even be considered a gift. I grant you exactly that boon this evening."

A disdainful sigh. "But beneath your gag, your mouth seeks to distort. You recoil, as would many, perhaps branding my methods corrupt and depraved. Human experimentation is, for some reason, an unspeakable taboo. And yet, your world has become reconciled to the Petri dish of warfare. In Leningrad, the methods applied were labelled strategy and taught to the most honourable, the officers and generals. And those methods were effective. At its height, twenty-thousand died each day of cold and hunger. Thousands were convicted of cannibalism; starvation insanity led some to eat their own flesh, others to make soup from the hands of dead children. But

Stalin and Hitler, those great powers of history, looked down upon a mountain of frozen corpses, a mountain containing my own parents, and continued their game.

"But you know this.

"Social and environmental experimentation is your established order, premature death the frequent consequence. My work shares that consequence, but balances it with the extension of both knowledge and human life itself. If you remain unconvinced, I do not truly care. Perhaps you feel the ethical choice for me is to simply accept my term and die, to show my solidarity with the herd. But now you understand: I rejected that bargain once before. Choosing to die for the ethics of others is not admirable. However you, Mr Lorimar, you *are* worthy of admiration, for at least the ethics you will die for are your own."

Footsteps receded. A door hinge squealed. The voice called back. "Until this evening my friend. The gag and mask will be needed for our performance, so you will forgive me if I leave you wearing them."

When the door banged shut, Andy wrenched at the straps binding his arms. He knew now with certainty. If he did not free himself, he would die here.

43

A SUPPORT ACT

FRIDAY 23RD SEPTEMBER, 17:52

Five minutes passed. Then he froze at a grunt of pain. Something had been dragged through the door, was scraping along the floor. Sokov's voice. "I bring company, Detective."

Then another voice raised in protest. Shrill. Angry. Desperate. "My last hours? Stuck with a gimp in a gag and blindfold?"

They'd only exchanged a few words before, but it sounded like Nick Cochrane. "Please Yurik! C'mon. If it wasn't for this bastard, we'd still be on the same side. Let me at least speak to the shithead. I've got a few things to bloody say!"

A grunt of assent and then Andy flinched against a blaze of light. He gasped cool air as the gag was untied. "OK Nick, last request. Show in three hours. I come back fix you both later."

When the door swung shut behind him, Andy examined this unexpected companion. Nick's limbs were bound in silver tape, secured to the arms and legs of a plastic garden chair. He was pale, but angry. "I developed software for them." He spat the words. "Made the brain-dead mistake of finishing it!"

The man's mouth tightened in pain. "They slammed my leg in the van door. Knee is bloody agony." Then he shouted "You promised me pills!" He jerked his arms against the tape, his mouth loosing a keening noise that finally resolved into expletives. "Fuck. Fucking dead. Fuck!" He stared at Andy. "Don't worry, I won't steal your glory. They'll do me in seconds. But you'll get a full fifteen minutes of fame. I'm just the support act."

Perhaps this arrival was a setup, but there was nothing to lose by taking it at face value. "And our performance is what? Getting carved up by a mad old Russian?"

Nick adjusted his position, grimacing. "Max is a citizen of the world nowadays. But this is his idea of team building. Potentially cathartic given the right mindset."

"Watching innocent victims die? Cathartic? Try evil."

Nick snorted. "Were Rome's citizens at the Colosseum evil? What about people who paid two shillings for a grand day out at a public hanging? Look, I'm a technologist, a rational man. Evil is a fully resilient system: there's a little bit in all of us." His sneer collapsed. "And less of the 'innocent victim' bollocks. This is capital punishment. It happens to people who threaten society. You insisted on threatening ours, so fuck you."

Andy pushed his forearms deeper into the straps, restarting his attempt to stretch or break them. "But what made you a threat? Did you object when they killed your father?"

Nick grimaced, looking away. "If you had only fucking dropped it. You had perfectly plausible explanations dangled in front of you."

"Murders. Disappearances. Buildings blown up and torched. Attempts to kill police? And that's just the stuff we know about. Plausible doesn't cut it. There are some cracks you can't paper over."

"It got out of hand. Max is losing it in his old age."

"What age is he?"

"Nobody knows for sure. Older than he looks."

The things Andy heard when blindfolded simply couldn't be true. But doubt was meaningless. He was caught in an insane web and about to be eaten by an impossible spider. "The story he told me—"

"Might even be real, some of it, but you can never tell with him. I was firmly inside the circle of trust until Yurik arrived with his duct tape." Nick thrashed in his chair, tugging at his arms. "Fucking shit!" But then he froze, noticing Andy's movements. "How are they feeling? Those arm straps I mean?"

"The right-hand side might be slackening a bit."

Nick's eyed widened. "Reynolds got his right arm out. Keep focusing on that side. Probably beneath the old bastard to try to fix it."

Andy redoubled his efforts. "Any other tips?"

"Maybe. But I'd keep working that strap for now." Nick had probably seen more than just Reynolds trapped inside this thing. But now wasn't the time to point out what a sick bastard that made him.

"What do they have over you then? Young, wealthy, highly skilled. What dragged you into this?"

"You know about my dad's condition."

"What condition?"

"Don't be coy. You mentioned Lou Gehrig's disease in your text message. I didn't want my parent to die. What would you do?" When Andy didn't respond the younger man continued. "And Max says it's familial. Since only he can treat it, I had two reasons to join the club."

Andy continued pulling and flexing his forearm against the strap. "If you really believed you could achieve these things, why not share it? Do some good?"

"Hofler tried leaking research. Max brought him back in line. The cleanup was messy."

"Prague?"

"What d'you know about that?"

"I know Dirk Müller was never seen again."

The younger man whistled. "Christ. You *were* close. That explains the hasty scheduling."

But that didn't make sense. Max couldn't know his thinking on Müller. Then it hit him. "Hang on. You saw my text message? About Lou Gehrig's disease?" If his arms had been free he would have slapped his own forehead. "My communications, my location ... even my favourite tea! You hacked my phone! That day in your father's office!"

When Nick shrugged it was confirmation enough. Then he nodded towards the right armrest. "Your strap looks loose enough now. Reynolds angled his arm away from his body. He clipped the backboard, but he got free."

Andy tried, but almost shattered his elbow. Lancing pain shot through his forearm. He bit down hard to avoid screaming. When the pain receded to a numb tingling he steeled himself to try again, this time forcing a more extreme angle. He clipped the wood and almost cried out, but his arm came free. Between gritted teeth he said, "Result at the second attempt."

"Don't get cocky. Reynolds managed it with knives through his hands."

That unpleasant detail conjured a memory: a luminous blue spatter mark on a stone wall. He unbuckled his other arm. "What about this panel over my chest?"

"There's a couple of latches, at the back of the chair."

Andy stretched backwards, but he couldn't feel anything like a latch. "I can't reach."

"But I can. If you can pull the tape off my arm."

Andy began scratching at the coils of silver insulation tape. He couldn't even find an edge. "This will take forever."

"Find a way. Because we definitely don't have forever."

44

THE GATE

I t was a pull, like the draw towards an audience member during mediumship, but on geographical scales. Doirin couldn't determine actual directions or specific roads, but the slackening tension of moving closer was vastly preferable to the growing squall of heading further away. She guided Ilsa at every junction.

The drive had not taken long, perhaps forty minutes outside of the city, but already the setting was quiet, deeply rural.

The car stopped on dusty ground in front of a tall chain-linked gate. Behind that gate, a rough track gouged through a field before ending at a cluster of old buildings. The place looked abandoned.

A faded sign tied onto the rusted wire shifted in the wind. The original markings no longer visible, just the graffiti scrawl: *Vinya Enverinada.* Ilsa frowned. "Maybe I read about this place. Once they made wine here, but there was something bad in the soil."

The gates were pulled shut, a padlock broken on the ground. "He's here," Doirin said. She held Ilsa's gaze, tugging a scrap of paper from her purse. "When you're safely home, call this number. It's Miguel Cova's family, but ask for Brian Nesbitt. Tell him where we are."

Ilsa recoiled. "I don't leave you alone! How you get back?"

The words Doirin spoke were gentle, but not her own. *"Zsa Zsa? Remember Clovenstone. Be safe and go home."*

Ilsa's eyes grew wide. And then glistened. She nodded mutely as Doirin left the car. The vehicle turned, dragging a plume of dust into the distance.

Doirin faced the gate and the heavy silence of the dead earth. With no idea what she needed to do, she threaded her fingers through the wire mesh and pushed. And rocked. And pushed again. The heavy gates scored deep wounds into the dirt, but soon she forced a gap wide enough to squeeze through. She followed the track towards the disused buildings.

45

FATHER'S DAY
FRIDAY 23RD SEPTEMBER, 18:21

Father waxed his moustache in silence while Sara waited for an answer. She no longer understood his dedication to these events. If there were a concrete threat, and on this occasion she had doubts even around that, it would surely be quicker and cleaner to simply dispose of it and move on. She wondered whether their beleaguered company could bear many more of his hastily arranged theatrical 'lessons'. Nick would be the fourth of their colleagues to die. Everyone was surely wondering who would be next. Rene, who balanced nervously beside Yurik on an overturned barrel, was a case in point. He'd been recruited by Thomas Hofler, but had outlived his mentor.

All the mentors, all the lieutenants, all were dying and no one was safe. This was madness.

But she had flown here at Father's request, and tonight would proceed as he planned. This was not the moment to challenge his methods, nor to debate strategy. That would come later. She repeated her point. "My Norwegian contacts used CAS9 rather than retroviral vectors, and have achieved far greater precision when modifying immune cells."

The stroke of the polished moustache comb remained even. "Interesting," he said, although his detached tone suggested nothing of the sort.

She chose to persist. Even an absent-minded acceptance would allow her to move forward. "Rene mentioned the growing capability of the team in Vyborg. I would like to engage with them on an exercise to trial the technique. I'd anticipate a less than twenty-percent impact on their research time."

The comb stopped. "The Vyborg team are fully engaged with tasks I have assigned. Their virology focus is ameliorating viral impacts on the ageing immune system. To be specific, my immune system. Their skills are exclusively directed towards the reversal of immune depletion and rejuvenation of the thymus."

"But this will augment their skills. Adding the Norwegian technique will enhance our therapeutic capability in a key direction and attract more clients."

His eyes hardened. "For a twenty-percent delay in progress I require? No. This technique is of some value, but from my own perspective relatively unimportant. The work is me, and I am the work. Vyborg should not be disturbed." He returned his comb and wax to a leather bag. "Now, to our performance. Did you remember your costume?"

SARA CHANGED in the rented minivan. The winery building was dirty and damp, and she needed a break from Father to regain her composure. She fitted the glittering eye mask carefully. He was disproportionately concerned about stage presentation and needed to be indulged. She was now ready to admit her role here: pandering to the enthusiasms of a selfish child.

Father claimed to protect their work, despite recklessly endangering it. Did he conjure these threats, she wondered, only to trap them in his magician's box, saw them in half and make them disappear? The last few months had been a whirlwind, each decision drawing dangerous scrutiny, each attempt to evade that scrutiny raising even more.

She checked the canvas bag containing her cards, knives and props, all the paraphernalia he'd trained her to handle since she was a child. She never forgot her fail-safe set, a duplicate of his own. Father was cautious and meticulous, except in matters of authority. Dissent was put down, brutally, irrespective of the consequence. Joan Wood, gone. Thomas Hofler, gone. Daniel Cochrane, gone, his son soon to follow.

She'd heard rumours, unwisely started by Joan but growing in strength since her removal. Rumours about Father's judgement, about his recklessness. Rumours that his replenishment process had repaired some deficits while allowing others to burgeon. Even, that their method might plant a seed of madness, which time would bring to bloom. It was a bleak prognosis. Surely it was wrong?

She must convince Father to adopt the innovations of traditional science. The work was powerful, and had been decades ahead of its time, but now? It was stagnating. Worse, it had already begun to decay.

Father simply commanded Marc be murdered, but had not questioned her further. Her secret act of rebellion had made something plain: he could not conceive of the possibility she might disobey him. Father had taught her to defer to no one, to consider no man her superior. No man, that is, save one.

But as things stood, with no access to replenishment, Marc's death sentence would play out slowly, and her defiance would have been for nothing.

No.

She would travel to Vyborg and initiate Marc's project in spite of Father's objection. Who would question her? And if Father objected they'd repeat their discussion in private and this time she would give no quarter. He needed to start listening or this endless cycle of reaction and reprisal would be their undoing.

Light flooded the van as she opened the rear door and stepped out onto dirt. This abandoned winery was emblematic of their strategy: it was falling apart. They must move beyond these ruins. Father would need her guidance more than ever to ensure that happened.

But a flicker just past the corner of an outbuilding caught her eye. Warily, she craned her head to see around the crumbling obstruction.

A woman was coming. On foot. Walking the dirt path between the vineyards.

This woman wasn't anyone Sara recognised. She had no reason to be here, so must have lost her way.

Sara straightened her mask and shouldered her bag, then strode forward to meet the stranger. She shouted. "Estás perdido? Are you lost?"

The woman kept walking. She was some years older than Sara, and paler than most of the locals. Disquiet clenched her stomach. This shouldn't be happening. The location was chosen to avoid this. Sara tried again. "Propiedad privada! This is private property!"

But the woman shook her head and continued towards the buildings.

46

THE RIGHT PLACE

FRIDAY 23RD SEPTEMBER, 18:47

Doirin had always known this was the right place. But what she felt now was something more. There was something very specific about this young woman in the mask. She appeared dressed for a masked ball, but the battered leather backpack she carried clashed with the glitter of her outfit. Doirin sensed a connection associated with this person, but it was far, far back, drowning in a tumult of internal noise. Lacking time to explore that, she simply ignored it and pressed onwards.

But the woman immediately blocked her path. "You can't be here," she said.

Doirin replied, "I'm here for Andy Lorimar. I won't leave without him." The woman stiffened, and peered down the dirt road towards the gate. "Don't bother straining your neck. There's nobody with me."

When the woman grasped Doirin's hand, the plaintive vibration strengthened, but remained impossible to reach. Maybe with a couple of stiff gins, but Doirin had the horrible suspicion it wasn't going to be that kind of party.

When they reached the largest building, it became obvious that it had been empty for some years. The earthy plaster was riven with cracks, as much of it on the floor as on the vandalised walls. They took a staircase, heading down, the young woman directing Doirin to walk ahead. Under her mask, it was obvious she was tense, ready to act, anticipating violence. But Doirin hadn't hit anyone since she left school, and decades-old experience of tuck-shop rough and tumble wouldn't help her now.

"Who did you say you were here for again?" The masked woman smiled as she spoke, but the question was dishonest. Outside, the tensing of her jaw had betrayed the briefest hint of panic. It was suppressed quickly, and without close observation, it could easily have been missed. But Doirin had always been a good observer. She knew what was really going on here.

"I'm looking for Andy Lorimar. You or your friends brought him here out of the city."

Again, a flicker of disquiet, cloaked by a smile. "You must be mistaken, but we'll check."

The staircase ended in a dark hallway, and they walked on. Stacks of blackened barrels were mounted against thick stone walls. The stacks gave way occasionally for access to a doorway or an open storeroom. The whole place smelled of damp and vinegar. "We're through at the end here. You go in first." The woman smiled again, still primed for conflict.

As Doirin entered that room, the turmoil in her mind reached a sharp crescendo, and then fell away. Was this it? The eye of a storm that had blown her and Andy out of their everyday lives? An old man in a white morning suit?

Yes.

His was the impression she had felt in the coffee shop: a man in white, the heart of it all. But he wasn't alone. Another man, perhaps African or West Indian, rose warily from his barrel seat at their arrival. The older man spoke first. "An unexpected guest. Who have we here?"

Doirin's chaperone answered, feigning uncertainty. "This lady appeared on foot. Says she is here for ... an Andy Lorimar?"

He waved dismissively. "Now, my dear, we need no secrets. Of course we have Mr Lorimar here. And of course, this lady will join him."

Doirin chilled to hear those words, and to know immediately what they meant. She always believed spirit would place her where she needed to be, but this was a room filled with murderers. Her fingers began to tremble, so she clenched her fists.

The older man continued. "This new arrival brings forward our plans, and I fear we must proceed without our audience." Audience. That word was the trigger. Panic took root in her gut and began to rise.

The man smiled. "Rene, could you fetch the stretcher? We will vacate this fine building sooner than expected." His smile broadened as he turned to Doirin, but his eyes were cold. "And not all of us will be walking."

Doirin began to scream.

47

HALFWAY FREE
FRIDAY 23RD SEPTEMBER, 18:50

Blood seeped from Andy's cuticles as he tore the last strip of tape from Nick Cochrane's right arm.

The younger man flexed his fingers. "Getting there. Now the other one."

Andy pushed against the panel covering his chest. He was two inches short of reaching the tape on the other arm. "We're stuck unless we can make do somehow."

Nick grunted. "I need to lean back. One arm holds your chair and stops me tipping. One works the catches."

They'd achieved halfway free but trapped in every sense that mattered.

Andy considered their situation, the distances involved and his own range of motion. He visualised Nick's tilting chair. The leg of the plastic seat should briefly move into grabbing range. "On three. You lean back, and when you begin to tip, I'll catch the front leg of your chair." There were no other options.

Nick grimaced. "Please. Don't fucking miss. One. Two. Three!"

Andy's lunge rattled the chest panel. He barely caught Nick's chair leg, but managed to arrest his fall. With a click, one side of the panel shifted, and he gripped hard to cope with the changing weight as Nick leaned towards the other catch.

The panel shifted without warning. Andy's ribs flared at the sudden pitch forwards, and Nick's chair toppled in a torrent of whispered expletives. With his first act of freedom, he rummaged in his trouser pockets and dry-swallowed two of his painkillers. Then, undoing his leg straps, he headed for a far corner of the room.

Seeing Nick's face squashed awkwardly against the vinyl floor sheet, left Andy oddly conflicted. The man deserved no sympathy, but their shared purpose had created an uncomfortable bond, and he wouldn't abandon him to die here.

He walked back with a curving length of wood. "I spotted this earlier."

Nick's words were muffled from eating the flooring, but still intelligible. "It's a barrel stave. They're everywhere here."

"This one had a glint at the top. Look. Probably part of the hoop around the staves. But the metal's ragged. Might be sharp enough to cut tape." He hoisted the younger man upright.

"So you're not leaving me at least."

"What? And have them kill you before your trial?" He scraped at the silver tape on the left hand side of the chair. A strip frayed and parted within seconds. "This'll speed things up nicely."

Soon the entire left side was free and Andy began working on the right leg. When Nick swore and rose, Andy assumed he'd nicked some skin.

Until he heard the footfall behind him.

Yurik Sokov stood inside the door. His eyes moved from Andy, crouched on the floor, to Nick, one leg still taped to the cumbersome plastic chair. As Sokov's expression hardened, Andy made no attempt to hide his fear. It was difficult enough shielding the oak stave with his body without giving a facial performance as well.

When Sokov launched himself, Nick recoiled and lost balance, tumbling backwards. But then Andy rose and twisted, his ribs screaming. He took a flash of satisfaction from the shock on his assailant's face as the barrel stave arced into view. Sokov's arm rose defensively, but too late. It redirected the swing away from his torso, straight onto the side of his head. He crashed into a wall, fell to the floor and lay unmoving.

Andy stooped and slashed the remaining tape from Nick's leg. "We need to move. Now."

Leaving the makeshift theatre they entered a long gloomy corridor of rotting barrels. Their shadows were thrown into occasional relief by the scattering of freestanding security lamps. Andy, unconscious on arrival, had no idea which direction to take. But Nick pointed. "Main staircase." Then he began walking gingerly, favouring his good leg.

Andy followed, but froze at a faint mewling from somewhere down the hallway. "What's that?"

With one foot on the bottom stair, Nick whispered, "People you don't want to meet. Come on."

But it was more than that. Someone was in distress. Andy wanted to lash out with the stave, but instead whispered. "Shit. It's Doirin."

His companion shrugged. "Good luck with that." Andy watched his hopes of bringing Nick Cochrane to justice limp around the bend at the top of the first flight of stairs. But he couldn't leave her. What was she even doing here? Had she been kidnapped as well?

None of that mattered. He had to get her out. He ran towards the weakening voice, until he found its source, and plunged through an unmarked doorway.

It was a lot to absorb.

Doirin struggled in the grip of Rene, so generous with his spiked tea at the waterfront. An older man in white, the same person seen at the Balrannoch, stood in front of her, pressing a black handkerchief over her mouth and nose. A masked woman, disturbed by Andy's arrival, reached into her bag.

Three of them. Woman on the left, Rene on the right, old man in-between. The numbers were against him, but at least he'd come prepared. He hefted the wooden cudgel. "I'll fight if I have to. Give me my friend."

Doirin's struggles were lessening by the moment.

Everyone looked to the old man. Eventually he smiled, as though the situation were entirely normal. "Your friend? But of course." Andy recognised the voice of Maxim Vorsky. The man removed his handkerchief from Doirin's face and tucked it into his breast pocket. Then he pushed her forwards in a lifeless swoon. She would have hit the floor hard if Andy hadn't dropped the barrel stave to catch her.

She was still breathing, but she was a dead weight. "What have you done to her?"

Nobody bothered to answer. Rene picked up the discarded length of oak. The odds had just shifted for the worse.

48

THE BETWEEN

Doirin stood on a plateau between two banks of mist. The black handkerchief was gone. Perhaps it had fallen from her face?

But she was here now, not there. That cellar room was far behind her.

A single step forward revealed a ragged cliff edge and she stooped, her fingers curling around the broken edge. This was the boundary we all ran towards; the final drop at the end of our days. Closing her eyes, she saw the image she'd carried through adulthood, all fear of the transition melting from the faces of those who soared from here unburdened, free, transformed. At least that was what she'd always believed.

She'd spent so many years guessing, constructing a story from the hints offered by her gift and her intuition. But now, perhaps. Now she might find proof.

She shouldn't remember these surroundings; she'd never been here before. But all around were echoes of familiarity. She knew this place, somehow. The rock was bleak, the landscape colourless, but a suggestion of vibrancy lay ahead, a spectrum glimpsed across vast distances.

And then she understood. This was a between place. The source of her whispers lay below.

And suddenly she was down, at the foot of the rock, standing on fallen scree, the forgotten remnants of countless lives.

She watched for some moments, taking in a marvel of formation and loss. Little messages scratched into the stone. Single words, fragments of thoughts. Hopes. Fears. Farewells. Sometimes images would crystallise, sepia memories cast against the rock face. But within moments each would vanish, drawn back into the implacable granite.

The silence here was absolute.

Such unnatural quiet puzzled her. She wasn't struggling to decode whispers across the divide; she was here, at the root. But her hands were shaking. Tremors rising from a deep fear. For herself. For Andy. For everything. And it was a fear that covered her senses like a shroud.

Focus-pocus.

She couldn't control what was happening back in that room. That wasn't part of her task anymore. Whatever happened, she shouldn't waste this opportunity. She clasped her arms around her body and squeezed and rocked and clung, reaching out, grasping for a point of connection.

On the side of her face she felt it; a tiny sigh from the tiniest lips.

And immediately she was aware of the throng. A milling, surging crowd. Pressing against her, so many, each one a life lost, each one trapped in the between. And they surrounded her, even though she felt rather than saw them. With no connection, no relationship to guide her, she was caught in a storm of anger and pain.

She stumbled, sliding on the brittle scree, found herself jostled and dragged and propelled. The spirits grabbed, pulling with a ferocity that alarmed her. She had no idea how to help them, no clue what they expected from her.

She sensed it then, sensed that she did not belong here, that they could not keep her. This close to the threshold, she could release her ties to the cellar room and leave this place. That simple act of letting go would move her onward, towards transformation and reunion with her own who had gone before. With Daddy. With Flora. And Rosie, when she joined them soon.

But no. He needed her. She couldn't leave Andy.

Andy

An immediate pull rose from the strongest connection. It called a clear voice to her side.

Marie

Marie Lorimar was with her. The mother who lost her child, drawn by Doirin's thoughts of the child who lost his mother. This particular loss, this love torn and stolen, it resonated here as a kind of bond. And in this swarm of souls, there was another who shared this pain. Another trapped at this border, tethered by the same sorrow.

Doirin let Marie lead her. Through the buffeting throng, to a place of grief. And in Doirin's mind, a name formed.

Mẹ-Mai

49

IN THE ROOM

FRIDAY 23RD SEPTEMBER, 19:16

Andy held Doirin for a moment, nearly overwhelmed by what he had caused. She wasn't the first woman he had drawn into the darkness.

But this wasn't the time for guilt. If he continued to crouch on the floor, Rene would overcome his hesitation and use the oak baton. He laid her down gently, and rose to his full height.

From the older man's demeanour it was apparent he expected the others to act on his behalf. The woman stared coldly from behind her mask, one hand still fishing blindly inside her leather rucksack. Andy prayed she didn't have a gun. Rene brandished the barrel stave but nervously, unwilling to engage. The old man said, "Finish him."

Andy faced Rene. "Give up. You're no fighter."

Rene inched forward at the challenge, so Andy roared, and he recoiled again. Good. Work on that. "Don't die for a lunatic." He held his arms forwards, his gesture open, placating. He doubted he would convince Rene, but his real plan was to block any swing, hopefully not break any bones, then wrest control of the club. It involved too much luck to qualify as strategy, but it was his best hope of getting Doirin to safety.

The masked woman produced a many-buckled strap from her bag. As she tied it around her waist, Andy's heart sank. Those metallic glints weren't buckles at all. She had just put on a knife belt.

She removed a silvered blade and balanced it in her hand. It glinted in the beam of a security light.

Maxim smiled. "Impalement artistry usually thrills through the narrow avoidance of injury. But our variant operates somewhat differently. Rene, you have thirty seconds to avoid humiliation or my daughter—"

While Rene was distracted by the old man's taunting, Andy pounced, grabbing the end of the stave. The broken metal band sliced skin as easily as tape, but shedding blood of his own choosing was better than waiting until the magician's homicidal assistant began lobbing daggers. He wrenched the club, dragging a wide-eyed Rene towards him. If he pulled him close, perhaps she would hold off—

A blade thunked into the wall beside his head.

Since Rene wasn't prepared to release the barrel stave, Andy pulled him into a wrestling hold, trapping the finally dropped stave with his foot. It didn't take self-defence training to recognise Rene was not here as an enforcer. Manipulating his adversary into a head-lock was reasonably straightforward, and he turned Rene around as first line of defence for any projectiles. "Drop the knives or I break his neck." If they called his bluff he was stuck, but perhaps the threat could end this.

But the door crashed open, and Yurik Sokov staggered inside, bloodied and swearing. With him, he dragged the broken body of Nick Cochrane.

Maxim applauded. "Whatever happens to Rene's neck is your business, Detective Lorimar. But these knives have a job to do, and I shall see that they do it."

Those bloody odds again.

He'd been riding his luck so far. But although Sokov was staggering slightly, it seemed unlikely he could be overcome again.

Then he heard the soft whispering behind him. To add to the many variables already present, it seemed that Doirin was waking.

50

THE SONG

Whe Sara watched Lorimar interpose Rene as a human shield, she realised this would not be ended with her knives from a safe distance.

Her anger rose at yet another unnecessary descent into chaos. For what? They'd had no certainty that Lorimar would continue to cause trouble. Indeed, to all outward appearances, Daniel Cochrane's confession had been accepted by the local police and the investigation had already begun to dwindle. Against that backdrop, Father's hunch might more properly be described as a grudge. And once more, his unilateral decisions had brought them close to ruin.

When the door burst open, she allowed herself a moment of relief. If anyone could finish this at close quarters, it was Yurik Sokov.

But her relief evaporated when the woman in the corner rose and began to sing.

What she sang was impossible. This melody was Sara's secret shame, the dream song that made her weak and brought her tears and pain.

The woman, Doirin, halted to speak. *"Pain not from the song, only its loss."* Then her refrain continued.

Sara reasoned that this must be some form of hallucination, but the expression on Father's face showed he recognised it too. Which meant it was real. What she was feeling was real.

Doirin suspended her song to speak again, and Sara calmed herself enough to properly listen. *"We did not lose each other, my daughter, con gái tôi. Our time was stolen, Bởi một tên trộm ác."*

In Sara's head the words shifted phase, becoming a polyphony of language and accent. English and Vietnamese and the woman's Scottish dialect unified, bonding into an inconceivable certainty: the words came from her mother.

Father signalled to Yurik, still glowering from just inside the door. "Ignore Lorimar. Kill the woman. Now."

Sara spoke without thinking. "Yurik—No! Leave her!" And Sokov froze, probably out of shock. He had never heard her contradict her father before. But lest he recover his composure and carry out Father's order, she drew two knives from her belt.

She was unsure where this was leading, but she was falling now, tumbling down a dark slope, negotiating unforeseen obstacles. Obstacles that were impossible, but nevertheless present. An unknown woman from a small, wet country was singing her mother's song, a song nobody had heard for over thirty years.

And Doirin was pointing now, pointing at Father. *"Con gái, anh ấy đã ăn tôi."*

Sara heard the crazy words in her mind: 'Daughter, he ate me'. She knew what they meant. And she found it credible, because it explained so many things. She turned to her father. "You used Mẹ-Mai as a template? A donor for your own replenishment?"

Father reacted as though struck. She recognised indecision play over his features, the same indecision she had witnessed whenever she asked questions about her mother. Something she now realised stemmed not from painful recollection, but from bloodless fabrication. "It ... it was not that simple."

But it was that simple.

Nowadays they would never mix genders between donor and client, but decades ago, as he evolved the method? His desperate expression conjured the ghost of a memory. Of being with her mother, of trying to leave. No, that wasn't the correct term, and father had taught her the importance of lexical precision. The correct term was escape. They had been trying to escape.

Doirin was smiling now, and cradled her arms to begin the song again, this time as though to an infant, presenting a tableau Sara had tried her whole life to remember.

And the emptiness inside her filled with unfamiliar emotion: rage. Free-flowing, it coursed molten hot, and she welcomed it, inviting it to consume the walls of cold rationality imposed by her upbringing, letting it form the crucible she needed, one where love could transmute to hate.

She could ponder later how a quest to prolong life had brought so much death. But for that to change, perhaps more death would be required. And she would meet Father's metric: she would act both because she must, and because she believed it to be right. Fittingly, she would use the methods he gave her, ones her mother would never have permitted he teach a child.

Father reacted to her silence, pressing on with smiles and reassurance. She nodded as though listening, and stepped towards him. As he seemed to relax, she darted forward, severing his left carotid artery.

His surgeon's hand grasped to apply pressure, attempting to slow the plume of arterial spray. But she was not finished. Swiftly, she brought the other knife to bear, plunging the blade into her father's eye socket. Seeing Sokov in motion, she pushed the old man forward to land face down, driving the dagger deep into his brain.

She raised her eyes and held Sokov's gaze. His loyalty had been unswerving. But he needed to understand: his old source of patronage was gone. He might expect to overcome her, but only if he could bring his strength to bear. For she was fast, and knew precisely where to cut.

As Sokov gazed at the spreading pool of his old master's blood, his face twisted with unfamiliar emotion. But he halted.

It was time to end this. "Detective Lorimar. You will release Rene unharmed. My friends and I will leave. This man," she kicked her father's corpse, "has orchestrated our troubles. But his time has passed. You cannot prosecute a cadaver."

"I can prosecute his accomplices."

Sara sighed. "Please. Allow me to conclude this without further harm."

Hope and doubt battled on the detective's face. "If I release Rene, what stops Sokov killing us?"

Sara understood. She was unsure if she could trust Father's man herself, and she certainly didn't need his skills for what she wanted her organisation to become. But right now he brought the balance of power she needed to leave unchallenged. "He will take this body outside now." Yurik stooped to lift the corpse onto his shoulder. The old man's blood surged for a moment, before trickling slowly down the Russian's back. She caught his eye. "We will meet at the van."

Sokov nodded, and Sara waited until his footsteps retreated down the corridor. "I cannot force you to believe me, but I have no desire for pointless skirmishing. Do not come outside until we are gone. Yurik belongs to the body he carries. I cannot promise to control him." She indicated Doirin, who stared unnervingly into the middle distance. "I would not see this woman harmed further. Her sedative will fade. We were caught in the adventures of a madman. Some of us for longer than others."

"He was ... mad, wasn't he? That story he told me? A surgeon during the second world war would be, what? A hundred? Older?"

How much of Father's story Lorimar had heard, she was unsure. But it didn't matter. That story was over. She paused at the door. "Doirin is also from Edinburgh? What is her full name?"

Lorimar pushed Rene towards her. "No. You don't need to know that. You don't need to know anything about her. Just go. Get in your car and—"

"It's Chambers, lassie. Doirin Chambers. But leave now. There'll be other police here soon."

The detective gave his friend a look of purest disbelief, but Sara nodded and left.

51

BACK OF A VAN

FRIDAY 23RD SEPTEMBER, 21:03

Later, when the Mossos d'Esquadra had arrived with Brian Nesbitt, Andy sat in the van encouraging Doirin to fill in the gaps. "What about the masked woman? Did you get the daughter's name?"

Doirin lowered her eyes, a likely signal that she wasn't really keen on the question. "It doesn't always work like that."

"But did it work like that this time?"

She looked away, and tapped her forehead. "You know what? I'm quite woozy. I might miss the start of the party."

"Party? Jesus, Doirin! You're going to the hospital!"

Doirin shrugged. "I met her, you know."

"Who're we talking about now?"

"Your mum."

He froze, unable to respond.

"You weren't responsible. For any of it. She wants you to know that." Doirin took his hand. "And what you saw ... with him and her? It's nothing to do with how things are between people. He never deserved you. That's why you never knew."

Andy looked into her eyes. He'd never get used to this, never fully believe it. But he tried to smile.

The rear door sprang open and Brian Nesbitt thrust his head inside. His eyes darted between the two of them, his face flushed and sweating. "That place is a bloodbath! Ilsa made zero sense! I have no clue why you ended up there, what Doirin did to find you, or how you got out in one piece!" He put his arms around both of them. "But screw that. You're OK." He allowed himself to smile. "And on the plus side, Migs' family now think I'm a god of global policing."

Andy laughed. Probably the onset of hysteria. "I've got just cuts and bruises Brian, but they drugged Doirin with something. Can we get her checked out?"

Doirin's eyebrow took a dim view of this idea. "So that was a natural snooze that brought you out here, was it? I'm fine. He was drugged worse than me."

Andy mumbled, "You didn't hear me singing in Chinese."

"I'll take that as a thank you. And it was Vietnamese, but since you're still half-deaf, I'll forgive you."

Nesbitt raised a hand for silence. "A drunk in Palamos was found with your wallet and phone. How does that fit?"

Andy sighed. "He'd have been lifted for murder when my body was found. Another charming misdirection."

"Well, thankfully we found their bodies, not yours. Our last loose ends: Nick Cochrane and Yurik Sokov, both dead."

Andy recoiled. "What? Sokov isn't dead!"

"Tell that to the person who cut his throat. He was found behind the outbuilding."

Doirin nodded. "That's where I saw the woman's van." She rubbed Andy's hand "It's over. They're gone."

"But what are we doing about the others?"

Nesbitt shook his head. "They'll be pursued by the local police. We've done our bit." He exhaled slowly. "Right. Step 1, I don't care who was drugged worse. You're both going to the hospital. Step 2, I'll arrange trauma counselling. Step 3, if I like it, I might even organise some for you guys."

EPILOGUE
FRIDAY DECEMBER 16TH, 6:52 P.M.

E dinburgh is home to many types of wind. But on that Friday evening it wasn't the friendly sort; it was the kind that came at you with a hammer. Between that and the treacherous slicks of frost that December had spilled on the pavements, the concept of pretending to be in South America seemed utterly ridiculous. What the hell had he been thinking?

Still. It was Doirin's birthday. And Christmas birthdays were often short-changed. Or so he'd heard; he'd never been much for celebrating these things. But then, he'd never had much reason to, not for a while at least. After the horrors of the vineyard, then losing her sister in October, she deserved a treat.

He reached her close on London Road with both literal and figurative cold feet. But the tyranny of a table reservation forced him to continue upstairs and ring the doorbell.

When Doirin answered, her eyes widened. "You scrub up well."

She was just being polite. "Don't be daft. You put me to shame." And she did. He'd never seen her in a going-out dress before, and she wore the perfume he remembered from the first time they'd met.

"I don't get many mystery nights, so I'm making the most." She smiled, her eyes narrowing. "Is that a brand new suit?"

Andy felt his cheeks redden. Simple question, simple answer. "Yes. I suppose it is."

As they walked outside, Doirin said, "And where are we headed on this fine tornado night?"

Andy reached over to turn up her collar. "We're going to eat Brazilian, drink Brazilian," but he hesitated, suddenly grasping the enormity.

She smiled, her eyes softening into mischief. "Oh God. Please don't say wax Brazilian."

His face was already red from the cold. It hopefully disguised the fact he'd just flushed beetroot. "Sorry! Dance Brazilian! They teach you ... or me, I mean, I suppose you won't need any lessons." Maybe she would hate it. "Is that OK?"

She stretched up on her tiptoes and kissed his cheek. "Detective Andrew Lorimar! You've excelled yourself."

It was nice how she did that. She was in his space and he was in hers and everyone was where they wanted to be. His smile began just hanging around, without even having to force it. He could swear he got a funny look from the driver as he flagged down a black cab.

It was cosy inside the vehicle, and the noise of the engine gave a semblance of privacy. Doirin asked, "You didn't fancy driving us tonight? Was it the weather?"

"Ach. I'm feeling an unusual amount of social anxiety so I'll have a drink. I won't be able to resist chamomile long-term, but one day at a time. Anyway, Brian was right. That stuff nearly killed me."

She pulled herself close. "Don't worry. I'll get you back safe. I'm sticking to mocktails."

"How come?"

She smiled and tapped her imaginary earpiece. "I fancy it being just the two of us."

The menu proved so tempting they selected a range of small plates to avoid missing out. After ten minutes the dishes began to arrive: mushrooms, empadas, cassava, prawns, cornbread, chicken. They landed in a ramshackle order but nothing disappointed. Perhaps not quite Mig's standard, but tasty and different and far better than anything Andy ever found in his evening Tupperware box.

He chose a cocktail arbitrarily because of the mint leaves, but it tasted as good as any of the SodaStream inventions he remembered from Ilsa's kitchen. They were worryingly easy to drink. He'd never developed much of a taste for beer or lager, and probably never would, but in a different life he might have been the first Edinburgh detective with a Mojito problem. Then again, who was he kidding? Someone would have beaten him to that years ago.

"Mojitos are Cuban, you know, not Brazilian." Doirin said. "But the way you keep hiding the evidence I doubt it much matters." She obviously knew a fair bit about the Latin-dance scene. And like many forms of social humiliation it seemed to exist in symbiosis with booze.

Andy was out of practice on that front. He suspected he was drinking too quickly, but was unsure whether he could afford to pace himself. The DJ was already setting up, and that meant the dance lessons were imminent. Worst of all, the dance floor was not, as he'd hoped, in a secluded area. Instead, it threaded a brazen path, cavorting through the dining booths, tables and bar area. There'd be no way to keep this embarrassment private. He poured another Mojito from the pitcher and prayed for the onset of lowered inhibitions.

The lesson plan proved ruthlessly straightforward: an athletic couple did impossible things while a bully in a tropical shirt heckled people to keep up. This style of torture may have been designed to create the desire to dance unsupervised.

If so, it worked.

Doirin was a far better instructor than Captain Coconut. Although Andy was clueless about musical styles, she gently guided him through the uncharted lands of Samba, Rumba, Salsa. Despite each variation demanding a physicality he simply didn't possess, she seemed to enjoy his attempts.

But there was something else.

The music was sinuous and undulating. And although he didn't move that way, not being Mick Jagger or Justin Timberlake or what-ever this generation's snake-limbed freak was called, it forced an unfamiliar intimacy. One pitcher of Mojito later, however, and it wasn't something he was in any hurry to give up. As Doirin danced, and he stumbled along, he considered the mystery of being here with her.

When the bar lights flashed for closing time, they gathered their things and headed into the street. The wind had lessened, but remained icy. "Happy Birthday, Doirin." He leaned forward to kiss her. And she reciprocated.

Eventually, she looked back towards the restaurant. "Thanks for this. It's not been a few months I'd want to relive, but I'd put tonight on replay no problem."

Tonight on replay.

He liked the phrase. It felt like an aspiration. Perhaps even the key to a mystery, one usually uncovered earlier in life. A reason, perhaps, for why people chose to be together.

They talked all the way to Doirin's flat on London Road, and stopped at the foot of her stair. Andy said, "I'm not doing anything this weekend. I don't suppose you're free for lunch tomorrow?"

"I am," she replied, "and breakfast."

Squeezing his hand she shushed his objections and guided him upstairs. "You're pissed, and it's bloody freezing. I saw some public information thing about hypothermia. I'm not saving you from murdering psychopaths to lose you to a stiff breeze from the Baltic."

It was the first time either had mentioned it, although he was sure she'd thought about it as much as he had. What they'd experi-enced together, what they'd shared, what they'd survived.

Their trauma was lessened because each helped the other make sense of it. The fact she put herself in such danger wasn't something he'd ever forget.

What she did for him wasn't something he could have expected from any civilian. But he could finally admit to himself, she wasn't just any civilian. You could allow some relationships to have their full meaning.

When the door closed behind them, there was awkwardness and closeness, laughter and tears and comfort.

And in the morning, everything was different.

AFTERWORD

First things first: Since this is my first novel it would really help me if you could take the time to write a review. Reviews not only help readers to find books, and they're also a great way to show the author some tough love (gulp). Whatever you have to say, I'll try my best to learn from it.

Once upon a time, many years ago, this novel was a short story. It described an unfolding nightmare for an audience member at a late-night show in the dying hours of the Edinburgh Festival. I knew from feedback it made readers feel something. That would normally be good, except mostly they felt the desire to punch me in the mouth. The complaints were multiple: why the event happened was never explained, good did not triumph over evil, revenge was a dish not even on the menu. Like I said, unfolding nightmare.

Eventually I set myself the task of turning that story into something more coherent and potentially publishable, something that answered some of those challenges.

I remembered as a child seeing, but not fully understanding, the traumatic pictures of the exodus from Vietnam that began towards the end of the seventies. The UN High Commission for Refugees estimate that resultant deaths at sea have numbered in the hundreds of thousands. Such mass-migrations and the attendant loss of life obviously continue to the present day, and as populations we don't seem to have any answers, beyond wanting such events kept off our radar and out of our backyard. I started to wonder about a character who looked at such matters differently, seeing not tragedy, but opportunity, not problem, but exploitable resource. I wondered what historical context might help form such a person, and what their goals might be. Those thoughts and my old story came together in what you've just read. I'm grateful you stuck with it.

ABOUT THE AUTHOR

G.P. Ritchie was born a Glaswegian but was never terribly good at it. After a misspent childhood hanging around libraries, falling into the company of the wrong sorts of books and comics, he began writing primitive software on a ZX Spectrum. He studied computer science at University, unwisely taking no gap year for lion-taming, mountain climbing, or any of that exciting stuff proper authors get under their belt before writing one of these descriptions. He has made his own chocolate a few times, so there's that.

Upon moving fifty miles to work in software development, he discovered he'd most likely been an Edinburgher in disguise all that time. But what to do with all those hours he'd previously reserved for friendly conversation with strangers? Mostly he played scrabble, but nowadays he's using some of them in the service of fiction.

He's written mostly computer software, but has also crowbarred some material onto radio and stage. He lives in Edinburgh with his wife and son.

Find out more at: https://nightsborder.com

ACKNOWLEDGMENTS

The fiction-writer's habit of just making things up has consequences, as some readers will undoubtedly spot. If you find yourself throwing socks at your e-reader or paperback, apologies, mea culpa, and it-was-me-wot-did-it. Occasionally though, I did muster enough sense to ask some questions, and a number of people deserve thanks for helping me out.

For invaluable information on law, policing and housing, I owe a debt of gratitude to David Dickson, Peter Sparrow and Lydya Okroj. For generous help on spiritualist beliefs and mediumship, thanks are due to Ann Treherne. Guidance on the tides around Cramond Island came from Arabella Kuszynska-Shields of the RNLI Queensferry Lifeboat team. On the topic of boats I should also recognise Aynsley Law, and a friendly but anonymous boat owner who offered some insights while painting his vessel. For the inside track on top hotels, I owe thanks to movement maestro Iain Dunn. A shout-out for writing support and advice goes to Sophie Cooke, Lynne Dickson, Helen Fowler, MaryAnne Hunt, Gill Connolly and all the gang from Skriva. For selflessly bar-crawling the Balrannoch in the name of research (and also not punching me in the mouth), Joe McShane. And deeply persnickety thoughts on measurement could only have come from David Coffield.

Beta readers are brave and hardy souls arriving at a manuscript before it is properly ready to receive guests. Thanks go to Jenny

Halpin, Stephen Richards and Sophie Cooke. It got better with every review guys, cheers.

Finally, for playing the deranged drill sergeant to ensure I hit 1000 words per day every day for two weeks I have to thank my son Sam. Everything else, I owe to Jenny.

Printed in Great Britain
by Amazon

45595607R00239